Other works by
Robert J. Alvarado
www.rjalvaradobooks.com

Non Fiction

Elfego Baca Destined to Survive
2013 Sunstone Press, Santa Fe, NM

Fiction

Young Pistolero Series
Young Pistolero
2014 Sierra Press, Queen Creek, AZ

STAR OF THE YOUNG PISTOLERO

Printed in the United State of America

IBSN-13: 978-0991477715
IBSN-10: 0991477715

SIERRA
PRESS

Published by Sierra Press
Queen Creek Arizona
First Printing, August 2014

Cover art and design by John Flinn
Graphic art by Daniel David Alvarado

DEDICATION

This book is dedicated to Irene Delores "Lolo" (Arambula) Gradwell, who was taken from our family too young. Her bright smile and love will be in our hearts forever.

ACKNOWLEDGEMENT

First and always, I owe more than thanks to my wife, Ellen, for her unending hours of critique, review, and clarity. A great artist and longtime friend, John Flinn, designed the book cover and art for the Young Pistolero Series.

Chapter 1

Chiwiwi's black eyes flashed a seductive look back at Rafe, before she ran around the corner of the whitewashed church in the middle of the Isleta Pueblo. Midday sunlight reflected off the front wall of the church and made him blink. Rafe's eyes caught a wisp of black hair as it curled around the corner of the church and she disappeared. Yes, he was sure it was Chiwiwi running away from him, teasing him as always, and beckoning him to follow. Rafe's loins stirred from the anticipation of holding his beloved Chiwiwi. He could feel the touch of her velvet skin and the scent of her hair. It smelled of lilacs. Her playful nature was always a surprise to him and one of the things he loved about her.

"Chiwiwi!" Rafe called as he raced after her, hoping to catch her before she hid. Rounding the corner of the church, he came to an abrupt halt. Chiwiwi was caught in the arms of the *gachupín*, the Spaniard Benicío. In his eyes, evil lived. Blood dripped from Chiwiwi's tunic and her head hung to one side. Benicío snarled a cruel grin and his devil eyes met Rafe's.

A low growl roared from Rafe's throat. Benicío released his grip and Chiwiwi slumped to the dirt at his feet. With his right hand, Benicío slowly drew the slender, sharply pointed rapier that hung at the side of the tattered pants of his dusty *traje*.

Chiwiwi's limp body sprawled on the dusty ground and blood stained her light deerskin tunic. Rafe knew she was dead. Instinctively, Rafe's hand reached for his gun, only to find a knife at his side. Benicío whipped the slender blade side to side, extending it from his hand. The devil with the sword sneered, approaching with the long blade. Rafe was no match without his guns, but he could find no peace until he killed this devil of a man or died.

"Desgraciado," Rafe growled at the *gachupín*, calling him a miserable wretch. "I will send you to your father in hell!"

"Me cago en esa India puta." Benicío growled back that he would shit upon the Indian whore

"Rafe, despierta." Rafe heard a voice from what seemed like inside a tunnel. "Wake up!" the voice said over and over, becoming clearer and louder each time and his body shook from side to side. The evil eyes and long rapier were fading into blackness, then suddenly, the devil's face and his beloved Chiwiwi were gone. Opening one eye, the devil's face was replaced with the face of his friend, Carlos Zuniga.

It had been four months since the battle at the Anaya *hacienda* in Corrales, New Mexico – the fight that took Chiwiwi's life and where Carlos killed his own brother, Benicío. After the tragedy, Carlos went with Rafe and George Summers, Rafe's adopted father, to build a new life in Santa Fe.

He and Rafe worked at George Summers' weapons foundry. In the evenings Carlos took care of Rafe's breeding horses while he looked for a teaching job. Carlos often had nightmares of the day he killed his brother, but woke to know it was the only way to end his brother's madness. Lately, the nightmares were less frequent, but he knew his friend Rafe was not so lucky. He had watched as Rafe slid further into despair.

At first, it was periods of forlorn silence. Rafe rode up into the hills and did not return for several days. Then the drinking started. Carlos smelled the tequila and saw the effect in his friend's behavior. If he tried to talk to him, Rafe grumbled and would often lunge at him in anger. He hoped time would heal Rafe's heart, before the alcohol killed him or he died in a drunken brawl. Carlos knew George Summers was extremely worried about Rafe, but they both felt helpless to intervene. Rafe was a man and had to resolve his grief in his own way. It had been over a month since they last saw him.

Three days ago, George asked Carlos to find Rafe and bring him home, because Rafe's uncle Jose had arrived from El Paso. "Do whatever you need to do," he told Carlos. "Just bring him home."

Methodically, Carlos searched the many *cantinas* and saloons in Santa Fe. He talked to bartenders, *vaqueros,* and whores. Some looked at him suspiciously and Carlos wondered if they were telling the truth. His description of Rafe sounded like just another drunken Mexican. He worked his way farther and farther to the outskirts of Santa Fe, getting more and more frustrated. Finally, late in the afternoon of the third day, a *vaquero* told him he saw a man fitting Rafe's description drinking at a *cantina* called El Coyote several days ago. Finding the *cantina* named El Coyote, Carlos described Rafe to the bartender.

"Yes, he was here yesterday," the bartender said. "He's been spending time with the owner's niece, but I haven't seen them today. I've never seen Elena so stuck on a man. She raves and throws bottles, if he doesn't show up," he continued. "She works here most days and lives with her brother. Her uncle knows where she lives, but he's not here." The bartender only knew they lived in the neighborhood, but not exactly sure where.

"Her last name is Montoya," the bartender added, "if that helps. Be careful crossing Elena. She can be a wildcat," the bartender warned.

Carlos waited at El Coyote Cantina until after midnight, but Rafe did not show. Finally, he rode back to the Summers' ranch to get some sleep, returning shortly after sunup. With the help of some locals, it did not take long to locate the house where Elena and her brother lived. Carlos was relieved to see it was a small, tidy house on one of the better streets in the *barrio*. He watched the house and waited, not wanting to start any trouble. It was midmorning before a young man opened the front door.

"Buenos días," Carlos said good morning walking up to the front of the house. "I'm looking for my friend. The bartender from El Coyote said he might be here with your sister." Carlos waited for a response and saw the young man, who he assumed was the girl's brother, sizing him up. "Is he here?" Carlos asked.

Rodrigo studied Carlos' face. It sported a long white scar from his right eye to his chin, somewhat hidden by several days growth of a dark beard. The slender man carried no gun and was dressed in a gray wool suit with a wide tie. The scar belied his otherwise dapper appearance. Shrugging, Rodrigo stepped aside. "He's in the back bedroom."

Walking into the dimly lit bedroom, Carlos found Rafe asleep with a young, naked woman in a tangle of sheets.

"Wake up," Carlos repeated over and over. Wanting to wake his friend gently, he pushed Rafe's shoulder trying to waken him. Slivers of sunlight cut through the daytime darkness in the small bedroom. The naked girl snored softly and they both reeked of tequila. The normally handsome face of his friend looked gray and gaunt.

"Go away, go away," Rafe said in a low whisper pushing his friend with his arm. Even his own voice amplified to a crushing throb inside his head.

"Rafe, you have to get up," Carlos said taking a few steps back. The stale smell of tequila and sex filled the room. Several empty bottles lay on the floor with their rumpled clothes.

Slowly, Rafe sat at the edge of the bed bent over with his hands on his throbbing head. His dark hair fell in stands across his bony fingers. Carlos waited patiently. He noticed the girl's brother followed him and stood motionless by the bedroom door, watching.

Rafe hated waking up to the pounding in his head and the sour taste in his mouth, but liquor was the only way for him to forget what happened to his beloved Chiwiwi. However, it did not stop the dreams – the dreams reliving the *desgraciado*, Benicío, killing her. He wanted to kill Benicío in the dreams, but something always managed to rouse him before he took revenge. In the end, he just wanted to die in the dreams, and be with Chiwiwi, and never wake up.

"Rafe, *don* Jorge wants you home," Carlos said quietly using Rafe's respectful name for his adopted father, George Summers. "Your *tío* Jose is here in Santa Fe." Rafe did not respond. He sat, still holding his head, until Carlos wondered if he had fallen asleep again.

"I can't go," Rafe finally whispered. "I can't let them see me like this."

"You must. I'll help you. Where is your horse?" Carlos asked.

"Tequila," Rafe demanded. "Get me a bottle. It will help."

"No, you need a bath, food, and strong coffee. Where is your horse?" Carlos repeated.

Rafe looked up, with dark lifeless eyes, but did not answer. Carlos handed him his trousers. Rafe moved slowly and groaned with each movement. Picking up his leg to pull up his pants, he fell backward onto the sleeping girl.

"*¿Arghh qué pasa?*" she moaned. Carlos pulled Rafe up and handed him his shirt. The girl lifted her head and looked at them through tangled strings of long brown hair. She started to say something else before she dropped back on the mattress.

Rafe turned and looked at the comatose girl and said, "I can't leave her like this."

"No *amigo*, we have to go. Her brother is here."

Carlos helped him up and buttoned his shirt. He helped his unsteady friend step into his boots. With Rafe somewhat dressed, Carlos shouldered him through the house and out the front door.

"Where is his horse?" Carlos asked the girl's brother.

"Around back," he responded. "I'll take care of my sister." Rodrigo was happy to see Rafe leave. His sister was crazy about him. It was not that he disliked Rafe, but his sister had fallen back into the bottle and it worried him. Drinking was her way of dealing with their past. He had helped her stay sober before Rafe caught her heart. Rodrigo did not know what demons possessed Rafe. He just knew Elena was crazy in love with him, and he knew she was imagining a future with this man. Rodrigo saw no future, only sorrow.

Fall was in the air and in Santa Fe that meant cold mornings. It was not the cold, but the bright sunlight that seared into Rafe's brain as he and Carlos stepped out the front door.

"*¡Mierda!*" he cursed stumbling against Carlos.

"Come on. We must go."

"*Mis pistolas,*" Rafe muttered remembering his guns. He turned around and went back inside the house. Carlos heard Rafe yell at the girl's brother to give him his guns. Shortly, Rafe stumbled down the front steps with his gunbelt around his hips. Rodrigo stood on the front step and watched the two mount up and slowly turn down the road.

When Elena woke she would be furious, but Rodrigo hoped Rafe would not come back. He wanted to get his sister sober again. Most of his young life seemed fated to be responsible for his family – first his father, now Elena. Rodrigo reached back through the open door and retrieved his hat. Closing the door, he walked down the road toward El Coyote Cantina. He would tell his uncle, in person, Elena would not be to work today.

Although anxious to get Rafe back to the Summers' ranch, Carlos set a slow pace. He knew the horse's gait would hurt every part of Rafe's body. Carlos led the horse while Rafe bent forward on his saddle. Neither of them spoke. Carlos hoped Rafe could just hang on. Soon a light rain started falling. Carlos felt the chilly drops on his neck, but Rafe seemed asleep or oblivious.

Slumping on the horse's neck and trying to hang on, Rafe mumbled to himself, "I don't want to see *don* Jorge or my *tío* Jose, not now or ever. Why can't they leave me be?" All he knew was he could not get the image of Chiwiwi out of his soul, no matter what he did, and he did not want to live without her.

CHAPTER 2

By the time Carlos and Rafe reached the Summers' ranch, rain was pouring down. Using the back door to the house, Carlos helped Rafe to the room with the tub just off the kitchen. Juanita helped him strip Rafe's wet and filthy clothes and get him into a tub of hot soapy water.

"Let him soak in the hot water," he told Juanita. "Keep the tub hot."

Carlos headed out the kitchen door crossing the distance to the foundry in the rain. He entered the foundry dripping water and completely soaked to the skin. Shaking water from his hat, he hung it on a hook and went to find George in his office.

"You found him?" George asked.

"Yes," Carlos replied. A look of relief washed across George's lined face.

"How is he?"

"Not good. He needs time to clean up and get food in his belly, then we will see what is left. Juanita is caring for him."

George came around his desk and grabbed Carlos around the shoulders. "Thank you." Releasing his grasp on Carlos' wet shoulders he told him, "You better get yourself out of those wet clothes."

When Carlos returned to the main house, Juanita was scrubbing Rafe with a soapy brush. Rafe flailed his arms toward the woman and she gave Carlos a frustrated look. Slapping the soapy brush into Carlos' hand, she stomped back to the kitchen.

"Calmate amigo," Carlos spoke to Rafe in a low voice telling him to calm down. He hardly recognized the pitiful man in the tub as his friend. Rafe's cheeks were hollow, his skin pulled over his ribs, and his eyes were vacant.

"Why did you bring me here? I need tequila," Rafe grumbled.

Carlos was not a drinker, but he had watched some

of his brother's *vaqueros* try to dry out and knew it was bad. Rafe was suffering from both tequila and a broken heart. This was a man ready to give up on life.

"Rafe, your uncle is waiting to see you. Here scrub yourself," Carlos said handing him the brush, but Rafe only half-heartily attempted to use it.

Carlos went off to the kitchen and asked Juanita to serve up hot soup, tortillas, and strong coffee. When he returned, Rafe was sitting naked on the edge of a bench, bent over with his head in his hands. At least he looked reasonably clean.

"*¿Todo bien amigo?*" Carlos asked if he was doing better. Juanita had left a clean pair of pants and a shirt beside a towel. Picking up the towel, Carlos attempted to dry him, but Rafe simply grabbed the towel wrapping it around his shivering shoulders. "Here, put these on," Carlos told him placing the clothes in Rafe's lap.

Rafe took the clothes, but did not move to put them on. Patiently, Carlos helped him pull up the pants and wrapped the shirt around his shoulders. Carlos led him, still damp, to the kitchen table where Rafe slumped into a chair. Juanita placed a serving of soup, tortillas, and coffee in front of each of them.

"Eat," Carlos urged Rafe. "You need to get food into that empty belly of yours."

Picking up a tortilla, Rafe obediently tore off a small piece and put it in his mouth. He took another bite and then another. His brain knew the food was good, but it had no taste. He looked up to see Carlos devouring the soup and decided to keep eating. After a few spoonfuls, the taste of the flavorful soup started to awaken his taste buds.

Carlos finally relaxed as he watched Rafe eat. The soup in Rafe's bowl disappeared and the hunch of his body straightened a bit as he finished the food.

"Feeling better?"

"*Poco a poco,*" Rafe whispered. His head still throbbed, but the food had settled his stomach.

Carlos helped Rafe upstairs to his bedroom and helped him onto the bed. "Sleep and you will feel better when you wake up." Carlos sat on a chair and watched Rafe relax into sleep. He would not leave him alone, not yet.

Sitting there watching him sleep, Carlos' mind wandered. He fingered the scar on his face remembering the first time he met Rafe in El Paso. Carlos' brother Benicío had beaten and cut his face with a rapier. Rafe had attempted to help him. Carlos wondered many times, if it was fate he and Benicío had fought in the street of El Paso that day, stopping the wagon driven by Rafe and George Summers. Four years later, it was Rafe who found him left for dead on the trail south of Albuquerque. Rafe took him to the Isleta pueblo and the Indians tended to his wounds. No, it was not fate; it was the hand of God that led Rafe to save his life. He watched his friend sleeping and thanked God for helping to find him and bring him home.

It was a little over four months since Carlos' brother, Benicío, kidnapped Chiwiwi and her friend Laapu from the Isleta pueblo and took them to Rubén Anaya's *hacienda* in Corrales. Chiwiwi and Rafe were in love – young and passionate and good love. Benicío destroyed it. By Benicío's hand they were all dead: Rubén, Chiwiwi, and Laapu. No matter how much Carlos tried to justify what he did to stop his out of control brother, he had killed him. He had killed his own brother.

After the siege at the Anaya *hacienda*, Carlos came to Santa Fe with Rafe and George Summers, the man Rafe called *don* Jorge. On many days, Carlos fared no better than Rafe in his sorrow and guilt. Sometimes the weight of his guilt felt like it was crushing him. In those times, he held on to the lessons he had learned at the seminary in Madrid, Spain. God gave us his only son, Jesus Christ, who was sacrificed for all our sins, past, present, and future. This was the grace of God as he was taught. God forgave him, but Carlos could not seem to forgive himself. With each passing day, his faith slowly gave him peace, but his final reckoning would someday be with God.

Carlos' life had been simple when he lived in peace with his family near Los Lunas, New Mexico. After the Mexican-American War, like many other Spanish families, the Zuniga's land was taken by the *Americano* lawyers. His brother Benicío watched the *Americanos* kill their father and drive the family off their land. Carlos was a student at the seminary in Madrid when his father was killed. With no money to pay for his continuing studies, he returned to New Mexico – to a life forever changed. Benicío went crazy after losing his birthright and turned into a murderous outlaw. Carlos had little choice, but to join him.

Benicío, the oldest son, and Carlos, the second oldest, were starkly different. Benicío – strong, arrogant, and proud, and Carlos – studious, quiet, and religious. Benicío tolerated little, barely tolerated Carlos. He belittled his younger brother at every opportunity. Theirs was a bond of blood and not a bond of friendship. Carlos' bond with Rafe was different. In the past four months, they bonded like brothers. The man sleeping on the bed had unselfishly saved his life, and it led to a chain of events that caused the death of Chiwiwi, but Carlos never felt any blame from Rafe.

George Summers took Carlos into his home giving him shelter, food, and work. With his training at the seminary, Carlos was looking for a teaching job in Santa Fe, but meanwhile he worked hard for George.

Now looking at Rafe sleeping peacefully, Carlos sighed. It had been difficult over these last several months to watch Rafe withdraw into his grief. No amount of seminary training had helped Carlos find a way to stop it. Relaxing in the chair, Carlos finally fell asleep.

Rafe stirred on the bed and stretched, slowly opening his eyes to the familiar green wallpaper of his bedroom. His head throbbed and his stomach cramped. It was the tequila. The rot-gut stuff he drank with Elena numbed his brain, but not his soul. Vaguely, he remembered the ride home in the rain. He was home, but he wanted to bolt, to run again and keep running, but his body would not respond.

Moving his throbbing head slowly, he stared around the room. Carlos was sleeping in the chair. Hung on the bedpost were his double-action GSW pistols *don* Jorge gave him so long ago. On another bedpost the arrow quiver

Chiwiwi gave him, trimmed in beads and turquoise, was holding the sawed-off shotgun he designed himself. Looking at the arrow quiver always put a stabbing pain into his heart. He had not been able to save her from Benicío. He failed her and she was gone, forever. Hanging around the quiver was a silver star amulet with a turquoise stone mounted in the center, strung on a leather cord. The amulet was a gift from Letoc, Chiwiwi's uncle, chief of the Isleta Tiwa Indians. These were the only things he had left of her – and his memories.

He stretched on the bed not wanting to close his eyes again, afraid Chiwiwi would be there in his dreams. He would fail to save her and Benicío would kill her again. The dream replayed in many different ways, always with the same ending. Chiwiwi was dead and he could not save her. Now he had no tequila to numb his mind and soul.

Running away was his only solace. At first, just running to the hills on Rayo his Appaloosa stallion helped, and then running to the bottle worked better. He remembered Carlos saying his *tío* Jose was in Santa Fe. Why? Jose wrote he was having problems getting Rafe's mother and sister out of Mexico. Perhaps he had more news. Rafe tried to get up, but the shooting pain in his head forced him back to the mattress and he closed his eyes.

The last time he saw his mother and sister was over four years ago, at *don* Bernardo's *hacienda* in Torreón, Mexico, where he grew up. His sister was curled up on the floor of their small hut, sobbing, after *don* Bernardo beat and raped her. Rafe exploded in a rage and grabbed his father's old flintlock pistol vowing to avenge her. His mother begged him not to go. "Nothing can be done," she pleaded with him.

Going to the main house, his feet moved up the polished stairs to the second floor bedroom. *Don* Bernardo, the *haciendero desgraciado*, was on his bed and *doña* Carmela's eyes went wide when she saw the gun in Rafe's hand.

The explosion and gray smoke from the gun still felt real to Rafe when he remembered how he killed *don* Bernardo that day. After the shooting he jumped on Rayo, *don* Bernardo's prized Appaloosa, and fled north to El Paso leaving his mother and sister behind.

He was trying to remember their faces, but his brain was not responding. Exhausted, he fell back to sleep.

CHAPTER 3

Tiny cinders snaked across each other before dispelling into nothingness. Crackling explosions from the fire created new ones, only to be short-lived partners in the dance of the fire. George Summers stared into the fireplace with one foot on the hearth, not really paying attention to the miniature fireworks. Rafe was upstairs sleeping. He was finally home, but would he stay?

George had a scar where an Apache arrow pierced through his leg in the desert of west Texas over four years ago. He and his partner, Frank, were ambushed and Frank was killed. God sent Rafe to save him. There was no other answer. Rafe was just seventeen years old then. He had shot the *haciendero* who raped his young sister and was on the run from Mexico. Rafe found George almost dead in the Texas desert and saved his life, and George now loved him like a son.

George's own son, Gregory, would be almost seventeen now, if he had lived. Gregory was buried by the oak tree in the yard. It nearly killed George when his son died of influenza at eight months. George raged at God and was angry at his wife, Josefina. It was not her fault, he knew, but he was filled with grief and unable to comfort her. He still found it hard to talk to her about Gregory, wanted to, but could not find words. When Rafe came to Santa Fe four years ago, he seemed to fill a void for both of them.

Rafael Ortega de Estrada, who George called Rafe, grew up in Torreón, Mexico, as a *peón* on a large *hacienda*. Rafe had nothing, was on the run, and yet he saved George's life. He used to wonder why a Mexican boy on the run had not just ransacked the wagon and left an almost dead man to die in that desolate desert. It would have been easy, easier than saving him. Peasant or king, George believed men were either fundamentally good or bad. Rafe was good.

George understood pride and honor – Rafe possessed both qualities. When George brought Rafe to Santa Fe, he learned English quickly, and learned the foundry business. He worked tireless hours on both. George's wife and daughters shared in loving Rafe and Josefina bustled over him, teaching him manners and social graces. By the time Rafe was twenty-one, he was a budding member of Santa Fe's society and was breeding Appaloosa horses on land George helped him buy. George wondered if he could be any prouder of his own son Gregory, if he had lived.

Smoke from the fire irritated George's already puffy eyes. He had slept only fitfully in the last several months, worrying about his adopted son's behavior since the gunfight at Corrales and the death of Chiwiwi. At first, he tried to give Rafe time and space to grieve. Rafe disappeared into the mountains for days on his Appaloosa, Rayo, only to return looking tired. George tried to get him engaged in work at the foundry, but Rafe was disinterested. Carlos told him Rafe was drinking, and then Rafe disappeared for almost a month. George was heartsick. He remembered Rafe carrying Chiwiwi's dead body out of the gates of the burning Anaya *hacienda* and placing her body at the Isleta chief's feet. Benicío killed her with a bullet meant for Rafe. Carlos killed Benicío, his own brother, but too late to save Chiwiwi.

After the battle at the Anaya *hacienda*, the trip home to Santa Fe was spent mostly in silence. Rafe slouched on his saddle, head hanging, not saying a word. Carlos dealt with his sorrow no better than Rafe. There were no words George could say to either one of them.

George remembered it was dusk when they arrived home and without saying a word, Rafe put up Rayo, and often slept in the loft of the horse barn, alone. Since then, George had many sleepless nights. Much like the time after Gregory's death, his only solace was working at the foundry. Josefina told him not to worry about Rafe. "He needs to grieve on his own," she told him. In reality, she worried about Rafe, too. George heard her praying to Saint

Christopher, asking the saint to keep their adopted son safe, and a candle stayed lit in front of the saint's miniature statue.

Sometimes George did not know what to make of Benicío's brother, Carlos. A well-bred young Spaniard, Carlos had studied at the seminary in Madrid. According to Carlos, Rafe saved his life, too. Carlos asked for little, and helped a lot. George thanked God for Carlos' help while Rafe was grieving. The young Spaniard stepped in and helped him, even though he had no experience in metalworking. Besides working in the foundry, Carlos looked after Rafe's horses, especially Rayo and the young colts.

Now, Rafe was safe at home and resting upstairs. George felt the pressure lift off of him, but Rafe's uncle Jose brought bad news. He worried whether Rafe, in his fragile condition, could deal with the news his uncle brought from Torreón.

The afternoon light was fading. The autumn rain had stopped, but puffy light gray clouds still scuttled along the skyline. A shaft of sunlight cut through the dim parlor. George sat back into his large leather chair and tried to relax. He instructed Juanita to prepare a large feast for supper. She was busy all afternoon in the kitchen and Josefina and the girls were helping. Light footsteps sounded in the hallway and the maid tapped lightly on the open door.

"Yes." George looked up.

"*Señor*, the boys are awake."

"Go and tell Jose to join me," he told the maid.

CHAPTER 4

The rain stopped while Rafe and Carlos slept away the afternoon. The setting sun cut shafts of light across the walls of the bedroom. An unknown sound jarred Carlos awake. His body ached from slouching in the high-back chair. Stretching his legs, he slowly stood up and looked at Rafe sleeping quietly on the bed. His face looked less haggard than it had this morning.

Walking to the bed Carlos pushed Rafe's shoulder gently. "Wake up," he said quietly. The sleeping body moved a bit, then settled back.

"Rafe, time to get up," Carlos said a bit louder and rocked his shoulder.

"Huh."

"Wake up. Time for supper. George and your uncle are waiting for us."

Rafe rolled over and opened his eyes, exhaling a tired breath. He looked at his friend's face. At the corner of one eye, a white scar cut down his face to his chin. Rafe remembered the day Benicío gave him that scar – the day he first met Carlos in El Paso.

Rolling to one side, Rafe sat up on the edge of the bed. He swayed slightly to one side, holding himself steady with his hands.

"How's your head?" Carlos asked.

"Is that the thing sitting on my shoulders and pounding?" Rafe retorted. Carlos laughed. It was good to hear his friend joking.

"Yes, and it needs a shave before supper. Are your hands steady enough to not cut your throat?" Carlos grinned enjoying the friendly banter.

Rafe shuffled to the dresser and splashed water on his face. The face staring back at him from the mirror looked thin and pitiful. The brown eyes looked dull. A scraggly beard covered his cheeks and chin. He could not remember the last time he had shaved. Although twenty-one, his beard remained sparse and soft, not like the heavy, dark beard of his father. His father's beard was so dark and heavy, even when he shaved his cheeks looked a shade darker than his dark skin. Rafe's eyes were a soft brown, unlike his father's eyes that were so black you could not see the center.

"Are you going to just stare at that face or shave it?" Carlos chided. He picked up the soap and beat it to a lather in the shaving cup, handing it to Rafe.

Rafe took the cup and lathered his chin. He decided to leave his mustache and a V-shaped beard under his lower lip. When he finished, he splashed his face with water and wiped it with a towel. Staring into the mirror, a new face stared back. The face looked like a Spanish *caballero*, a Spanish gentleman.

"What do you think?" he asked turning to face Carlos.

"I think you'll scare the girls."

Dipping his fingers into the water, Rafe ran his hands through his unruly hair several times to slick it down, hoping to make himself presentable. He changed his shirt and tucked it into his pants. Bending to put on his boots his head throbbed, forcing him to sit on the bed.

Sitting on the bed until his head cleared, Rafe finally stood steady on his feet. Remnants of the headache lingered and his mouth was dry, but his stomach was demanding food and that was a good feeling. Straightening his back and shoulders, he looked into the mirror again one last time before he turned to Carlos.

"*Vámonos.*" They walked out of the room together and down the main stairs of the house, Rafe taking the lead. His uncle was here in Santa Fe. Rafe hoped he had good news about his mother and sister. They heard voices and followed their ears. Rafe led the way into the drawing room. Carlos, walking behind, saw him square his shoulders before turning the corner. George and Jose looked up as they entered.

"*Tío,*" Rafe called out as he went to hug his uncle Jose.

Jose was shocked by Rafe's looks. Where was the proud, robust, young man who had ridden into El Paso just a few months ago and battled the Reynolds to regain Jose's ranch? Standing before him was a thin and drawn shell. *"Mijo,* you don't look so good."

"It is nothing," Rafe responded and Jose let it pass. George had explained the heavy grief consuming Rafe since the death of Chiwiwi.

Turning to George, Rafe said simply, "Hello, Father." George wrapped two strong arms around Rafe and pulled him into his chest.

The sound of clicking heels sounded in the hallway. Dolores and Elizabeth Summers burst into the room. "Rafe!" girlish voices called out. The two daughters of George and Josefina Summers loved Rafe like an older brother and they missed him terribly over the last several months. Suddenly, arms and kisses fell all over Rafe, grabbing him from their father's hug.

When Rafe arrived four years ago at the Summers' home, the girls were eleven and nine. At first they were shy, but Rafe loved to tease with them and soon they bonded like natural siblings. The girls liked to jump on him and play tug of war with his arms. He spent long summer evenings playing hide and seek on the property, always letting them win. He called Dolores, Lolo, and Elizabeth, Lizzy. Now young teenagers, the two girls were growing into lovely young ladies. Lolo favored more of her mother's Spanish features, while Lizzy had light brown hair and freckles and an infectious grin.

"Help!" Rafe exclaimed. The girls only laughed and continued their onslaught. Lizzy pulled at Rafe's mustache and laughed. "You look funny."

"Ouch," he cried out, but knew it was useless to defend himself. Behind him, he heard more shoes clicking on the floor.

"Mother, look at Rafe. He looks like your grandfather's picture in the hallway," Lolo called to her mother. Josefina Summers hurried into the room and the girls twirled Rafe around to face her. She smiled and wrapped Rafe in tight hug. This woman was his adopted mother for the past four years. Like her husband, her home and her arms were open to him. Rafe felt a rushing of both love and shame for his behavior lately.

"Mother, I'm sorry if I hurt you," he whispered in her ear.

"It only matters that you are safe," she murmured into his neck and held him tight. In her heart, Josefina understood his grief. She still carried grief for her son Gregory who died suddenly of influenza at eight months old. One day he was there and one day he was not. His small grave was marked beside a tree in the backyard. It had almost killed George's spirit and she stayed alone most nights. In her grief, she was tempted at the time to return home to Spain, but God had intervened and she became pregnant and Dolores was born, two years later, Elizabeth.

Josefina had watched the tree grow tall and green in the yard and imagined how her son would have grown tall. George seldom talked about him, but she knew it was just his way. He adored the two girls and was a wonderful father. When he brought Rafe home four years ago, she knew God sent this young man to them. Rafe saved her husband from certain death. Rafe could never replace Gregory, but Josefina had faith, that like the grief which still stung in her heart, time would mend her adopted son.

"Supper is served," Juanita announced. Lolo and Lizzy grabbed Rafe and demanded he sit between them. Wrapping an arm around each, Rafe led them to the dining room.

Eight candles lighted the long Spanish colonial table. Large platters of meat cooked with chile sat on the sideboard. Bread and squash were arranged on plates. The family stood behind their high-back chairs and George gave the blessing over the meal, the same blessing Rafe heard so many times before.

"Lord, bless us your humble servants. We give thanks for this food which you have provided. Keep us safe in your arms and let us be servants of your will, Amen."

"Amen," they all chimed in and then the girls made a

dash to be first to fill their plates.

Rafe was anxious to ask his uncle about his mother and sister, but knew this was not talk for the dinner table and it had to wait until later. Josefina and the girls talked about the autumn festival and dance at the church in two weeks. They wanted new dresses.

"New dresses? What boys are you trying to impress?" Rafe taunted the girls. Lolo gave him a teasingly disgusted sigh.

"I want lace around the bodice and sleeves in peach taffeta, just like the one we saw in the catalog," Lolo said excitedly to her mother.

"Lace around the bodice? Isn't that a bit improper for a girl of your age?" Rafe asked, looking quite serious.

"Stop it, Rafe. I'm almost sixteen, and besides it's 1870 and all the girls are dressing this way," Lolo said, but he saw her face blush. "Sylvia O'Hara told me you better be there and dance with her," Lolo teased him back.

The playful banter continued throughout dinner. His taste was no longer numbed by tequila and he savored each mouthful of the spicy meat and his stomach approved. The autumn squash was cooked with sugar and lots of cinnamon. Rafe ate double portions and with each bite, he seemed to feel better. By the time Juanita served dessert, Rafe's headache was gone. Being around his family was good – very good.

After dinner, Josefina shooed the men out of the dining room and they returned to the parlor. George offered Jose a cigar.

"Tell me about my mother and sister," Rafe said anxiously to his uncle before they sat down.

"When I went to Torreón to bring them to El Paso, your mother told me she won't leave," Jose said looking at the cigar in his hand.

"What do you mean she won't leave?" Rafe's eyes widened and his heart skipped a beat.

"You will not like what I am going to tell you." Jose raised his dark eyes to look directly at his nephew. "María has a four-year-old son, a two-year-old daughter, and another baby on the way."

"What! Who did she marry?"

"She is not married. The children belong to *don* Bernardo. You didn't kill him." Jose saw the color drain from Rafe's face and his jaw tighten.

Silence filled the room.

"*¡Cabrón!*" The curse growled from Rafe's lips as he jumped out of his chair. Rage filled him, swelled him. "I can't believe that *bastardo* is still alive. I killed him!"

"*No mijo*, he survived and took María as his mistress. Your mother won't leave your sister and the children. They are living in the guest house of the *hacienda*. María is young and thinks *don* Bernardo loves her and the children. She does not want to leave."

Rafe slammed his hand against the fireplace mantle. "That *desgraciado* keeps people like they are horses. He thinks he owns them and takes his pleasure with my sister," he growled.

"Your mother was so pleased to know you are alive and well. She said she prayed to Saint Christopher everyday for your safety. She said God has now answered her prayers, but she told me to tell you not to come to Torreón. *Don* Bernardo will kill you if you do," Jose warned him.

Rafe sagged into an overstuffed chair near the fireplace. The roaring fire crackled, popped, and spit tiny embers beside him, but Rafe took no notice. His brain swirled in fury from the bad news. He could not accept what his uncle told him. *Don* Bernardo was alive and forcing his sister to have his bastard children.

George looked over at Rafe and said, "I'm sorry, son. I know this is not the news you wanted."

Rafe blamed himself for not killing the monster, *don* Bernardo. He watched the *desgraciado* fall after he shot him with the flintlock pistol and always assumed he had killed him.

"I must go to see for myself and speak to my mother."

"That's not a good idea, Rafe," George said. "It's not

safe."

"No, you must not go," Jose added. "*Don* Bernardo has many loyal *vaqueros* and they will recognize you."

"Perhaps, I can go?" George interjected. "*Don* Bernardo doesn't know me."

"No, I have to go," Rafe insisted.

"He will have you killed," Jose warned him.

"It's been almost five years since I left the *hacienda*. I have changed. He won't recognize me." Rafe tried to assure them.

Listening to them argue, Carlos understood Rafe's dilemma and thought about how he could help and came up with an idea.

"I will go with you," Carlos stepped into the conversation. "You told me *don* Bernardo was a horse breeder. Perhaps we can go there pretending to buy horses. I will pose as a *haciendero* from New Mexico and you will be my head *vaquero*," Carlos said looking at Rafe.

"Yes!" Rafe exclaimed. He jumped out of the chair and pounded his right fist into his left hand. "Look at me, *don* Jorge. I am not the same boy you brought here to Santa Fe. Would you recognize me?"

"I don't like it, Rafe. You can't go. It's too risky. If *don* Bernardo sees you with your mother and sister he will remember," *don* Jorge admonished him.

"I agree *mijo*. I saw *don* Bernardo. He is hunched over at the waist and they say he is meaner than ever." Jose warned.

"I must go there. I will not rest until I get them away from that dreadful place where they are slaves of the devil. You know I can't let that stand *tío*," he said directly to his uncle.

"I spent most of my time at the *hacienda* with *don* Pablo, the horse master, in the barns. *Don* Bernardo didn't see much of me, only when I shot him. It happened so quick, I don't think he will recognize me. I have to go!" He had made up his mind.

CHAPTER 5

On a ridge near his *hacienda* in Torreón, Mexico, *don* Bernardo Reyes sat on his horse surveying the valley below him. His disfigured back was aching, but he learned to ignore it after years of pain. He watched his neighbor, *don* Miguel Santos, and a few *vaqueros* rounding up stray cows in the valley below. He and Miguel had been neighbors and *amigos* for over thirty years.

Miguel and his wife, Juana, often visited Bernardo and his wife, Carmela, on holidays and invited them to *fiestas* at the Santos *hacienda*. Miguel was a tall and lean man who looked more distinguished each year as his hair grayed. Juana was not as pretty as Carmela, but she was here and Carmela was not.

Bernardo's wife Carmela was gone. She left him and his injured body after she found out his *peón* mistress, María, was pregnant with his bastard. It was all the fault of María's *bastardo* brother, Rafael, who shot him the day he raped María for the first time. It was months before Bernardo could walk again and by then Carmela had left him.

Sitting on his horse and watching *don* Miguel in the valley below, his stomach churned. He had pondered what he planned to do today for over a year. It was not something he relished, but his *hacienda* languished while the Santos' *hacienda* flourished. Business was business. Friendship was a commodity for fools.

Over the years, Bernardo would meet Miguel Santos, sometimes by chance, riding the hills. They would stop and talk about politics and the French, curse the *peóns* and their slovenly work habits — the talk of two *gachupíns*, Spanish gentlemen. For weeks Bernardo rode these hills each day hoping to meet his old friend. Today, he watched from the top of a ridge with the afternoon sun behind his back. Bernardo was not a patient man, and after weeks of frustration he hoped Miguel would see him waiting.

Finally, he saw Miguel wave to his *vaqueros,* who were corralling a small group of cows. Miguel turned and rode toward his direction, alone. Bernardo patted his horse and moved slowly down the ridge. He wanted to meet Miguel on the rocky escarpment.

"*Hola viejo,*" Miguel greeted him as they met on the trail, calling Bernardo an old man.

"*Hola baboso,*" Bernardo cajoled his friend.

"How's your old body today," Miguel asked.

"My *garrancha* still works. How about you?"

"Hey, don't worry about me. I get my share of young *chicas.*"

They chatted about cows and horses – the talk of *hacienderos.* Bernardo kept one eye on the *vaqueros* in the valley below moving the cattle toward the Santos *hacienda.*

Miguel noticed the afternoon shadows of the short and stubby trees were casting long down the hill. "We better get off this hill before we lose our light," he said. Carefully, he turned his horse and took the lead. Bernardo followed behind. Up ahead was a part of the trail where it dropped off steeply to the left.

Bernardo had one last look into the empty valley, before he quietly slipped his *riata* from his saddle. Bernardo's horse was better trained than Miguel's and Bernardo a better horseman, but Bernardo knew he only had one chance to time his throw – one chance to catch Miguel off guard. He twirled the lariat and let it fly. Bernardo threw the lariat perfectly over Miguel's chest and pulled back tightly.

His knees ordered his well-trained horse to stop. After years of tracking and catching wild ponies, the horse obeyed even the slightest verbal or physical command. As soon as Bernardo was sure the momentum of Miguel's fall would carry him down the cliff, he loosened his grip on the rope and let it go.

Miguel's body tumbled down the steep hill with a spray of dislodged rocks following behind. Bernardo watched until it landed in a heap about fifty feet below. Miguel's riderless horse skittered a little way down the trail and stopped. Bernardo sat his mount watching the body. Miguel did not move.

Grunting, Bernardo dismounted. He knew this would be the most tiresome task. In his younger years sliding down an embankment was easy, but since the *bastardo* boy shot him, nothing was easy. Slowly, he picked his way down the side of the hill. He slid about twenty feet, losing his footing and almost twisting his ankle. Finally, he made it to where Miguel's body lay bloody and crumpled. Miguel's leg looked twisted and broken. Blood oozed from a jagged gash on his temple and dirt covered his once proud *traje* and face.

Bernardo pushed at Miguel to loosen his *riata* and pulled it from under the body. Miguel groaned and opened his eyes.

"*Ayúdame,*" he begged for help. Bernardo jerked back at Miguel's voice, thinking he was already dead. Pulling his lariat free, he wound it and laid it on the ground. He assumed the fall would kill Miguel and pondered what to do. His careful planning made sure no gunshot or obvious evidence of foul play could be discovered when Miguel's body was found. It would look like Miguel's horse had misstepped, throwing him to his death on the rocky slope. Just an accident, the authorities would assume.

"Why?" Miguel whispered to Bernardo, his dark eyes still clear.

Bernardo stood looking down and laughed. "Your money, your land, your wife," Bernardo told him. "It is the way of *gachupíns*. We take what we want."

"Please, please don't do this. I will give you money, if you want it," Miguel begged.

Bernardo picked up a large rock and moved it beside Miguel's head. Grabbing Miguel by the hair, he lifted his head and pushed the large rock under it. Bernardo looked into Miguel's eyes, and then crushed his head back against the rock. He bashed Miguel's head four or five times until life left his eyes.

Bernardo stood up, winded. He lifted the bloody rock and hurled it down the slope watching it loose smaller rocks as it fell. Catching his breath, he picked up his lariat and scratched out the footprints he made near the body. Slowly, he climbed back up the slope to where his horse patiently waited.

The old *don* finally reached the trail and grunted in pain as he climbed up on his horse. His energy was spent. It was getting dark, but his horse knew the trail well. Turning back, Bernardo headed back up the hill and home. When the body was found, he would console *doña* Juana Santos in her grief.

CHAPTER 6

"*¿Por qué?* Why didn't you stop him?" Elena Montoya yelled at her brother Rodrigo.

"Stop it *pendeja*. His friend was determined to get him out of here. I couldn't stop him. Besides, you were dead drunk," Rodrigo responded.

"If he doesn't come back to the *cantina*, you know I won't be able to find him," Elena yelled at her brother.

"Good. He was no good for you. All you two did was drink and fuck."

Elena responded by throwing a large, brightly painted jar at him and stomped off. The jar shattered on the hardened clay floor.

Rodrigo shook his head thinking she was so much like their father. Born to a wealthy Spanish family, Francisco Montoya de Archuleta y Rosas drifted, tending to a life as a *picaro*, a gambler and a womanizer, who had lived off his charm and wits. Rodrigo and Elena were his oldest children, born to a striking young Tewa Indian girl. In Santa Fe, only his uncle Nico knew they were half-breeds.

Fair haired and light skinned, Rodrigo resembled their Spanish father. However, he had none of his father's charm and was quiet and withdrawn. Elena, even as a young child, was a beauty. She inherited all of their mother's loveliness, but her Spanish side gave her a light olive-colored skin and golden brown eyes. Her brown hair shone gold in the sunlight and cascaded in waves down her back. Like their father, she had a wild side – she could be charming and knew how to use it.

She flirted with the men at the *cantina* and several tried to court her. Then one day, Rafe walked into the *cantina* and Elena was smitten. Rodrigo could not see what she saw in Rafe. The man was obviously withdrawn and unhappy.

Elena slammed the bedroom door and threw herself on the bed sobbing. Her brother did not understand why she loved Rafe so much. Rafe, his name, that was all she knew about him. She remembered vividly the first day he came into the *cantina*.

She was tending bar. The tan-skinned young man was completely self-absorbed when he sided up to the bar and took no notice of her. Finally, he looked at her with vacant eyes and asked for a shot of tequila. Her soul, her very being, took a tremendous jolt. She had no control over her feelings for the quiet stranger. He finished his drink and left. She shrugged off the feeling and quickly engaged the other customers.

Three days later he came back to the *cantina*. Elena had her back to the door when he walked in. Just his presence in the room sent a jolt through her. Before she turned around, she knew he was there.

He walked to the bar and tossed down a coin. He looked forlorn. She slid up in front of him.

"Tequila," he grumbled hardly looking up. Elena's heart thumped, but this man did not even notice her. His woven cotton jacket and vest were well tailored, but wrinkled and dirty. His eyes were brown and dull. She could not understand the power this man commanded over her heart.

"*Hola*, my name is Elena," she spoke quietly to him. "You look like you lost a friend."

He looked at her with his dull eyes, then looked down at his drink, but Elena did not move away. Slowly he tipped the drink into his mouth and set the glass down and Elena refilled it.

"I lost everything," he mumbled quietly never looking up.

"Hey Elena, we need drinks over here," a big man at the end of the bar yelled at her.

"I'm coming," she replied. He did not look up when she walked away. He stayed for a couple more drinks and then left.

"*¿Quién es ese hombre?*" she asked her uncle Nico if he knew the man.

"*No sé,*" Nico replied.

The following night was slow. The weather was rainy which kept a lot of the regulars at home. The batwing doors swung open and a man clad in a black slicker and black Stetson walked in. Sluggishly, he unwound the slicker and hung it and the hat on a peg by the door. Elena caught her breath. It was the man.

As he approached, Elena moved around the bar and slid up next to him. "Nico, bring us two tequilas," she said to her uncle.

"Rainy night," she said to the stranger.

"Yeah," Rafe replied. Her chest was thumping and her hands shook. Again, she tried to get his attention by moving in close to him, but he shifted away preoccupied with his thoughts, making it clear all he wanted was to drink, not talk.

Elena tried every trick to engage him. Why did she feel this way? By the looks of him, he was just a drifter, lost and miserable. She wanted to dismiss him, but something kept a hold of her. Something pulled her to him like a magnet and would not let her go.

"¿Eh, qué te pasa, eres maricón?" a frustrated Elena asked him touching his arm.

"¿Huh, qué?" he muttered finally looking at her. Next to him was a beautiful young woman obviously trying to get his attention.

"I asked if you were queer?" Elena goaded him.

"No! Why are you bothering me?"

"Don't you think I'm beautiful?" she purred. She threw her brown hair away from her pale face with the back of her fingers and pouted her painted red lips.

He turned, took the glass and tossed the tequila down his throat, saying nothing. Finally, completely irritated with his rebuke, she drew back and slapped him across the face. He grabbed her arm with all his force and pulled her to him.

"Don't ever do that again," he growled at her, nose to nose.

"So, that's how I get your attention. You like to get hit?" Elena laughed at him.

Pushing her away from him, he signaled to the bartender to refill his glass. This infuriated her. No man ever pushed her away. All men wanted to get close to her; it was she who pushed them away. At least she had gotten a response from him.

"You are a *maricón!*" she yelled loud enough so everyone in the *cantina* could hear.

"Get away from me," he sneered at her. He took the refilled glass of tequila and tossed it down, then flipping a coin on the bar he headed to the door. Elena panicked, knowing she insulted him; she followed him across the room.

In a soft, sweet voice she said, "Please, don't go. I'm sorry. I acted terrible and insulted you." She pulled on his arm. "I just want to meet you, but you keep ignoring me," she pleaded.

"Look, I'm in no mood to get to know anyone, let alone you." He tried to get away from her, but she held his arm tightly. He had been drinking most of the day without much food and his head swam a bit.

Outside it was pouring down rain and cold. He turned around to face her while donning his slicker. The lights by the door danced on her hair and it glinted with gold. She was beautiful or maybe it was the tequila.

"What is it you want with me?"

"I think you are handsome and I want to get to know you," she responded with the same sweet voice as she held onto his arm. "I live close by. My carriage is out back and I'll make you a good meal. That's all."

Rafe stood there staring at her beautiful face, not wanting to go with her, but the tequila said, "Go ahead, go." He was too tired and too lost to resist her and she seemed to sense it.

"Get your horse," she told him. He put on his Stetson and walked out into the rain. When her carriage came around the corner from the back of the *cantina*, he tied the brown horse to the back of the carriage and climbed on. Elena drove them to her house.

True to her word, she cooked a hot meal for him of

chili and potatoes and she kept his glass of tequila full. She hummed a tune in the kitchen and asked him no questions. It was enough that he was here with her. She touched his hand when she handed him the plate of chili and electricity shot up her arm. He seemed oblivious to it, but she tingled all over.

He ate mostly in silence, but finished the food and tequila. She wrapped an arm around his shoulders and helped him to his feet. He followed her slowly into her bedroom.

Rafe allowed Elena to help him out of his clothes and he lay back on the soft bed with his eyes closed. Soon he felt Elena's hands on him. They were tender the way Chiwiwi touched him – soft and gentle. Elena's hair fell on his bare chest as she leaned over to kiss him.

His tequila-soaked mind drifted to the bed of soft skins that he and Chiwiwi shared. Chiwiwi was holding him. He felt her straddle him and he groaned. Her hands pushed against his chest. Tenderly, he caressed her breasts and rose to kiss each one. His manhood was sheltered in her, warm and firm. He rocked her slowly and firmly. He looked at her hands resting on his chest and wondered why she was not wearing her silver cuff bracelet. His rhythm gained momentum until she cried out.

He wrapped his beloved Chiwiwi in his arms, cupping her butt cheeks in his hands. He thrust and withdrew until he exploded into her softness. "Chiwiwi," he groaned into her hair. Elena heard him whisper the name and vowed to make him forget. Rafe saw Chiwiwi's face in his mind and then darkness enveloped him.

Rafe woke up to the smell of bacon cooking. Elena came to the bedroom with a tray of breakfast and a smile on her face. He looked at her confused. His head pounded and his mouth was dry.

"What's your name?" she asked him.

"Rafe. You?"

"Elena."

A shaft of sun cut through the small bedroom. Vaguely, he remembered leaving the *cantina* with her last night. After that, he did not remember much. Rafe leaned back on the pillow. His will to fight was gone. Elena put the breakfast tray between them.

The memories of first meeting Rafe faded away as she heard Rodrigo sweeping up the broken pieces of clay. She should not have thrown the jar at him, but she was hurt and angry. She was stuck on the lonely, unhappy, young man and Rodrigo did not understand why. For the last month, she and Rafe spent most of their time here at the house. She told herself she was helping Rafe forget Chiwiwi, whoever she was. He would not talk about her. Each night they drank tequila until he was drunk and then they spent the night in bed together. Soon, Elena was as drunk as he was, often sleeping all morning. She seldom went to El Coyote to tend bar and Uncle Nico was mad she was not coming to work anymore.

Rodrigo finished sweeping the floor and was drinking coffee when Elena came out of the bedroom looking sullen, her eyes puffy and red. Her once immaculate beauty was growing dull and pasty. Rodrigo was worried. He wanted a good life for her, for both of them. He bought them this small house and gave her money to buy nice things. He worked hard to provide for them after their father had died. He was glad the man she called Rafe was gone. Good riddance.

"You have to help me find where he lives," Elena demanded when she walked into the room.

"Why, don't you know? You think you're so clever and you don't even know where he lives. For all you know he's a drifter. He was a bum," Rodrigo went on rather enjoying his sister's dilemma.

"No! You're right. I'm stupid in love with him," she answered and slumped into an overstuffed chair. "I didn't ask him a lot of questions. I just wanted to be with him."

"How am I going to find him? Why didn't you ask the man who came to get him where they were going?" she asked more meekly.

"How was I to know what to ask? He said his father needed to see him and something about his uncle, so I guess he must live around here somewhere." Rodrigo looked at Elena draped over the chair. She looked so young and vulnerable. Her brown hair, usually brushed and shiny, was disheveled and she only wore an old worn-out house coat and was barefoot. She was so much like their father – flighty and irresponsible. He had watched his father ruin his life, and theirs, and vowed to keep Elena from making the same mistakes.

First, he needed to get her sober and off the tequila. "Have you eaten anything yet?" he asked.

"No, I'm not hungry."

"You need to eat. Go take a bath and I'll fix breakfast for you. If you stop the tequila, I'll try to help you find him." Rodrigo knew he was sort of lying, but he needed to get her sober, then hopefully she would move on.

Elena sighed and stood up. "Ok, scramble some eggs."

When Elena returned, clean and dressed, she still looked forlorn. She sat down at the table. Rodrigo scooped a heaping mound of eggs, beans, and two corn tortillas onto a plate and set it in front of her. He poured a cup of strong coffee.

Elena stared at the food. "Eat," he said. She picked up a fork and put a bite of eggs in her mouth. "Finish all of it and I'll help you find him. What's his last name?" Rodrigo asked.

"I don't know."

"What? What do you mean you don't know?"

"I told you, I'm crazy in love with him. All I care about is being with him. The rest of the world can go to hell." Tears welled in her red-rimmed eyes.

"His name is Rafael, but he goes by Rafe. That's all I know and he lost a girl that he loved named Chiwiwi. I was trying to make him forget her."

"Rafe. I don't know anyone by that name, but I'll ask around. Someone might know." Elena was scraping the plate and the food was gone. She looked pale. "Go back to bed and sleep it off," Rodrigo said picking up the dirty plate. "I'll tell Uncle Nico you might be back to work tomorrow night."

Elena burst out in tears. "Please . . . find him. You don't understand. I need him." She dropped her head into her hands and sobbed.

Rodrigo shook his head. He would try, but not very hard. Hopefully, Rafe would not come back.

CHAPTER 7

Carlos and Rafe sat in the Summers' parlor beside the fire scheming a plan to go to *don* Bernardo's *hacienda* near Torreón, Mexico, to rescue Rafe's mother and sister. George and Jose had given up several hours ago trying to persuade the two young men it was folly to go on this dangerous mission.

Rafe needed time to regain his health and to add a few pounds to his skinny, tequila-slogged body. Nevertheless, it was early October and they needed to get started soon before the cold New Mexico winter set in. Jose was leaving in the morning, needing to get home to his family in El Paso.

Rafe still could not process that his sister María had two children and one more on the way. That *don* Bernardo fathered her children was unthinkable and made him rile at the thought.

Jose told them he had been scared to stay very long at the *hacienda*. *Don* Bernardo was a cruel and mean man who did not like or trust strangers. Uncle or not, Jose was unwelcome.

Carlos' plan was a good one. They argued over who should be the horse buyer and who the *vaquero*. Rafe was concerned Carlos did not know enough about purebred horses to negotiate with *don* Bernardo. Carlos worried *don* Bernardo would recognize Rafe. Finally they agreed, Carlos would pretend to be an arrogant aristocrat who left the details to his trusted *vaquero*. Exhausted, they let the fire burn down. Tomorrow, they would start planning the details of the trip in earnest.

Rafe stretched out on his bed in the upstairs bedroom. His now tired body screamed for tequila. He noticed while he was downstairs talking to Carlos, his hands were shaking. The tequila had dulled the pain in his soul and Elena had soothed the longing in his body, but nothing could bring Chiwiwi back.

Elena was pretty and he did like the way her hair glinted in the sunlight, but they spent little time in the sun. Most of the time was spent in her darkened bedroom. He did not think she was a *puta*. He never asked her, but she was no virgin either.

For the past month, he had stopped at the *cantina* to find her for a night of drinking and rowdy lusty sex, and then more tequila and more sex until they were exhausted. He would hardly call it lovemaking, but she did not seem to mind. It was not like making love to Chiwiwi – not passionate and tender. Sex with Elena was hurtful and raw, like animals. Somehow though, it appeased his anguish. After a couple of weeks, he stayed drunk at Elena's and no longer came home. She kept his glass of tequila full and the drinking made him numb. Numb to his pain, numb to his guilt and numb, just numb.

Sometimes, he woke as Elena slept beside him and his mind wanted to leave, but his body would not respond. He did not love her, of that he was sure, but she made him forget and that was enough.

A quiet knock sounded on the door. *"¿Estás bien?"* Carlos' voice came through the door asking if he was all right.

"Sí, buenas noches," Rafe said goodnight.

Autumn had come to Santa Fe and the night air was cold and even fully dressed he shivered. Sitting up he removed his boots and crawled under the blankets. *"Mierda,"* he cursed and wondered why he was so cold. He tucked the blankets tightly around him, but the shaking did not stop.

His stomach growled, but it was late in the night and it would have to wait until morning. He wanted a shot of tequila. His body craved the amber liquid, knowing it would stop the shaking. He twisted out of the blankets. Pulling off the last blanket, he stood up next to the bed and took a couple of wobbly steps in the dark. His legs buckled and he reached out blindly grabbing at the bedpost. His hand grabbed at a leather string and he closed his fist around it. Still unsteady his hand slid down the string until something poked into his palm. Even in the dark, he knew what it was – Chief Letoc's silver and turquoise star amulet. Letoc told him the amulet would keep him safe.

He pulled himself back onto the bed still holding the amulet. "I don't need tequila," he mumbled to himself. If it called to him again, he would not answer. Wrapping himself in two blankets, he curled up on the bed. Slowly, the shivering stopped and he fell into a deep sleep.

"Wake up, son, wake up," a voice said. A hand pushed his shoulder and he groaned. "Wake up. Jose is leaving and wants to say goodbye."

George stood over him smiling. "How do you feel?"

"I've been better."

"Jose is waiting to see you before he leaves."

Rafe struggled into his boots and followed George downstairs to the parlor. Jose turned and reached out his arms. "We will be waiting for you to come to El Paso. Wire me if you need anything for the trip to Torreón. I will have it ready when you come."

"Safe journey, *tío*. Tell *tía* Lupe I am looking forward to seeing her."

The entire Summers' family waved goodbye as Jose turned down the lane. Rafe knew Jose would ride hard to get home to his family, but the trip would still take several days on the trail.

Lizzy and Lolo wrapped their arms into Rafe's and they walked him into the house. "Juanita made cinnamon rolls for breakfast," Lizzy said. "I'm going to eat them all and you won't get any," she teased.

"Not if I can stop you," Rafe teased her back. They tugged him to the dining room and the smell of food awakened his stomach. After two large helpings of cinnamon rolls, eggs, ham, and coffee, Rafe was finally full.

"I'm going riding today," he said to his adopted father. "I'm feeling better, and I have some things to work out in my mind. I will return tonight."

George nodded thoughtfully. "Be careful."

Early October in Santa Fe brought color to the surrounding hills along with a chill in the air. Rafe wore a heavy wool coat and a black Stetson pulled down over his eyes to shield the sun. He strode to the corral with purpose. Surrounded by mares, he spotted the tall Appaloosa with the white and brown rump.

Rafe whistled. The Appaloosa jerked his head high with ears perked forward. Rayo knew Rafe's call. Their bond was more than horse and master. With tail high, Rayo pushed the mares aside to greet Rafe. His large face and powerful brown eyes stared two inches from Rafe's.

"*Hola amigo.*" Rafe patted Rayo's face as the Appaloosa nudged at his chest. The large stallion suddenly jerked his head and almost pushed Rafe over. Stumbling a bit, Rafe righted himself and Rayo pushed again.

"You are mad at me, I see." The Appaloosa kept nudging Rafe with his nose, snorting and whinnying. Rafe had never neglected the horse for any length of time since Rayo was a foal at the *hacienda*. He saw him every day since the horse had been born, until this last month.

Rafe dug into his coat pocket and pulled out a red apple. Holding it out to Rayo, the horse snorted. "I know you're mad. I'm sorry," Rafe said softly, holding the apple under the horse's nose. Rayo looked at him, jerked his head up and down and pawed his front foot, then accepted the peace offering from Rafe's hand.

Rafe rubbed the horse's spotted face and ran his hand down his dark shoulders. Splayed across his rump, a distinctive array of dark brown splotches stood out against white. Rayo's coat was shiny and his dark brown mane and tail brushed. Rafe knew Carlos had cared for all of his horses while he lost himself and he was grateful.

Rafe talked to all of his horses, but most of all to Rayo. He swore the horse understood what he said. "I see you have been taking care of the ladies *señor caballo,*" Rafe teased Rayo. He could tell one of the mares was pregnant. Come spring he would have another foal for his herd.

"Soon we will leave on a very important trip, but now you and I are going for a run. You are looking a little soft to me," Rafe kept talking to the Appaloosa. Rayo pawed at the dirt while Rafe saddled him. "Hold still."

Once saddled, Rafe jumped onto the horse's back and Rayo took off at a full gallop. Like one being, Rafe and Rayo surged east away from the ranch toward the snow capped Sangre de Cristo mountain range. Rayo knew the trail and Rafe let him take it at whatever speed the Appaloosa wanted. Rafe held on and enjoyed the speed, feeling the biting wind in his face as they entered the foothills.

Rayo was more than his horse; he was his friend. The powerful horse sensed Rafe's every feeling and action. Rafe was helping *don* Pablo on the stormy night Rayo was born at *don* Bernardo's *hacienda*. The mare was having trouble. The horse master said it was dystocia and he thought the foal was a bit sideways in the birth canal. *Don* Pablo reached in and tried to correct the position of the foal, but still the mare struggled. Suddenly a *rayo*, a thunderbolt, struck just outside the barn. The tremendous crack and brilliant flash of light jolted the mare enough to force the foal out like a shot. *Don* Pablo and Rafe stood staring at a beautiful newborn Appaloosa foal and Rafe named him *Rayo*, after the powerful thunderbolt.

Rafe was fifteen the night the Appaloosa was born. When the young colt was not nursing or following the mare, Rafe played chase and grabbed its tail to get his attention. Rayo would whinny and play the game. They ran with each other, sometimes for hours. For two years, Rafe spent his free time caring for the Appaloosa colt.

The day he shot the *haciendero desgraciado, don* Bernardo, who beat and raped his fifteen-year-old sister, Rafe stole Rayo and fled north. He was seventeen, a murderer and a horse thief, and on the run. He remembered that day like it was yesterday. He was full of rage and only focused on revenge. By a twist of fate, his escape from Mexico brought him to Santa Fe with George Summers, the man he called *don* Jorge and now, Father. That was over four years ago.

Never a day went by that Rafe did not think about his mother and sister. He had left them. His mother would forgive him, but his sister? She was young and he left her even more defenseless. He still could not believe *don* Bernardo was alive. The *bastardo* continued to rape María, fathering her children. Guilt flooded him. "It's all my fault," he grumbled to himself. The *haciendero* lived and his mother and sister were prisoners of the devil.

Rafe spurred Rayo to go faster. The power and beauty of the animal never ceased to amaze and delight him. Both he and the horse seemed to be shedding anger and frustration. Soon the clouds started building over the Sangre de Cristo range and the warmth of the sun was leaving the valley floor. Rafe turned Rayo back toward the ranch.

He had to go to Torreón to rescue his mother and sister and find a way to bring them and the children to Santa Fe. "This time I will make sure I kill that devil, *don* Bernardo," Rafe swore to himself.

CHAPTER 8

The early morning sun cut through the shutters into the dark bedroom where *don* Bernardo Reyes sat on a chest at the foot of his bed. His manservant was helping him dress in his best *traje* for an appointment in Torreón.

"*Ayeee pendejo,*" *don* Bernardo cursed at the manservant. Dressing was difficult and painful since he had been shot. It infuriated him that he could not dress himself anymore. The dark brown suit trimmed in silver, the one he used when he pranced his horse on the plaza of central Torreón, had been altered to fit his disfigured body. He lived with pain every day since that miserable boy, María's brother, shot him almost five years ago. He cursed the wretched boy everyday and blamed him for all his troubles.

Once tall and proud, the bullet shattered a vertebra in his lower back leaving him stooped and deformed. It took months of pain and agony before he walked again. *Doña* Carmela, his wife, nursed him and ran the ranch while he was bedridden. At first, she seemed her usual, contrite self. Then one day, she came into the bedroom white with anger.

"Your *puta* is pregnant!" she screamed. Carmela was barren. It was a source of discord in their marriage. *Don* Bernardo needed heirs and she wanted children. They blamed each other. She refused to watch his *puta*, María, give him a child. Although she knew it was not the first time he strayed from her bed, she decided it was the last. She looked down at his broken body and laughed.

"Your *puta* can have you," Carmela said and by the next morning she was gone. Bernardo could not get out of bed to stop her. Now, over four year later, the main house of the *hacienda* was dilapidated and the curtains were shabby and dusty. Without his wife to run the servants, the house was slowly deteriorating. His health and mobility left him unable to manage the *vaqueros* and *peóns* properly. They grew lazy and full of disrespect for him. Some ran off and he was unable to muster enough command to find them and it nurtured discontent on the ranch. The years had not only deteriorated the *hacienda*, his money was nearly gone.

Today, *don* Bernardo was meeting with his *abogado*, Nicolás Jiménez, at the lawyer's office in Torreón. *Doña* Carmela finally sued him for a civil divorce in Mexico City, wanting her share of the horse ranch. She threatened him before, but he was always able to appease her with a substantial bank draft. Jiménez told him to expect a fight and her *abogado* would not be bought off easily. *"¡Desgraciada!" don* Bernardo cursed her, and resolved to give her as little as possible, even though he built the horse business mostly from her first husband's money.

Don Bernardo remembered when he met Carmela. He was a brash, young *caballero*; she was married to an older, wealthy banker in Mexico City. Her husband, *don* Leonardo Bustamante, invested his money on silver explorations in and around Zacatecas. The exploration ventures were mostly failures, but when he had success it yielded him a small fortune. However, the man dedicated himself to his silver ventures, ignoring his beautiful young wife, Carmela. Young Bernardo first saw her on the *paseo*, riding a carriage with the sister of his friend, Ignacio López.

Behind the white laced fan, he saw the bluest eyes, the shade of the darkest blue sky he had ever seen. Bernardo was smitten.

"¿Cómo se llama esa mujer?" Bernardo asked Ignacio her name.

"Su nombre es doña Carmela. Es mejor que tengas cuidado con ella," Ignacio warned him that she was married to a very influential man and to get any ideas he had about her out of his head.

"No worries, *mi amigo,"* Bernardo laughed.

"I'm not worried, but I have a feeling *don* Leonardo should be," Ignacio responded, knowing his friend only too well.

Pain shot up *don* Bernardo's leg jarring his thoughts away from the past to his painful dressing ordeal. His manservant lifted his foot to put on his left boot, almost knocking the *don* off the bench.

"*Baboso,* be careful you idiot," *don* Bernardo hissed at the servant. The man lowered his head waiting to be hit, but *don* Bernardo restrained himself.

"*Lo siento,*" the manservant apologized.

The manservant put on the boots, buffed them to remove any fingerprints, and helped his master stand up.

"I will call for the carriage, *patrón,*" the manservant said and hurried from the room.

Don Bernardo looked at himself in the long mirror, which stood in the corner of the bedroom. Trying to straighten as much as possible, he wanted to see a proud *caballero* in the reflection, but only saw a stooped old man.

"*Me cago en el hijo de puta,*" he cursed. He swore he would someday shit upon the son of the whore who shot him. *Don* Bernardo knew Rafael would come one day for his mother and sister. On that day he would kill the *bastardo* and get his revenge.

Rafe's mother, Celiá, was weeding the small vegetable garden next to the *casita* just outside the main house courtyard wall.

"Antonio," Celiá yelled out at her almost four-year-old grandson. He took off after a rabbit that was digging under the squash plants in the garden. The boy glanced back at his grandmother, but continued his pursuit. He carried a small stick, waving it, and yelling. The rabbit was in no danger and hopped away. Full of energy, the boy was determined to run it off.

Looking up, Celiá saw *don* Bernardo's carriage coming down the lane from the main house.

"Antonio! Come here," his grandmother called sharply. She knew the *don* hated to see children running or behaving wildly. He would punish María for letting the children loose. Hearing the tone in his grandmother's voice, the child turned and quickly came back to her.

"*Nana, pero el conejo está todavía aquí,*" he complained pouting and pointing to the rabbit hopping back toward the garden.

Antonio was named after his grandfather, Celiá's

husband, Antonio Escalante de Estrada, who was killed in the war against the French. In May of 1862, the French were defeated at Puebla and stopped from marching into Mexico City. Her husband, Antonio, was sent to Puebla along with many newly recruited soldiers to reinforce the Mexican army. Again, the French attacked Puebla with a much stronger force and defeated the Mexicans. Antonio died fighting for Mexican freedom at Puebla. After his death, Celiá raised Rafael and María, alone. That was eight years ago.

Celiá, now going on forty with graying hair and dark complexion favoring her Indian heritage, was on her hands and knees as the carriage approached. She kept a hand on the boy's arm while the carriage rode by. The *haciendero* would not be aggravated today.

From the carriage, *don* Bernardo saw Celiá in her garden. Slim and shapely, she was still a handsome woman, even at her age. When she was young, she was a beauty. He watched her kneeling with her young grandson, his son, Antonio. Her daughter, María, was his mistress and Antonio's mother. María was beautiful like her mother had been when she was young, but María was more timid. Celiá was feisty and proud. He thought about her sometimes when he was with María, remembering a day in the past – a day when he was not old and bent.

His *garrancha* stirred. His back might be hunched, but he was not dead, not in that way. María was carrying his third child. He decided to call for her tonight to appease his anger. Although María's belly was swelling, she was still able to satisfy him.

As the carriage went by, Celiá kept her hand on her grandson until it was far down the lane and then let go. *"Ve por el conejo,"* she said and he laughed and sped off to try to find the rabbit.

Antonio reminded her so much of her Rafael at the same age, both in looks and demeanor. *"Gracias a Dios,"* she crossed herself. Rafael was alive. Jose brought the news from El Paso. She prayed every day since Rafael shot *don* Bernardo and fled, hoping her son was alive. Jose said he was a fine young man, tall and handsome, and living in Santa Fe, New Mexico. Jose told her many things she could hardly understand, about a *gringo*, and how Rafael saved the *gringo's* life. Rafael bought Jose's ranch in El Paso and supplied Jose with money to take them to Santa Fe. She did not understand how Rafael could have so much money.

"*Nana, Nana,*" Antonio yelled for her. She looked up and he was now chasing a black crow with his stick. The crow swooped and screeched at the boy.

She waved and laughed at her grandson. If she blinked, she could picture her Rafael wielding a stick as a young boy. Although she longed to see him, Celiá hoped Jose would keep him away from Torreón. *Don* Bernardo swore to kill him, if he ever came back. Celiá believed it was one reason why he kept María as his mistress – revenge against them for Rafael's actions. She had begged Rafael that day almost five years ago, but understood and accepted his passion and honor. Many times she asked God why the *don* had lived to torment them.

It broke Celiá's heart that the *don* abused María, working her hard by day and abusing her sexually at night. She knew it was only time until the old *don* tired of her daughter, casting her aside for someone younger or prettier. María, young and naïve, believed the *don* loved her.

Celiá sighed knowing there was nothing she could do about the old *don's* ways. She loved her two grandchildren dearly, regardless of their father, just as she loved Rafael.

Jose said Rafael had money to take them from the *hacienda*. Celiá only knew life as a *peón*, a slave. Her husband was buried on the far hill. She knew nothing of freedom or life outside of the *hacienda*. Besides, the *don* would never let his children leave, of that she was sure. Since Jose's visit, her daily prayers changed from, please let my son be alive, to, please do not let him come.

María, almost twenty now, was six months pregnant with *don* Bernardo's third bastard. The *don* first raped María when she was fifteen – the day Rafael shot *don* Bernardo in revenge and fled.

Several months later, *doña* Carmela left the *hacienda*

when the news spread through the *peóns* that María was pregnant. *Don* Bernardo was bedridden. With *doña* Carmela gone, the *don* forced María to tend him, caring for his every need. Celiá noticed bruises and her daughter was exhausted at the end of each day. Her daughter did not need to tell her that the *don* continued to rape her.

Only for the few weeks after Antonio's birth did he allow her to rest. With time, María accepted the *don's* abuse and raged against her brother. "It's Rafael's fault," she would say. "He had no right to shoot the *don*. I hope he comes back and the *don* will shoot him." Celiá knew María's words came from the *don's* mouth. While María worked in the main house tending to *don* Bernardo's needs, Celiá raised the children.

Antonio was four and looked so much like Rafael did at that age. Beautiful Alicia was two years old now. Alicia's skin was pinkish with light brown hair. There was no doubt, she was *don* Bernardo Reyes' daughter. After Alicia's birth, María begged the *don* to move her and the children to the main house. He finally moved them to the guest cottage. María was ecstatic and danced around the new cottage in joy. "You see, *Mamá*, the *don* loves me." It was bigger than the old *jacal* and the *don* allowed Celiá to plant the little garden on the side of the cottage to grow vegetables for the family.

Despite the gift of the larger house, Celiá internally cursed the *desgraciado* who raped her sweet, young daughter and then kept her as his mistress for revenge. There was no justice for *peóns* and she knew nothing could be done.

Now, María was pregnant with the *don's* third child. She was having a hard time carrying this baby. She was sick most days and miserable. She came home from the main house exhausted and sick and had barely put on any weight. At night she could not get out of bed to take care of the little ones. Celiá worried for both her daughter and the unborn child's health.

A month ago Jose came with the news that Rafael was alive – alive and living in Santa Fe. Jose had money to take her and the children to the United States. It was a miracle, a miracle from God.

Celiá and Jose talked to María about leaving the *hacienda*. "No, I won't go," María insisted. "The *don* loves me and loves the children. You can go *Mamá*, then maybe the *don* will move us to the main house."

Celiá knew only too well the ways of *hacienderos*. They took what they wanted from the *peóns* and then tossed them out like trash. Celiá knew it was only a matter of time before *don* Bernardo tired of María, revenge or not. She was no longer a radiant, young girl. Celiá heard rumors that the old *don* moved a pretty, younger girl into the main house to work in the kitchen. According to the servants, the *don* was attentive and kind to the girl. There was also talk that the *don* wanted to court a wealthy widow whose husband died when he fell off his horse. Celiá knew María's position at the house was in jeopardy, but her naïve daughter could not be swayed.

Antonio startled her from her memories. "*Nana*," he said tugging at his grandmother's shoulder. He pointed to a hawk flying high in the sky. Looking at his sweet face, she knew she could never leave. Celiá prayed to God every day to keep Rafael away, but her heart told her he would come for them. They could not leave; the *don* would not allow it and Celiá would never leave her daughter and grandchildren. The thought of *don* Bernardo killing Rafael flooded her eyes with tears. She prayed to God to protect them all.

CHAPTER 9

John B. Sutton slammed down the shot of rye and chased it with a long drink of cool beer. John only drank rye, not the red-eye bourbon drunk by his drovers. Yet, there was a time in his younger days he drank his share of the rot-gut. Standing at the Crystal Palace Bar, just on the outskirts of Austin, Texas, Sutton was drinking alone. All of the local drovers and cowhands knew him and steered clear. A few of them worked for the hardened cattleman; none of them wanted to drink with him.

Sutton ignored the usually rowdy crowd drinking and laughing around him. Marta's whores were hitting on cowboys wanting them to buy drinks and trying to lure them upstairs for a quick roll. A few of the painted up whores approached him, only to move on when he rejected them. Cinnamon Baker was the only whore for him.

For the past ten years, Sutton ran his Circle B Ranch near Austin, Texas, running about four thousand head of Texas long and short horn cattle. He was a Texas cattleman, born and bred. A special breed of men raised on the Texas plains, beaten by wind, sun, and weather. He had driven hundreds of thousands of cattle across the wilds of Texas, fought Indians and Mexicans, and buried many good and bad men on the frontier. Hard work and hard times were mostly all he ever knew. His leathery skin was as weathered tough as his heart.

John's mother died giving birth to his youngest sister when he was nine. From then on, any semblance of a home was mostly atop a horse working cattle with his father. He had three years of schooling before his mother died, just enough to learn to read and write, but John knew the cattle business, through and through. His father taught him how to command and keep respect of men with an iron fist. "They're too stupid to think fer themselves," his father told him. "Always do the thinkin for em, but yew gotta let em raise hell on Saturday night."

John watched his father demand respect from the cowboys, and if they complained or disobeyed, he either fired or shot them without hesitation. For almost thirty years he worked with his father, driving cattle across the Texas plains, growing tougher with each passing year.

When he was young, he hung out with the other cowboys, drinking and canvassing the saloons for whores. The long tiring hours on the saddle evaporated into a whiskey bottle. Drinking, soft women, and killing went hand in hand with the cowboy life. When the pent-up cowboys got to a town, they got blinding drunk and would shoot at anything and everything. If anyone tried to stop them, they shot first and talked later.

John remembered the night in Lawton when he was fifteen. A rangy cowboy pushed him at the bar. They were both drunk. John pushed back and the older cowboy cursed at him. Although taller than John, the man fell back when John punched him. The cowboy staggered up and his hand went for his gun. John pulled his pistol and shot him through the heart.

Three days later his father made bail, paid a fine, and John was released on the agreement with the sheriff that it was a fair fight. They mounted up and his father never said a word about it. It was the first man John killed, but not the last. Now, at almost fifty, those days seemed like a distant memory and he had lost count of how many men he killed. He did not even consider adding the Indians and Mexicans to the tally. Neither amounted to much more than killing dogs, in his mind.

Those days on the range were over and now he was the boss and sold his cattle to others who drove them to market. The Circle B was a respected cattle supplier and Sutton had built a reasonable amount of wealth over the past ten years. His plan was working well, until the state of Texas came around wanting him to pay taxes for the use of state range land. He told the greedy government assholes to go to hell.

"Texas is free territory," he told them. "Free grazing!" It was free land and free grazing since the Texans fought Santa Anna and took Texas from Mexico.

"New laws," they told him. Texas needed money and the state wanted to control the lucrative cattle business – his business. He was not going be taxed for what was already his right. The local cattlemen's association agreed. They hired a prominent lawyer, but the law was passed and there was nothing the cattlemen could do.

He poured another shot of rye into his glass. Behind him he heard cussing and a chair slam to the floor. He glanced into the mirror above the bar and noted a tussle at the roulette wheel. Someone thought he was being cheated. Of course he was cheated. All the roulette wheels in town were rigged.

John caught his reflection in the mirror. He was not a handsome man, never had been. He was short and stocky and his once dark hair, now had steaks of gray showing at the sides. A droopy mustache covering his upper lip was almost completely gray. The skin on his face looked like brown crinkly leather. Today, a bristly salt and pepper beard covered his chin – more salt than pepper. He only bathed and shaved on Saturday afternoon for Cinnamon and today was Wednesday.

John dressed more like a drover than a man of means and anyone looking at him would not be impressed. That suited him just fine. He did not give a hoot what people thought of him. The only person in this whole blasted town he cared for was Cinnamon Baker.

For the last several years, John visited the Crystal Palace every Saturday afternoon and paid Madam Marta for Cinnamon's time and body until midday on Sunday. At first he thought she was just another whore, but learned she was different, and soon became her regular. Cinnamon was his dream of how a woman should be. Her curly auburn hair fell over her green eyes. She was stunning even with the paint washed off her face. But it was not her looks, so much as her way. To him she was an angel. John felt safe and happy with her and he never felt happy or safe.

After working hard at the ranch all week, John would ride to town. People in town had started to realize you could set your watch on his Saturday ritual. At three, he soaked in a hot bath at Thompson's Barbershop and Tonsil Parlor. He scrubbed the week's dirt and sweat off his short, stout frame. His left arm had a long scar from a tangle in a knife fight some years back. His right shoulder had a circle scar from an Apache arrow, but it was his stomach that was the worst. A chunk of his right hip was all but missing. A longhorn had bucked him over its head. The wound had festered and a doctor had to butcher him to save his life. Drying from his bath, he would put on his best suit and step to the front room. Ted Thompson kept a chair open for him. If the barber was cordial, he knew the tough old bird would pay him double for the trim, shave, and a splash of lavender.

By five o'clock, John would stride into the Crystal Palace. Marta knew he was coming. She knew to have Cinnamon available and ready. John liked it best if Cinnamon was waiting at a table for him, dressed in green. He liked green on her the best and over the years he bought her many fancy green dresses. Green matched her eyes, and well, he just liked her in green.

On Saturdays he liked to sit with her and let people see them together. Occasionally, a stranger in town would try his luck at interfering with an older man and the best looking whore at the Palace, and more than once they carried the stranger out – dead. The locals knew you did not want to cross paths with John B. Sutton when he was with Cinnamon, or when he had his back up. They saw it in his eyes and those who did, gave him wide berth.

However, this was not Saturday; it was only Wednesday evening. John was dressed in his working clothes and not his suit. Tonight he was more determined, than angry. The anger at the Texas politicians had dissipated several months ago into a plan.

He had made up his mind and tonight he needed to see Cinnamon. He knew tonight was her night off and that was why he came. Marta said she was upstairs and he had to wait. He hated to wait.

"She'll be down soon," Marta said. "You can't go up,

John. You know the rules."

So he waited with shots of rye, trying to put himself more at ease. John was excited. He had alternate plans; he called them his contingency plans. To hell with paying those politicians his hard-earned money. To hell with Texas. It hurt his soul to give up his cash to those slick, good for nothing, carpetbagging sons of bitches.

He and men like him had made Texas habitable. His father, Cyrus, fought with Sam Houston to defeat General Santa Anna at San Jacinto, the famous battle winning independence for Texas from Mexico. Cyrus instilled a love for Texas in his son. He also instilled a distrust and dislike for Mexicans. "Shiftless greasers," his father always called them. Cyrus had died on the Texas prairie he loved so much with a Commanche arrow in his gut. John and the cowhands buried him somewhere out on the plains. The exact location was blown away by the Texas wind. John thought he would die here too, but now he had decided to leave his beloved Texas.

John's plan was to drive his herd to New Mexico. He bought land near San Marcial, just north of Fort Craig. The valley there was lush, just west of the Rio Grande. San Marcial provided an ideal climate and land was cheap, and best of all there was plenty of open range. The railroad and army were paying top dollar for beef to feed the troops and workers in the west. Today, most of his Texas cattle were sold in Kansas for shipment and sale in the east. John knew he could make more money selling his cattle in Cheyenne, Wyoming.

Over a month ago, John sent half his herd to his new ranch near San Marcial with his trusted foreman, Bill Payton. Once he settled his affairs in Austin, he and the rest of his drovers would drive the remainder of the herd to New Mexico. Staring at the glass of rye, John thought the plan was a good one, at least financially. He hated leaving Texas, but knew he could make it big in New Mexico.

One thing grated at him – New Mexico was still mostly Mexican. "Bunch of stinkin greasers," he had heard the talk. "They even run the towns and the law," he was told. Well, he would put a stop to that. When he got there, things would change.

"John B what are you doing here?" Cinnamon purred in his ear. Her voice startled him, as he was lost in his thoughts. Cinnamon liked calling him John B.

"Cinnamon, I need to see you tonight," John said looking into her green eyes.

"John B, you know this is my night off. I only get one night off a week." Cinnamon was wearing her coat and only a little makeup. John liked her that way and liked when she called him John B. "I'm on my way to see my mother and won't get back till late."

John's face fell and his shoulders sagged. Cinnamon knew something was wrong. "What's the matter, what's happened?" she asked wrinkling her brow.

"I need you girl. I need to talk to you. It's important to me. I'll pay you double and pay Marta double," he begged.

"But, my mother." She looked away. Double her usual fee would help her pay for her mother's care. It was getting more and more costly to care for her mother's needs.

"Please girl, I need you," he said as he held her by the shoulders.

"Triple my fee and I'll work it out with Marta, but this better be important," she answered sternly, pulling his chin up and looking him in the eyes.

"It's very important," he assured her.

Cinnamon spoke with Marta and returned. Taking John B by the arm, together they walked up the stairs to her room. Her scent lingered on his arm. She smelled of roses in the summer. He knew she was a whore. He knew she was with other men during the week, but he thought of her as his. He loved her. He loved feeling safe in her arms and thought she loved him, too. After all he had money. Lots of money and she knew it. He was no ordinary drover. Sure, he was more than twenty years older, but he was a kind lover and always bought her gifts.

With care she stripped his clothes. He allowed her,

enjoying the tenderness. Cinnamon knew what John B liked, even though it disgusted her. He loved for her to rub his body with her hands – his leathery, shriveled body. It was what he craved more than sex. Almost like no one touched him when he was little, or something odd. Most men usually just wanted to ride her and be done. He sighed and smiled when she touched him. His skin felt like a snake – scaly and dry. His arm had a long scar, but that was okay. It was his grotesque hip that revolted her. It was half-missing and the skin around the injury was ragged and ugly.

Stretched out on the bed, he relaxed to her touch. Even his small penis stayed limp until she worked it. Cinnamon knew John B liked her on top. She enjoyed it too, except for the feeling of his ragged hip on her thigh. Normally, he liked her to work slowly, luxuriating in even the smallest tenderness. Tonight, she pumped his penis with her hands to make him hard and mounted him quickly.

While she brought him to a climax, Cinnamon was thinking of the new hat she saw in the milliner's window. Now, she could afford it, so perhaps this was worth it. After she satisfied him, she sat up and leaned against the headboard.

"Now, tell me what's got you all a tatter?" she asked.

"I'm leaving Texas," he responded in a low voice.

"What? What do you mean leaving Texas? You mean leaving on a cattle drive?" she asked casually inspecting a fingernail on her left hand that was rough.

"Just what I said. I'm leaving Texas for good."

"But, you can't. This is your home. What about your ranch?"

"Those sons of bitches at the land office are forcing me to pay for ranging my cattle on land my father fought for and won against the Mexicans. I won't get fleeced for running my cows on my own land," he grumbled.

"You have lots of money, John B," she said. "It hardly seems a reason to leave." Of course, Cinnamon had heard the talk at the bar. Cattlemen had been grumbling about it for months, but she did not know anyone who wanted to leave Texas.

"My father fought for Texas independence for the same reason – the Mexicans were over taxing the people. Now, our asshole politicians are doing the same to me," he growled. She knew he was getting riled and used her soft voice to keep him calm.

"Where will you go?" she asked quietly rolling over and walking her fingers on his chest. Realizing he was serious, her mind flicked with worry about her steady source of money from him.

"New Mexico," he replied. "There's a lush valley there where my cattle will flourish. New Mexico is cooler and has many mountains, not flat like Texas. It's not far to Wyoming where the army is buying beef at high prices. I'll be richer than ever."

John was trying to paint a lovely picture for Cinnamon. He knew she was not in love with him, but she did love his money. He loved her for how she made him feel – safe, and he hoped to use his money to entice her.

After a pause he said, "I want you to go with me. I'll build us an empire there. Just you and me. Nothing will stop us from getting rich. You'll have a new life in New Mexico, a respectable life as my wife."

Cinnamon was stunned. Whores just did not get this kind of an offer. She thought he was just saying goodbye tonight. Her, go with him? She always ignored his old, worn, pathetic body, because she was a whore and he had money. It was her job to make him feel good and she was good at her job. She lied to him about his limited love making, flattering him because of the extra gifts and money he gave her, but now he was asking her to go with him, forever. She thought about her true feelings – he revolted her. There was no way she wanted to spend the rest of her life with this wizened excuse of a man, money or not.

"Cynthia, come with me to New Mexico and I'll make you an honest woman." She was shocked when he used her given name. Cinnamon was not her real name. It was Cynthia Barkett. She took the name Cinnamon Baker, because she liked the way it sounded. Only a few people knew her real name. She did not even remember telling him and even more surprised that he remembered.

Being a whore was no great life, but leaving forever with John B was terrifying. Thinking fast she said, "I can't John B. I can't leave my mother." This was true. Her mother needed her here. Whoring was paying all the bills and paying for her mother's care.

"We'll take her with us," he answered immediately. "Cynthia, I need you with me. I need you girl and I'll make you happy and rich." John picked up her left hand and held it up. "I'll buy you a diamond ring," he said kissing her ring finger.

John knew Cinnamon was stalling and probably did not want to go with him. He had worked out a contingency plan for that, too. First though, he appealed to her greedy nature.

Panic was building up in Cinnamon. Her heart was thumping, making it hard to breathe. She stiffened up, but not enough for him to take notice. She pulled her hand from his and jumped off the bed.

"Oh, John B you do know how to flatter a girl, don't you?" She splashed cool water on her face from the wash basin and fanned her face with her hands. He lay on the bed staring at her. His eyes always looked at her kindly, like he was looking at her now. He never beat her and was always gentlemanly. It was his body that revolted her. When they made love, she kept her eyes closed, but could feel his ragged hip.

"That sounds like a fine idea, John B, but I can't go until my mother gets well. She can't travel now," she responded coyly, "and I owe Marta money. She'll never let me leave."

"I'll pay Marta," John told her. "I'll pay for both you and mother to travel in style to New Mexico. We'll make sure she gets the best care."

"When are you leaving?"

"In a couple of days. Half the herd is already gone. I have some details to finish up."

"A couple of days! I can't leave in a couple of days,"

she exclaimed.

"I'll leave with the herd and send for you."

Cinnamon decided to play along. Once he left town, she would make more excuses until he gave up. "I'll go tell my mother the good news. I still have time to go visit her tonight, if I leave right now," she said. Quickly she started dressing, while he took pleasure watching her.

She was lying. He knew it, but she would come to New Mexico. He was sure of that. He would work it all out with Marta.

"Thank you, John B," she purred and kissed him. "Now, get dressed and go on home. I'll write you and let you know when mother can travel," she told him.

John hummed as he dressed knowing Cinnamon would come to New Mexico. She did not know it yet, but she would come.

CHAPTER 10

Each day Rafe felt stronger and the shakes were almost gone. Juanita, the cook, was pleased to see him eat double portions at each meal. By the end of the week, Rafe's cheeks were no longer sunken and his pants were fitting better.

Rafe, Carlos, and George sat many hours in the Summers' parlor planning the trip to Torreón, Mexico. The plan sounded simple. Carlos would pose as the son of a prominent *gachupín* family from Los Lunas, New Mexico. His name would be *don* Alejandro Martinez de Lunas, an aristocratic *haciendero*. Rafe would go as *don* Alejandro's trusted *vaquero* and keep his hat pulled low. Rafe's name would be Juan Romero.

In front of the fire, Carlos pantomimed meeting *don* Bernardo and introducing himself as *don* Alejandro Martinez de Lunas in formal Spanish, reciting his heritage and social credits. Rafe watched his friend transform into a *caballero*, a Spanish gentleman, before his eyes – the manners, the square of his shoulders, and the aloof look on his face. Carlos was right. He could convince *don* Bernardo he was a man of means.

Carlos could tell *don* Bernardo the *Americano* army had bought most of his quality horse stock and he was looking to find quality stock in Mexico. They agreed it was unlikely that *don* Bernardo was aware of life or business in New Mexico and less likely to know whether the army was buying horses or not. Rafe said *don* Bernardo was a greedy man and only cared about money and not politics.

Carlos and Rafe would travel to Torreón by wagon. Rafe wanted to stop in El Paso and see his uncle Jose and family. Carlos wanted to stop in San Marcial and visit his cousin. He thought his cousin, Tomás, might be able to provide him with a *gachupín traje* and silver saddle. His own was worn and shabby. To meet *don* Bernardo, Carlos needed to dress like a prosperous Spanish aristocrat.

They discussed the details of the plan trying to prepare for contingencies. The problem they seemed unable to solve, was how Rafe could meet with his mother and sister without drawing attention.

In his zeal, Rafe just wanted to kidnap the women and children, throw them in the back of the wagon, and ride hard for Texas. George and Carlos both laughed at him.

"You must keep a calm head, son," George admonished him. He worried Rafe would have a hard time keeping his rage under control, once he was face to face with *don* Bernardo.

Rafe tried to remember everything about the *hacienda*, but his memory was fuzzy to many details. Uncle Jose said his mother and sister were living in the guest cottage. Rafe remembered it as a small house just outside the courtyard walls on the main road. It would be in full view, so slipping in or out would be difficult. Besides, Rafe told them, the *peóns* see everything.

"Nothing goes on at the *hacienda* that is secret," Rafe told them. Rafe was sure *don* Bernardo paid *peóns* for information – there were eyes everywhere.

"It would be better if we get my mother and sister away from the *hacienda*, so I can talk with them, but I don't see how," Rafe said. *Peóns* seldom left the compound. The cooks went to town for market, but Rafe knew the only time his mother went to town was on Sunday for Mass. "We'll have to find them at the church."

Meeting in a public place was risky, but they could devise no other plan. The church was large and busy on Sundays. The square in front of the church was usually busy with horses, wagons, and people from the surrounding area. If he could get his mother to follow him to a quiet spot, they could talk. He would have to convince her to leave with him.

George wanted them to drop off a shipment of GSW guns to John Grady's General Store in Albuquerque. Frustrated by delay and inaction Rafe bristled. "This is not a business trip."

"You can't get there in one day, son," George reminded him. "You are businessmen on a trip, besides you need to stop and rest the horses."

Rafe paced the room. "When can we get started?" It was Monday afternoon and Rafe was anxious to be on their way.

"I'll have the gun shipment ready tomorrow and we can get the wagon packed," George said. "Your mother wants to have a big dinner before you go."

"Then we will leave Wednesday morning," Rafe asserted. George's heart was heavy at the thought. There was trouble in Torreón for Rafe and Carlos and he knew it, but he also knew Rafe had to go.

CHAPTER 11

John B. Sutton stopped and turned his horse east for one last look at the outline of Austin, Texas. It was all but invisible through the dust his herd of cattle kicked up as they trailed west to New Mexico. It had been years since he had joined a cattle drive. In his younger years it was the only life he knew. Now, the dust was making him cough and his butt was already sore.

The early October weather was still warm, just as he had expected. John meticulously made all of the preparations for the seven hundred mile drive to San Marcial. He made up his mind to leave Texas last spring when the asshole government assessor came demanding taxes for his grazing land.

"I'll be damned if I'll pay taxes to use free grazing land," he kept telling himself. All of the cattlemen were angry, but most were resigned to pay. "What else can we do?" they said at the cattlemen's association meetings, but John would not pay. "Refuse and fight," he told them.

Most of the cattlemen were businessmen and some were eastern dandies. "Lilly-livered cowards," he called them. A few men, like him, hardened by years of cattle ranching in Texas, agreed with him, but without solid opposition the government won. John refused to pay and the government put a lien on his last cattle sale. Infuriated, he decided to leave Texas. Never again would the government flat out rob him. He meant it too; no politician would take his hard-earned money.

Leaving his ancestral homeland of Texas grated deep in his soul. He was Texan – born and bred. Hell, his father fought with Sam Houston for Texas's independence. One of his uncles died at the Alamo, when a Mexican cannonball made a direct hit on a stockpile of munitions near his position. His mother's two brothers were executed by the Mexicans after Santa Anna overran the Alamo. He hated those money-grabbing Texas politicians as much as he hated greaser Mexicans.

His only home had been the wild and often lawless Texas, a place where only men as tough as nails survived and John was tougher than most. Now, the damned law was taking over. Hell, just last spring the sheriff jailed several of his cowboys for getting rowdy in town. All they did was shoot at some greaser's kids who were running in the street. John paid the bail of ten dollars for each man. Highway robbery for nothing.

The cowboys worked hard all week and deserved to blow off steam on Saturday nights. It was normal to have some busted up tables and shot out windows in the fun. Occasionally, someone got shot in a fight. More and more, sheriffs were posting signs reading, no firearms in town.

Last year one of his men shot a store clerk in the arm by accident. Well, not exactly by accident. The store clerk was making Ponyboy George wait while he served another customer. Ponyboy got twitchy and winged the man. It cost Sutton twenty dollars for Ponyboy's fine and he did not take it out of his pay. Ponyboy, though a hothead, was one of his dependable drovers and had been with him for maybe fifteen years.

John paid his cowboys well and was a tough, but fair boss. He expected a lot from them and for those who were loyal and hardworking, he took care of their needs. Good and loyal cowboys were getting harder to find on the Texas prairie and John knew it.

When he told the cowboys of his plan to move to New Mexico, all but one agreed to go with him. He had expected it. Cowboys were a shiftless breed of men and their only home was the open range and the bunkhouse. They banded like brothers and for most, John's ranch was the only home they knew. They would go where he asked them to go. John knew some were outlaws from Missouri, Louisiana, and other places – men with a past. Their only future was to die from a bullet, or an arrow, or from just plain hard work.

On Saturday nights the men went to town. Sometimes they took a bath, sometimes not. They needed whiskey and women to make their life worth living. The saloon keepers overcharged them for rot-gut whiskey and the whores made extra money. The Faro dealers and roulette wheels were all crooked, and by the end of Saturday night most of the cowboys had spent or lost their weekly pay. This was life in the frontier towns.

John could see change coming. It would not be long before Austin became more civilized, beset with new laws and social graces. He had been to St. Louis and Chicago and even Baton Rouge. He saw the ladies in their fancy buggies. He went to the restaurants and saloons where you had to be dressed in your Sunday best. No guns were permitted and no rough talk or rough play was allowed.

Yes, John saw the future of Texas and he did not like it. Men like him were a dying breed. Well, he was not staying.

During the Civil War he and his fellow Texas Confederates invaded New Mexico. He spent almost six months at Fort Craig south of Socorro, New Mexico, along the Rio Grande. When he decided to leave Texas, he remembered San Marcial, a hamlet just north of Fort Craig. There was good grazing land there and good water along the Rio Grande.

The Territory of New Mexico was still wild and free. The range was open and only a few large herds had pushed that far west. Last June, John sent his lawyer to search for land near Fort Craig. The lawyer's stage stopped in San Marcial and he learned that someday it would be on the train route from El Paso and north. John's lawyer negotiated a bargain price for a large stretch of land bordering the Rio Grande south of San Marcial, surrounded by good grasslands. San Marcial had the two main requirements for his cattle – grass and water. In summer, the valley was lush with blue grama grass and in winter rabbitfoot grass was abundant. His long and short horned Texas cattle would flourish.

The lawyer told him the old town of San Marcial washed away in the big flood of 1866 and was rebuilt on higher ground west of the Rio Grande. The town had a saloon, a small hotel under construction, a livery and other merchants to support his needs. Except for the saloon, the town was primarily run by Mexicans. That bit of information grated on John, but he would deal with it when he got there.

It was a start. The land had been used by the army during the war and some old corrals and shacks could be used by his cowboys. He sent half the herd to San Marcial led by his foreman, Bill Payton, and a group of drovers over a month ago. Now, on his way with the rest of the herd, his dream of becoming the cattle baron of the Territory of New Mexico would become a reality. The Circle B would be known from New Mexico to Wyoming, and he, John Burke Sutton, would put San Marcial on the map.

"Hey, Boss, where yew reckon we shud pull up tonight?" Rip rode up beside John and startled him out of his thoughts.

John studied the sun for a minute and then replied, "There's a water hole bout ten miles up ahead. Start herdin the strays."

Rip rode off shouting orders to the others and John took one last look toward Austin. He thought about Cinnamon and the long nights on the trail he would have without her. He had hoped Cinnamon would accept his marriage proposal willingly, but he suspected she was stalling. He paid Madam Marta a handsome sum to throw Cinnamon out and smear her name in Austin so she could not work at the other saloons. It cost him dearly, but he hoped it guaranteed Cinnamon would come running to him.

She was a whore, but he would make her a lady. He loved her and she could start a new life in San Marcial with him, as his wife. He would be good to her and she would learn to love him, if only for his money. The thought put a smile on his face as he turned and rode to catch up with the herd.

A cowboy rode up in front of him interrupting his thoughts. "Gotta calf with a broken leg."

"Shoot it and give it to Shep," John responded. Shep, the cook, would bleed and hang the calf for food in the coming days. They would lose at least fifty cows on the trail, if they were lucky, more if they had bad weather.

He hoped to make Abilene in less than two weeks. It would be well into November before they reached San Marcial. Then John would show the New Mexican greasers how a real cattleman operated.

Chapter 12

"Hey Ponyboy, we goin on over to Big Ed's ta bend an elbow. Yew comin," Butcherknife Bill Payton yelled over at George who was trying to bind a broken part of the corral fence. Like many cowboys, George was always called by his nickname, Ponyboy. Most of the time no one knew where the nicknames started, but they stuck. Bill was called Butcherknife. His nickname started because he was good with his castrating knife. He got the nickname many years ago when he was riding for the Three Bars outfit.

"Shur nuff, but gotta fix this post first," Ponyboy replied. "Won't take long."

"Hur . . . ry up," Pewee stuttered. "I'm . . m . . . d . d . dry as a b . b . bone."

A few days ago Butcherknife Bill and the cowboys settled the Circle B herd onto the land purchased by John B. Sutton. The valley was bordered by a volcanic hill on one side and the Rio Grande on the other. It had been a long, hard drive from the Circle B ranch south of Austin, Texas, to this new ranch site southwest of San Marcial, New Mexico.

Twenty Sutton cowboys, with a cook and scout, started with about two thousand head. They lost more steers than usual coming over the mountains. Bill Payton, head drover for the Circle B outfit, was responsible for the drive. He knew Sutton would be angry with the extra losses, but Sutton was not expected to be coming with the rest of the herd for another month. By then the herd would be scattered on the open range. Counting head would not matter.

Bill led the drive according to Sutton's instructions. When they arrived, the old shacks and corrals were in worse shape than Bill expected. Sutton had painted a better picture. The cowboys, though, were happy to be settled after more than a month on the trail. The herd was set loose to roam the escarpment and fertile river valley, but the horse corrals were practically falling down and the bunkhouse was not much better. Bill ordered the cowboys to get the corrals fixed first, so they could hold the horses. They hurriedly fixed the smaller corral in a makeshift manner. Ponyboy, with several others, was working on the larger corral and hopefully they would have it finished by tomorrow. With luck they might get the bunkhouse fixed before winter set in.

The new ranch site was about ten miles downriver from the small village of San Marcial, New Mexico. At least there was a decent saloon and the boys could get their fill of liquor.

Sutton told the men he was moving his spread to build the largest cattle operation in New Mexico. "The Union Army out west pays double for beef," he told the cowboys. Sutton offered the men double pay for this last drive and a bonus after next summer's auction. Bill knew Sutton was leaving Texas because of new open range taxes. Surveying the pathetic broken down bunkhouse, Bill thought Sutton was a fool. He sold his big spread in Austin to escape paying a few extra dollars to the government. It would take years to rebuild here in New Mexico.

"Let's go," Ponyboy interrupted Bill's thoughts. He gathered his saddle and walked over to his roan horse that was tied to a tree. It took only a few minutes to saddle his horse. A competent cowboy prided himself in getting the saddle hitched in a hurry. Often it was a matter of life or death, but today it was only whiskey.

"Maybe we can git us one of them sen'o'ritas," Jed said with a wide grin showing stained teeth.

"Them sen . . . sen . . oritas don't wawa . . want the li . . likes of yew," Pewee teased Jed. Jed was one of the toughest cowboys in the Sutton bunkhouse. Pewee would not be teasing the hardened cowboy, were he not on horseback.

"Shut yer big bazoo, Pewee. Yew know I can whup yew with one hand," Jed responded gruffly.

"Yew two gonna r'gue or yew comin?" Ponyboy shouted.

The two cowboys glared at each other until Jed swung up into his saddle.

"Cum on then, let's go kick up a row." Bill whirled his horse around and they broke into a gallop heading north.

San Marcial was a small, dusty village set along the Rio Grande. Bill had been in plenty of these small towns in his life, but this one was full of greasers. Sure there were Mexicans in Texas, but they were beaten and they knew their place. Bill hated greasers. One of his older brothers was killed in the war with Mexico and his father was wounded, bad. Bill had worked his father's small farm to feed his mother and sister. His father slowly withered away until he died of his injuries in fifty-six. Watching his father die slowly cemented Bill's hatred for Mexicans.

Here greasers ran the town and stores. *Gracias* this and *gracias* that. Hell, Bill wished he was back in Texas.

He and the boys had only been to the town once before. Twelve of them rode into the village with guns blazing. They treed San Marcial good that day shooting at dogs, cats, and anything that moved. The Spanish settlers heard the gunfire and scattered like chickens. Stupid greasers deserved no respect from him.

The only good thing about San Marcial was Big Ed's Saloon. Big Ed's was owned by Ed Seeley, a retired Union soldier from Fort Craig. Seeley decided to stay in New Mexico after retirement and used his muster-out pay and savings to open a saloon and hotel in new San Marcial. Seeley told the Texans that the usually tame Rio Grande flooded several years back and the original town was washed away. The town decided to rebuild on the west side of the river, the high side, where it would be safe from future floods. Ed built the saloon and had a half-finished hotel attached to it.

Bill and the four cowboys covered the ten miles in short order, riding into the dusty, quiet hamlet late in the afternoon. The few Mexicans on the street scurried into alleys and doors when they saw the Texans coming.

"Yew better skedaddle greasers," Butcherknife Bill

yelled out. He and the cowboys pulled their pistols and fired into the air. They stopped in front of Big Ed's, dismounted, and tied the horses to the post. Climbing the wooden steps their Texas spurs jingled as they stepped into the saloon.

"Hey Big Ed, set em up," Bill shouted to the man behind the bar. Big Ed Seeley, tending his own bar, smelled the Texas cowboys before he looked up. At the door, the five cowboys all wearing wide leather chaps, flaring out at the sides over heavy cotton pants, were reloading before holstering their pistols. They wore dirty checkered wool shirts and all had wide loosely-tied bandanas around their necks. Bill, the ramrod, stood a few inches taller than the rest, and looked even taller with his wide-brimmed, ten gallon hat.

"Sure enough boys," Ed responded with a smile He quickly brought out a bottle and five shot glasses, setting them up on the bar.

Ed Seeley was glad for the business. After retiring from the army, Seeley built his saloon catering to the army, locals, and caravans on the El Camino Real. Merchants hauled their goods from Mexico City to Santa Fe up and down the trail. It was not a steady income, but it kept him alive as a businessman. He started a hotel attached to the saloon, but did not have money to finish it.

Now, a Texas cattleman bought a big spread southwest of town and his cowboys were coming to San Marcial for supplies and liquor. Big Ed was already starting to count his good fortune. His business would double or even triple. Those Texas cowboys liked their whiskey and he was happy to sell it to them. He did not like their behavior, but did like their money.

As usual, the merchant trade was dwindling with winter approaching. The business from the cowboys would keep him afloat this winter. He would sell them watered-down whiskey and beer and he hoped to buy a cow from them for slaughter, from time to time. On their first visit to town, the cowboys rode up and down the street shooting and hollering. The locals were scared and he did not blame them.

The locals were his friends, as well as customers. Ed had lived in New Mexico for over twenty-five years. Originally from Indiana, he joined the army and spent twenty years in the cavalry. His last assignment was at Fort Craig. He had grown to love the turquoise skies and mild New Mexico weather and so he stayed when his enlistment was over.

Ed was not the only Anglo merchant in town, but there were only a few. The village's government was run by members of local prominent Spanish families. The families were descendants of Spaniards who settled this area in the early 1600s. The people were mostly hard working, gracious, and friendly. They banded together against the elements, strife, and Indian attacks. On Sunday, Ed joined them at the small Catholic Church.

"Seen any sen'o'ritas round here tday?" Ponyboy asked Big Ed.

"You boys stay away from the girls here. The Spanish are very protective of them," Big Ed warned the cowboys.

"Aw, we ain't scared of no stinkin greasers," Ponyboy jawed, "but ol Pewee here shor is scirt of talkin to gals. Ain't yew Pewee?" Pewee was shy around girls because he stuttered when he was nervous.

"Yew . . . yew . . . sh . . shhut yer big ba . . ba . . baaazzzzoo Pony, or I'll c . . c . . c . . clean your p . . plow," Pewee shot back. The cowboys laughed. Pewee drained his glass in one gulp and slammed the glass on the bar top.

"Give the boys a bottle," Butcherknife ordered. He was standing at the bar working on the second half of a bottle. The cowboys were Seeley's only customers. Ponyboy George and the others started a game of poker at the front table.

"Tain't no fuckin action round here?" Butcherknife Bill complained to Big Ed

Big Ed listened to Bill complain. He had a piano, but no player, except occasionally when a young soldier from the fort, who played a little, came to town. On Friday and Saturday nights Gerardo dealt Faro, but Ed was not sure if he would, now that the Texas cowboys were here.

"Yeah, weekdays are usually quiet," Big Ed replied. It was a lie. Weekdays were slower, but some locals normally wandered in and out. Not tonight. The locals knew the Texans were in town.

"Hey, git nuther bottle of that tornado juice over heah," Jed hollered from the table.

Big Ed reached under the bar and walked over to the table. Picking up the empty and replacing it with a new bottle he said, "That'll be two dollars."

Jed reached into the pot in the middle of the table and handed Big Ed the dollars. Ed sure did like the cowboys' money. Taking the money, he headed back to the bar.

"Lookee here boys, thar goes a sen'o'rita," Jake hollered suddenly. Through the front window, Jake saw a young girl passing along the boardwalk in front of the saloon. The four cowboys jumped up from their game and headed for the door.

"Hey thar missy. Cum in and have a drink," Ponyboy called to her over the batwing doors. The young girl did not speak English and did not understand the words, but she knew from the talk in the town that she was not safe around these bad men. *"Hombres malos,"* her father warned her.

"¡No!" The girl turned into the street and ran across to the other side.

"Cum back! We jes wanna see yer purdy face," Ponyboy bellowed. The young girl hurried quickly and turned into the mercantile store.

"Looks like ol' lover Ponyboy just got the mitten," Jake chided.

"Yeah, guess she jes don't think yew hansum nuff," Jed said and the cowboys all laughed at Ponyboy's rejection.

"Jes yew shut the hell up. I'll git me the next one," Ponyboy grumbled. He hated being laughed at. "Yew ain't doin no better cause there ain't no whores in this shitheel town."

In Austin, a whore could be had at any saloon in town. The best whores were at the Crystal Palace, but were too pricey for a cowboy's pay. Ponyboy usually hung out at the Devil Dog Saloon and Dance Hall. The whores there were not really too pretty, but they were cheap and willing.

Tomás Armíjo stood inside the mercantile just finishing with his order when young Enriquita Sanchez burst into the store, breathless.

"Ayúdame por favor, los Tejanos me están molestando," she cried for help from the menacing Texans. Tomás and the storekeeper, Arturo, comforted her.

Tomás peered out of the store's window and saw some men hanging out in front of the saloon. The cowboys were in town and drinking at Big Ed's. One of the cowboys was standing in the street yelling and waving a bottle of whiskey.

Tomás Armíjo was the recently elected *alcaldé*, mayor of San Marcial. In reality he did not want the job, but the people voted for him unanimously. Beside, no one else would do it. He was part of the Armíjo clan, the founding family of this area, but had grown up and been educated in Santa Fe. When his grandfather died, Tomás inherited a large piece of the original Armíjo Spanish land grant. He decided to move his family to San Marcial and manage the *hacienda*.

He was taller than most men in the village and was of pure Spanish blood. Tomás' eyes were bluish and his hair was brown. When he dressed in his Sunday *traje*, he looked like his grandfather's picture, which hung at the Armíjo *hacienda*.

When he accepted the position of mayor, Tomás thought it was just a ceremonial position. Now, the Texans had come to town and the villagers looked to him for guidance and help. He was the mayor and the only government or law in the small hamlet. The sheriff was in Socorro. Tomás sent a letter last week to inform the sheriff of the potential for trouble, but he might not hear anything back.

The night after the Texas cowboys showed up in San

Marcial last week, and wildly rode up and down the main street shooting and hollering, the shopkeepers and the padre showed up at Tomás' home. "Do something," they said. Tomás did not know what to do. He was not the law, nor even carried a gun, but he was no coward.

Tomás took a long look at the cowboys across the street. Taking a deep breath, he came out of the mercantile with an armload of goods.

"Hey greaser, yew got a sister?" Ponyboy yelled out at Tomás.

Tomás stepped to the street. "You men, you cannot be scaring our women," he said in perfect English. "Go back to your drinking in the saloon."

"Hey greaser, yew speak English, eh?" Ponyboy said. Tomás turned to walk away hoping to make his point, and not start a conflict with the drunken cowboy.

"Hey greaser, I'm talkin to yew." Ponyboy strode across the street and grabbed him by the arm and pulled Tomás around to face him. The packages in Tomás' arms scattered to the ground.

"We want no trouble with you or your men," Tomás said looking him in the eye.

"Hey boys, this here greaser don't want no trouble," Ponyboy called back to the cowboys standing in front of Big Ed's.

"Well, yew got trouble," Ponyboy hissed into his face. Tomás smelled the rank whiskey breath of the drunken Texan.

"Yeah greaser, yew bess listen to ol' Ponyboy," one of the other cowboys yelled.

Ponyboy pulled his revolver and took a couple shots at the canned goods scattered on the ground.

"¡Baboso!" Tomás cursed the cowboy, calling him a drooling idiot in Spanish.

"Hey Ponyboy, he jes called yew a baboon," Jake hollered across the street.

Ponyboy saw fire in the greaser's eyes and he did not like it. No greaser was going to challenge him and get away with it.

Bullets hit the dirt beside Tomás' feet. "Dance greaser!" Ponyboy growled.

Ed Seeley heard the shots and moved to the saloon doorway. He saw one of the cowboys holding a gun on his friend, Tomás Armíjo, in the street. "Damn cowboys," he muttered to himself. At six foot two inches, Seeley's frame filled the doorway. In his hand he carried a shotgun and was not afraid to use it, but all he wanted was to make money. Gun play was not going to make his saloon and hotel a success. The cowboy called Butcherknife Bill followed him out of the saloon and was standing to his left.

Tomás did not move, but glared defiantly at the crazy cowboy. When the cowboy fired his sixth shot, Tomás lowered his shoulder and drove it into the cowboy's chest. They fell into the dusty street.

"Cum on," Jake said to the other cowboys and started to move off of the wooden boardwalk to help Ponyboy.

"I wouldn't if I were you," Seeley said behind them. Jake and the cowboys whirled around to see Big Ed holding a shotgun on them. "It's a fair fight now," he said.

Ponyboy raised a fist and hit Tomás in the chest knocking him back. Tomás responded by pummeling him in the gut with both fists. Ponyboy was stronger, but he was also drunk. Pushing Tomás off him with a swift knee jerk, Ponyboy threw a right hook into Tomás' cheek. Blood spurted from his lip and pain shot into Tomás' right eye.

"Gi . . . git im P . . P . . Pony. Gi . . git im g . . g . . . good," Pewee stuttered.

Ponyboy reached around to his back and pulled a knife. Seeley saw the knife and feared for Tomás' life. Rushing into the street, he ran toward the two fighters with his shotgun raised.

Pointing the shotgun at Ponyboy he demanded, "Stop now!" Seeley waved the shotgun at Ponyboy to back away from the bleeding man on the street.

Ponyboy looked up at the shotgun and slowly stood up. He put the knife back into the sheaf attached to his gunbelt and raised both hands slightly. "All good," he said grinning at Big Ed.

"You boys have had your fun now. Go back to the saloon and I'll buy you a drink on the house."

"Yew a greaser lover?" Ponyboy sneered at Seeley.

Ponyboy gave Tomás a kick on the ribs and stomped off muttering, "Stinkin greasers."

"Git the bottle and let's git outta here boys," Butcherknife Bill ordered his men standing in the saloon's doorway. He hated greasers just as much as any of the cowboys, but it was his responsibility to keep his crew alive. No need to cause a killing or getting one of his men killed tonight. Soon they would have the rest of Sutton's men in camp and then they would own this shitheel town.

The five Sutton cowboys mounted their horses and fired at store windows and doors as they rode out of the village, heading back to their camp. Ponyboy shot out the window of the mercantile. From inside he heard a young girl scream and he chuckled.

"Are you all right?" Ed asked Tomás as the Texans rode off.

"Yes, thank you."

"Come on in the saloon and have a drink. We'll get you cleaned up." Ed helped Tomás to his feet, and then picked up the cans and packages Tomás had dropped.

CHAPTER 13

Wednesday brought colder weather to Santa Fe. The wind howled and blew a light powdery snow swirling around the wagon as Rafe and Carlos finished loading it with supplies. It was late October and winter was showing itself on the mountains – white rocky crests and barren trees. A cloudy vapor snorted from the noses of the two team horses, floating off in the wind as they stood patiently waiting to begin their work.

George watched quietly as the two young men finished loading the wagon. For two days he had been barking orders at the foundry and hovering like a mother hen over the packing of supplies in the wagon. He made sure his orders were followed.

The wagon was the same one George and his partner Frank used when they were attacked by Apaches. The same one Rafe found in the remote desert of Texas with George barely clinging to life. The same one he and Rafe rode to Santa Fe over four years ago. It had been repaired and was in good working order.

"I loaded two double-action rifles and an extra shotgun in the secret hiding place," George said to Rafe as he tapped at the removable panel just behind the seat.

"Good, what about ammunition?"

"There is some in there and plenty more in your supplies." he responded. "I also put in plenty of black powder, in case you need it."

Josefina and the girls hurried out of the house with sacks under their arms. "Here's food sacks for the trip," Lolo said.

"Juanita made plenty of tortillas and red chili. There's slab bacon, dried beef and plenty of coffee and staples in the food bins," Josefina added.

Rafe could tell Josefina was chattering nervously, knowing full well he knew where all the supplies were kept. He walked over to his adopted mother and wrapped her in a big hug. She buried her head in his shoulder. "God be with you," she whispered.

When she finally let go of him, Lolo and Lizzy grabbed at him from either side. With a strong arm around each girl, he kissed them on the cheek. "Now, you behave until I get back," he said laughingly. Lolo giggled.

"We'll light a candle every day," Lizzy said looking at Rafe with serious eyes and hugged him tightly.

"I'll be back before Thanksgiving," he said.

Rafe walked over to George. He wrapped his arms around the man to whom he owed his new life. "We'll be careful, *don* Jorge," he said using his personal name for the man who was now like a father to him.

George sighed, "Send a telegraph as soon as you can. You know Josefina will worry." Rafe knew George would worry just as much as Josefina and the girls.

Rafe and Carlos climbed into the wagon seat. Rafe adjusted his hat and looked at Carlos. Carlos nodded an agreement and snapped the reins. Slowly the wagon groaned into movement. Rafe gave *don* Jorge a nod. Josefina and the girls were on the porch waving at him. He tipped his hat and gave them a big smile. He scanned the Summers' home and his adopted parents and sisters one last time, with the nagging thought he might never see them again. Returning to Mexico was risky, but his mother and sister needed him. It burned a hole in his heart that he had left them there in the hands of *don* Bernardo.

The wagon lurched, picking up speed, as the rig turned and started down the lane. Behind the wagon Rayo and Sombra trailed along. *Sombra* meaning shadow in Spanish, was a two year old black stallion sired by Rayo. Carlos would ride Sombra into Torreón, pretending to be a horse buyer. The stallion was a beauty and *don* Bernardo would be impressed. The wagon moved under the GSW sign and headed south, Carlos driving, with Rafe at his side.

They rode in silence until the town of Santa Fe was well behind them, both lost in their own thoughts. The morning sun was not giving any warmth and the patchy clouds were being pushed by the wind. Rafe finally reached back and grabbed two buffalo hides, handing one to Carlos.

"Hope it's warmer in Albuquerque," Carlos said. The first winter storm always felt colder. By the time they got back, Santa Fe would be wrapped in winter.

"We should be able to make Algodones," Rafe said. He knew from previous trips there was a decent stage stop in Algodones. "We'll need to keep a good pace, though."

Carlos clicked the reins a little harder and the horses picked up the pace. He remembered the Algodones stage stop. Carlos' brother, Benicío, and his band of outlaws had robbed it once, while he held the horses. The memory jolted through his brain. It had been a cold night and the travelers were in the main room eating their supper. Benicío took their money and took the women's rings and broaches. Carlos was thankful no one was killed that night. Benicío kept most of the money and gave the trinkets to his men. Later, they exchanged the trinkets for sexual favors with whores. The poor travelers were left with no more than the clothes on their backs. Carlos was not proud of those days and glad they were over.

It was a long day to Algodones. Rafe and Carlos talked a bit about their plan, but spent many of the hours in silence. It was almost dark when they reached the stage stop. Rafe put up the wagon and horses in the barn. The supper was good and hot.

"We'll start right after breakfast," Rafe said. "We need to be in Albuquerque by the afternoon." Rafe knew Carlos would be ready to go early. He knew his friend's habits. Carlos rose before the sun and spent an hour in prayer every day.

The sleeping rooms at the stage stop were small, but clean. Rafe pulled off his boots and hung his jacket on the bedpost. He tapped his chest and felt the silver and turquoise amulet which hung around his neck. He wore it for good luck. He needed luck on this trip, even if the amulet reminded him of Chiwiwi. Stretching out on the small bed, he wrapped a blanket around himself and hoped Chiwiwi would not come in his dreams. She had not for three days, but dreams of *don* Bernardo's *hacienda*, dreams of his mother and sister and of his youth, replaced her. Some good dreams, some bad.

The morning brought sunshine and blue skies. The wind was blowing and it was chilly. After a hot breakfast, Carlos and Rafe tied Rayo and Sombra to the back of the wagon and headed south, wrapped in the buffalo hides. Rafe took the reins and snapped the team horses to attention. "Yehaa," he called to them.

"We will get to Albuquerque by midafternoon," Rafe said. "The Grady mercantile is on the plaza. I want you to make the delivery."

Carlos looked at his friend. "Why?"

"Carlos, there is a girl. A girl named Susan Grady. She's the daughter of John Grady," Rafe started, but paused, "She . . . I . . . she likes me."

"Rafe, the lover boy," Carlos said laughingly.

"No, it was not like that, but we were beginning to get close. It was before I met Chiwiwi," Rafe went on. "I made her a promise to come back and didn't."

"Soooo, you don't want to see her now?" Carlos asked with a grin.

"No, and we don't have time to stay. Mr. Grady will ask us to supper."

"You have so many women, Rafe, and I have none. I don't feel sorry for you," Carlos said laughing out loud.

"Come on *amigo* that's not true." Rafe responded. There was only one woman for Rafe, Chiwiwi, and now she was gone.

"What about the one I found you in bed with? Then a red head came to the house asking about you one day when you were up in the hills. Now, you're telling me you have one in Albuquerque who loves you?" Carlos asked looking at Rafe with raised eyebrows and a quirky grin.

Rafe looked down and said, "Carlos, I'm not ready to see her, not just yet. Please, just do the delivery," he pleaded.

"Where will you wait?" Carlos asked accepting Rafe's dilemma.

"I'll take Rayo and ride ahead. I'll wait for you south

of town."

"Are you going to visit Chief Letoc at the Isleta pueblo?" Carlos asked.

"No, I can't face him or Chiwiwi's sister, not yet." Rafe's said turning away.

CHAPTER 14

"Why are you doing this to me?" Cinnamon Baker screamed at Madam Marta. "The bum you set me up with last night had three months of stench on him and stiffed me for five dollars."

Cinnamon was used to her elevated status at the Crystal Palace. Marta gave the bums to a couple of the other girls and kept Cinnamon for the better customers. Cinnamon was the prettiest girl at the brothel and thanks to John B. Sutton had the nicest dresses.

"You take them as I see fit," Marta said to her in a huff.

"I'm the best money maker in this lousy joint," Cinnamon screamed at Marta.

"Not anymore. Now that Sutton's gone, you are just another whore to me." Marta had deliberately been giving Cinnamon more than her fair share of the lousy customers. Sutton paid Marta handsomely to force Cinnamon out of the whoring business. He wanted to marry Cinnamon, but the stupid whore refused him.

Cinnamon knew John B paid double for her from Saturday afternoon to Sunday afternoon. It was a lot of money – more than another girl made in a week. Cinnamon thought she was special, better somehow, than the rest. All the men wanted her.

"The rest of the girls have been taking the bums for too long while you set yourself up like a princess on Sutton's money," Marta egged the girl on. She knew Cinnamon would come complaining to her and this was her opportunity to do what Sutton paid her to do. He paid her a thousand dollars to fire Cinnamon. "Make sure no one else will hire her either," he said. "Spread some rumors."

"You'll have to work on Wednesdays from now on too, to make up for the money," Marta continued.

"Wednesday! You know it's the only day I can take

care of my mother." Marta knew Cinnamon was a responsible daughter. She supported her ailing mother by whoring. If Sutton had not told her that he planned on taking both of them to New Mexico, Marta would not be firing Cinnamon.

"I won't do it!" Cinnamon growled. "I don't care what you do, I won't do it!"

"Don't talk to me like that, Cinnamon," Marta admonished her.

"I'll talk to you any way I want. You're no better than I am. You were a whore before you started this joint." Cinnamon wagged a finger at Marta.

"Get your things and get out!" Marta growled at her.

"You can't fire me!" Cinnamon screamed back at her.

"I said, get out of here, and don't come back," Marta said turning on her heel.

"What am I suppose to do now?" Cinnamon screamed at Marta's back.

"That's not my problem," the madam said as she walked away.

Cinnamon knew Marta started as a whore in New Orleans. Like Cinnamon, Marta had a sugar daddy who paid her extra for spending special time with him. She played the man for extras and when she had enough saved, she took off in the middle of the night for Austin, Texas. Marta had sworn to herself she would never end up an old, worn-out whore. Marta had a good head for numbers and she knew the real money was paid to the madam, not the girls.

When she arrived in Austin, she started a new life. She even changed her name to Marta from Margret. She made friends with a politician who helped her buy an empty two-story building, just outside of the city limits. The building was not in bad shape and Marta hired a carpenter to build a bar and the rooms upstairs. She bought pretty fabric for curtains and beds for the upstairs rooms. She wrote letters to girls she worked with in New Orleans and offered them good wages. It did not take long for the Crystal Palace to become a vibrant brothel. It had been

twenty years since she arrived in Austin. The town had
grown and her business prospered. The Crystal Palace was
now considered the best saloon and brothel around Austin
and it had made her rich. Now in her late forties, Marta's
ample figure pushed at the seams of her dress and her
swelled bosoms drooped. Her face still showed most of her
youthful beauty, even with the tired lines of the years.

Marta knew Cinnamon frittered away most of her
extra money on dresses, shoes, and hats. She was lucky that
John Sutton wanted to marry her. Most whores would
jump at the chance to live a respectable life. Marta did not
understand why Cinnamon refused Sutton's generous offer
to take her as his wife and to support her ailing mother, but
that was not her problem. Sutton paid her handsomely to
throw Cinnamon out on her ear and Marta had earned the
money. No one would hire Cinnamon, not any saloon in
this town.

Up in her room, Cinnamon saw her life coming apart
and fell over the bed, loudly crying her heart out. A part of
her wanted to go back downstairs and apologize to Marta,
but anger boiled up through the tears. She refused to whore
to these dead-beat ranch hands and smelly trail bums. Tears
blinded her as she gathered her clothes and belongings
from the small room at the top of the stairs. It would be
easy to get a job at one of the other saloons. She might
have to start at the bottom there too, but soon she would
be back on top hustling the high rollers. She would show
Marta.

Cinnamon lugged her suitcases down the back stairs.
She did not want to say goodbye to the other girls and
Jackson, the bartender. She just could not face them.

Trying to muster some sense of pride, she slowly
walked along the dusty boardwalk in front of the closed
storefronts. Her mother lived in a small house on the far
end of the city.

"*¿Cinnamon dónde va?*" She heard a voice behind her. It
was Pedro, a local Spanish-Texan. He was a driver for
Marta and had often driven her to her mother's house.

"Can you take me to my mother's?" she asked him.

"¿Qué te pasa?" Pedro asked her what was wrong.

She understood and replied, *"Nada,"* and left it at that. She was mad, but most of all she was scared. The thought of having to take care of her sick mother and not having the income she enjoyed from working at the brothel overwhelmed her.

By the time they reached her mother's house, Cinnamon was shaking. She quickly said thank you to Pedro and handed him a nickel.

She hurried into the house throwing the suitcases on the floor. Her mother was sitting at the kitchen table having coffee. Cinnamon was not sure what was wrong with her mother. She took her to doctors and they could not help. Sometimes she was normal and sometimes she was just gone, as if lost in a different world. When she was normal, her mother would remember things, feed herself, and keep house. When she was sick, well, she did none of those things. Cinnamon paid an older Mexican woman to check up on her every day. If she was having a bad day, the woman would make her something to eat and put her to bed. It cost Cinnamon a lot of money, but she loved her mother dearly.

"What's the matter Cindy?" her mother called out. She shuffled her way into her daughter's room and found her face down on the bed.

"Why is that Mex bringing you here on a Friday? Why have you packed your suitcases?" she asked.

"I was let go," Cinnamon replied between sobs.

"But, but you were the best and the prettiest," her mother said. Cinnamon sighed and was glad that today was a normal day for her mother.

"It doesn't matter. Madam Marta said I had to go."

"What about your friend, that Mr. Sutton?"

"Momma, I . . . we can't go with that man. I only used him for his money. Besides, he moved to New Mexico."

"It will be all right, Cindy. You have money saved," her mother said. "I can take in sewing."

Cinnamon remembered when her mother was an

expert seamstress in New Orleans. That was before she started having the spells.

"Yes, don't worry Momma. I'll get another job at one of the other saloons."

In reality, Cinnamon had little money saved. Between taking care of her mother and spending most of her extra money from John B on dresses and pretty things, she was almost broke. Cinnamon got up and dipped a washcloth in the water basin. She scrubbed her face clean. When she looked into the mirror, she saw a beautiful fresh face and wondered why she painted it. She was only twenty-four years old.

CHAPTER 15

"Hey Boss, yew want me ta post an extree guard tonight?" Rip asked John B. Sutton. The drive had been on the trail for nine days, nine long days. A small band of Comanches were keeping them under a watchful eye, but had not attacked. John tried to tell his men they were just making sure the herd was passing through and not settling, but he was nervous and agreed with Rip to post extra guards.

They should have been in Abilene by now, but the cook's wagon lost a wheel and a sudden hail storm scattered part of the herd. It cost them at least three days. The Comanches had been following at a distance for the last two days. Red Tate, Sutton's most trusted scout, had been keeping an eye on their movements.

John had been on many drives through Comanche territory. He never understood Indians. Sometimes they attacked viciously and other times let cattle and wagons pass peacefully. Each night John rotated his drovers on guard duty around the horses and campsite. The already weary cowboys accepted the extra work without complaint. It was all part of the job.

Today was especially tough with a strong wind blowing from the west. They ate dust for ten long hours and even here in camp the dust blew constantly. When John had been young these things seemed to just be part of a drive, but now at his age every mile seemed five times longer. The first three days he could barely walk after the long day of riding was done. He hated how it made him look weak and old in front of his men.

"Red says the Injuns are still out there, Boss," Rip told Sutton when he came into camp.

"They're probably more interested in the horses than the cows, so post a guard on both sides. Tell the men to stay alert and no drinking and keep that fire high."

"Shur nuff, Boss."

John sat wearily down on his bedroll away from the men. He remembered the nights he was just one of the cowboys on the trail. The men sang and joked while the fire burned. Mostly they told stories before they settled down for some well deserved sleep. He was the boss and no longer welcome to their circle. Tonight, he was just as happy to rest his worn out body.

God he missed Cinnamon. After Cinnamon hedged on his offer of marriage, he left Marta with a thousand dollars to run her out of a job and out of town. Marta dared not cross him. John stretched out for the night listening to the night critters chirp and the talking of his men. He closed his eyes trying to picture Cinnamon in his favorite green dress and promptly fell asleep.

"Clang!" The sudden noise woke him with a start. His eyes blurred as they opened to the approaching morning. The cook had dropped a heavy skillet. Stretching, he groaned quietly with pain from his aching back. A little over an hour later, he and the drovers were saddled and moving the herd northwest. They would cross the Brownwood River sometime later today. Tomorrow they would reach Abilene, if all went well.

At least the wind stopped and they made more miles today. Minutes stretched into hours, each the same, except for the movement of the sun in the sky. It was October and the sun kept the days warm. Red Tate was riding hard in his direction. John stiffened in the saddle.

"Comanches on the move," Red said. "Bout twenty of em, best I can count."

"Where are they?"

"Jes tother side of the Brownwood. They all painted like a war party. Got rifles."

John knew there was no other route. Their only path was across the shallow crossing of the Brownwood to Abilene. They needed supplies for the rest of the trip. If they headed west from here, there was nothing until Big Spring – just hundreds of miles of nothing.

They rode along in silence for a few minutes until Sutton said, "Whatcha think?"

"If they wanted to attack, they probly woudda already," Red replied. "They awaitin for us at the river."

Rip saw the scout talking to Sutton and swung behind the herd to join them.

"What's goin on?" he asked when he reached them.

"Comanches waitin at the Brownwood," Red replied.

"War party?" Rip asked.

"Painted up, but waitin."

"Rip, keep the herd moving. Spread the word, but tell the men to keep their rifles down. I don't want to spook them Indians. When we get to the river we'll stop and see what they want," Sutton said having made his decision. He had twelve well-heeled men who could handle a fight, but he didn't want to start it.

"Got it, Boss." Rip jerked his horse to the right and loped away to the herd.

"Red, ride ahead and keep a sharp eye. Lemme know if they cross," Sutton ordered.

A couple hours later the Sutton herd was stopped on the south side of the Brownwood River. Across the water, mounted on horseback, were twenty-one Comanches. The Indians waited on the other side, all carrying rifles. Some of their ponies nervously moved side to side and John could see paint on both the horses and braves. Near the middle was a feathered brave, who appeared to be the leader. Around his naked chest, he wore a beaded chest plate. Out of his headband, long feathers loosely flapping in the breeze.

"Rip, tell the men to stay ready, but not to start anythin unless them redskins attack," Sutton ordered his ramrod. "Red, let's go powwow," he said to his scout. Red Tate spoke a little Comanche, hopefully enough.

When they started into the river, three Indians, including the leader, broke from the group and did the same. The two parties met in the middle of the shallow Brownwood.

Red raised his hand in a greeting. The Comanche riding in the middle did the same. The other two held their rifles up.

Red and the Comanche leader exchanged some words. John heard only a few words of Comanche he knew: *puc*, *piajunubi* and *cuhtz*. John knew *cuhtz* was the Comanche word for buffalo.

Red turned to Sutton. "They hunt buffalo, but can't find any. They want ten steers and five horses to let us cross in peace," the scout translated.

The cattle were no problem, but they did not have five extra horses. "Tell em ten cows, two horses, and two bottles of whiskey."

Red turned to the leader and relayed the message by holding up his fingers. The leader said something to his braves and then raised his feathered-adorned rifle high over his head. *"Haiiee,"* he yelled. Two braves started across the river toward the herd. The leader turned back and walked his horse to the far side of the river.

"I guess that means yes," Red said to Sutton. They turned and followed the Indians to the herd. Sutton ordered his men to cut ten cows from the herd and push them across the river. The Indians took two young horses and two bottles of whiskey and returned to the group waiting on the other side. As soon as they forded the river, the Indians rode out of sight.

"Saddle up," Sutton barked to his men. "We gotta pull foot and git movin."

Tomorrow, he would resupply and buy a couple of extra horses in Abilene and sleep on a soft bed. His men could have fun in Abilene blowing off steam, before the long push to New Mexico.

CHAPTER 16

Don Bernardo Reyes waited impatiently in the outer office of his lawyer, Nicolás Jiménez. He hated waiting for anything. Jiménez was busy with a client accused of taking land from a *mestizo* farmer. *Don* Bernardo heard heated words and some of the conversation, even through the closed door. Finally, Jiménez finished and called *don* Bernardo into his office.

"I'm sorry to keep you waiting, *don* Bernardo," Jiménez said greeting him. The old *don* gruffed at him and sat down.

"So, tell me what the *hija de puta* wants?" *don* Bernardo cursed. "You said she has a lawyer."

"*Sí*. Here is his letter," Jiménez said handing it to him. "She wants money, twenty thousand *pesos*, but not the *hacienda* or land, and she knows how much the *hacienda* is worth. It says she will pay to have the marriage annulled in the eyes of the Catholic Church."

Don Bernardo had been sending *doña* Carmela a monthly allotment for the past four years. It was enough money to keep her in a fairly lavish lifestyle in Mexico City. She had threatened him a couple times before and he paid her extra. Actually, he wanted to be divorced from her, but he would not let her rob him.

A divorce would allow him to marry the wealthy widow *doña* Juana Santos, who now owned a large piece of land adjacent to his south pasture. The marriage would make him one of the largest land owners in the area and give him much needed funds. He stifled a chuckle at the thought of *don* Miguel Santos' accident, orchestrated by his own hand. Now his widow, *doña* Juana, was wearing black and grieving, and not yet ready for courting. That suited his plan perfectly, as he needed to get divorced before he could begin an official courtship.

In reality *don* Bernardo was almost broke. His wealth had dwindled each passing year. He did not have twenty thousand *pesos,* not even close. "Carmela is a greedy *puta,"* he cursed to the lawyer. "The land is not worth nearly that much. What she wants is blood money." Blood money – yes, he knew it. Blood money for the murderous deed they planned so many years ago when they were young lovers.

Bernardo Reyes was a young *caballero* when he met Carmela. She was married to *don* Leonardo Bustamante, a wealthy banker in Mexico City who was almost twice her age. Bernardo was a brash young man who grew up in the northwest town of Torreón. His father and mother came to Mexico when he was an infant from Córdoba, Spain. His father, *don* Luis, sold his small cotton farm just outside of Córdoba. He carefully packed cotton seed and he, his wife, five-year daughter, and infant son made the trip across the Atlantic to Veracruz, New Spain. On the trip from Veracruz to Torreón, Bernardo's mother and sister died of yellow fever. Only he and his father survived the trip.

Despondent with the loss of his wife and daughter, *don* Luis worked incessantly. Bernardo was raised more by servants, than by his father, but he hardly cared. At the age of fourteen, his father enrolled Bernardo at the diocese school of Tlaxcala in Puebla to give him a formal education. His father sent Bernardo a handsome monthly allowance, more than most of the other boys. At the end of Bernardo's first year, the diocese expelled him for drinking and fighting.

His father then bought Bernardo a spot at the Military Academy in Mexico City. Bernardo excelled in his studies, but failed in discipline. He and his cadet friends controlled their classmates with their fists. There were rumors floating around, the boys were hanging out at a *cantina* at the edge of town near a whorehouse. The rumors were true and young Bernardo was financing the drinking and whoring. The *comandante* at the school disciplined Bernardo, threatening him with expulsion, but each time his father paid whatever the price to keep young Bernardo in school.

By the time he was seventeen, his father was the wealthiest cotton farmer in Torreón, and Bernardo was incorrigible. He left school, but continued receiving his father's monthly bank draft. Roaming Mexico City with money and bravado, Bernardo spent most of his days in *cantinas* drinking and most of his nights in the arms of a *puta*.

Bernardo was almost eighteen when he received word his father was in poor health and wanted him to come home to Torreón. The years of neglect and separation from his father left Bernardo empty and within three months his father died. Bernardo put his inherited cotton farms up for immediate sale. Farming cotton was not his future, but the farms sold handsomely, providing him money and plenty of it. With his newly inherited money, Bernardo raised his status. He attended prominent social gatherings in Mexico City and bought a fine horse and silver-trimmed black saddle. He was *gachupín* and he started living the life with Mexico City's upper socialites. Instead of *putas*, he set his lust upon many of society's fine young *señoritas*.

Lucinda Vargas caught his eye and the brash young Bernardo arranged secret meetings with her. Although promised to Frederico de Reynoso, Lucinda was smitten by Bernardo's daring. Their reckless behavior started rumors and soon Frederico challenged Bernardo to a duel. Bernardo paid Frederico's representative handsomely to short-shot Frederico's pistol and Bernardo shot him dead.

It was about a month later when Frederico's representative told the real story and Bernardo was chased out of Mexico City. Though the law did not prosecute him, society did. Disgraced, and his inherited wealth dwindling, he returned to Torreón and bought land for a horse ranch. Within four years, he had a small horse ranch in Torreón and was making a tidy profit.

On a trip to Mexico City to deliver a stud stallion, he met Carmela. Bernardo could not keep his lustful eyes away from her, but she was married to a prominent banker. Bernardo and his friend, Ignacio, visited the *paseo* every day, strutting their horses alongside the carriages and flirting with the *señoritas*. It was like the old days, but Bernardo only had eyes for Carmela. Each time he saw her, he wanted her more. Her smoldering eyes said, yes.

"Why is she here when she's married?" Bernardo questioned Ignacio.

"She comes to the *paseo* with her friends when her husband is away at the silver mines," Ignacio told him.

Bernardo was now twenty-four years old – brash, handsome, and fearless. For two nights, he followed Carmela home and spied from the shadows until early in the morning. On the third night, Bernardo scaled the wall using sturdy vines up to the second floor balcony. A faint light shone from her bedroom. A smile came to his face when the balcony door opened freely.

His *garrancha* stirred at the thought of having his way with the beautiful Carmela. Quietly, he opened the door, his rapier ready in his hand in case he miscalculated and encountered trouble. In the dim light he saw Carmela covered in only a sheer nightgown. The sheer material clung to her firm breasts and shapely legs, and between them nested a puff of dark hair. Blood rushed to his *garrancha*. For a moment, he stood near the bed admiring her beauty. Carmela's deep blue eyes opened and her mouth started in a scream, but Bernardo covered it with a light kiss.

"*Silencio, por favor no grites. Soy Bernardo,*" he told her not to scream. Bernardo felt her body tense and saw wide blue eyes looking at him, then, she relaxed.

"*¿Por qué estás aquí?*" What are you doing here she asked.

"You are the most beautiful woman in Mexico City and your beauty has trapped my heart."

"But my husband . . . " she trailed off as he reached under her gown and spread her legs.

"Is not taking care of his precious wife," Bernardo whispered.

His hand stroked between her legs and she moaned and spread her legs for him. He put his lips to hers. She reached down and found his *garrancha* fully engorged.

Pulling her nightgown off, Bernardo gasped at her naked beauty. Her breasts were milky white with bright pink nipples, her dark pubic hair silky and moist, and her pouty lips hungry for his kisses. He slowly and passionately caressed every part of her body. Carmela moaned with exquisite pleasure.

When he finally entered her, he felt his *garrancha* grow even more. Slowly, he luxuriated in the slow and rhythmic thrusts until she matched him with every stroke and they exploded together.

Bernardo held her in his arms, stroking her hair and letting his hand wander lightly on her body. Every inch of her was alive with desire – a desire she never knew possible. *"Mi corazón es tuyo,"* she whispered quietly that her heart was for him as her head rested on his chest.

"Tú eres mío," he told her, she belonged to him.

"Esto no es posible," she told him it was not possible, because she was a married.

"No me importa," he told her he did not care.

Taking her face in his hands, he brought her lips to his. Lightly at first, and then deeply he kissed her until she could take no more. Her body arched in arousal. His lips moved to her breasts, kissing and biting them tenderly. Her hips rose in response and she groaned in delight, "Don't stop."

They made passionate love three more times, each time with more fervor. Her hands clawed at his back as she met his every thrust. Carmela's lust was awakened and she lost control. All she knew was she wanted more.

They became lovers. Carmela would get word to Bernardo when *don* Leonardo was away at the silver mines. After dark, Bernardo scaled the wall to her bedroom, finding Carmela waiting for him. Each night grew more passionate and their lust was intoxicating. She desperately wanted to be free of her marriage and it was Bernardo who devised a plan to kill her husband.

"What do you want to do, *don* Bernardo?" Jiménez asked interrupting his thoughts.

The truth was *don* Bernardo still loved Carmela. He always had and was angry that she left. It was his *gachupín* right to take a mistress. At least María had given him a son, bastard or not.

"The horses sired by Santiago are fetching two hundred *pesos* each. Others are fetching one hundred and fifty for a stud and one hundred for a mare," *don* Bernardo said. "If I sold all my horses it would bring five thousand. That is all I have."

It was not as much as the horses might actually bring him, but it was a lot of money. He had stolen much more from Carmela's inheritance of *don* Leonardo's wealth after his death. A death planned by Bernardo and Carmela, leaving the lovers free to marry.

Don Bernardo remembered the day he killed *don* Leonardo as if it was yesterday. Carmela got word to Bernardo about *don* Leonardo's next trip to his silver mine in Zacatecas. Bernardo put his plan in motion to make sure Carmela's husband did not return.

On the trip homeward, *don* Leonardo and the driver stopped for mesquite broiled *carne asada* and wine in Ojocaliente at a *cantina* south of Zacatecas. From Ojocaliente the road grew steeper and more treacherous as they wound down the mountain. Bernardo waited as the carriage rounded a sharp curve, hidden by small mesquite trees. The driver never saw Bernardo's arrow which pierced his chest. He slumped to one side and then fell off the driver's seat to the dusty road. The mules spooked as the reins jerked in the dead man's hand, sharply to the left. *Don* Leonardo wrenched sideways as the carriage began to bounce along the road. He yelled out of the window to the driver, but got no response.

Picking up speed, the mules galloped along the winding road with the carriage bouncing crazily behind. At the next sharp curve, the carriage flipped on its side and skidded over the crest. It tumbled down the drop until it came apart at the bottom of the hill, smashed into pieces.

Bernardo, on his stallion, rode behind the carriage and watched it fall. Carefully, he circled down to the bottom and made sure *don* Leonardo was dead. He robbed him and whacked his head with a machete to make it look like *bandidos*. He and Carmela were free.

Bernardo quickly made his way back to Torreón. As they had planned, Carmela waited for her husband's return. In a few days, a traveler found the driver and the wreckage. Carmela played the grieving widow. It was torture to wait for his beloved Carmela, but Bernardo was very patient for this prize. It took time for the lawyers to sort out *don* Leonardo's business dealings and for her to lawfully inherit his wealth. While he waited for her, Bernardo looked for a large and better parcel of land for a bigger *hacienda*. They would be rich, but they both had blood on their hands.

"Five thousand is not much, but we can claim she has no rights to the *hacienda*," Jiménez interrupted *don* Bernardo's thoughts. "If she refuses, do you want to fight her in court?"

"What are my chances of winning?"

"Her lawyer says she has damning evidence on you, and not just the adultery," the lawyer said as he looked over his half-cut spectacles.

Don Bernardo knew what it meant. Carmela would tell how he murdered *don* Leonardo. She would claim she had nothing to do with it and that he forced her to move to Torreón. Rage swept him into a fury. *"Me cago en esa puta,"* he growled the Spanish curse. She could ruin him.

After several long minutes he finally sighed and said, "Offer her the five thousand *pesos*. I cannot go higher."

Feeling old and angry, *don* Bernardo had trouble getting on his horse when he left the lawyer's office. He agreed to the settlement knowing he did not have the money. He vowed to not pay Carmela and hoped to ruin her, and he thought he knew how. He needed money, though, money to pay someone handsomely for the deed. He pondered his problem on the ride back to the *hacienda*.

Outside the courtyard, he spotted his young bastard son, Antonio, playing in the dirt near his grandmother's garden. He thought about the new kitchen girl. She was very young and pretty, but he would call for María before dinner. He needed her tonight and needed his release.

Chapter 17

Rafe stretched out on a buffalo hide under a tall cottonwood tree on the west bank of the Rio Grande waiting for Carlos. Rayo lazily munched on grass near the river. Although midafternoon, there was a chill in the October air. He buttoned his jacket over his chest and pulled up his collar. While Carlos made the delivery in Albuquerque at Grady's mercantile, Rafe rested.

The effect of the month long binge on tequila still lingered in his body. He tired easily and sometimes felt a crawly feeling in his stomach. Closing his eyes he slept lightly, awakening easily to the squeals from hawks high in the sky. He watched them soar and then land high atop the cottonwoods. Along the banks of the Rio Grande, white egrets stood like statues hoping for an unwary fish to pass by.

From where he rested, he could see the top of the whitewashed chapel at the Isleta pueblo, the place where he first met Chiwiwi and where she was now buried. It seemed like yesterday, and yet, it seemed unreal. When he thought of her, guilt choked him. He wanted to see Chief Letoc, but needed more time. He could not face the Isleta chief and his wife, Shuren, Chiwiwi's sister. Someday, not yet. He had failed all of them.

"*Mierda*," he whispered a curse. He had failed his mother and sister, too. While he was safe and happy in Santa Fe, *don* Bernardo was fathering María's children. He should have stayed. He should have stayed and made sure he killed *don* Bernardo. It was his duty to protect his family. His father left him in that charge, but he ran and they suffered. Now, he had to make things right. The guilt in his heart burned with rage. A rage that would see *don* Bernardo dead, and his mother and sister safe.

In the distance he spotted a dust cloud. Several wagons had already rolled down the road, but as this one grew closer he recognized Carlos. Rafe stood up and collected the buffalo hide.

"*Eh, amigo,*" Carlos yelled out when he saw Rafe and pulled the wagon off the trail.

"How did it go with Mr. Grady?" Rafe asked.

"Fine, of course he asked about you and George. I told him you were busy at the foundry and George asked me to make the delivery."

"Did you see Susan?" This was the obvious question Rafe wanted to know.

"No, she wasn't there. I left the mercantile as soon as I unloaded the guns."

Rafe tied Rayo securely to the back of the wagon and climbed up to the seat. "You drive," Carlos said handing over the reins.

Clicking the reins, Rafe started the team and the wagon lurched forward heading back onto the trail. The sun was dropping lower in the afternoon sky and Rafe estimated it was about three o'clock.

"Los Lunas has a hotel," Rafe said. "I thought we might stop there and have a good meal. The hotel has a good restaurant."

Carlos knew Los Lunas well. His father's *hacienda* had been only a few miles to the east from the village. He grew up in Los Lunas and the people knew him. They also knew Benicío. His brother and his band of outlaws terrorized the small town many times. He knew he might not be welcome there.

"I think we can make Belen," Carlos replied not wanting to tell Rafe the reason for not stopping in Los Lunas. "It is only about another two hours and it will make tomorrow's trip to San Marcial shorter." They planned to stop in San Marcial to visit Carlos' cousin, Tomás Armijo. Carlos wired ahead and asked Tomás to get him a fine *caballero traje* and matching saddle. He did not explain in the wire, but knew his cousin would be happy to see them.

Rafe stared down the trail as they passed the turnoff to the Isleta pueblo. He took a last look at the whitewashed steeple of the Isleta Mission Church where Chiwiwi was buried. Pain stabbed his heart. "Chiwiwi, forgive me," he whispered under his breath.

Carlos sensed Rafe's emotions and kept quiet. This stretch of the King's Highway held scars for both of them. It was not too long until they were passing the spot where Benicío had robbed and burned some freighters and left Carlos for dead – the spot where Rafe found him and saved his life. Carlos watched for evidence of the exact location, but the elements had erased it.

Finally, Carlos decided to break the quiet tension. "Rafe, what do you know about your Spanish heritage?" Carlos asked.

"My Spanish heritage? I'm a *peón* from Mexico. You know that."

"Where do you think your ancestors came from?" Carlos asked him teasingly.

"Torreón. They lived there for generations," Rafe replied.

Educated in Spain, Carlos tried to explain. "In the 1500s the Spaniards conquered the Aztecs and other native tribes in Mexico. They called it New Spain then, now, it is Mexico. A Spaniard born in Spain was called a *gachupín*. My family was *gachupín* since my ancestors came from Spain. Spaniards not born in Spain, but of pure Spanish blood, are called *criollo*. I am a *criollo*, because I was born in New Mexico. For centuries, the *gachupíns* and *criollos* controlled New Spain. They owned the land granted by the Spanish royalty, just as my father did."

Rafe knew the word *criollo*. Every Mexican knew of Padre Hidalgo. He rebelled against Spanish rule. "Padre Hidalgo was a *criollo*. He fought for the peasants and Mexico became free from Spain," Rafe said proudly.

"Yes," Carlos replied, "and the peasants who fought with him were Indians and *mestizos*. The children of mixed Spanish and Indian blood are called *mestizos*. You are a *mestizo*," Carlos said. "You have both Spanish and Indian blood in you. One of your ancestors was a Spaniard."

Rafe did not think of himself as a Spaniard. He had never thought about it in that way. He was Mexican. A Mexican *peón*.

"Are all *mestizos peóns?*" Rafe asked.

"Unfortunately the wealthy land owners in Mexico, *gachupíns* and *criollos,* have controlled the *mestizos* and *Indios* for centuries. Without land and money the peasants have little choice but to work as slaves," Carlos continued.

"Yes, and the *hacienderos* take young girls and make them no better than whores." Rafe responded bitterly.

"Look, there's the lights of Belen," Carlos said pointing ahead to lights beginning to twinkle in the darkening evening.

Chapter 18

Elena Montoya choked, almost throwing up her breakfast. She felt sick every morning for the past week.

"What's wrong with you?" her brother Rodrigo asked.

"I don't know," Elena replied. "I just can't eat breakfast. It's disgusting."

"You always like bacon and eggs," Rodrigo said.

"I know, but the smell is making me sick."

"You haven't been to the *cantina* for three days. Uncle Nico is worried about you."

"I just can't go. I can't stand the smell of the *cantina*." More than the rank odor in the *cantina*, it was almost three weeks since she had seen Rafe. He did not come back to the house or the *cantina*. Every time the batwing doors opened, she looked up expecting him to walk in, but was disappointed.

"No, it's that *pendejo*, Rafe," Rodrigo said.

"I know. I keep waiting for him to come and I can't stand it," she replied.

Rodrigo kept the promise to his sister and made inquires about the young man around Santa Fe. Finally, an old Mexican blacksmith said he knew a young man named Rafe. The blacksmith told him Rafe worked for the GSW foundry. It was a prominent business in Santa Fe. The blacksmith said Rafe had been by several weeks ago to have a set of wagon horses shod and a wheel fixed. Rafe told the blacksmith he was going home to Mexico.

Rodrigo was relieved. "Good riddance," he muttered to himself as he left the blacksmith. In his mind he knew the young man was nothing but trouble for his sister. When he got home, Rodrigo lied to Elena and told her he had gone to the GSW foundry.

"He's not coming back. I told you he left for Mexico," Rodrigo said trying not to gloat.

Elena was heartbroken at the news about Rafe. She

prayed every day that it was not true. Now, she was sick and Rafe was gone, forever.

"You can't keep drinking that rot-gut tequila. No wonder you're sick every morning," Rodrigo grumbled at her.

"Why would he go to Mexico?" she blurted out. "I didn't know he was from Mexico. He spoke perfect English."

Elena choked again when she looked at the food sitting on her plate. She pushed it aside. She knew her nausea would finally pass by midmorning, but would the torture in her soul ever pass?

"What did the foundry man tell you?" she asked again.

"I've told you twenty times," Rodrigo said. "He worked at the foundry and he packed up and left for Mexico."

"Where in Mexico?"

"I don't know!" Rodrigo bellowed. "He's gone, Elena. He's gone."

Elena's head fell into her arms on the table, sobbing. She did not know why she loved Rafe so fiercely, but she did. She heard Rodrigo pick up her plate and scrape it onto the floor for the dogs.

Rodrigo came behind his sister and wrapped an arm around her shoulders. "Go back to bed, *hermanita,*" he said affectionately. "I'll come back at noon to make lunch for you."

"*Gracias,*" she said softly. "Tomorrow, I'll go home to the pueblo. Mother will take me to her medicine man, like she used to when we got sick as little kids."

CHAPTER 19

After spending the night in Belen, Rafe and Carlos left early heading to San Marcial. A cold wind howled from the north. They took turns driving, each huddled under a thick, warm buffalo skin. It had been a long day and it was Rafe's turn to drive.

"Carlos," Rafe yelled over the wind, "I see the mountains to the west."

Carlos peeked from under the buffalo skin and sat up. "Yes, those are the San Mateo's. The turn to San Marcial will be marked with a sign."

It was late afternoon and the sun's rays were casting a shadow off the highest peaks of the San Mateos. Even though it was still daytime, the temperature was dropping with the mountain's shadow.

"The San Mateos were a landmark for the Spaniards coming from Mexico City. Travelers on the Kings Highway used the mountains to tell them they were getting close to Socorro. Socorro was the first large settlement in southern New Mexico," Carlos explained.

"Why did the Spaniards come here?" Rafe asked.

"They were looking for gold and silver," Carlos said. "King Phillip II of Spain commissioned Juan de Oñate to lead the first expedition in the late 1500s. He and his colonists followed this same route north and eventually settled Santa Fe."

"That was a long time ago," Rafe said. "How did they survive?"

"They traded with the Indians, grew crops and some livestock, but it was a very hard life," Carlos said.

Ever since Carlos explained that Spanish blood flowed in him, Rafe had been pondering his life. He knew his grandfather owned a small farm near Torreón, but never thought much about it. Rafe only knew his life as a *peón*, working for *don* Bernardo with no future. Carlos explained he was *mestizo*, mixed Spanish and Indian blood.

He wondered if it mattered, now that he was an American.

"There's the sign," Rafe said seeing a rough-hewn sign along the trail.

They followed the road into San Marcial. The town looked new. The painted wooden store fronts were well kept and the paint was not weathered. Behind the storefronts were adobe houses in various shades of brown.

"I thought you said San Marcial has been a stop on the King's Highway for hundreds of years?" Rafe asked confused by the sight of the new-looking town.

"The old town was washed away in the 1866 flood. They had to rebuild the town on higher ground," Carlos explained.

The streets were deserted. As the wagon drove by Big Ed's Saloon, two rough-looking cowboys glared at them from the door. Rafe's mind flashed back to El Paso and Lilli Jean's Saloon. El Paso was bigger, but the scene was familiar.

"There, turn left toward the river," Carlos said pointing to a narrow road. They followed it to an iron archway with the name Armíjo designed into the pattern across the arch. Rafe drove the wagon into the courtyard of the main house and pulled up near the front steps.

Carlos bounded from the wagon and knocked on the door. It was dusk and the shadow of night was beginning to darken the courtyard. Candlelight poured out when a young woman opened the door.

"Carlos, bienvenidos a nuestra casa," the woman welcomed him.

"Tomás, mira quién está aquí," she called out to her husband to come and see who had arrived.

Carlos hugged the woman, before he called for Rafe to come in and introduced him to her. *"Teresa, este es mi amigo Rafael Ortega de Estrada."*

"Estoy a su servicio, señora," Rafe gave her the customary greeting saying that he was at her service and bowed slightly. She acknowledged him and ushered them into the warm living room and closed the door to keep out the cold.

Tomás walked into the room limping. The left side of his face had a big purple bruise extending from his left eye to his chin. On his lip was a crusty scab.

"*¿Tomás qué te pasó?*" Carlos asked his cousin what happened.

"*Un vaquero de Tejas me golpeó,*" Tomás responded that a Texas cowboy beat him.

Rafe knew his intuition was right. This was not El Paso, but the Texas cowboys he saw in front of the saloon were no better.

"*¿Por qué?*" Rafe asked why.

Tomás told them a Texas cattleman bought grazing land just south and west of San Marcial. He said his cowboys were grazing the cattle on the common land used by the Spanish for many generations. "They are also taking or killing our livestock," Tomás said.

"They beat you because of that?" Carlos asked.

"No. They scared and chased a young girl in town. When I told them to stop it, one of them beat me."

"*¡Desgraciados!*" Carlos exclaimed bitterly.

"Where's the sheriff?" Rafe asked.

"We don't have a sheriff. I am the *alcaldé* here. The people look to me for answers."

"What can you do?" Carlos asked his cousin.

"Nothing. They have us out gunned," Tomás answered bitterly. "The people here are farmers and ranchers, not gunfighters. I sent a wire to the sheriff in Socorro. Someone will be here tomorrow, hopefully. Come, let's not worry about that now. We must toast to your safe arrival."

Tomás led them to the dining room. A servant set glasses and a bottle of tequila on the long wooden table. The three men sat down on high-backed, ornately carved chairs. Rafe looked at the tequila bottle and cringed. He had not had a drink for several weeks, but knew it would be rude to refuse.

Tomás poured tequila into small glasses. "*¡Salud!*" he said. Rafe picked up the glass and tossed it into his throat. The smooth amber liquid burned only slightly. He was surprised by the taste – smooth and light. The tequila he drank at *El Coyote* with Elena had a raunchy after-taste.

"Tomás, the tequila is excellent," Rafe said.

"This tequila is from Jalisco. The Sauza family has made tequila for generations. They age it for many years. The rot-gut tequila sold in most saloons is cheap and tastes awful. I have a merchant who brings me bottles of Sauza and I keep it for special occasions."

The warm tequila spread through Rafe's sides. Suddenly he was no longer cold or weary, and his body called out for more.

Teresa instructed the servant, carrying large platters of mutton, corn, and tortillas, where to set the platters on the table. The mutton steamed and the smell of the spices filled the room. Teresa sat down at the far end of the table.

"Tell me about your trip to Mexico," Tomás said.

Between bites, Rafe explained about his mother and sister at *don* Bernardo's *hacienda*. He told Tomás of his sister's rape and her children by *don* Bernardo. Tomás nodded an understanding as he listened.

"It is the old way, I'm afraid," Tomás said. "*Haciendros* use the *mestizos* and *Indios* as slaves or worse. Although the people won freedom from Spain, the old ways don't die easily."

Rafe and Carlos explained the plan and how Carlos would pose as a *gachupín* horse buyer from New Mexico and Rafe a *vaquero*.

"Did you get the *traje* and saddle?" Carlos asked.

"Yes, the saddle is my grandfather's. I use it on special occasions. I had the *traje* made to your specifications," Tomás said. "You will look like a *grandee gachupín.*"

"*Gracias.* I will take good care of the saddle and return it on my way back north."

Tomás picked up the bottle of tequila and started to pour another round. Rafe waved him off. "I'll look after the horses," he said.

CHAPTER 20

Crowing roosters asserted authority declaring their turf, just as the sunlight poured over the eastern mountains. The ritual happened here at San Marcial, like most rural towns, every morning to get people moving to start their day.

Rafe woke, about an hour before the roosters saw sunlight, worrying about *don* Bernardo. The old *don* was still alive. The *haciendero* was mean, ruthless, and well trained in swords and guns. No *caballero* in Torreón dared cross him. Rafe bested him, only because the man was taking *siesta* and unarmed. When he shot him, Rafe was a *peón*. Now, he was confident of his guns and skills, but *don* Bernardo would not be bested again so easily.

Rafe lay covered up, keeping the morning chill at bay, until he heard clanging from the kitchen. Carlos and Tomás stayed up long into the night talking. Carlos slept soundly, snoring on the small bed on the other side of the room.

Outside the house Rafe heard voices, then a banging on the front door. Apparently, Tomás' day was about to start.

Pulling on his boots, Rafe walked over and pushed his friend's shoulder. "Wake up, we have a long day ahead," Rafe said. Carlos rolled out of bed and put on his boots trying to shake the cobwebs from his head. Together, they walked downstairs into the living room, just as several men were leaving the house.

"*¿Problemas?*" Carlos asked.

"*Sí,*" Tomás answered. "The cowboys shot up the saloon again and some of the store windows. They even shot several of Florita's chickens.

"*Desayuno,*" Teresa announced breakfast.

"You can't wait for help from Socorro," Carlos said over breakfast. "They probably won't come anyway."

"I know," Tomás said. "I am only one man. What can I do?"

"We are three now," Carlos said looking at Rafe. "We will go to where the Texans keep the herd and talk to them."

"Are you sure?" Tomás' eyes widened.

"Yes, I will talk to them and ask them to respect the people and property of San Marcial. I will ask them to live in peace here," Carlos said.

Tomás and Rafe looked at him, and then each other, and shook their heads.

"Carlos, you can't reason with Texas cowboys," Rafe said. He knew from experience that only a six gun could reason with a Texan. "They'd rather kill a Mexican than talk to one."

"I agree with Rafael, Carlos. You are only asking for trouble," Tomás added.

"We must try to reason with them without fighting," Carlos insisted.

"Well, I will take you there, but you better be armed. What about you Rafael, will you go?" Tomás asked looking at Rafe.

"No, please don't go. There will be trouble," Teresa spoke out overhearing them.

"Yes, we have to show them we are not afraid of them or they will not stop," Carlos said. "We have time before we go to Torreón." Carlos searched his friend's face and Rafe reluctantly agreed.

After breakfast, they gathered their belongings and packed the wagon. Rafe gathered his guns and the short-barreled shotgun he carried in the quiver Chiwiwi gave him. Carlos surprised Rafe with his willingness to confront the cowboys. He knew it was naïve of Carlos to think that he could talk them out of harassing the people in the village. Putting on his gun belt, Rafe knew the only way to deal with Mexican-hating cowboys was with guns. He was ready.

Rafe saddled Rayo and Sombra for Carlos. Once saddled, the horses pranced in anticipation. They had not been ridden in a couple days and welcomed the exercise.

Tomás took Rafe and Carlos on a tour of San Marcial, pointing out how they had rebuilt the town on the west side of the Rio Grande after the flood. It was Saturday morning and all was quiet at Big Ed's Saloon and partly constructed hotel. A few locals walked and talked along the main road. They waved at Tomás and he returned their greeting. A few stopped the trio and Tomás introduced them to his cousin Carlos and Rafael. No Texas cowboys were in town.

It was a glorious October morning. The wind from yesterday had calmed and the sky was a deep turquoise aqua. They rode south through the village toward Fort Craig. Tomás led them up on a mesa overlooking a grassy valley. From there they saw a vast herd of cattle grazing along the river. Carlos was surprised at the size of the herd. Cowboys on horseback milled through the herd and chased strays. Carlos tried to count the number of cowboys, but only ten were visible from atop the mesa. Carlos turned his horse down the mesa, but Tomás stopped him.

"No Carlos, there are too many of them," he said. "Besides they are just cowboys and not the boss." Reluctantly, Carlos agreed.

By the time they returned to San Marcial it was past noon and they stopped at Big Ed's for lunch and a beer. The saloon had a long bar and five tables where meals were served during the day and cards were played at night. One of the tables still had playing cards and chips left from last night's game. A tall man was sweeping up glass. Two broken chairs were pushed to the back of the room. One of the tables was on its side with a broken leg. He looked up as they entered.

"Hello Thomas," he said.

"Hello Ed. This is my cousin, Carlos, and his friend Rafael," Tomás introduced them to Ed Seeley.

"Glad to meet ya," Ed greeted them.

"I see you had some trouble last night. I heard about it this morning," Tomás said.

"Damn cowboys," Ed said. "They get liquored up and all hell breaks loose."

"What'll ya have?" Seeley asked wiping the bar.

"We'll have ham and cheese sandwiches and a beer,"

Tomás ordered.

"Hey Thomas, how's the face?" Ed asked while fixing the sandwiches. Rafe noticed Ed Seeley called Tomás by his English name, Thomas.

"Getting better. It's not as sore as it looks anymore." Tomás fingered the purple-bruised area on his cheek where the cowboy had hit him.

"I don't like seeing the cowboys acting up, but they bring me good business," Ed responded.

"Don't worry Ed, we will work it out with them," Tomás answered. "I wired the sheriff in Socorro."

"Sure, sure that will help. We need some law around here," Ed went on. "You boys staying long?" Ed asked Carlos and Rafe.

"No, we're on our way to Mexico," Carlos answered. Rafe observed and stayed quiet. He liked Ed Seeley. He looked you in the eye when he talked to you.

"Good of you boys to stop here. Hope you do again on your travels back," Ed said.

"We will be back in a couple weeks," Carlos replied.

They finished their lunch and had just mounted their horses when gunfire erupted. They saw dust before they saw five cowboys riding hard into the village shooting up and at buildings. Twice the cowboys rode up and down the street shooting, before they came to a dusty halt in front of Big Ed's.

"By gad, Butch did yew see them greasers scoot?" Ponyboy George yelled out at Butcherknife Bill laughing as they dismounted.

"We dun scirt da hell outta em," Bill laughed back at him. The other three cowboys finished shooting up into the sky, before they dismounted. The cowboys stood near their horses reloading their pistols as Carlos got down off his horse and went toward them unarmed. Rafe slowly dismounted and found a strategic spot in case there was trouble.

"You men have to stop shooting at houses and animals," Carlos said stepping up to the closest cowboy.

"Say what?" the cowboy stopped on his heels, turned,

and stared at Carlos in disbelief.

"I said you have to stop that shooting. Somebody might get killed." Carlos stood directly in front of the dusty cowboy.

"I be damned! This here greaser wants us to stop havin fun," Butcherknife Bill said looking at Carlos, but talking to his friends. "Hey Ponyboy what shud we do with this here greaser?"

"By gummie, I licked that other one afore. Maybe he wants me to crawl his hump again," Ponyboy answered pointing to Tomás. "Let's make them two greasers dance the bullet dance."

Tomás moved behind Carlos and grabbed his sleeve. "Let's just go," he hissed.

"Yer friend knows how to dance, do you?" Butcherknife placed a couple of well aimed shots at Carlos' feet. Ponyboy and the other cowboys were hooting and hollering behind Bill. Carlos did not move. He stood his ground and looked straight at Butcherknife Bill defiantly.

Rafe was amazed and proud of Carlos. He had not seen this side of Carlos, but Rafe knew words were cheap and guns did the talking to Texans.

"Lookin ta go to the bone yard greaser?" Butcherknife raised his pistol and aimed it at Carlos' chest and was about to palm the hammer.

"That's enough." Rafe stepped up from behind Rayo. He stayed back just far enough to have every one of them in his view. His hands hung loose and ready at his sides.

Bill looked over at the man behind the voice and saw Rafe with his two six-shooters and the top of a shotgun hung on his back. The looks of the well-heeled Mexican stopped Bill for a second.

"Yew stay out of this greaser or yew'll get the same as im," Butcherknife growled.

"Put that gun down," Rafe told him. Bill held his gun, but Rafe sensed he was thinking about his odds.

"Yew, where's yer gun," Butcherknife asked Carlos waving his pistol at him.

"I don't carry one," Carlos answered.

"You don't carry one. In Texas only chickens don't carry a gun," Bill chuckled.

"Yeah, only chickens don't carry no gun," one of the other cowboys chimed in making clucking sounds.

"I love to shoot chickens," Butcherknife threatened Carlos.

"You pull that hammer, and that will be the last thing you'll do before I put a bullet in your head," Rafe warned the cowboy, pulling his pistols. Rafe knew his double-action revolvers had the advantage over the cowboys' single-action pistols.

Ponyboy and Jake pulled their pistols. For the moment it was a standoff, until Butcherknife went to palm the hammer on his pistol. Rafe shot the hat off of Butcherknife's head in a blink of an eye. Ponyboy's eyes went wide, but he instinctively tried for his pistol's hammer. He looked up to see Rafe's gun aimed at his chest and not his hat.

"Drop those guns," Rafe ordered. "Don't come to this village shooting again. Like my friend says, someone could get hurt, maybe someone like you."

"*¿Comprendes?*" Rafe added in Spanish.

The cowboys were shocked. They were used to treeing Mexican towns and never had any greaser attempt to stop them. Treeing was their word for having fun – shooting at anything while they galloped up and down a town hooting and hollering.

"Cum on boys," Bill said, slowly putting his gun back into his holster and picking up his hat. He looked at the hole in his hat as he walked to his horse and mounted.

Bill glared down at Rafe. "Yew and me'll meet one day," he warned.

Bill whirled his horse, not waiting for a reply, and the five cowboys galloped back to their camp.

CHAPTER 21

"Is that you Cindy, honey?" Cinnamon Baker's mother called out from the back bedroom when she heard the front door of the house slam shut. Her mother had been bedridden for three days.

Tears ran through the smeared black mascara under Cinnamon's eyes. "Yes Momma," Cinnamon called out trying to sound happy.

For two weeks Cinnamon canvassed Austin for work, anything. Even the Yellow Rose Saloon would not hire her and it was the worst saloon in town. In her best dress and using her given name of Cynthia, she tried to find work in a shop or business. No one in or around Austin would hire her. Unbeknownst to Cinnamon, Madam Marta had ruined her prospects in Austin just as John Sutton paid her to do.

Cinnamon's meager savings were dwindling and last week she had to call the doctor for her mother. She walked to the kitchen and dabbed her face and eyes trying to remove the smeared mascara. Dirty dishes were piled in the sink. A half of a pint of milk sat on the kitchen table, spoiled. Her mother had forgotten to put it back in the ice box.

The doctor said her mother was getting senile – could not remember things. Last week her mother had been in a bad spell. Cinnamon was afraid to leave her to look for work, and she could no longer pay Rosa to look in on her.

Pushing at her mother's door, Cinnamon put on a smile and walked into the dim bedroom. "Hello Momma. How are you feeling?"

"Cindy, darling," she said. "You haven't been home for days. I've missed you."

Cinnamon left her mother early this morning. The doctor said part of her condition was an inability to judge time and to play along so as not to upset her.

"I'm here now Momma," she responded. "Are you hungry?"

"No, I just ate," her mother replied. Cinnamon knew this was not true, but true in her mother's mind. Her mother grew skinnier and more frail from forgetting to eat. If she could get her to eat properly, maybe she would get stronger.

"Well, I'm hungry and I'll fix us something," Cinnamon told her. "Come out to the kitchen and talk to me while I cook."

Cinnamon helped dress her mother and put on her slippers. Padding beside her like a docile lamb, her mother sat in a kitchen chair.

"Why aren't you at work today?" her mother asked.

Cinnamon told her mother a hundred times that she was fired, but her mother could not remember.

"Today's my day off, remember."

"I like your new blue dress," her mother said, "the one with the puffy bows. You look real pretty in that one. Why don't you wear that one tomorrow?"

When she was twelve, her mother bought her a pretty blue dress for Easter. It had been one of Cinnamon's favorites until she developed breasts and outgrew it. For some reason, at times, her mother remembered her as that little girl in the blue dress.

"Yes it is pretty. I'll wear it tomorrow," she played along knowing her mother would not remember tomorrow.

Cinnamon hummed while she cooked up some ham and biscuits. Her mother toyed with a cup of coffee at the table, seemingly lost in another place and time. These last weeks at home every day made Cinnamon realize how sick her mother was. When she had been working and only coming for occasional visits, she seemed much more normal. The doctor said it would get worse and worse.

"Here Momma, eat," she said putting a plate of ham and hot biscuits on the table. Her mother looked up at her and smiled.

"Thank you dear, but I'm not hungry."

Cinnamon buttered a biscuit and spread jam on it hoping to entice her to eat. Placing it in front of her mother she said, "Momma, you have to try the jam made from the berries behind the house. You know they are your favorite."

Finally, her mother picked up the biscuit and started eating. "Grandma used to pick those berries for jam," her mother replied. "She taught you to make the jam when you were a little girl."

At least her mother was eating even if her mind did not remember where she was. Her grandmother's house with the berries in the back yard was in Ohio. It was the house where Cinnamon's mother grew up and learned to make jam from the berries. Cinnamon was getting used to the confused world of her mother and understanding how to manipulate her, even to eat.

A few hours after supper, Cinnamon put her mother back into bed. Her mother clung to her hand. "Cindy, don't leave me again," she pleaded.

"I won't Momma. I'll be here in the morning when you wake up."

Cinnamon Baker walked into her bedroom and flung herself on the bed. What was she going to do? Tears burst and ran down her cheeks falling onto the rumpled bed cover. "Why, why?" she said over and over. "Why did Marta fired me?"

Yesterday, she went to the Crystal Palace and tried to make amends with Marta, but the madam would not even look at her. Cinnamon was infuriated and left cursing. Even the other whores, her old friends, ignored her.

She pondered going to Fort Worth. She heard it was a booming cattle town. Surely, she could find work at a saloon there, but taking her mother to a new town, finding work, and a place to live, scared Cinnamon. The only option was to go back to New Orleans. She knew people there. At twenty-four years old, she was not as desirable as the younger ones, but she would be able to find work.

Cinnamon wiped her nose on her embroidered handkerchief and slid off of the bed. In the bottom drawer of the dresser she kept a box. In it was all the money she had. She pulled it out, sat it on the bed, and counted it again, praying somehow it would be more than yesterday. A little over twenty-three dollars was all she had in the box. It was not enough to go to New Orleans. Not enough to go anywhere and start over.

Cinnamon fell on the bed, tears pouring down her cheeks and sobbed. She only had one solution to her problem – John B. Sutton. The deformed older man repulsed her, but he had asked her to marry him and promised to take care of her and her mother. He was really a good man, she knew that. He was rich and had plans to become richer in some no-name town in New Mexico.

She swallowed hard deciding to accept John B's proposal. She could care for her mother and never have to worry about money for the rest of her life. As far as sleeping with the repugnant little man, she would act as his whore, just like before. She would paint herself up and pretend she cared for him. After all, isn't that what whores did?

Sitting by the oil lamp, she wrote a letter to John B asking him to send money for a stage ticket for her and her mother to El Paso. She wanted to be married in Texas, she wrote.

The next morning she took the letter addressed to John B. Sutton, San Marcial, New Mexico Territory, and gave it to the postmaster. With her, she carried a suitcase containing her best dresses and hats. She knew she could sell them to some of the whores at the Crystal Palace for half of what they cost her. It was not much, but would keep her and her mother alive until she heard back from John B.

CHAPTER 22

Orange, pink, and gray lit up the eastern sky five days out of San Marcial. Rafe and Carlos crossed the Rio Grande yesterday and were now in Mexico. At first, Rafe had misgivings. It felt strange to be standing on Mexican soil, his homeland, but this morning the beautiful sunrise gave hope to all those traveling south on the Chihuahua Trail.

Rafe and Carlos stopped briefly at Rafe's uncle Jose's ranch north of El Paso. They left Rayo and took a chestnut stallion. Rafe would use the stallion when he pretended to be Carlos' *vaquero* in Torreón. His uncle Jose also provided a pair of *vaquero* chaps, a soft worn jacket, and a single-action pistol. He warned Rafe not to take his GSW pistols or shotgun. "A *vaquero* would not have such weapons," he told him.

Rafe and Carlos were covered up under the buffalo hides, still fighting off the chill until the sun warmed up the chilly morning. The last two nights they made camp on the trail and slept in the wagon. They agreed it was better to keep clear of any large towns until they reached Torreón.

"Even the hills have eyes," Rafe told Carlos. Rafe held the reins and had the horses at a steady pace. Today they would get to Chihuahua and pick up more supplies.

"Think those cowboys in San Marcial will behave themselves?" Carlos said through chattering teeth, worried about his cousin Tomás in San Marcial.

"Don't think they will. I bet I made them hate Mexicans even more," Rafe replied knowingly.

"Well at least you scared them with your gunplay, but I'm worried about Tomás."

"Believe me Carlos, Texas cowboys don't scare, they get even," Rafe warned.

"That's what I'm afraid of," Carlos said, teeth still chattering.

"We'll stop there on our way home. Right now we

have more trouble awaiting us in Torreón," Rafe said. Carlos heard urgency in his friend's voice and knew Rafe was worried about what was to come.

Rafe was impressed by Carlos' bravery in San Marcial. He stood up to the Texas cowboys, unarmed. It was foolish, but very brave.

"What made you stand up to that cowboy without a gun."

Carlos thought for a minute before answering, "Pride, honor, and some anger. Spaniards are very brave by nature. It is in our souls."

Since Carlos explained to him that he was a *mestizo*, part Spaniard and part Indian, Rafe pondered the idea. He still did not quite understand or believe it.

"You see, many years ago the Moors conquered Spain. The Moors followed the prophet Mohammad and the Spaniards were Catholic. It was in the year 711. For more than seven hundred years the Spanish battled the Moors, until the year 1492, when the last of the Moors were driven out of the city of Granada." Carlos looked over at Rafe to see if he understood.

Rafe did the arithmetic quickly in his head. "That's seven hundred and eighty-one years! They fought the Moors that long?" Rafe asked.

"Yes, it is said the common people in Spain dropped their plows, closed their shops, and closed their classrooms to pick up arms to go fight the Moors," Carlos said. "It was not just a battle of armies; it was a battle of the people – all the people," Carlos said with pride. "For generations the people fought the Moors. It became like the air they breathed and part of their spirit. It is in your spirit, Rafe, and mine."

Rafe listened intently and was impressed by the tenacity of the Spaniards. "You mean I stood up to *don* Bernardo because Spanish is in my soul?" Rafe asked still confused.

"Pride, honor, and bravery, yes, it is all part of you."

"But, *don* Bernardo is a Spaniard and he has no pride or honor or bravery," Rafe grumbled. "He is a *desgraciado*."

In Mexico, ruthless men like *don* Bernardo and other *haciendero*s controlled the government, the military, the police, the laws, and most of all controlled the peasants. They used *peóns* for work and raped the young girls for pleasure. These were the Spaniards Rafe had known in his youth in Mexico.

"Men are men," Carlos replied. "Some are good and some are bad. My brother was a bad man. It is the way of men, but without bravery, the Spaniards would not be in Mexico."

"What do you mean?" Rafe asked.

"After defeating the Moors in 1492, the King and Queen of Spain financed Cristóbal Colón to find a passage to the orient by sailing west from Spain. Colón and his men sailed thousands of uncharted miles into the unknown and landed near Cuba. At that time, most people thought the world was flat and the sailors thought they would just fall off the earth," Carlos said laughing.

"I can see why they thought that," Rafe said pointing to the flat landscape around them. Rafe had never been on a boat or seen the ocean, but he read about it in his studies in Santa Fe. "Were the boats large?" he asked.

"Oh no, they were really quite small," Carlos replied. "The voyage across the Atlantic was extremely difficult and fearsome, but the Spaniards called upon their faith in God to see them through. After Colón found the Americas, Spain sent more explorers.

"In the early 1500s, Cuba was settled as the Royal Government of New Spain. The governor sent expeditions west and they discovered what is now the mainland of Mexico. They also discovered the local Indians had gold. Just like it is now, gold was very valuable. In the year 1519, Hernando Cortés commanded an expedition to the mainland. He took about six hundred soldiers and sixteen horses on eleven ships.

"Cortés was a brave soldier and a cunning warrior. He and his small expedition fought their way into the mainland. The native Indians had never seen horses and thought the Spaniards on horseback were one being or

Gods. Once Cortés defeated a tribe, he befriended them and made them his allies. He learned the mainland of Mexico was ruled by the Aztec Prince Moctezuma. The Aztecs under Moctezuma ruled most of the smaller Indian tribes and took the conquered tribes as slaves and for human sacrifices. The smaller tribes hated the Aztecs," Carlos continued explaining the history of Mexico.

"The Aztecs sacrificed other Indians?" Rafe shuttered a bit at the thought.

"Yes, they cut out their beating hearts as sacrifice to their Gods. The Indians told Cortés, Prince Moctezuma had a fierce and great army and would eat the Spaniards, if they were captured."

"Eat them?"

"*Sí, eso es cierto,*" Carlos said it was true. "The Aztecs thought they seized the power of their enemies, if they defeated and ate them. The Spanish, their horses and weapons, were very powerful and the Aztecs wanted that power."

"What did Cortés do?" Rafe asked.

"The Aztecs ruled the land from a large city called Tenochtitlán. It is believed that Tenochtitlán was larger than any city in Spain, with tens of thousands of people," Carlos explained.

"Ten . o . ch . tit . lán," Rafe tried to pronounce the word.

"It is the city we now call Mexico City," Carlos continued. "Cortés moved his army and Indian allies toward Tenochtitlán. He was told the Aztecs had golden idols and great wealth. Cortés hoped to set up trading between Moctezuma and Spain, but he was not afraid to fight. Cortés entered Tenochtitlán and eventually defeated Moctezuma and the Aztecs. It took many battles, but the Spaniards finally won."

"How many men did Cortés have?" Rafe asked.

"He had maybe five hundred men."

"He only had about five hundred soldiers against the entire Aztec empire?" Rafe asked amazed by the bravery of Cortés.

"I told you the Spanish are brave," Carlos chuckled. "He also had Indian allies who helped him defeat the Aztecs."

"I like that man Cortés," Rafe said. "It seems good fortune and luck followed him."

"And faith," Carlos responded. "Cortés and his men had great faith in God. They believed the warrior saint, Santiago, followed them into battle, and helped them win."

Rafe knew the Catholic saints from the Catholic lessons at the *hacienda* and from his mother. Santiago, the legend of the warrior saint, was the reason *don* Bernardo had named his prize stallion, Rayo's sire, Santiago.

"Yes, I know the legend of Santiago," Rafe said. "He is a great warrior saint on a white stallion with a fiery sword."

"You know the rest of the story, Rafe. You are part of it. As much as you dislike Spaniards, like *don* Bernardo, you are part Spaniard. It is your history, too," Carlos finished.

Rafe reflected on the history of the Spanish Carlos had been telling him, and his Spanish heritage. He thought about Cortés and the great defeat of the much larger Aztec empire. *Don* Bernardo was but one man, but Rafe knew he was going to need all his bravery to confront the *don*, especially without his GSW pistols. He vowed to himself that he, Rafael Ortega de Estrada, with Spanish blood and bravery, would kill the *desgraciado*, *don* Bernardo, and rescue his mother and sister.

CHAPTER 23

Several weeks after Rafe and Carlos left San Marcial, Tomás Armíjo walked into Big Ed's Saloon on a Thursday afternoon. A few locals were drinking at the bar.

"Hello Ed."

"Howdy Thomas."

"How's business?"

"Slow. The locals are afraid to come. No one comes on the weekends when the Texans are in town. Wanna a beer?"

"Gracias."

Ed Seeley was not happy about losing the local business, but understood. He did not blame the locals for being afraid. He witnessed the cowboys beat Thomas and witnessed the confrontation between the Sutton ramrod, named Butcherknife Bill, and Thomas' cousin. If Carlos' friend had not shot Bill's hat off and held his gun on the other cowboy, Ed was sure Thomas' cousin would be dead. Ed had seen fancy shooting, but had never seen anyone as fast and sure as the young Mexican.

"Thomas, who was that young man with your cousin – the one who bested the cowboys?" Ed asked.

"Rafael Ortega de Estrada."

"He sure is fast," Ed said. "I hear the cowboys talking about him. They are still teasing Bill about getting his hat shot off. Bill swears he'll kill him next time." Tomás nodded knowing Rafael would be a target of the cowboys, if he came back to San Marcial.

"I also heard the cowboys talk about the boss man coming to San Marcial and bringing the rest of the herd with him," Ed said. "Word is he will be here today or tomorrow. I got a letter for him from Austin, Texas. His name is John B. Sutton."

"John B. Sutton, huh? Well, I hope he will calm his cowboys down," Tomás said and rose to leave.

"See ya soon," Ed said as Tomás headed for the

door. He hoped Tomás was right and the boss man would control the cowboys, but he knew it was just a wish.

Friday morning John B. Sutton and his drovers broke camp and started the herd on the last leg of the drive. Dust clouds rose up from the trampling herd of cattle coming up a trail near the Rio Grande. It was an impressive sight which could be seen for many miles. People in San Marcial already knew the herd was coming. The cowboys were talking in the saloon, and in the stores travelers told of the moving herd.

The herd was about ten miles south of San Marcial. John sent Red Tate, his scout, ahead to notify Bill Payton the herd was coming, and to ask Bill to send extra men to help get the herd settled. John B. Sutton was an exhausted man.

John and his drovers had been on the trail for over five weeks and John was dog tired. They had more than their fair share of broken wagons, lost and sick cattle, and Indians. But worse, was the trouble in Abilene. Two of his drovers shot a drunk Mexican and landed in jail. The boys were just blowing off steam, shooting at things like they always did. Stupid Mexican tried to stop them and they shot him dead.

The sheriff took Burt and Frankie to jail and threatened to hang them. "Hang em for shooting an old greaser?" Sutton blustered to the sheriff. "Cold blood," the sheriff said. "Mex wasn't packin."

"What kind of stupid law protects Mexicans," Sutton complained.

"The American law," the sheriff replied. "Mexicans are citizens, just like everyone else in Texas."

"Hogwash," Sutton growled.

"A killin is a killin. Don't matter what color does the killin or what color gits hisself kilt," the sheriff said in response. The sheriff did not really give a hoot about Mexicans, but knew he could fleece the big boss to get the two cowboys off the hook.

When Burt and Frankie sobered up and the sheriff told them the law, they begged Sutton to do something.

Sutton did not really care about either of the two men; they were just cowboys, but his men cared and they expected him to handle the matter. Sutton could not afford to lose his men's trust in the middle of a long cattle drive. It took a hundred dollars each to bribe the sheriff into releasing Burt and Frankie.

"Get out of Abilene, now. You, your men, and your cattle and don't come back," the sheriff told Sutton, smirking and pocketing the money.

John fumed at the price. Two days later when they reached La Mesa, Texas, the burn was a rage. Damn Texas lawmen. Damn Mexicans. Two hundred dollars for killing some old Mexican was just highway robbery. Camped outside of La Mesa, the last fairly-decent sized town before the New Mexico border, John gathered his men. He knew La Mesa was a smaller, mostly Mexican town.

"Let's tree it," he told his men. "Tree it good." John and his men left the camp after sunset and headed into the dusty village. When they were done, not a window or door did not have several bullet holes. John and Burt rode their horses into the *cantina* and shot up the bar. As bottles shattered, spilling their amber liquid, the bartender grabbed a shotgun from under the bar. John shot him dead.

By the time they returned to camp, John's fury was spent and his body weary, but they started the herd immediately. Sleep would have to wait. He was glad this damned drive was almost done and glad to be leaving Texas.

"Hey, Boss." Butcherknife Bill rode up to John Sutton interrupting his thoughts.

"Hey, Bill." Sutton grinned and was relieved to see his top man.

"How's it goin with the herd," Sutton asked.

"Fine as cream gravy," Bill replied. "We got em settled on good grass near the river."

"These cows are pretty spent," John replied, "Been pushing pretty hard." He waved his hat at the incoming herd.

"Yeah, it's a tough trail. I'll take the herd in fer yew,"

Bill said.

"Good, been on the saddle too long." John's face was covered in trail dust and he puffed hard on his stub of a cigar. Bill noticed the boss looked his age and then some.

Butcherknife Bill rode off to the herd and Sutton rode north, alone. John let his horse lope at an even pace. The horse was just as tired as he was. He was relieved to hear from Bill the herd was well settled. Bill was a good man and a good ramrod.

John rode casually into the village of San Marcial. Curiously, he noticed the streets were almost empty even though it was midday. It was not much of a town, yet. John smiled imagining the dusty little hamlet as a booming cattle town. He pulled up in front of Big Ed's Saloon and slid wearily off his horse, flipping the reins around the post. Stiffly, he went up the steps to the saloon door and walked in.

"Howdy! Who's the big bug here?" John demanded loudly puffing out his chest. It was almost noon and Ed had just finished setting up the bar and unlocked the front door.

"Why, I guess I'm the big bug," Ed answered with a smile at the Texas talk. "What can I do for you?" Ed asked, guessing this was the boss man from Texas.

"I'm John B. Sutton," he said reaching out to shake hands with Ed.

"I'm Ed Seeley, owner of this place." Ed took his hand.

"Glad to know you Ed. Yew got a nice place here."

"You look thirsty. Beer or whiskey?"

"Cold beer, then make it a rye," John replied.

"You must be the big boss man from Texas," Ed said. "Your boys've been talking about you bringing the rest of the herd."

"Yep, from Austin, Texas," John said with pride. John drained the rye in one gulp and chased it with the beer. "That sure tastes good. Yew got any vittles?"

"Sure, got bacon, eggs, and coffee already made up."

"Sounds good." John looked around the empty

saloon. "Come sit and eat some breakfast with me," he said to Ed. "We got r'selves some bidness to discuss."

"Yes sir, a batch a eggs and heap a bacon coming up."

John liked Ed Seeley. Seemed like a decent sort. More than John expected in this little town. Ed returned with a platter of food and they sat down facing each other. John dug into the hot food like a starving man and drained his coffee cup before he spoke.

"Mighty good." He wiped his mouth with his sleeve. "I'm gonna need me a hot bath and then a room. I'll be staying here in town for awhile," he said looking at Ed.

"Yes sir. I got three rooms upstairs. The tub is back of the kitchen and there's an outhouse out back." Ed was delighted. Steady money for a room each day would greatly help his sagging bar sales. John B. Sutton seemed a likable man. He was definitely more mannerly than Ed had expected.

"I be wantin to hire a crew to build me a ranchhouse," John continued.

"I run a crew that's building my hotel here, only crew in town, unless you go get one from Socorro," Ed informed him.

"Tell yew what, yew let me have that crew of yers and I'll make it worth yer while," John said looking straight into Ed's eyes.

Ed did not have to blink to decide. He had run out of funds to finish the last part of the hotel and glad to hire out his crew.

"That can be arranged Mr. Sutton. Right now, my crew is just about done with the first part of my hotel. I guess I can spare them some. You're gonna need a supervisor to get the job done right, though" Ed offered.

"Call me John. Do yew know where I can git one?"

"That'd be me. Did a lot of construction in the Army. Do you have an idea on what you want built?" Ed asked.

"Yes, I do. How soon can yew git started?"

"Soon as I can get somebody to spell me here, I reckon," Ed replied. He was elated by his sudden windfall –

hotel room, food, drinks, and supervising the building project. Ed knew this man had money and Ed imagined a bunch of that money coming his way. Yes, he liked this man.

"Want another cup a joe?"

"Yep. Who's in charge of this here town or is that yew too?" John asked raising his eyebrows.

"No, that'd be Thomas Armíjo. He's the mayor," Ed told him.

"Where kin I find him?" John asked. Damn Mexican running the town. Well he expected it. That would have to change.

"Most mornings he usually comes in here first thing for coffee and a chat. Ain't seen him today though, so he's probably at his ranch," Ed said.

"By the way, I have a letter for you, arrived last week," Ed said suddenly remembering the letter. He went around the counter and brought the letter back to the table and handed it to John.

John caught the scent when Ed handed him the letter. It was Cinnamon's perfume, no doubt about it. He grabbed the letter from Ed's hand. Quickly he opened it and read her short letter. A huge smile lit up his face under his month-old droopy mustache. The long miles felt lifted from his weary body. His plan had worked. Cinnamon was going to marry him. John was grinning with joy.

"Good news?" Ed asked.

"Yes sirrie, boy! I's gonna need yew to work hard to get that ranchhouse built quick. Looks like I'm a gettin married," John said excitedly. Plans raced through his mind. He would have a beautiful wife and grow the largest cattle ranch here in New Mexico. New Mexican politicians would come flocking to him and he relished the thought. He would control the town and the cattle business in the territory and he would have Cinnamon to share it with.

In the letter, Cinnamon told him to wire her money for the stage to El Paso. She wanted to be married in Texas before she came to New Mexico. She and her mother were ready and as soon as she got his reply, they would catch the stage for El Paso.

Marta had done a good job. Cinnamon was desperate. She did not even have money for the stage. He would wire her the money and tell her to go to the Stratton Hotel in El Paso. Hell, he had no problem going back. It would be his last official act in the state of Texas. "To hell with them money-grabbing politicians. He'd bring his bride to New Mexico and start a new life here. A bigger and better life than he had in Austin," he told himself.

"How bout that bath," John said. "It sure would feel mighty good."

CHAPTER 24

Rafe woke to the screeching of a hawk and looked around the wagon. Carlos was already up saying his prayers and cooking breakfast. They camped near Bermejillo, a town about twenty miles north of Torreón. Today they would arrive at their destination. Rafe crawled out from under the buffalo blanket and jumped off the end of the wagon. To his surprise the morning was mild and warmer. Being used to the colder weather in Santa Fe, he had forgotten how temperate this part of Mexico was in the fall.

They had picked up supplies in Chihuahua and Carlos had the coffee pot going on top of the fire as bacon sizzled in a pan.

"*Buenos días,*" Carlos said looking up.

"Is that coffee ready?" Rafe asked.

"Should be. Breakfast is almost ready."

Sitting by the fire last night, they talked of their plans once they arrived in Torreón. Rafe knew it was important to arrive in Torreón in character, because word of strangers would spread quickly.

After breakfast, Carlos dressed in his *traje*. The black jacket was cut to the waist and trimmed with tooled silver buttons on the cuffs and down the front. The pants were of a fine black cloth. The bottom of each bell-shaped pant leg was cut open showing the white lace of the inset. The pants were trimmed in matching silver buttons down the outsides. Around his waist Carlos tied a red sash over a crisp white shirt.

Rafe looked at Carlos and said with respect, "I am at your service, *don* Alejandro." They began using their adopted names yesterday, when talking to each other. Carlos was *don* Alejandro Martinez de Lunas; Rafe was Juan Romero.

"On your feet Juan. We must be going," Carlos said in a stern voice playing his part, and then he smiled.

"How was that?" he asked.

"Bueno," Rafe replied.

Rafe dressed in the well-worn *vaquero* clothing his uncle Jose gave him. The brown jacket was cut short at the waist with lighter brown embroidery in front along with small silver clasps. It had the same embroidery on the sleeve cuffs. His legs were covered with a pair of leather chaps. Small silver studs adorned the sides. He tied the soft leather leggings around his calves and over his boots. All this fit over simple, white cotton *pantalones*. He tied a thin kerchief around the collar of his shirt and put on his straw sombrero with a wide flat brim. The hat's crown was tall and flat on top with a leather band.

Rafe tucked a pistol under his belt with the grip pointing to his right and stood up straight. Carlos nodded an approval. Rafe was now Juan, *don* Alejandro's trusted *vaquero.*

They broke camp and hitched the wagon. Carlos started to help, but Rafe warned him against helping. Carlos must be *don* Alejandro at all times.

They rode for about an hour without speaking, each thinking about what was to come. Finally, Rafe broke the silence. Not wanting to talk about what was waiting in Torreón he asked, "How did your family get to New Mexico?"

"My great-great-great-grandfather was from Madrid. He and his wife traveled to New Spain to start an import business. At that time all products had to be imported from Spain. It was very costly for the colonists to buy all of their goods from Spain, and very lucrative for the importers. It was a good business for several generations of my ancestors. Then Spain engaged in ongoing wars against France and England, using gold and silver mined in New Spain and taxing the colonists. The wars were costly and the colonists in the New World were tired of being taxed and getting nothing in return. My great-grandfather decided to move his family to New Mexico. At that time, colonists who lived on the northern frontier obtained the status of *don*, which means *de origen noble*, and were exempt from paying taxes."

"But," Rafe interrupted, "they were *gachupíns*. Weren't they already *dons?*"

"Yes, they were *gachupíns* because they were Spaniards born in Spain, but they were merchants and not considered noblemen. Spain's social *casta* system is quite complex. My great-grandfather was given a large Spanish land grant near Los Lunas. He started a cattle ranch. That is where I was born."

"What happened to your land? Why did you lose it?" Rafe asked.

"The United States was pushing west. It is a very long story, but General Santa Anna lost almost half of Mexico to the United States." Carlos stated. "Texas, New Mexico, and most of California were bought by the United States under the Treaty of Guadalupe Hidalgo."

"Yes, but why did you lose the land in New Mexico?" Rafe asked again.

"After New Mexico became an American territory all of the laws changed. The treaty stated the Spanish landowners were protected, but newcomers didn't care what the treaty said. One day an official from the new government came to our Los Lunas ranch and told my family to leave. They killed my father in the courtyard as my brother and mother watched."

Rafe was stunned. He was not sure what to say, and then said simply, "I'm sorry."

"We are Americans now, you and me. The past is over and nothing can be done," Carlos finished.

Nothing can be done. Those were the words his mother spoke to him on the day he shot *don* Bernardo for raping his sister, but Rafe no longer believed it. The old *don* was still alive and this time Rafe would finish what he tried to do over four years ago.

They crested a ridge and the city of Torreón popped up on the horizon. Their fake lives were beginning – *don* Alejandro and Juan. Carlos sat up tall, proud, and nonchalant while Rafe drove the wagon. Rafe had butterflies in his stomach as they entered the city plaza expecting to be recognized immediately. He drove the wagon to the central plaza where the Hotel Bilbao was located. Curious people on the plaza stared at them.

Carlos jumped down and dusted his *traje* with a glove. He strode into the hotel and announced himself.

"Buenos días. I am *don* Alejandro Martinez de Lunas from New Mexico. I will need two rooms. I wish your best room for myself and a suitable room for my *vaquero."*

"Sí señor," the hotel clerk said crisply, "I am sure you will find our rooms to your satisfaction."

"Where is your bank? I have business there," Carlos asked the clerk.

"Sí, it is on the other side of the plaza," the clerk replied.

Rafe walked into the hotel and stood quietly near the door. He carefully set down their satchels on the floor by his feet. He kept his hat low to cover his face.

"I will have your belongings taken to your rooms," the clerk said.

Carlos barked at Rafe, "Juan, see to the wagon wheel and the horses." He turned on his heels and swept past Rafe without a look heading to the stairs.

Rafe took the wagon to the livery. He asked for the wheels to be checked, even though he knew nothing was wrong. He paid handsomely for *don* Alejandro's horse to be brushed and fed extra oats. Everything they did was carefully planned to announce, *don* Alejandro Martinez de Lunas from New Mexico had arrived.

Rafe walked to the plaza and found Carlos sitting in the patio of a restaurant facing the *paseo.* They sat outside near the edge of the cobblestone *paseo,* where they enjoyed a meal of *carne asada* and a cool beer. It was four o'clock in the afternoon and people were just ending their *siesta.* The shops were getting busy and the *cafés* were filling. Even though it was a Tuesday, the plaza was busy with activity.

Along the plaza flowers hung heavy from the balconies. Reds, purples, and yellows attracted bees and butterflies. Rafe was enchanted by the women's brightly colored dresses and the sights and sounds of his home town. He did not remember it being so pleasant. Down the street the sound of a strumming guitar floated in the wind.

He and Carlos talked of horses, so that anyone overhearing their conversation knew why they were here. After their meal, they walked to the bank. Rafe kept a slight distance behind Carlos and kept his head down. Carlos looked magnificent in his *traje* and walked with confidence. When they arrived at the bank, Carlos turned to go inside and Rafe waited outside.

"Buenas tardes, *señor*," the teller greeted Carlos when he entered the bank. The bank was small, but the wooden teller counter was well polished and the brass doorknobs shone brightly.

"*Buenas tardes. ¿Esta el gerente?*" Carlos asked for the manager.

"*Un momento, señor.*" The teller walked to an office in the back of the bank and spoke to someone.

A well-dressed man in his forties walked out from the back room of the bank, with his glasses halfway down his nose. He looked over them at Carlos.

"*Señor, soy don Alejandro Martínez de Lunas de Nuevo México.*" Carlos introduced himself. He casually removed his gloves and snapped them into his left hand.

"*Mi nombre es Gregorio Zamora. ¿Qué puedo hacer por usted don Alejandro?*" The bank manager introduced himself as Gregorio Zamora and offered his services in typical manner. Carlos could feel the banker's eyes studying him. Each detail of his person would be assessed.

"I am from Los Lunas, New Mexico and here to buy horses. I wish to deposit money in your bank for the transaction," Carlos told him in Spanish, his voice arrogant and aloof. Carlos saw the banker's eyes flicker and knew *don* Alejandro was approved.

"Very well, you have come to a good place in Mexico for horses. *Don* Bernardo Reyes is the best breeder and has quality horses for sale. I would be happy to make the introduction for you," the banker offered graciously. It was customary for business introductions to be made formally by an intermediary and Carlos knew this was a crucial piece of their plan.

"Muchas gracias," Carlos replied. "That would be most helpful."

"Tomorrow morning I am free and can take you there and make the introduction," Gregorio said. "I will send a messenger to *don* Bernardo."

"You are most gracious, *señor.* I have one thousand American dollars I want to deposit in your bank. More will be transferred from El Paso when the transaction is completed. Is that acceptable?" Carlos handed Gregorio a leather wallet containing the money. Gregorio counted it and wrote out a receipt.

"Where are you staying *señor?"* the banker asked.

"The Hotel Bilbao."

"I will meet you at the hotel at eight o'clock," Gregorio told him with a slight imperceptible bow.

"Hasta mañana señor," Carlos replied and walked out of the bank.

Although Carlos and Rafe had discussed plans and possibilities, each step was venturing into the unknown. Carlos set a casual pace on the sidewalk and Rafe walked just slightly behind.

"The banker will take us to *don* Bernardo's *hacienda* at eight o'clock tomorrow morning," Carlos whispered just loud enough for Rafe to hear.

"Good," Rafe replied. "Any problems?"

"No, he said *don* Bernardo was the best breeder in the area. The banker will make the introductions."

Caballeros on the sidewalk looked carefully at the well-dressed *grandee.* He was a stranger, but the men nodded a customary greeting to Carlos, who acknowledged with a slight nod. No one took much notice of the *vaquero* at the *grandee's* side.

"Let's take a walk around the plaza," Rafe said, feeling more comfortable that no one gave any notice to him; he was just another *vaquero.* Rafe was surprised when he realized the plaza in Torreón was larger than the plazas in Albuquerque or Santa Fe. Graceful stucco, two-story homes surrounded the plaza on two sides. From the second story iron balconies, heavy baskets hanging with flowers burst with color. The *Catedral de Nuestra Señora de Carmen* stood at the east end. The center of the plaza had many large trees and several fountains. Rafe remembered when *fiestas* filled the plaza with music, treats, and dancing. Shops and small *cafés* circled the plaza and wagons and carriages were moving along the *paseo*.

A jolt gripped his gut when Rafe spotted *don* Pablo, the horse master from *don* Bernardo's *hacienda*, coming in their direction carrying a sack of supplies. Rafe's heart pounded, sure that his mentor from the horse barns at the *hacienda* would recognize him. When they passed each other, the horse master nodded his head at *don* Alejandro as he walked by, ignoring Rafe.

"That was *don* Pablo from the *hacienda*, the horse master," Rafe caught his breath and whispered to Carlos.

"Do you think he recognized you?"

"I don't think so. He would have stopped. He and I were very close."

"It's a good thing you grew that mustache and patch under your lip," Carlos chuckled.

As they continued strolling the plaza, Rafe recognized familiar shops and saw faces of a few shop owners who he remembered. "We should stop at the saddle and tack shop," Rafe said.

"Yes, it will announce our intentions. Word will spread," Carlos agreed.

Walking into the saddle shop, Encarnacion, the owner, greeted Carlos, *"Buenas tardes, señor."*

"Buenas tardes. Soy don Alejandro Martínez de Lunas de Nuevo México," Carlos introduced himself.

"I am happy to meet you *señor*. How may I be of service?"

Rafe had visited this shop many times with *don* Pablo and he had spoken to Encarnacion when he was a boy. The last time was five years ago. It was the year he shot *don* Bernardo. After greeting Carlos, the shop owner nodded in Rafe's direction and then ignored him.

"I am here in Torreón to buy quality breeding stallions from *don* Bernardo Reyes. The saddle maker in

Socorro is not to my standard," Carlos said with mild annoyance in his voice. "I am told you make fine quality saddles." Rafe watched as the saddle maker puffed with pride. Carlos knew exactly how to portray an aloof and distinguished *haciendero*.

"*Gracias, señor.* I make only the finest quality saddles and use silver of the highest grade," the saddle maker responded. "When will you need the saddles?"

"*Señor Zamora* has offered to introduce me to *don* Bernardo tomorrow," Carlos explained.

Lowering his voice, even though no one else was in the shop, the owner said, "I must tell you, *don* Bernardo is a clever and cunning negotiator. He will try to cheat you."

Carlos nodded an acknowledgement. "*Gracias, señor.* I will be back to buy saddles, if I am satisfied with the quality of *don* Bernardo's horses."

It was late in the day when they left the saddle shop. The church bells rang for the final mass of the day. Rafe and Carlos headed for the *Catedral*. A few people joined them as they walked up the steps into the church. When they walked into the cool chapel, Rafe was almost overcome with emotion. He had been baptized in this chapel and came many times with his mother. The *hacienda* had a small chapel, but his mother insisted they travel at least once a month and on holidays to Torreón's *Catedral de Nuestra Señora de Carmen*. "They have a real priest," she would say.

The afternoon light shone through large stained glass windows on either side of the alter. A large wooden image of the crucifixion hung on the wall behind it. On the left side, the encased replica of *Señora de Carmen* had many lighted candles at her feet. Elaborate candle-lit fixtures dimly lighted the chapel on both sides. Rafe and Carlos dipped their fingers in the holy water and made the sign of the cross before finding an empty pew in the middle of the chapel.

Rafe recognized the nun who taught him catechism before his first holy communion. He recognized *doña* Cholé, a widow who spent all her time helping the church since her husband's death. She was sitting several rows in front of them. Through the service, Rafe started to relax. No one recognized him. Carlos was right. As a *vaquero*, Rafe was invisible. During the mass, he prayed to Saint Christopher to help him in his task to rescue his mother and sister. He skipped the part about wanting to kill *don* Bernardo. He watched as Carlos was lost in his own prayers.

Later that evening, they sat outside on the plaza enjoying a few drinks and platters of food. A few *señoritas*, in their open carriages, teased the young *caballeros* in the Spanish tradition. The *caballeros* pranced their horses alongside, trying to get the young women's attention. Watching, Rafe thought it looked almost like a dance. It would have been a pleasant evening, if dread did not hang heavy in Rafe's heart. Tomorrow he would see the *desgraciado, don* Bernardo, again.

He visualized the *hacienda* – his boyhood home. Rafe knew the layout of the stables, the *vaquero* quarters, the *jacals* where the *peóns* lived, and the grounds around the *hacienda*. He had never been in the *casita* where his mother, sister María, and children now lived. The only time he entered the main house was the day he shot *don* Bernardo.

"Carlos, the *hacienda* is located northeast of here about ten miles, near a small lake. A spring from a nearby rocky hillside feeds the lake," Rafe began describing the area in an effort to stop worrying. "The *hacienda's* land is large enough for *don* Bernardo's horses to roam and it is not fenced. The property is marked with stone markers. Most of the horses will be in the hills and canyons," Rafe said quietly to Carlos. Rafe went on to describe the main house, the horse barn, and the grounds.

"Tomorrow, we will set the plan into motion," Carlos replied. "I am sure *don* Bernardo will invite me into the house, while you remain outside. It will give you time to find your mother and sister."

Rafe thought about tomorrow, with both anxiety and excitement. Tomorrow, he would see his mother again. Tomorrow, he would face *don* Bernardo again. Rafe dreaded tomorrow, but prayed for tomorrow to come quickly.

CHAPTER 25

John B. Sutton hummed a tune as he waited for the stage to El Paso. Last week he wired the money to Cinnamon and checked the stage routes. She and her mother ought to be in El Paso waiting for him by tomorrow. Everything went as planned. The herd was settled in the valley, Ed Seeley started work on the ranchhouse, and Cinnamon was marrying him. John was a happy man.

Since arriving in San Marcial, John made his presence known. The greaser merchants treated him with respect and fear, exactly what he wanted. He was sure the so-called mayor, Tomás Armíjo, could be bought or intimidated, allowing John to do anything he wanted.

The only problem – the town had no whores. His men were grumbling. Last weekend he let some of them ride to Socorro. When he got back to San Marcial after the wedding, he planned to talk to Seeley about it. His men needed both whiskey and women.

Dust rose in the distance as the stage approached. No one got off in San Marcial. When the stage was ready to go, John joined two women and a man traveling to El Paso. John settled into the seat and closed his eyes imagining Cinnamon's soft breasts.

Butcherknife Bill and Ponyboy George were catching strays before nightfall. Riding the ridge, Ponyboy called over to Bill, "Damn, Sutton's gonna have a whore, and we git nuttin." Ponyboy had been grumbled constantly to Bill, and although he agreed, Bill was tired of listening.

"Yew bess not be talkin thata way round Sutton. He'll kill ya. Let's git back to camp afore we cain't see," Bill said to Ponyboy and turned his horse down the ridge.

Butcherknife saw two riders heading their way as they rode toward camp. He knew it was Jed and Pewee checking in for night guard duty. The guards listened for odd sounds and rode the edges hoping to catch predators coming in to get a free dinner of prime beef. Occasionally a large bobcat or mountain lion sneaked in, caught a calf, and dragged it off to its den. Even roaming bands of coyotes could kill a young cow.

John told Butcherknife to post sentries every night. Bill put the cowboys on a rotating schedule, but they did not like it. Riding at night was hard work and more dangerous to both the horse and man. They never had these problems back in Texas. It was bad enough that winter was coming and the bunkhouse was not yet completed.

"Hell, Sutton don't care. He's livin like a thoroughbred stud at the hotel in town," Bill grumbled to himself. "Hey Ponyboy, let's git on over ta Big Ed's and lift a few," Butcherknife hollered to Ponyboy.

"Shur nuff, maybee that greaser Mescan will be thar an we can give im a good ass whuppin," Ponyboy answered.

"He's mine, I tol yew," Bill growled. "When I find im I'll get that curlywolf greaser and teach im good."

"Ya an iffin he ain't thar we kin maybee get us a sen'o'rita."

"Yew know Ed don't have no whores. No whores in that stinkin shitheel town," Bill grumbled.

"We shud go back to Texas," Ponyboy suggested. "Afore the snow starts flyin." Bill agreed and they yelled and shouted on their way to town. "Yehaa, Texas here we cum."

By the time they reached the small hamlet, their venting was spent. Butcherknife and Ponyboy rode quietly into the sleepy town of San Marcial. Bill, as always, kept a keen eye for the greaser's Appaloosa stallion. Only one horse looked like that. A dim light glowed from Big Ed's saloon and the place was empty as they walked in. Big Ed was behind the bar cleaning glasses and looked up.

"Howdy Big Ed, a couple a shots," Butcherknife spoke first.

"Hey boys haven't seen you round lately," Big Ed said, setting up two shot glasses and filling them up to the rim. It was Monday evening and Ed had spent most of the day out at the site of Sutton's new ranchhouse. He had several of the locals leveling the spot and digging foundation posts. The local Mexicans were none too happy to be working near the Texas cowboys, but there had been no trouble.

"Been busting our ass building line shacks and looking after the herd," Ponyboy stepped up and answered.

"Two more," Bill ordered. Both men had thrown down the first shot and felt the warm flow of the red-eye burn in their throats.

"You betcha." Ed poured two more. This time they took it with two swallows.

"Seen that Mescan round?" Butcherknife asked.

"Which one, there's lots of them around here?" Ed knew who they meant, but kept a casual tone.

"Yew know. The one who shot my hat off," Butcherknife looked at Ed, while he pointed at the shot glasses. "Hit us again."

"No, ain't seen him around here lately." Ed knew Rafe and Carlos had left San Marcial, but wanted to keep that information quiet. He thought it might keep the Texas cowboys in check, if they thought Rafe was a local resident.

"What ya want him for?" Big Ed asked while he poured a third round.

"We gonna tree that curlywolf greaser," Ponyboy sneered.

"Ya, we gonna beef that greaser and plant im permnent like," Butcherknife chimed in.

"Bill's gonna plant im fer sure." Ponyboy slapped Bill on the back laughing.

"You boys best be careful with that man. You're liable to get hurt. He's mighty fast." Big Ed pushed them a bit.

"We ain't scared of that greaser. Hell, I kin take im by myself," Ponyboy blurted out letting the red-eye speak for him.

"Shut yer bazoo Ponyboy! Don't listen to im, Big Ed. That's just a lot of blow. I'm the best draw in this outfit,"

Butcherknife bragged. The two cowboys kept on bragging to each other. Ed left the bottle in front of them, but kept track of each shot they took.

The front door opened and a young couple walked in. With hat in hand, the young man tentatively walked up to the bar keeping nervous eyes on the cowboys.

"I yem lookeen for *señor* Seeley," the young man said in broken English.

"I'm Seeley," Big Ed said looking up from behind the bar.

"*Bueno*, I yem Lucas Gomez. I haf lumber load and supplies you order from Socorro," the young man said. The woman stood by the door with her bonnet in her hands. They both looked to be about twenty years old. The woman was slender and wore a slightly too big, blue checkered dress.

"Well now. Are you the carpenter?" Big Ed asked, as he came around the bar and extended his hand to Lucas.

"*Sí, soy carpintero,*" Lucas replied he was the carpenter and took Ed's hand.

"Park your wagon around the back and I have a room for you," Ed told him.

"I haf two wagons, *señor*. *Mi esposa*, Carmen, drove the other one," Lucas said waving his hand toward his wife by the door.

Ed looked over at the young woman as she looked up and blushed. "*Buenas tardes*, Carmen," Ed said to her.

"Come with me and I'll show you where to park the wagons," Ed said walking with Lucas to the door. "I'll check them over in the morning." Ed and Lucas walked to the street. Carmen stayed quietly by the door. She clutched her woven shawl tighter around her shoulders.

"Damn greasers everywhere," Ponyboy grumbled to Bill. "That one sure is purdy though," Bill replied. Ponyboy looked at the young woman and agreed.

"Howdy thar sen'o'rita, cum on over and have a drink with us," Ponyboy said loudly waving his arm in an arc at the woman.

Carmen looked down. She did not understand the

man and wanted no part of him.

"I said, cum over here and have a drink. Cain't yew damn greasers be sociable?" Ponyboy said pushing away from the bar. He staggered over to the woman and grabbed her around the waist. Carmen's screams floated to the back of the saloon. Hearing her scream, Lucas and Ed ran in the back door and saw Carmen push one of the cowboys away from her. His arm was wrapped around her waist.

"Come on purdy gal, just one drink." Lucas heard the cowboy sneer at his wife. Crossing the room, he grabbed Ponyboy away from his wife. Ponyboy staggered and threw a drunken right cross at the young man, but missed as Lucas ducked the blow.

Ed stepped in between them. "That's enough of that boys" Big Ed warned the cowboys looking at Ponyboy.

"He was only foolin, Big Ed," Bill slurred out laughing.

"Ya, I's only foolin," Ponyboy laughed. "We jes asked the purdy gal to have a drink with us."

"You boys can't be bothering people like that," Big Ed warned them, and pulled on Ponyboy's shoulder.

Ponyboy pushed Ed away, "Stay outta this Big Ed. Let's see what yew got greaser." Ponyboy swung another punch in Lucas's direction.

"I told you boys to get back," Ed yelled at them, pushing Ponyboy hard. "Get out. Get out now."

Bill grabbed Ponyboy's arm and the two cowboys staggered from the saloon, grumbling.

Ed took Carmen's arm and walked the young couple upstairs to their room. "What's wrong with those men?" Lucas asked Big Ed as they climbed the stairs.

"Don't worry about them. They just had a little too much to drink. I will take care of them." Opening the door to room number three, Ed lit the oil lamp. A slow glow filled the small room. "I hope this room will be comfortable for you."

"*Sí, gracias,*" Lucas replied.

"I will need you to be ready to deliver the lumber and supplies to the work site first thing in the morning." Ed left them and closed the door behind him.

"Tengo miedo," Carmen said she was afraid and broke into tears as the door closed clinging to her husband.

"Don't worry *querida, señor* Seeley will help us," he assured her. Lucas held her tight until he felt her relax a bit. He too was worried, but did not want to scare his wife more. Socorro had its share of cowboys and Lucas knew they had little regard for Mexicans.

Gently, he pulled Carmen away from his chest. "Look at this nice room," he said. Tears were still streaming down her face. She looked at the big soft bed and tried to smile. "This is a good job and we can start our life here. Isn't this better than living with your family?" Work was scarce in Socorro even though Lucas was a master carpenter. They had been living in her parent's small home for the past six months.

"Sí." Carmen nodded. "Hold me," she said wanting to feel safe in her husband's arms. Carmen thought she was pregnant, but wanted to be sure before she broke the news to him. This job was important to them, if a baby was on the way.

The two cowboys were gone by the time Ed returned downstairs. He found the bottle of whiskey gone and no money. "Damn cowboys," he cursed. Something was going to happen someday, something bad. He just knew it.

CHAPTER 26

Rafe and Carlos rode with Gregorio Zamora, the bank manager, to *don* Bernardo's *hacienda* at eight o'clock on Wednesday morning as planned. Rafe thought Carlos looked grand in his shining *traje* and the black stallion's silver saddle jingled with each step. Carlos, posing as *don* Alejandro, introduced Juan Romero as his trusted *vaquero* to the banker, and then they ignored Rafe.

Riding slightly behind Carlos and the banker, Rafe's stomach turned into knots with each passing mile. His mind wandered as he recognized the terrain where he once ran and played as a boy.

Gregorio turned under the archway onto the road leading to the *hacienda*. Memories flooded Rafe's brain. *Jacals,* the mud picket houses, where the *peóns* lived on either side of the road looked even smaller than he remembered. On his right was the one where Rodolfo, his boyhood best friend lived. They spent much of their time hunting and fishing when they were not working. They made their First Holy Communion together along with his sister, Consuelo. She was a year older and loved to annoy Rafe by wanting to hug him every time she saw him. He wondered if Rodolfo and Consuelo would recognize him. Both danger and excitement pumped inside his chest making it hard to breathe.

To the right was the trail to the lake – the lake where he and Rodolfo fished and swam. To the left of the lake trail was the large garden for the *hacienda*. A jolt hit his stomach when he saw the *jacal* where he, his mother, and his sister had lived. It was small and shabby. The once white stucco a dirty tan, weeds grew in the yard, a broken table was dumped on one side, and the blanket across the door was torn. His mother had always taken pride in the small hut. Now, in its doorway stood an older, rotund woman.

As they approached the main house, Rafe saw the

horse barn and corrals. Only a handful of horses stood in the corral. The main house was a U-shaped, two-story building with balconies on the upper level. Baskets of mostly dead plants hung from the balconies, instead of the lush flowers *doña* Carmela always tended. An eight foot wall surrounded the courtyard and the main house was white washed including the wall. It too looked dirty and cracking. A small house, the guest *casita,* was located outside the courtyard close to the walled entrance to the main house. In front of the *casita* was a small garden.

As the trio approached the main house, a servant came out. He took the reins and helped Carlos and the banker dismount. Rafe climbed down and played his role, standing quietly with the horses.

A man, bent at the waist and limping, came out of the front door. Yesterday afternoon Gregorio sent a messenger to *don* Bernardo bringing news that an *Americano* was looking to purchase breeding horses. Their arrival this morning was expected. The old *don* had hardly slept last night anticipating his good fortune. Gregorio said the *Americano* had money and more in El Paso. *Don* Bernardo greeted the banker and accepted the introduction of *don* Alejandro Martinez de Lunas.

"*Bienvenidos a mi hacienda señor, yo soy don Bernardo Reyes, a su servicio.*" The *don* welcomed Carlos to his ranch and offered his services in the formal Spanish greeting.

Rafe felt like a thunderbolt struck him in his heart at the sight of the old *don,* looking old and somewhat frail, but his voice still had a force of authority to it and it shook Rafe to the core. His hands holding the reins of the horses shook and it took every ounce of his being to remain motionless and calm. Every fiber of his body wanted to pull his pistol and shoot the old *bastardo* where he stood on the veranda.

"Yes I have breeding horses, but first let us go inside and have a refreshment," *don* Bernardo offered and escorted Carlos and Gregorio into the house.

Rafe guided the three horses to a water trough. While the horses got their fill, he scanned the courtyard and stole furtive glances at the guest *casita,* hoping to see his mother or sister. His brain raced with possibilities. Now that he was here at the *hacienda,* it eluded him how he could talk to his mother and sister without being noticed. It had all seemed so much easier when he and Carlos had discussed their plans.

Servants around the *hacienda* were going about their duties. A wagon carrying hay came down the road and headed to the barn. Several women carried wood in blankets on their backs to use for firewood in the kitchen. Some young children, walking behind them, carried baskets with vegetables. Life at the *hacienda* was not much different than when he was a child.

After a little while, a man drove a one-horse buggy across the yard and stopped in front of the guest *casita.* A young boy came out, who looked about four or five years old, and ran to the waiting buggy. Then, two women came out. The older one held a toddler in her arms, and the younger was obviously pregnant. Both climbed into the buggy. It was his mother and sister, with her children.

Rafe stood and gaped. His heart wanted him to run to them, but he held back. He watched the buggy head to the gate. His mother was driving while María held onto the younger child on her lap. The boy sat proudly between the women. It reminded Rafe of days in his youth when he sat beside his mother on the way to town. Rafe watched the buggy as it drove off down the lane.

"Juan!" Gregorio, the bank manager, called out. Rafe did not respond. "Juan!" he yelled again startling him out of his thoughts.

Rafe jerked his head up and said, *"Sí."*

"Don Alejandro wants you go to the bank with me and bring back money for him."

"Sí señor," Rafe answered with his hat in hand and bowing his head slightly.

As they mounted up and headed down the same path as the buggy, Rafe tried to contain his excitement. God had sent him an answer to his problem. On the way back from the bank, he would find the buggy, talk to his mother and sister, and arrange the escape.

Not long after Rafe and the banker rode under the main gate, they galloped past the buggy. Rafe tried hard not to look at them as he rode by, but caught the eye of the young boy. His sister's head was down, her dark hair covering her face, talking and cuddling the younger child. His mother looked well, her graying hair flying in the wind as she drove the buggy. Seeing them again, his heart pounded with joy.

At the bank, Gregorio asked Rafe to sign a receipt. Rafe signed only an 'X', pretending to be illiterate, and looked up at the banker with a question in his eyes. The banker sighed, nodded, and folded the paper.

"Take this directly to *don* Alejandro," the banker said. He handed Rafe a pouch with one thousand U. S. dollars in gold, which Rafe tucked into his shirt.

"Sí señor," Rafe answered.

Rafe thanked Gregorio and walked out of the bank. Swinging up onto his horse he spurred it away from the plaza and raced back toward the *hacienda* – back on the road to find his mother and sister. He watched, expecting to catch sight of the buggy over every rise. Soon he was past the point where he knew he should have overtaken them, but they were nowhere in sight. His stomach churned as he circled the horse looking in all directions hoping to spot them.

"Where can they be?" he screamed into the wind, frustrated because he could not waste too much time looking for them. Carlos and *don* Bernardo were expecting him back. He rode up a small knoll to scan the area hoping to see them, but saw nothing.

"Mierda," he cursed. His spirit sagged. He had been so sure he would find them. Turning, he spurred the horse and raced down the road toward the *hacienda*.

Carlos and *don* Bernardo were waiting on the shady veranda when Rafe arrived at the main house. Pulling his hat down a bit after he dismounted, Rafe walked up the veranda steps and handed the pouch containing the gold to Carlos, with a slight customary bow, then stepped back.

Carlos spread it out on the table for *don* Bernardo to see.

"*Bueno*," *don* Bernardo said satisfied and ready to continue the transaction. Carlos gathered the coins and tucked the pouch in his waist sash and stood up.

"Come to the barn," *don* Bernardo said.

Don Bernardo was elated. Here was the solution to his problems. One thousand dollars and more, much more. The *haciendero* from New Mexico was only vaguely familiar with horse breeds and *don* Bernardo was sure he had the chance to overcharge him.

Walking into the barn, *don* Bernardo said, "Here is only a sample of my horses. Most of my stock is in a boxed canyon not far from here."

Rafe saw *don* Pablo standing near the back of the barn. He was quietly listening to the men, but making himself look busy.

"Juan, have a look," Carlos ordered Rafe. Rafe walked to the closest stallion and gently took hold of the horse's ear with his right hand and with his left hand brought the stallion's face eye to eye. "*Tranquilo caballito*," Rafe whispered to the stallion. The horse remained calm to Rafe's touch and did not balk to Rafe checking his teeth. The young *vaquero's* manner shook Pablo. It was the same method Pablo taught his apprentices on how to approach a horse. A slight smile pulled at the corners of Pablo's lips as he studied the face of the *vaquero Americano*.

Rafe ran his hands over the horse's shoulder blade in an S-motion along the muscle, then down the knee and pulled up the hoof. Just for effect, Rafe walked to another horse and checked it knowing this was an insult to the *don*.

"They are acceptable, *jefe*," he said looking over at Carlos.

"These are fine stallions," *don* Bernardo roared. "Pablo, are these not the finest horses in all of Mexico?"

Hurrying to his *haciendero's* side Pablo said, "*Sí señor*. These are the finest stock. *Don* Bernardo only raises the best of breeds." Rafe kept his head behind the rump of the nearest horse. The horse master was standing only three feet away from him. He knew every line on the man's weathered face after years of working with him here in this same barn. Rafe marveled that *don* Pablo did not recognize him.

Carlos turned casually to *don* Bernardo and said, "Very well. Juan will pick the seven best stallions and twelve breeding mares from your stock. I trust his judgment. I will pay two hundred for the stallions and two fifty for the mares."

"*Me insultas señor,*" *don* Bernardo blustered pretending to be shocked and insulted. "These are the finest stock in Mexico, *señor.* Each mare will foal you thirty quality young. The stallions are sired from only the top Spanish breeds. You insult me with such a price."

"I do not wish to insult you," Carlos said using an aloof tone. Rafe knew from watching George Summers negotiate business deals most of this was an act. "The young mares are not verified and the stallions may be wild. It will take me years to foal a quality breed."

"There is no better stock in Mexico. I will make sure half of the mares are with foal."

"My *vaquero* will verify the mares. I will go two fifty for the stallions and three hundred for the mares with foal," he offered *don* Bernardo.

"I will take nothing less than three hundred for the stallions and four hundred for the breeding mares. The young mares will be three fifty."

"I will not go such a price. Come, Juan," Carlos huffed. Rafe's heart sank. They had to buy the horses. They could not just leave, but he followed Carlos' lead and fell in step behind him.

As they turned to leave, *don* Bernardo said, "Wait. Three hundred for the stallions and three fifty for the mares. You must pay me in gold."

Carlos stopped, acted annoyed, and then said crisply, "Very well. It will take a few days to transfer the rest of the money from the bank in El Paso. Juan will inspect the breeding mares and stallions. He will pick the best ones."

"*Bueno, don* Alejandro. We agree then," *don* Bernardo said. "I must take my leave now for some important business that needs my attention. Send me word when the gold is in the bank."

"*Bueno*. When the gold arrives, I will send Juan to inspect and cut the best from the herd. I will follow in the afternoon with the payment in gold," Carlos said. Rafe's heart jumped at the thought of coming back to the *hacienda* alone.

"*Adios, don* Bernardo. I will send word soon." Carlos snapped his gloves and turned. "*Vámonos, Juan,*" he ordered Rafe.

Rafe and Carlos walked briskly from the barn. Rafe held Carlos' horse while he mounted, then mounted his own. *Don* Bernardo did not exit the barn. Turning the horses, they headed down the lane. Rafe rode ahead, but Carlos caught up to him.

"Slow down. I don't want to give the wrong impression. What is the matter with you?" Carlos asked. Rafe slowed and let Carlos set the pace.

"My mother and sister are out there somewhere in a buggy. I saw them leave before I went to the bank with Gregorio. We must find them before they get back to the *hacienda,*" Rafe explained. "It is my chance to talk to them."

As soon as Carlos and Rafe were out of the *hacienda* gates, they rode swiftly down the road. Scanning the horizon from every knoll, they saw nothing.

"Where could they go?" Carlos asked.

"I don't know. If they were headed to town I should have passed them earlier," Rafe replied. "We must find them."

CHAPTER 27

John B. Sutton arrived in El Paso a happy man. Cinnamon should be waiting for him at the Stratton Hotel. All his plans worked perfectly. The herd was settled in New Mexico, Ed Seeley was working on his ranchhouse, and Cinnamon would be his wife.

Jumping down from the stage, John hurried to the hotel. He nodded at the clerk, turned the registration book around, and scanned it with his finger.

"Sir, can I help you?" the clerk clucked quite annoyed.

"Oh, yes, I'm looking for a guest. Miss Baker," John said.

"We have no guest by that name registered." The clerk grabbed the book and turned it away from John.

"Impossible, she and her mother should have arrived yesterday by stage from Austin," John blustered.

"Oh, you mean Miss Barkett and her mother," the clerk replied.

"Cynthia Barkett?" John asked surprised that Cinnamon used her given name.

"Yes, Miss Barkett and her mother. Who are you, sir?"

"John B. Sutton. I'm a gonna marry that girl."

The clerk looked at the weather-beaten, older man and raised his eyebrows in disbelief.

"I'll need a room. The best yew got and have this bag taken up," John ordered placing his satchel by the desk. "What room is Miss Barkett in?" he asked in a more contrite voice.

"Room ten, sir."

John turned and took the stairs two at a time. He knocked on the door marked ten.

"Just a minute," a voice called out. John took off his hat and dusted his shoulders. A few seconds later the door partially opened and green eyes peeked out through fallen tendrils of auburn hair.

"John B! You're here!" Cinnamon opened the door fully. John's eyes took in the woman who was to be his wife. She was clad in a simple dress and her hair was curled into a knot in the back. Without makeup she looked pale, but her green eyes were still fetching.

"You look lovely. A vision," he said embracing her.

"Thank you John B," she said a bit formally pushing away from him. Cinnamon had steeled herself for this moment. She was here, she was going to marry John B. Sutton, and she would make him happy, even if she did not love him. She left her old life to live a proper life as a rancher's wife, and to never have to worry about money again.

"Who's here Cindy?" her mother asked from the bed.

"John B, Momma. Go back to sleep," she replied.

"Cinnamon honey, I got us another room," John whispered.

"Not so fast, John B. I want a proper wedding and I'm not Cinnamon anymore. I'm Cynthia. Cynthia Barkett, and I will be Cynthia Sutton. I'm not your whore anymore. I'll be your wife and be respected," she demanded.

John had not thought much about it, but he understood. "Cynthia, my dear," he said softly and tipped his head. It made him smile to see her proudly hold her head up to him. Yes, she had the makings of a good rancher's wife.

"And," she continued, "there won't be any wedding until I go shopping and buy a new wardrobe. Now, go to your room and clean up and I'll get ready."

John walked out of the room a bit stunned, but happy. Cinnamon, now Cynthia, was here and giving him orders. She was lovelier now than ever, and she would be all his.

Much to John's impatience, it took six days to complete the arrangements for the wedding and to satisfy Cynthia she had enough proper clothes to assume her role as rancher's wife. She called it her trousseau – hats, gloves, dresses, a warm coat, high laced boots, and then more shoes, day dresses, traveling dresses, riding pants, the list went on. John let her buy whatever she wanted to make her happy.

On the next Saturday afternoon, Cynthia walked down the stairs inside the Stratton Hotel, a vision of loveliness in a lacy white dress. She insisted on wearing white, because nobody knew her in El Paso. She held a bouquet of pink and white flowers in her hand. John was dressed in a new dark blue suit with a flower pinned to the lapel.

Waiting next to John at the bottom of the stairs was Terrence Howard, a prominent El Paso banker, acting as the best man. His wife stood next to him. Sutton knew Howard from past dealings and liked the banker. Howard was more than happy to attend this wedding for a wealthy cattleman, such as Sutton. He hoped to negotiate to be Sutton's banker for the new cattle business in New Mexico. "No bank in San Marcial," he told Sutton. "I can handle everything." It was a good proposition for both parties. Looking up and seeing the beautiful woman descend the stairs, Howard wondered what such a beautiful young woman saw in an older man like Sutton. "Money buys happiness," he whispered in his wife's ear.

Cynthia reached the last step and forced a smile under the veil for all to see. Her mother stood across from John. Thank goodness her mother was having a good day. It made her happy to see her looking like the old days and not a limp rag in bed. Mr. Howard and his wife stood beside John. Cynthia stepped down the last step and took John's extended arm. Together they turned and walked up to the preacher. She knew this was forever. Forever married to this repulsive older man. What the hell, she thought, maybe forever would not be so long. She would make him happy and reap the rewards. Oh yes, she would reap the rewards. She would make John B pay dearly for her.

John B. Sutton was grinning as he walked Cinnamon to the preacher. He still thought of her as Cinnamon, even if he called her Cynthia as she demanded. He did not care that she had been a prostitute. He loved her. He needed her. Best of all, her beautiful body belonged to him now, and no one else.

Without much fanfare they said, "I do," and were driven on a buggy decorated with trailing shoes tied with long strings of twine. The buggy horse was decorated with a few flowers sticking out of the harness. Mr. Howard organized a reception for them at his house and invited some prominent El Paso citizens to help the newlyweds celebrate their marriage.

Later after the reception, Cynthia put her mother to bed upstairs in the hotel. John wrapped his arms around her and whispered, "I can't wait to see yew slowly strip out of that white dress, darlin."

Cynthia kissed him, but pushed away, "The night's young John B. I want to go dancing."

"Dancin?"

"Yes, dancing. It's our wedding night, John B. A girl must go dancing on her wedding night," she flirted with him. She coyly ran her hand down his cheek. "Please John B."

He would do anything to make her happy. "Then let's go dancin, my sweet."

Cynthia changed from her wedding dress to one of her new dresses. John shed the suit for a pair of gray pants and a white shirt, no tie. Cynthia made sure her mother was asleep, before she and John walked down the stairs of the hotel and out to the street.

The only place open was Lilli Jean's Saloon down Stratton Street, not far from the hotel. The out of tune piano was echoing its dinky sound as they walked through the batwing doors. It was Saturday night and the saloon was busy. Cowboys lined the bar and all the tables were taken, but someone shouted, "It's the newlyweds!" Everyone cheered and two cowboys motioned them to take their table.

Lilli Jean brought over a bottle and set it on the table with two glasses. "Congratulations," she said. "The bottle is on the house."

John poured two shots. Cynthia sipped hers. In the old days she chugged the fiery liquid with the best of them, but that was Cinnamon, not Cynthia. Several people came to the table and talked to them, giving congratulations. It was a typical night in an El Paso saloon. Cynthia watched saloon girls flirting with cowboys. It made her cringe inside to see the rough-looking cowboys manhandle the girls. One older, well-worn looking woman worked a saddle-bum at the far end of the bar. Cynthia shuddered, thinking that would have been her fate, someday.

"Are yew cold, darlin?" John B asked seeing her shake.

"No. How about that dance John B?"

John stood up, bowed, and extended his arm. Cynthia quickly grabbed it and they began to twirl on the small dance floor. John was not a good dancer, but nobody in this saloon would care. They bumped into a cowboy dancing with a saloon girl, but they kept on dancing.

"Are yew happy, darlin?"

"Yes, dear," she lied. Well, she was happy right now. She wanted to enjoy this night. All she wanted to do was enjoy the evening and delay having to go to bed with him, just yet.

"That's all I want for yew, darlin. Yer happiness is all that is important to me," he assured her.

"You're a gem John B," she purred. The piano player changed tunes. This one was a slow ballad. John held her close as they danced.

Suddenly, a voice from across the room yelled, "Cinnamon!" The yell mingled into the noisy bar room. Neither John nor Cynthia heard it.

A rough hand jerked John's shoulder aside and grabbed Cinnamon around the waist. "Whatcha doin here in El Paso?" the cowboy asked. "Today's my lucky day, runnin into yew. Yew was the best whore in Austin. I gots lots of money girl. What say yew and I go upstairs?"

He did not get time for an answer. The cowboy felt John's gun butt smash into the side of his head before he blacked out, and then crumpled to the floor.

"Hey!" another cowboy yelled heading toward John and Cynthia. "Yew cain't do that!"

"I just did. Now, yew boys back off." John pushed Cynthia behind him and pointed his pistol at the two.

One of the cowboys went for his gun, but John fanned the hammer and shot the man in the shoulder. The other cowboy stopped on his heels.

"I coudda killed im," John warned pointing his gun at the other cowboy's gut.

"Yeah, well yew ain't gettin away with this. Why yew protectin a fuckin whore?" the cowboy asked.

"Yew go back to yer drinkin and take care of yer friend," John warned. He ushered Cynthia toward the front door, keeping one eye on the cowboy all the while.

Quickly, they crossed the street to the hotel and went up the stairs to their room. "I'm sorry John B." Tears cascaded down Cynthia's cheeks, thinking about the cowboy who ruined her wedding night. Maybe she would never be free from her past.

"It's alright my sweet. I'm sorry this happened," he told her. John gently wiped her face and kissed her cheek.

"You know I'm a whore and no telling how many times this will happen. One day you might get shot because of me." She looked at him, really looked at him, and saw something new. He was not a bad looking man, older, but not ugly. He had protected her and defended her.

"This won't happen in New Mexico. No one knows yew there," he assured her. "There, yew will only be Cynthia Sutton."

Cynthia smiled. "Yes, Cynthia Sutton. Thank you John B."

Slowly he wiped her tears and held her until the sobbing stopped. When he began to unbutton her dress, she let him gladly. He carefully hung her dress on the chair and began removing her petticoats, anticipating the treasure waiting for him.

CHAPTER 28

"I told you that woman was a witch. She will do you more harm than good, *mija*," Celiá said to her daughter, María. She did not like the so-called *curandera*, a healer, as the witch called herself, but María liked the old woman and insisted on seeing her.

It was a long ride to the *curandera's* hut and now they were making the long trip back to the *hacienda*. The baby was asleep on María's lap and Antonio slept between them. Celiá tried to go slowly over the bumpy road for her daughter's sake, but the old buggy swayed and jerked from every rut.

"She has no magic to help you feel better," Celiá said. Celiá knew something was not quite right with this pregnancy. María had been sick for months and lost a lot of weight. Her cheeks were shallow and she ate little. "The doctor in town is a good man and has good medicine," Celiá told her again.

"Mamá, yo no confío en el médico." María, like many of the locals, did not trust the doctor or the new ways of medicine. María went to him once and did not like how he put her on her back and made her spread her legs to look inside of her. She refused to go back. No one had the right to touch her there, only *don* Bernardo. Actually, the old *don* never did look at her down there; he just mounted her and rolled over when he was spent.

"I know you don't like his ways, *mija*. My friends say he is a good doctor. Already he has delivered forty babies with no problems. Even *doña* Ofelia likes him. You did not even try the medicine the doctor gave you for your sickness. The smelly drink the *curandera* gave you only made you worse," Celiá kept pressing her daughter.

"The *curandera* says I will get better. She threw the bones and cast a spell to drive off the evil in me," María replied. "She says I'm sick, because I'm not married. I'm going to talk to *don* Bernardo tonight." Celiá's chest tightened. She knew *don* Bernardo would never marry María. He was a *haciendero* and her daughter a *peón*, regardless whether she bore his bastards.

The sun was hanging low in the sky as they slowly wound their way home on an old wagon path. Celiá was not really concentrating on the road while trying to talk sense to her daughter. The horse knew the way home, anyway.

Suddenly, two men, a *grandee* and a *vaquero*, rode up to the buggy. The *grandee* put up his hand for her to stop and she quickly pulled on the reins. The *grandee* leaned over and grabbed the reins to the horse, while the *vaquero* jumped from his horse.

"*Señor*, we are on our way home to *don* Bernardo's *hacienda*," Celiá said. "Why do you stop us? We have nothing."

"*Mamá*," the *vaquero* said walking toward them.

Frightened, Celiá did not hear what the *vaquero* said. "*Por favor señor*, we have nothing of value. My daughter is sick and my grandchildren are asleep. *¿Qué quieres de nosotros?*" she asked the *grandee* again what he wanted.

Rafe removed his hat as he walked to his mother. Celiá had not really looked at the *vaquero* as he approached. "*Mamá, soy Rafael*," Rafe said drawing closer.

Celiá looked down at the *vaquero*. He was tall and lean and his shoulders were broad and full. He had a mustache and small beard under his lower lip. She looked into his eyes and looked into the eyes of her son.

"*Madre de Dios, Rafael eres tú*," she cried out choking back tears at the shock of seeing her only son again.

"*Sí Mamá, soy Rafael*. Follow us to those trees. We must get out of sight before someone from the *hacienda* comes along," Rafe told his mother in Spanish. Carlos guided the buggy to a clump of trees off the road.

When the buggy stopped, Rafael helped his mother from the seat. She grabbed her son wanting to be devoured in his *abrazo*. "Rafael, Rafael," she said over and over, tears cascading down her face.

María did not move from the buggy, still holding the

sleeping baby in her lap. She watched her mother hug Rafael and it grated her. Why had her brother returned?

"*¿Por qué has venido aquí?*" Celiá asked him why he came. "I told Jose to tell you not to come. It is dangerous for you to be here. *Don* Bernardo will kill you," she pleaded with him.

"*Mamá, don* Bernardo saw me today at the *hacienda*. He didn't recognize me." Rafe assured her.

"You must not go back. Please promise me."

"*Mamá*, I have come to take you and María and the children to live with me in Santa Fe," he told her. "I can take you away from here, away from *don* Bernardo. This is my friend Carlos. He is here to help us."

"*Muy feliz de conocerte, señora,*" Carlos told Celiá he was happy to meet her.

María was listening to her brother. "*Yo no quiero ir a Santa Fe,*" María grumbled saying that she was not going to Santa Fe. Defiantly, she stayed on the buggy's seat holding the baby tightly, glaring at her brother.

"María, you have to go. You will have a better life there," Rafe said as he walked to her side of the buggy. He put his hand on her arm. "*Por favor* María. Please, there is no life for you and your children here."

"No, my life is here at the *hacienda* with *don* Bernardo," she replied stubbornly.

"María, the *don* is a mean man. He will not take care of you and the children," Rafe explained.

"What do you care about us? You left us here and didn't care what happened. *Don* Bernardo took care of us and my children."

"I had to go because I shot him for what he did to you. I thought I killed him," Rafe continued. "I had to run or the *policia* would have killed me."

"Well, you didn't kill him. Now, I have his children and he takes care of us. Someday I will be his *doña*. I'm staying," she answered looking straight ahead and not at her brother.

"*Mamá*, talk to her," Rafe pleaded to his mother.

"I will not leave my grandchildren. Besides, *don*

Bernardo will follow and find us. He will not let his children go easily. What you say is true, but he does love the children." Tears flowed down his mother's cheeks and she looked away.

Rafe was so sure his mother and sister would go with him. His stubborn sister did not understand the way of *haciendos*. *Don* Bernardo was only using her until she grew older and someday would discard her for someone younger.

"*Nana, Nana,*" Antonio woke and cried out for his grandmother. Celiá walked to the buggy and lifted the child into her arms.

Frustrated by his sister's obstinate position, Rafe walked nearer Carlos and whispered, "We have to take them now."

"No, we need to stick to the plan," Carlos replied. "We cannot gather all our belongings, and the wagon, and make enough distance from Torreón in the dark to be safe. It would not take *don* Bernardo long to catch us."

Rafe lifted the boy back into the buggy and took his mother in a tight abrazo, wrapping his strong arms around her. "*Mamá*, meet me Saturday at the lake where we picnicked as a family when María and I were children. We have to talk alone, *Mamá*. Come at *siesta* time. Don't tell María," he whispered. "She must not tell the *don.*"

His mother nodded. "I will try."

"You better get back to the *hacienda* before it is dark," Rafe said. He helped his mother up onto the buggy's seat.

"I love you both," he said handing her the reins.

Chapter 29

Progress on John Sutton's ranchhouse was on schedule. Ed Seeley was more than pleased with the carpenter, Lucas Gomez, he hired from Socorro. The foundation was completed and the sides and roof were well started. Ed helped Lucas hire local men to provide labor and help with the bigger jobs. Lucas was a good manager and the men liked him. Ed was happy with the progress and was confident to leave the job in Lucas' capable hands while he worked at his saloon.

The house was located on the highest spot of the property with a good view of the river below. Looking east, one could see a wide cut of the Rio Grande slowly flowing south. To the west, the San Mateo mountain range cast its long shadow at sunset. The front veranda wrapped the house on three sides. In winter, the sun would keep the south and west side porches warm and pleasant.

Ed was getting paid double from John Sutton and he made sure to pay the workers well. He wanted John to be pleased when he returned from El Paso. All in all, Ed thought they were making great progress.

Carmen, Lucas' wife, was a great help hauling supplies from San Marcial to the construction site. Each day she and Lucas drove the first load to the site together. If more loads were ready, Carmen came back to town and carted the supplies back and forth. She often stayed at the site and fed the men. After a day's work, Lucas and Carmen ate and slept at Ed's hotel. They asked for little extra. If it was slow in the saloon, Ed and the couple stayed at a table and Ed gave Lucas a whiskey and they talked. Occasionally, Lucas worked late at the site and chose to sleep there. On those nights, Ed helped Carmen unhitch the wagon and they often ate supper together.

Tonight the three of them were sitting at a table discussing progress on the ranchhouse. "Are the cowboys giving you or the men any trouble?" Ed asked.

"No, the cowboys are busy with the cattle and building a bunkhouse. The cowboys are not so good at building. My workers say the bunkhouse will blow over with the first big wind," Lucas said laughing.

"I'll talk to Mr. Sutton after the ranchhouse is finished and maybe he'll pay to have a real bunkhouse built," Ed told Lucas.

One afternoon about a week later, Carmen drove the supply wagon to the construction site with a load of lumber. "I'll unload the lumber, then I need you to go back to town and pick up more wire," Lucas told his wife. "If you go now, you'll be back with the wire and then we can stay until dark and we'll drive back together."

After the wagon was unloaded, he helped his wife up into the wagon's seat and wrapped the warm wool blanket around her shoulders, before slapping one of the team horses on its rump. Slowly the wagon rumbled off down the bumpy road.

Earlier in the day at the site of the half-finished bunkhouse, the cowboys needed more nails to finish part of the west bunkhouse wall. The weather was getting colder and Bill was worried about getting the bunkhouse done before the snow started flying.

"Let's go to town and git some nails," Butcherknife Bill said to his friend, Ponyboy George.

"Yeah, we kin wet r whistles, too," Ponyboy replied. They saddled up and rode hard to San Marcial.

"I have no nails," the mercantile clerk told the two cowboys. "We won't get more for a couple days. All our supplies are getting used up at the ranchhouse's construction site."

"Whadda mean, yew ain't got no nails. This here shitheel town never got nuttin we need," Bill complained.

When the two cowboys walked out into the street still grumbling, Ponyboy said, "Ain't got no reason to go back. Let's go tip a few."

"Howdy, Big Ed," they said when they walked into the saloon. A few locals sat at the bar. The cowboys still made them nervous, but things were calmer since the day the young *pistolero* from Santa Fe bested the Texas cowboys to the draw. The cowboys were not harassing the local workers at the ranchhouse and they did not come into town shooting anymore. It was good for Ed Seeley's business and good for the town in general.

"Howdy fellers," Big Ed replied. "Whiskey?"

"Shur nuff, bring us a bottle."

The locals turned back to the bar and the two cowboys sat drinking at a table. Soon the bottle of whiskey was almost gone.

"You boys want another bottle?" Big Ed asked walking by the table.

"Nah, what we want is nails, but this here shitheel town don't got no nails," Bill said slurring his words a bit.

"Yeah, an there ain't no whores neither," Ponyboy chimed in.

"Nails," Big Ed said confused, ignoring Ponyboy's comment about whores.

"Nails for our bunkhouse. Cain't build a bunkhouse without no nails."

"There's nails at the construction site of the ranchhouse," Big Ed said. "Why don't you go borrow some from there until more get shipped in from Socorro?"

"Damn, Bill, why didn't yew think of that?" Ponyboy asked. "It all belongs to Sutton. Come on, let's go."

"Here, finish this here bottle," Bill said to Ponyboy filling the two glasses for the last time and draining the bottle. "Bring us a bottle for the road, Big Ed."

Ed watched the two cowboys weave toward the door. Ponyboy was leaning heavily on Bill's shoulder. He doubted much work would get done on the bunkhouse today.

The two cowboys rode out of town and headed down the road to the construction site of Sutton's ranchhouse. Riding slowly they passed the bottle back and forth between them. Ponyboy was bending Bill's ear. "I cain't do this no more. There ain't no whores in that shitheel town and winter's acomin. I'm ready to go back to Texas." Bill let Ponyboy jabber, thinking maybe he was right.

Carmen, on the supply wagon, was headed back to town for the load of wire when she spotted two riders coming on the road toward her. She could tell they were cowboys and held the reins a little tighter.

Butcherknife and Ponyboy rode up to the wagon and blocked her way on the road.

"*Buenooos tardees sen'o'rita,*" Ponyboy said showing a rotten toothy grin.

Carmen did not answer and clicked the reins hoping to get the wagon moving again, but their horses stood fast on the path.

"Whoa thar sen'o'rita. Now that ain't bein very friendly," Ponyboy slurred. "We don't git to talk to no purdy sen'o'ritas in this here town."

"*Por favor, déjame pasar,*" Carmen pleaded for them to let her pass. These were the same two cowboys who had cornered her in the saloon and she could tell they were drunk.

"*Por favor,* what?" Ponyboy replied sliding off his horse. "Yew want to do us a favor?" he said laughing and walked closer to the wagon. "Yeah, yew can do us a favor missy."

"*No, déjame en paz,*" she begged them to leave her alone.

As he approached, Carmen saw evil in the cowboy's eyes and when he got close to her, she snapped the end of the leather reins hard at his face. They cut across his cheek and he jumped back. Snapping the reins to the horses and pulling hard to the right she yelled to the team. The horses bolted off the wagon path and into the brush. Branches of creosote and willows scratched at her arms and legs, spooked the horses, but terrified she continued whipping the horses hoping to get away.

Bill sat on his horse watching Ponyboy rub his face and cursing. "Hell, let her go," Bill told him.

"The hell I will," Ponyboy sputtered. "No damn greaser whore will treat me thatta way." Ponyboy jumped to his saddle and whipped his horse, following the wagon into the undergrowth. Bill wheeled his horse and followed them.

Carmen drove the horses through the stinging bushes praying for a miracle. The back wheel hit a large rock and the wagon jumped crazily. Carmen barely hung on. If she managed to get back to the main road, she might outrun the cowboys back to town. Suddenly one of the horses spooked and reared back. She had no choice but to slow down and get the horses settled. In an instant, the cowboys were on either side of her.

Bill rode up beside the left horse and grabbed the reins bringing the team to a complete halt. The cowboy she had whipped jumped from his horse onto the wagon seat, but Carmen quickly jumped down from the other side. Her feet hit the ground and she started to run.

"Whar yew goin? Ain't nowhere to go," Butcherknife Bill told her still holding the reins to the horses.

Ponyboy jumped off the wagon and chased her grabbing her by the waist. "Look what yew dun," he said putting his face close to hers. His face had a red welt on one cheek.

Carmen smelled the whiskey on his breath. His clothes smelled worse. The more she squirmed in his grasp the tighter he gripped her.

"*¿Qué es lo que quieres de mí?*" Carmen asked them what they wanted with her.

"Me no speekee the Espanol," Ponyboy said. "Yew fuckin hurt me, now I'm gonna hurt yew."

Carmen swung her free arm at the cowboy's jaw. It was a glancing blow, enough to loosen his grip, but he managed to grab her wrist as she tried to escape. Wrenching her arm, she pulled it out of his grasp. As she turned to run, Ponyboy's large hand grabbed at her loose woven *camisa* tearing it off and exposing her bare breasts.

"*Déjame ir, déjame ir,*" she begged him to let her go.

"Now that's more like it," Ponyboy said. Holding her tightly by the wrist, his free hand tore her *camisa* completely off leaving her bare from the waist up.

"Yee doggies, I ain't seen a woman fer too long," Bill whistled looking at Carmen's firm, young, tan breasts with darker brown nipples. Greaser or not, he felt the surge of blood to his groin.

"*Ayúdame, ayúdame,*" she screamed for help into the wind, but there was no one to hear, except for her two tormentors.

"Grab her arms," Ponyboy said to Bill. He grabbed her legs off the ground and they carried the squirming young woman to a grassy area. Dumping her to the ground, Bill held her arms while Ponyboy pulled up her skirt and ripped off her loose *pantalones.* Carmen wiggled and squirmed, but the cowboys held her tight.

"*Ayúdame Dios,*" she prayed to God for help.

"I get her first," Ponyboy said with a growl. "She owes me for the whippin. Hold her still, Bill." Ponyboy unbuttoned his pants. He had not had a woman since they left Texas and he was damn ready.

Ponyboy's hands grabbed her breasts roughly, squeezing and pulling at them. Carmen screamed, but knew there was no one near enough to hear her. He was almost on top of her when she jerked a knee into his gut as hard as she could.

"Bitch," Ponyboy yelled in surprise and backhanded her hard across the face. He grabbed at her knees and pulled them apart. Spreading her legs, he pushed inside of her.

"*Ayeee,*" she screamed.

Ponyboy pumped her roughly in and out, while Bill held her tight. It was not long before he was spent and fell heavily onto her.

Carmen felt the heavy man fall on her. His greasy hair covered most of her face. The other man still held her by the shoulders, but she could move her face a little. Finally relaxing a bit, the cowboy on top of her moved his head to one side. Carmen saw her opportunity and bit hard at the top of Ponyboy's ear.

"Owwww, yew fuckin bitch!" Ponyboy pulled out his gun and butted her hard on the side of her head. Carmen's head lolled to one side and she went limp. He jumped off the listless woman with his limp penis still sticking out of his pants.

"Why the fuck did yew do that?" Bill asked.

"She fuckin bit my ear off," Ponyboy said. "Look!" Ponyboy pushed back his shaggy hair showing the blood dripping down his cheek from the top of his bloody ear.

"Damn, Ponyboy. Yew killed her and I didn't even get any yet," Bill complained.

"Go ahead and fuck her, Bill," Ponyboy replied. "She won't give yew no trouble now."

"I ain't gonna fuck no dead woman," Bill replied dropping his grasp on Carmen and standing up. Carmen's naked body lay on the ground at his feet. "Whatta we gonna do with her?"

"Leave her to the buzzards fer all I care," Ponyboy said. "Fuckin greaser."

"She'll be missed," Bill said. "She's that Mexican carpenter's wife and they stayin at Seeley's."

Ponyboy buttoned his pants and turned to leave.

"We can't leave her like this," Bill insisted. Even his whiskey-slogged brain knew they were in a lot of trouble. "What if she's not dead? She'll tell."

"Shutup. I'm thinkin," Ponyboy growled. He wiped a hand across the blood dripping down his face from his ear. In a sudden move, Ponyboy pulled his pistol, walked back to Carmen's body, and bashed her head again, harder. Carmen's head ricocheted off the dusty ground. "Just to make sure," he said. He put his pistol back into its holster.

"Damn Ponyboy, yer fuckin crazy. Now yew got us in a heap of trouble." Bill looked at the woman's head bashed in on one side and knew she was dead. Blood oozed from her ear and mouth.

"Quit yer jabbing and grab her arms." Ponyboy picked up her feet. "Over there," he jerked his head toward a thicket of low hanging willows. They carried Carmen's body and dumped it under the willow thicket and dragged dead branches to cover her body.

"What about the wagon?"

"We'll burn it, just like Injuns. The damn town will think Apaches burned the wagon and took the woman,"

Ponyboy replied.

Bill gathered their horses while Ponyboy drove the wagon back to the road about a mile from the body. They unhitched the horses and with a little help from dried grasses, the wagon was quickly engulfed in flames. Ponyboy mounted up and grabbed the team horse's reins. He would run off the horses on the way back to their camp.

CHAPTER 30

Dust from the speeding wheels of the stagecoach kicked up into the cabin even with the window blinds pulled down. The stage rocked and swayed crazily, but Cynthia seemed the only one to notice. Her husband, John B, was sitting next to her, sound asleep and snoring. There was an old Mexican man sitting across from them. His eyes were closed, but Cynthia knew he was not asleep. Her mother sat on the other side of John B staring at nothing and not saying a word. Today was not one of her good days.

Cynthia was happy to leave El Paso, in fact, she was happy to leave Texas. Too many men knew her there. Some knew more of her than she cared to admit, because she was good at her job. She had been a good whore; men remembered her. Now, she was a married woman, married to a wealthy man, and soon to be even wealthier, if John B's plans worked out as he wanted. John B raved about the ranch and the ranchhouse he was having built for her. She was excited to see it, especially the house.

So much had happened since Madam Marta threw her out of the brothel for no reason. She only accepted John B's proposal because she was desperate. When she left for El Paso, she dreaded marrying the man sitting beside her, but now, she looked at him differently. He defended her honor at Lilli Jean's Saloon on their wedding night, and he might have been hurt or killed because of her. John B treated her like a lady and no one ever did that before.

"Eh, hey beautiful, the dust getting to yew?" John stretched his shoulders and looked at her with sleepy, adoring eyes. Cynthia had a handkerchief covering her nose and mouth.

"It's not too bad as long as I have this handkerchief," she replied.

John pushed up the blind, looked out the window,

and recognized the terrain. "It won't be long now. We're coming up on Hot Springs. San Marcial is only another thirty miles, or so, from here."

"Good, the bumping and the dust are getting to me a bit," she complained. Cynthia smoothed her new traveling dress and dust flew everywhere.

John took her hand and dusted it off before holding it. "Have yew slept?" John asked.

"No. I tried, but I couldn't. Tell me again about the house."

"Yew'll be able to see the river from the kitchen window or sit on the veranda and watch the deer graze nearby. In winter, two sides of the house will git the warmin sun, and in the summer two sides will be cool. It has four bedrooms. One fer us, one fer yer mother, and two fer our children," he said squeezing her hand. "To the west the sun will set behind the San Mateo mountain range. I asked fer the well to be dug just outside the kitchen," he continued.

"By the way, can yew cook?" he asked with a quizzical expression. All he knew about her was the moist treasure between her legs that drove him crazy. Really, he knew little about her. It never crossed his mind to ask.

"Yes John B, I can cook. You won't starve," she said, and laughed, and then coughed from the dust.

"Sorry darlin, but I don't know nothin bout yew," he apologized.

"Just because I was a whore doesn't mean I can't do anything else."

"Don't call yerself that anymore. Yer through with that life and yer my wife now," John scolded her.

"Yes John B," she replied resting her head on his shoulder.

"Where were yew born?" he asked.

"I was born in Cincinnati, Ohio. My father worked on the river docks. There were eight of us in the family – four boys, four girls. The boys left home as soon as they were old enough to make a living. Two of my brothers died fighting in the Civil War for the Union," she said. "I guess you didn't know I'm a Yankee?"

John laughed, "No, didn't know that. I thought yew was a southern belle. I guess it don't matter much anymore, one way or tother."

"I was the youngest. Father was killed by a large crate when it fell on him while he was helping to unload it onto the dock. Mother had to work as a house cleaner and took in sewing to keep the family going. It was not much of a living. Most everything I owned was a hand-me-down. She worked hard to keep us children fed and clothed and we all went to school, but my life seemed to be going nowhere. Nowhere I wanted to go, anyway. When I was fifteen, a girl friend and I hopped a riverboat and made our way to New Orleans. We dreamed of being show girls. They said we were pretty and we thought they wanted us to join a show," Cynthia said picking at something on her sleeve. "Our money ran out. There wasn't much to begin with. A man took us to Madam René. She hired us immediately."

John picked up her hand and held it. "If it's too difficult, you don't have to tell me."

"No, I want to," she continued. "At first I was scared and wanted to go home, but Madam René took me under her wing and taught me how to be the best, and I was. I was special she told me, but I was just young and fresh. When I got into my twenties, I knew that I was just another whore. That's when I made my way to Austin." Cynthia kept her eyes on John B wanting to see how he reacted to her story.

"None of that matters to me," he said. "I'm the one who loves yew."

Cynthia rested her head on John's shoulder again. She was tired and drained. It seemed so long ago when she was a young girl in Cincinnati. She closed her eyes.

A short time later John felt the stage slow and nudged Cynthia. "Look, we're in San Marcial," he told her pulling up the window shade.

Cynthia looked out the window and was not impressed. All she saw was adobe houses, some were whitewashed, others left the brown adobe exposed. Much of the town looked brown. The buildings were brown, the dirt street brown with the brown dust flying off the wheels of the stage. The buildings looked newer, but plain compared to Austin or El Paso. It was late afternoon and only a few people were going about their business – people with brown faces.

The stagecoach pulled up to a two-story building and stopped. A sign hung over the door reading, Big Ed's Saloon and Hotel. The wood front of the saloon was freshly painted white with red trim.

A tall man came out to greet the passengers and was surprised to see Sutton step out of the coach. "Well, hello Mr. Sutton," the man greeted him before he saw her. The most beautiful woman he had seen since he left his hometown to join the army stepped out of the coach, taking John's extended hand. She wore a light green, ankle-length dress with a short, waist-length jacket. A black ribbon tied around her high collared blouse was secured by a large broach at the front of her neck. Her shining auburn hair was wound into a bun under a tailored hat matching her dress.

"Ed, this is my wife, Cynthia," John said proudly.

"Hello ma'am, I'm Ed Seeley," he greeted her tipping his head. "Welcome to San Marcial, Mrs. Sutton."

Cynthia looked up at Ed with her emerald green eyes. "Thank you, call me Cynthia," she told him. Cynthia reached her hand back into the stage and helped her elderly mother step down. The woman looked confused.

"Where are we Cindy, honey?" she asked.

"This is our new home, Momma. Remember I told you."

"I have a room for you, Mr. Sutton, and another for your mother, Cynthia," Ed said as he helped carry their luggage into the saloon.

"How's the ranchhouse comin along," John asked.

Ed cringed, but knew he had to relay the bad news. "It was going well after I hired a good carpenter from Socorro. The foundation is done and most of the walls and roof are done. His crew was working on the interior walls, but last week Indians burned his supply wagon and kidnapped his wife," Ed told Sutton as they walked upstairs. "The workers are scared and the carpenter is out searching for his wife."

"Indians!" Cynthia gasped. "John B, you didn't tell me there are Indians here."

"There, there, Cynthia. I'm sure everythin will be all right," John held her arm tighter. "I won't let anythin happen to yew, darlin."

"Can't yew git nother carpenter?" John asked a little annoyed hearing of the delays. "Don't yew have a contingency plan?" he asked with an authoritative edge in his voice.

"Sure, I got another carpenter, but many of the men are spooked. The new carpenter is studying the plans and getting to know what's left of the crew. Some of the crew left with Lucas to look for his wife. The poor man is out there looking for her everyday now," Ed answered.

"How dreadful," Cynthia said. "We must help, John B."

"It's not our affair," John said with irritation in his voice that quieted Cynthia. Turning back to Seeley he said, "Well, I want to take my wife out there first thing tomorrow to show her the site and see what's been done on the ranchhouse. Yew must hire another crew if yew have to."

"Yes, sir. I'll get hot water going for your baths and you all come on down for supper after you get settled," Ed offered. He left the luggage, handed John the key to the rooms, and hurried downstairs.

John looked at Cynthia and said, "Git yer mother settled, dear."

Chapter 31

"You must not tell the *don* your brother was here," Celiá warned María when they arrived home at the *hacienda*.

"Would serve him right if the *don* killed him," María pouted. She hated her brother for leaving them, but in her heart she did not want to see him dead.

"Your brother only wants what is best for us," Celiá said.

"You can go with him if you want," María retorted. "The *don* will take care of me and the children."

"*No, mija*, I will not leave you and the children, especially in your condition. I told Rafael to leave and not come back. It will cause us problems if the *don* finds out he was here. You must promise not to tell the *don*."

"*Sí Mamá*, I will not tell him."

On Saturday during *siesta*, Celiá secretly skirted the main house and corrals on her way to the lake. She had not slept last night thinking about him. He was no longer her boy; he had grown into a man. Several times she shook her head hardly believing it was true – Rafael was here.

Rafe watched his mother approach the lake. He watched from behind some trees to make sure she was alone and not followed. He noticed she walked with a light step, her head held up high, and looked much younger than her years.

Stepping out from behind a tree he simply said, "*Mamá.*"

Startled, Celiá stepped back and almost tripped, but Rafe reached out and caught her. Grabbing him, she held him close, trying to make up for the almost five years he had been gone. She was amazed at the change in her son. The mustache and triangular beard made him look like a Spaniard. He looked like his father when his father was a young man.

They talked about María and the children and about *don* Bernardo. Celiá told him that María would not agree to leave.

"You cannot let the *don* continue abusing María. You know there is no future for her here," Rafael reminded her.

Celiá knew in her heart Rafael was right and the *don* would tire of María, but leaving frightened her. "I am afraid, *mijo*. *Don* Bernardo has spies everywhere. How can you be sure we can escape? If the *don* catches us, he'll kill you and make our life more miserable."

"We have a plan *Mamá*. All you need to do is get María and the children to town on Tuesday morning and Carlos will drive you and the children to El Paso."

"He is a *grandee*. How can you trust him?" she asked.

"He is my friend. He came here to help me rescue you."

"The *don* will not let his children go," she said. "He will follow us."

"By the time he realizes you are gone, you will be over the border. He has no power there." Rafe hoped this was true, if the *don* was alive. Rafe had a plan to make sure *don* Bernardo could not follow them to the United States and would never hurt his family again.

"Trust me *Mamá*. You and María mean everything to me."

"*Sí, mijo*. I will try to do as you say."

"*Mamá*, you must go now before you are missed," he said tenderly. They held tightly in an *abrazo*. Celiá touched his face one last time before she walked away.

Don Bernardo sat in his high-back chair sipping brandy and pondering the last several days. Three days ago the *grandee* from New Mexico and his *vaquero* came looking for horse stock. "*Americano estúpido*," *don* Bernardo chuckled to himself with a rue smile.

Yesterday, he checked with the banker, Gregorio, and *don* Alejandro had cabled El Paso for the rest of the gold. *Don* Bernardo had demanded payment in gold and not in *Americano* dollars for the horses and Gregorio said the gold would arrive on the late Monday stage. Yet, something did not seem quite right.

The *grandee* said good horse stock was limited in New

Mexico. That might be true, but he had not heard of any shortage. It was obvious to him that the *grandee* did not know much about horse flesh and less about horse trading. Perhaps, the *Americano* army was buying horses at an inflated price.

The door to the living room opened quietly and a servant entered carrying a tray.

"More brandy, *señor?*" the servant asked.

Don Bernardo stuck out his glass, but said nothing in return.

"Anything else, *señor?*"

"*Nada,*" he replied. "Leave me alone." The servant bowed and quietly slipped from the room.

Don Bernardo knew the *grandee* was willing to buy twenty of his best stock and it was an outstanding price. He surely needed the money. Carmela refused his divorce offer and now wanted ten thousand *pesos*. The sale of the horses could bring him more than half that amount, but it was still not enough. He needed at least twice the amount to pay her off.

"Twice," he murmured to himself. If only he had more horses, perhaps he could sell more to the *grandee*. Rolling the brandy in his glass, something nagged at him. *Don* Bernardo rubbed the stubble on his chin. If he could sell directly to the buyers of the stock, eliminating the *grandee*, he could make more, much more. If the *grandee's* buyers needed good stock, he could buy it cheaply from some of the lesser breeders here in Mexico and sell them for a hefty price directly to the *grandee's* buyers.

The old *don* sat staring into his glass of brandy thinking about a better plan. How could he get his hands on the *grandee's* gold and still keep his horses?

Chapter 32

Tomás Armíjo, mayor of San Marcial, mulled the disappearance of Lucas Gomez's wife, Carmen. Three days ago workers from the construction site came galloping into town screaming about Apaches. They found the remains of the burnt wagon on their way home from the site. The information immediately spread like wildfire through the small village.

It was certainly not the first time Mescalero Apaches had attacked the settlers, but things had been quiet for some time. Ed Seeley had organized a search party. They rode to the burnt wagon and combed the area until dark. The next morning, Tomás wired the sheriff in Socorro.

Everyone in the village believed Apaches took her. Women held their children tighter and everyone was scared. Construction on the Sutton ranchhouse stopped. The workers refused to travel and work unprotected. Tomás did not blame the people, but something nagged at him. The Apaches had lived in peace with San Marcial since long before the big flood. They came to town and traded deerskins for supplies. It just did not seem obvious that they kidnapped the woman and burnt the wagon. He wondered if it might be renegade Apaches from another area.

At Big Ed's, the town council and most of the store merchants were having a meeting. Scared and angry, wanting revenge, the council declared, "The Apaches must pay."

"Do not start a war with the Apaches," Tomás warned them. "We need to be sure they did this, and then the soldiers at Fort Craig can handle it." Tomás knew the people were no match for Apache braves. Blood would flow on the streets of San Marcial, if the Apaches got riled.

Yesterday, Tomás asked Bartolo Lucero to go to the Apache camps to see if they had Carmen. Bartolo was Jacarilla Apache. He had been raised since a toddler by the

Lucero family in San Marcial. As an Apache, Bartolo was allowed access to the Mescalero's camps. Tomás asked the council to wait until Bartolo returned from his visits to the Apache camps, before taking any action.

"Indian lover," one of the men grumbled at Tomás. "Bartolo is a damn Apache. How can we trust what he says?"

"*Calmate,*" Tomás argued. "If the Apaches did this, we will have our revenge. I promise you." Finally, the men went home still grumbling, but resigned to wait.

Word of the Indian attack spread like wildfire throughout the river valley. Sutton's cowboys came to Butcherknife Bill ready for a fight.

"Bill, what are we gonna to do bout them damn redskins?"

Bill knew the Apaches were faultless, but was happy to perpetuate the fear. "Tell everyone to be on the watch and double the guard at night," he ordered. "If yew see any redskins, don't ask questions, jes shoot."

Later that afternoon, Ponyboy rode back to camp and found Butcherknife working on the bunkhouse. "My damn ear hurts like hell," he complained.

"Serves yew right," Bill grumbled. "Let me take a look."

"Owwww," Ponyboy yelled sitting on a stump behind the bunkhouse.

"Hold still," Butcherknife told him. Ponyboy's ear was looking worse each day. Bill cleaned it with an old bandana and water. Puss oozed from the scab.

"I think yew need a doctor," Bill said.

"Naw, it'll be all right. Besides, there ain't no doctor in that shitheel town."

Bill squeezed the infected ear and wiped the yellow puss. Sealing the wound with axle grease, he wrapped Ponyboy's filthy bandana around his head.

"There, keep the bandana tight."

"If the damn town had some whores, I woodna killed the bitch, and my ear woodna be bit off," Ponyboy groused.

Bill was none too happy at Ponyboy for killing the woman. Bill regretted it and did not want to hang for killing a greaser. All he had wanted was an easy poke. Bill made Ponyboy stay out of town and away from the camp. No need to have him be seen with part of his ear bit off. Besides, stupid Ponyboy might blab.

"Yew bess git back out on the range," Bill told him, "and keep yer mouth shut, yew hear. If someone asks yew about yer ear, say yew caught it on a bramble bush chasin a stray."

"Dun give me no shit," Ponyboy cursed, but mounted his horse and rode out of camp.

Bill had been in town yesterday. Everyone was sure the Apaches took the woman and burned the wagon. The locals and the mayor were having a meeting at Big Ed's. The locals wanted to attack the Indians, but the mayor calmed the mob down. Bill worried the mayor was not convinced the Apaches were at fault. Wanting to fan the fear, Bill told the mayor the cowboys would help them fight the Apaches.

Tomás wanted to let the army handle the Apaches, if they were at fault. He told the mob, "The woman will be found and then we will know who has done this." He told them the sheriff from Socorro was notified. Hearing this, Bill was worried. If they found the body, a trained sheriff might know it was not Apaches.

Late the next morning Bartolo returned from the Apache camps and reported to Tomás, "The Apaches do not have the woman and I believe them. They have other Spanish women, but they have been with them since they were children."

"You are sure?"

"*Sí,* I searched the camps," he said. "They had nothing to hide and were friendly."

"*Bueno, muchas gracias,* Bartolo."

Tomás was satisfied it was not the Apaches who took Carmen. He had not gotten a reply from the sheriff in Socorro and did not expect any swift action anyway. The sheriff in Socorro had hundreds of miles of territory to patrol and might not even be in town.

"Bartolo, come with me to scout the area where the wagon was found."

"Let me get a fresh horse and then we'll go," Bartolo replied.

It was midday when they arrived at the charred wagon. Hundreds of hoof prints surrounded the area. The search party had destroyed any evidence in their haste to find the woman.

Parts of the burnt wagon were dumped on the side of the road when the searchers sifted the debris. Bartolo carefully paced the area and sifted some of the charred dirt.

"I don't see any arrow holes or burnt tips. Tomás, you take the left side of the road, I'll take the right. We'll work our way to the turnoff to the construction site." Bartolo often scouted for the Army at Fort Craig and Tomás was glad to have him along.

Carefully, they worked their way south to the turnoff road and found nothing out of the ordinary.

"Let's work our way back to the burnt wagon. We'll go the same way we came, so we can examine the same terrain from the opposite way," Bartolo instructed.

From the west on a nearby mesa, Butcherknife Bill watched the mayor and a man searching the roadside. Bill had been keeping watch on the search for the last several days, but mostly the searchers were close to the burnt wagon site. These two searchers were methodically working their way along the road. Bill could tell one of them was a trained tracker. They disappeared from Bill's view for awhile, then they reversed course and came back toward the charred wagon.

Bill stayed atop the nearby mesa watching them. Tired and hot sitting in the sun, he worried they might eventually find the dead woman. He had contemplated moving the body, but it was too risky. Ponyboy started this trouble being just plain stupid, but Bill knew it was up to him to fix it.

Tomás and Bartolo slowly walked along the road re-examining the roadside for any evidence they may have missed the first time. When they reached the burnt wagon they regrouped.

"Bartolo, let us search from here to the village," Tomás said while they rested and drank water from their gourds.

Bill watched the two searchers stop and rest. He watched them mount up and each take a side of the road heading toward San Marcial. They moved slowly in and out of the brush, stopping and peering down. They were heading in the direction where he and Ponyboy hid the body. Bill pulled his rifle from the scabbard on his saddle and took aim.

Long shadows were creeping up on them. Tomás knew they only had another hour or so of daylight left. He noticed Bartolo stopped and was intently studying the ground. He pulled up his horse and waited.

Suddenly, a shot rang out toppling Bartolo from his horse. Tomás heard a second shot whizz above his own head. He jumped off his horse, ducking behind a small tree. He looked all around, but saw nothing, then up on the mesa he caught a glimpse of a rider on horseback, and then it was gone.

"Bartolo! Are you hit?" he yelled out.

"Sí"

Glancing to the mesa once more and seeing nothing, he got up and ran to Bartolo. He was bleeding from his right shoulder. "Bartolo can you ride? We have to get out of here," Tomás said.

"Yes, help me up."

Tomás ripped his own shirt and stuffed the cloth under Bartolo's shirt, pressing it on the wound. He helped him up and onto his horse and Bartolo clung to the horse's neck with his good arm. Tomás held the reins and led Bartolo's horse down the road walking him slowly. It was almost dark when they reached San Marcial. The only person who had any medical experience was Johnny Fields, a discharged medical corpsman from Fort Craig who married a local girl.

Johnny went right to work on Bartolo, removing the

bullet and cleaning the wound.

"How did this happen," Johnny asked.

"We were on the road looking for clues on the disappearance of Lucas's wife, when shots were fired at us from the mesa."

"Do you think it was the Indians?" Johnny asked.

"No. I don't think it was Indians," Tomás replied, but did not say anything about the man he saw on the mesa – a rider with a cowboy hat, the type worn by the Texas cowboys. He didn't want that information spread around town, not yet anyway.

"Bartolo, you keep that wound clean, and come see me in a couple of days," Johnny said finishing up.

"*Sí, muchas gracias,*" he thanked him.

Bartolo and Tomás walked down the road with their horses in tow. "Do you think this had something to do with the woman?" Bartolo asked.

"I think so. Tomorrow I'll go back and finish looking for clues."

"I'll go with you. You shouldn't go alone."

"No, no, you can't do that. You must rest. I'll ask Ed Seeley to go with me. You go home now," Tomás said and walked on to Big Ed's Saloon.

"Hey, Thomas," Ed greeted him when he stepped into the saloon. It was quiet except for a local down at the end of the bar.

"Ed, I need your help," Tomás said quietly. He wasted no time telling Seeley what happened to him and Bartolo out on the road where Carmen went missing, including the man he saw on the ridge.

"So, you don't think it was Apaches?" Ed asked quietly.

"No," Tomás answered.

"I have to finish searching the area. Will you go with me tomorrow?" Tomás asked.

"Well, I ah, ah, I don't know. Mr. Sutton and his wife asked me to take them out to see the progress on the ranchhouse. I guess I can take them in the morning and ride my own horse. I'll meet you at the burnt wagon about noon."

"I'll see you at noon," Tomás replied. "Please Ed, keep this between us for now."

CHAPTER 33

There was a bit of cool air blowing in from the open window just above the headboard. In the distance Rafe heard roosters crowing one after another. Only one was close to the hotel and he was the last to answer the call. Rafe had been awake for hours after a restless night.

Saturday, he met his mother by the lake just northeast of the *hacienda*. Together they hatched a plan to take María and the children to the doctor in Torreón. María adamantly refused to leave *don* Bernardo. She thought he loved her. His mother agreed with him that it was only a matter of time before María was replaced with a younger girl or the *don* died.

"How can she not see the truth?" Rafe had asked his mother when he met her at the lake.

"She's young and not thinking right," his mother had told him. "Forgive her. She's still angry at you for abandoning us."

The plan was simple or seemed simple. His mother would force María go to the doctor in town on Tuesday morning. After the doctor visit, Carlos would put them into the wagon and head straight north. By the time they were missed, Carlos would be well north or hopefully already into Texas. Rafe would meet them at Uncle Jose's ranch in El Paso and take them to Santa Fe.

"What if you do not come?" his mother had asked worried.

"I will not abandon you again," he adamantly insisted.

It was Tuesday morning and the gold had arrived late yesterday afternoon at the bank. Today he would go with *don* Bernardo to the box canyon and select the young stallions and mares for *don* Alejandro. It was a ruse, of course, and he worried the plan would fail, but most of all he worried his mother could not follow through with the plan. If she could not get María to the doctor in town, all their effort would be for nothing.

Rafe dressed in his *vaquero traje*. He laced up the chaps and tied his sash carefully. He pushed the pistol behind his waistband. All night long he kept reviewing details in his mind. He wanted to kill *don* Bernardo, but rescuing his mother and sister required restraint. When he was dressed, he met Carlos at the restaurant for breakfast.

"Eat," Carlos said. "It will be a long day."

"I know, but my stomach is in knots," Rafe replied. He managed to drink a cup of coffee and eat a sweet bun. "I wish I had one of my GSW guns. What if I have trouble? This old single-action pistol my uncle gave me will not be of much help."

"You don't want to raise his suspicions," Carlos replied. "Keep the gun in your saddlebag." Carlos could see Rafe's face tighten and knew he was worried. Every meeting with *don* Bernardo raised the chances that his real identity would be discovered.

"No, I'll be defenseless," Rafe retorted.

"Nothing will happen to you. *Don* Bernardo must bring the horses from the canyon to get his gold," Carlos reminded him, then changed the subject. "I don't want to worry you, but what if your mother does not show up?"

"I too am worried she will not be able to get María and the children to the doctor. Give her as much time as you can, but then you must get the wagon and ride hard for Texas."

"What about you?" Carlos asked.

"I will stay and find a way to get them out," Rafe answered. They did not speak further about the problems and risks they were both taking.

At the *hacienda*, *don* Bernardo's manservant helped him dress for riding. He mused while the servant laced his riding boots. Saturday he sent some inquires to New Mexico to find buyers for his horses. The gold he got from the *grandee* and selling more horses directly to *Americano* buyers in New Mexico would give him enough money to pay off the divorce. Once he was free of Carmela, he would marry the widow, *doña* Juana Santos, and join their two *haciendas.* It would increase his land holdings more than double.

Mariano knocked quietly on the bedroom door, pushed it open slowly and said, *"Patrón, el hombre ha llegado."* Mariano told *don* Bernardo the *vaquero* had arrived.

Picking up his riding quirt, he hobbled down the stairs. Mariano and the *vaquero* were waiting for him in the foyer.

Rafe watched *don* Bernardo struggle down the wide staircase. He was jolted back to the day he crept up those same stairs and shot the *don.* It was as he remembered – the large clock, the polished wood stairs, and the pictures hanging on the walls.

"Bueno, vamos," *don* Bernardo said without greeting Rafe in any formal way. Rafe lowered his head as the *don* walked by and he followed Mariano out the door.

A servant helped *don* Bernardo to mount his horse. Mariano led the way, followed by *don* Bernardo, with Rafe trailing. Rafe knew exactly where they were going. He and *don* Pablo had been there many times when Rafe was a boy, checking on the horses, or catching a young colt. His horse, Rayo, spent much of his first year in the box canyon.

Rafe was relieved *don* Bernardo took little notice of him. It was as Carlos had said, "You are only a *vaquero,* of no importance."

When they arrived at the mouth of the box canyon, they discovered the gate was open, allowing the horses to escape. Mariano quickly rode ahead to assess the situation and came back saying most of the horses were gone. It was all part of *don* Bernardo's plan. He came out yesterday afternoon, opened the gate, and drove the horses to a canyon deeper into the hills.

"Vamos a buscar los caballos," the *don* said to Rafe in an angry huff that the horses must be found. He told Mariano to go back to the stables and bring more men to help round up the horses.

The old *don* headed south into the canyons, setting an easy pace. Rafe followed a few paces behind as they wound through the shallow rocky canyons.

"*Mierda,*" Rafe cursed under his breath, and then relaxed. It did not matter how long it took them to find the horses. His mother and sister were to leave for town as soon as *don* Bernardo took him to the box canyon. They must already be in town or with Carlos. The longer it took at the canyons the more time Carlos would have to get away from Torreón.

Rafe continued following *don* Bernardo through several shallow canyons. Rafe knew these canyons well because he had searched them for strays with *don* Pablo many times. It appeared to Rafe that the old man knew exactly where he was going. The *don* urged his horse to the top of a ridge, and they spotted the herd of horses below them. *Don* Bernardo signaled Rafe to follow him down to the mouth of the canyon.

Following the *don*, Rafe wished he had his GSW guns. He wanted to kill the old *don* up here in the hills and leave him to the buzzards, as he deserved. He would do it slow. Laughing at the old man and telling him of his real name. He would say, "I am Rafael Ortega de Estrada. You raped my sister and sent my father to die. Now die and go to hell as you deserve."

Rafe lifted the flap of his saddlebag and fingered his pistol. *Don* Bernardo rode in front and was an easy target. Rage shook Rafe to the core. Visions of the day he found María raped and beaten flashed in his mind. Memories of the flash of the flintlock pistol and a body falling to the floor belied the view of the old *don* riding in front of him. Surely, Carlos had gathered his mother and sister and they were headed north. He could kill the *don* and ride hard to meet them in El Paso.

When they reached the mouth of the canyon there was a patch of small trees by a dry stream. "Eh, *vaquero,* help me down off this horse," the old *don* gruffed at Rafe. Rafe walked his horse to a nearby tree, dismounted, and flipped the reins around a branch. He turned and walked toward the *don's* horse, keeping his head down hoping the *don* would not get a good look at his face. He did not see *don* Bernardo pull his pistol.

When he reached the *don's* horse, it backed away a few steps. Rafe looked up at *don* Bernardo and saw a pistol cocked and pointed at his chest.

"*¿Por qué estás haciendo esto?*" Rafe asked the old *don* why he was doing this. Frantically, Rafe was trying to formulate a plan seeing the barrel of the *don's* gun pointed directly at him.

"*Para el oro,*" he said – for the gold.

Rafe was trapped. He had nowhere to run or hide. He moved side to side, opposite of *don* Bernardo's nervous horse. He watched the old *don* take aim. This was not how it was supposed to be. He thought of his mother and sister, praying Carlos would get them to safety.

A moment before *don* Bernardo fired at him, Rafe saw a slight hesitation in the old man's eyes. He wanted to yell out and curse the *desgraciado*, but the last thing Rafe heard was the explosion of the gun.

Chapter 34

Since Saturday, after she met Rafael at the lake, Celiá planned their escape. She was secretly giddy with excitement and fraught with fear. For two days Celiá had been adding *poawa* root to María's tea. She knew the root caused stomach pains, but was not harmful. María complained and held her stomach and Celiá told her daughter she might lose the baby.

"You need to see the doctor," Celiá told her.

"No, I won't go," María protested, but each day she grew worse. Last night María curled up in her bed holding her stomach, crying. Watching her daughter suffer, Celiá's heart ached, but she knew it was for the best.

The next morning, Celiá saw Rafael arrive at the *hacienda*. Once he left with *don* Bernardo, she called for the buggy.

"I'm taking you to the doctor," she demanded. María was too sick to refuse.

Readying the children, Celiá let her eyes wander around the small *casita* looking at her things for the last time. Although meager, the smallest of her belongings held memories of her life. She could not take anything, anything which would arouse suspicion.

"Here Antonio," she said handing him a blanket. "The wind is a bit colder today." She made María wrap up the baby in a warmer blanket, too. All the way to town, María complained to her mother about how the doctor was going to look at her.

"You are sick. He can help," Celiá said.

"I don't want to see that young doctor," María complained.

"It is for your own good and the baby you are carrying. That *curandera* gave you something bad. I don't trust her," Celiá said, keeping the ruse going.

They arrived at the doctor's house in Torreón. It was a small, but pleasant home off the main plaza on a side street. Celiá dropped the buggy anchor on the ground before she helped María to get down. She saw Carlos sitting on his horse down the street and noticed he was no longer dressed as a *grandee*.

"Here we are. Don't be afraid, *mija*. The doctor will not hurt you. He can only help you," Celiá assured her as she walked her daughter into the doctor's house. The doctor was busy with another patient and Celiá nervously settled her daughter in a chair.

Carlos watched the two women and the children walk into the doctor's office. He waited until a man walked by and turned the corner, and then casually rode to the buggy. Tying his horse to the back, he jumped into the buggy and drove it down the street. He had left his wagon behind the doctor's office earlier. Rafe told Carlos it was important that no one see him take them out of town.

Carlos drove the buggy to the livery. He explained to the liveryman that *don* Bernardo would send for the buggy in a few days. He paid the man a few *pesos* to feed and stable the horse and rode back to the doctor's house and waited around back.

The doctor called for María. She grumbled and handed the baby to Celiá. The doctor smiled at her kindly and took her into the back room.

Alone in the waiting area, Celiá bounced Alicia on her lap. Antonio played with a toy. Her heart ached knowing Rafael was with *don* Bernardo. What if the old *don* recognized him?

Before long, María came out of the office. She was lightheaded and embarrassed. "Keep her off her feet," the doctor told Celiá. "She is weak, but young and strong. I gave her a powder to settle her stomach. Give it to her twice a day," the doctor explained handing several paper pouches to Celiá.

"*Gracias,*" Celiá said. She gathered the baby and led Antonio and María out the door. Walking around the corner with the children, she met Carlos and the wagon waiting for them.

Carlos swung Antonio up into the back of the wagon.

"*Mija*, get into the wagon," Celiá told María.

Confused, María looked around for the buggy, then she looked at her mother. "*Mamá*, what are we doing?"

Without a word, Carlos picked María up and gently placed her inside the wagon. He helped Celiá, still holding the baby in her arms, up into the back and shut the tailgate. Quickly he jumped into the driver's seat, clicked the reins, and the wagon took off with a jolt.

"*No Mamá!*" María yelled out. She tried to get up, but the jolt of the wagon knocked her back.

"*Mija*, we are leaving to go live with Rafael. There is no future here in Torreón," Celiá said with a definite sternness in her voice.

"But *don* Bernardo . . . the children," María protested and began crying.

"*Don* Bernardo is going to marry *doña* Juana Santos," Celiá told her.

"*No Mamá*. He won't," she sobbed.

"Yes," Celiá said. "He wants her ranch now that *don* Miguel is dead. The new *patróna* will never put up with a husband's bastard children, especially belonging to a *mestiza.*"

María sunk to the seat, exhausted. She did not want to believe her mother. She wanted to believe *don* Bernardo would take care of her and the children. The last time she bedded him she asked, "Do you love me, *don* Bernardo?" He did not reply, and only patted her arm and laughed.

"*Mamá*, is everything you told me about *don* Bernardo true?" María asked.

"Yes *mija*, it is all true. You know the new *patróna* will send you and the children away. *Doña* Carmela would have done the same, if she had stayed," her mother said.

Stunned, María sat back crying. The lurching of the wagon made her stomach hurt worse and she curled into a ball.

Carlos headed north out of Torreón with the women and children hidden in the back of the covered wagon. He kept a steady pace until he was out of town, and then let the horses run at a faster clip. He hated to make the trip

rougher on the women, but wanted to put as many miles
between them and Torreón as possible.

CHAPTER 35

Don Bernardo stepped his horse close to the body of the *vaquero* from New Mexico. Awkwardly he got off his horse. Blood splattered the *vaquero's* chest and blood pooled behind his head. The *don* pushed at the body with his foot to make sure the man was dead. With some effort, he unsaddled the *vaquero's* horse and dragged the saddle behind a bush. With a slap, he ran the horse off. *Don* Bernardo took one last look at the body of the young *vaquero*. He pondered a second shot to be sure the *vaquero* was dead, but decided to let the coyotes finish him off.

Another man killed for money, just like he killed Carmela's husband and *don* Miguel Santos. He thought it ironic he had killed the *vaquero* and would kill *don* Alejandro because of Carmela. Four for the same woman. *"Puta,"* he cursed. "I'll be glad to be done with her."

With some effort he stepped up into his saddle and headed out of the canyon. *Don* Bernardo smiled to himself as he rode away. No one would find the body, except for the scavengers. Soon there would be no trace. He hoped killing *don* Alejandro would be as easy.

Don Alejandro would bring the gold to the house expecting to meet his *vaquero* with the horses. *Don* Bernardo would tell him the horses had been brought down from the canyon to the north trail and were waiting with his *vaquero*. He would graciously offer to lead him to the meeting place. Once he had the gold in his hands, he would make sure the *Americano* disappeared.

No one cared if a couple of *Norte Americanos* were lost in Mexico. Even if the Mexican authorities investigated, any evidence would be long gone or attributed to *bandidos*.

It was a good plan. The gold would be his, the horses would still be his, and *doña* Juana and her *hacienda* would soon be his, as soon as he paid off Carmela.

Riding out of the canyons, he stopped at the top of a hill overlooking a long valley. In the distance he saw smoke twirling to the sky from the widow *doña* Juana Santos' house. She probably would want them to live in her house after he married her. A woman liked her own things and he did not care.

Carmela had overseen all the details of running their main house and servants. *Don* Bernardo ran the *hacienda* and *vaqueros*. Theirs was a typical relationship. He assumed *doña* Juana would feel the same. Better they lived at her *hacienda*, so he could visit his *putas* at his. Yes, that would be a good arrangement.

Halfway back to the house, *don* Bernardo met up with Mariano and several *vaqueros* coming up the trail.

"Mariano, no need to search for the horses. The *vaquero* has taken the horses he selected, and is on his way to the north trail to wait for *don* Alejandro. Come, let us return to the house and wait for the *Americano*," *don* Bernardo said.

"*Bueno, jefe.*" The *vaqueros* turned and followed their boss back to the house.

Two young Chichimeca Indian brothers crawled along the canyon wall. They often played near the box canyon where they knew the old *haciendero* kept horses.

"Do not steal any horses from the *haciendero*," they had been told by the elders. "He is a very bad man." However, they were allowed to catch strays and bring them back to the village.

Yesterday afternoon the brothers watched the old *haciendero* take the horses from the box canyon and move them to the small canyon below them. Today they came looking for strays.

"We shouldn't take any," the younger of the two said. "They are still the *haciendero's*."

"They are free," the older one said. They tried to catch one yesterday after the *haciendero* left, but the horses were skittery. It was hard to catch one on foot. Today they would try to corner a young one. The older boy carried a rope harness.

The two boys stood in the rocks above the small herd of horses. They talked about how to sneak down and corner one of the young ones.

"I want a stallion," the younger one said. "Maybe that black and white one."

Below them, two men rode into the small canyon. The older boy recognized the old *haciendero*. The boys hid behind a clump of prickly pear cactus. They watched the younger man slide from his horse and tie him to a tree. The old *haciendero* pulled his gun and shot the younger man. He fell backward to the dirt.

Hidden by the cactus, the boys watched the old *haciendero* strip the saddle from the man's horse, hide it in the bushes, and drive the horse off. He kicked at the dead man, remounted his horse, and rode off. The older boy was sure it was the *haciendero*, because he was stooped and walked with a limp.

When the *haciendero* rode off, the older boy said, "Let's get that saddle." They scurried down to the bottom of the canyon.

"Search him," the older boy told his younger brother, "and see what we can take." He walked over to the bush and dragged the saddle out to the dirt. It was a good saddle. His brother put on the dead man's sombrero and started to search his pockets.

"*Ayeee!*" the boy wearing the sombrero cried and jumped back.

"The man is still alive," he said. "I heard him groan."

Blood soaked through the man's shirt near his heart. "See if he is dead," the young one wearing the sombrero said. His older brother knelt down and pushed the man's shoulder.

"Arrrgghhh."

The boys jumped back away from the injured man, looked at the man, and then at each other. "Let's take what we can and get out of here," the younger boy said.

"No, we can't leave him," his older brother said.

"He's going to die. What do we care."

"No, we must try to help him. Run, go get the medicine man who is staying at our village. Maybe he can save him. I'll stay here," he ordered his younger brother.

The young boy hesitated.
"Go!"

CHAPTER 36

It was near ten o'clock by the time John B. Sutton and his beautiful bride walked downstairs for breakfast in Big Ed's Saloon.

"Good morning," Ed said cheerily.

"Good morning," they both replied at the same time. John ushered his wife to one of the tables and held the chair for her.

"Eggs and biscuits, all right?"

"Shur," John replied.

After breakfast Ed had his buggy brought around for John to drive it to the ranchhouse. He explained he would not be returning with them, but did not explain further.

"Quite all right," John said. "I may take the Missus for a little tour."

"What about the Indians, John B?" Cynthia asked.

"Never mind, dear. I'll take care of yew."

Ed cleaned up the kitchen and closed the saloon for the day.

The morning was cold from the overnight rain and clouds lingered about, promising more rain. Ed led the buggy to the construction site. When they passed the remains of the burnt wagon, he walked his horse slowly. He heard Cynthia fussing at her husband about the Indians.

At the construction site, only a few men were working. The rest of the workers were too scared of an Indian attack. However, John seemed pleased with the progress.

"As soon as we clear up this Indian problem," Ed told him, "work will get back into high gear."

"Good," John said. He walked off with Cynthia to see the view from the back of the house.

From the ridge where he had taken shots at searchers yesterday, Butcherknife Bill watched his boss and his whore ride past the burnt wagon and continue to the ranchhouse's construction site. He recognized Cinnamon's auburn hair.

Sutton had married the whore and brought her here like a proper lady. "Shit, she's just a whore from the Crystal Palace. I coudda never paid her high price, miss high and mighty, but she's still a whore," Bill grumbled.

Bill had been keeping a sharp eye on the search for the woman's body. Last night's heavy rain washed away most of the tracks and Bill was relieved that the body would probably not be found.

"Hell, I better git back, case the boss comes a lookin fer me," Bill muttered. He turned his horse and galloped back to the cattle herd.

Ed left Sutton at the ranchhouse and headed back to meet Tomás at the burnt wagon. Tomás had not arrived yet, so Ed started looking around. Yesterday's rain washed all the tracks away and left a muddy mess. Pondering the muddy site, unlike Tomás, Ed was sure it was Indians who took the woman. He remembered Indian attacks when he served at Fort Craig. Sometimes they attacked for no reason.

Tomás came riding up the road. "Sorry I'm late. Mount up and I'll show you where we got shot yesterday."

"Did you see the buzzards up yonder when you came up the trail?" Ed asked Tomás. "Maybe we ought to go check that out first."

"Yes, I saw them. You're right. Let's follow them. Five or maybe six birds, you know it must be a large kill." Tomás swallowed hard and wished he had not used the term kill, but he was not expecting to find Carmen alive.

They turned their horses to the northwest. A flock of buzzards flew high in the sky, circling. The terrain was open with shrubby bushes and large boulders.

"Not many places to hide a body out here," Tomás said.

"Damn rain last night washed away any tracks," Ed replied.

Tomás kept turning in his saddle and watching the far mesa. He saw nothing, but the ambush from yesterday was still fresh in his mind.

"Trouble with tracking buzzards, is the damn things

keep moving. Just when you think you are getting to them, it seems they move farther away," Ed said.

"Over there," Tomás yelled. He watched one of the great birds swoop to the ground and then return to the sky. Tomás and Ed galloped to the base of a small rocky knoll.

"Up in those boulders," Tomás said pointing up. They tethered their horses and went on foot. The air was cool, but the sun was still warm on their backs. By the time they reached the top, they were both panting.

"Behind that big boulder." Ed pointed and they climbed the last few yards. "Caw," cried one of the birds unhappy with the intruders. The ugly birds hopped a few feet and then scattered into the sky. The cawing buzzards remained circling directly overhead. Ed walked around the boulder with Tomás close behind. A large, half-eaten antelope rotted on the ground. "Well, I'm glad it's not her," Ed said relieved. They turned and hiked back to their horses. As they headed back to the road, a stiff cold wind carried darkening clouds into the valley.

"We best be getting back," Ed said. A cold rain hit them before they made it back to the village. "We can start again, early in the morning, if you want," Ed suggested.

"I appreciate your help," Tomás replied. "I'll come to breakfast in the morning and we'll go from there."

Chapter 37

"A man is dying," the Chichimeca Indian boy wearing the sombrero said. The sombrero, several sizes too big for his head, kept falling over his eyes.

"My brother, Katu, says you must come," the boy tugged at the medicine man's sleeve. The boy bent over at the waist trying to catch his breath and the sombrero dropped to the ground. He had run the several miles from the canyon to his village.

"Calm down boy. Now, tell me again what did you see?" the medicine man asked. He handed the young boy a water gourd.

Pomac took a long drink. "A man shot another and left him for dead, but he is still alive," he said. "Come, I will show you. He needs help. He's still alive," he repeated. He took another long swig of water dripping some on his shirt.

The medicine man rose slowly and packed some small bundles into a leather pouch without saying a word. He wrapped a blanket around his shoulders. Pomac watched the old man. He was not a Chichimeca. He was not one of them. He had come here several weeks ago. Pomac heard people in the village saying the old man was a sorcerer, but his father said he just followed the old ways. His mother said he was an Aztec medicine man.

Xihuitl was a trained healer – a medicine man. He traveled the remote countryside and along the way he served the people's needs as a healer and in turn they provided rest and shelter. Sometimes he stayed for periods of time, and other times he quickly went on his way. Each tribe of these remote areas was different. Some embraced him and others were scared of his potions.

"Come now, take me there," the old man said, finally ready. He mounted his horse and pulled Pomac up behind him and pulled on a rope tethering a donkey. Pomac pointed the way.

When they reached the top of the mesa, Pomac

pointed down into the canyon. Xihuitl saw the man lying on the ground. He swung Pomac off the horse and said, "Go. I will walk the horse down." While Pomac ran, the old Healer slowly and carefully picked his way down the rocky slope pulling the donkey behind him.

Pomac reached the bottom of the canyon. "I brought him," he yelled to his brother. "Is he still alive?"

"Yes, but barely," Katu said playing with a pistol. "Where did you get that?" Pomac asked.

"I found it in his belongings," Katu replied.

When Xihuitl reached the boys, he found them playing with a pistol.

"Go over there," he said to the boys and pointed away. Xihuitl got down on his knees by the hurt man. The man lay on his back. Blood covered the front of his once white shirt and was beginning to crust. Xihuitl felt a heart beat in his neck. He took out his knife and cut the man's shirt carefully, lifting the material from his chest, hoping not to start more bleeding.

Xihuitl rocked back on his heels. Under the man's shirt he found a mangled silver star amulet hung on a leather string around the man's neck. Turquoise fragments, mixed with blood, splayed over the man's chest in the shape of a star about the size of his hand.

"Aahhh." Shocked, the old Healer fell back on his seat recognizing the star as a sign from the Goddess. "The Goddess Coatlicue, the preserver of life, is with you my young friend," Xihuitl said to the injured man.

Slowly, he rose and gathered bundles from his donkey. While he cleaned the wounds and applied his medicine, he told the boys to gather longs poles and get leather ropes from his gear on the donkey. Xihuitl collected the loose turquoise fragments and put them into a small leather pouch. The Healer knew the amulet had great power and must not be lost.

With the help of the two boys, he built a crude litter. Carefully, they lifted the injured man and lowered him onto it. When they lifted the man, Xihuitl noticed a large gash on the back of the man's head and blood on a rock. Xihuitl rolled his sarape and placed it under the man's head to cushion it. The journey back to the Chichimeca village would be long and bumpy.

Xihuitl told the boys to saddle the man's horse which had not run off very far. The old medicine man asked the boys to show him a way back to the village without traversing the canyon. They led the way riding the injured man's horse. By the time they arrived, the sun was getting low in the sky.

News had spread in the village that the boys and the medicine man found a wounded white man. The Chief stopped them outside the Chichimeca village as they approached.

"You cannot bring him here," the Chief asserted. "White men are not allowed in our village."

"He is blessed by the Goddess Coatlicue," Xihuitl pleaded. The old Chief shook his head. "You are welcome; he is not," the Chief insisted. No matter how much the Healer pleaded with the old Chief, he was not allowed to take the wounded white man into the village. He asked if the two boys could stay and help him. The old Chief agreed and turned back to the village.

CHAPTER 38

As they planned, Tomás went to Big Ed's Saloon for breakfast the next morning before they resumed the search for the missing woman. Mr. and Mrs. Sutton joined them at the breakfast table. Mrs. Sutton was a vision of loveliness and Tomás had time to study her over breakfast. Curly reddish-brown hair framed her face enhancing her dazzling green eyes. When she laughed, her eyes sparkled like emeralds. Mr. Sutton was a very lucky man. When Ed introduced Tomás, she said, "Call me Cynthia."

"Did you find the woman," John Sutton asked.

"No," Tomás replied.

"Dreadful, simply dreadful," Cynthia said. "I can't believe Indians are still on the warpath here."

Tomás assured her the Indians were not on the warpath. "If it was Indians, it was a rogue band from another area."

Ed told Sutton, he and Tomás were going after breakfast to search the area where the woman disappeared. Sutton said he was riding to the ranch to check on the herd. Cynthia wanted to stay at the hotel and tend to her mother.

"Do you mind if I use the kitchen to fix food for my mother," Cynthia asked Ed.

"Not at all," Ed replied.

Sutton rode a little way with the two men until he broke off to find the herd. Tomás and Ed rode up the road, but not as far as the burnt wagon. The road was soupy with mud and frozen puddles in the shadows from yesterday's cold rain.

"Bartolo and I were about here when the shots were fired at us," Tomás told Ed. "I think they came from a shooter on that mesa," he said pointing west. They scanned the mesa and saw nothing.

"Are you sure it wasn't Apaches?" Ed asked.

"No, but I only saw a silhouette when I looked into the setting sun, and I'm sure the man I saw wore a cowboy hat," Tomás said.

"Everyone thinks it was Apaches."

"Perhaps they are right, but we haven't had trouble with them for some time now. I sent Bartolo to their camps. You know Bartolo is Apache, don't you?"

"No, I didn't know that," Ed answered.

"He was raised in San Marcial, but the Apaches allow him to come to their camps. He came back and told me they have some Spanish women who have lived with them for many years, but they don't have Carmen."

"Is he sure? Maybe the Apaches were lying," Ed asked.

"They trust Bartolo. I don't think it was the Apaches. I think it was one of the Texas cowboys, but I hope I'm wrong."

"I know they are a rough bunch, but kidnapping or killing a woman is something I can't believe," Ed responded. "They always talk in the saloon about everything when they've had enough whiskey. I would have overheard something."

"Well, let's finish what Bartolo and I started. You take the right side of the road and I will take the left side. We'll search back toward San Marcial."

Slowly, they paced the horses at a walk. Occasionally they dismounted to get a better look at the terrain and search for tracks. An hour into the search, Ed was on foot leading his horse. Under a large cottonwood tree, he saw a wagon wheel track leading to a thicket near the Rio Grande.

"Thomas, over here," he yelled out.

Tomás galloped over and joined Ed. The trees had preserved the tracks from the recent rains. Slowly, on foot, they followed the indentation of the wheel track, losing it at times and then finding it again. Under the shade of the trees, thin ice crusted shallow wet indentations. They walked lightly and tried not to damage any evidence. Carefully, they picked their way, stepping on rocks and branches whenever they could, rather than sink in the wet, sandy soil.

"There's another track," Tomás said pointing right.

Not saying a word, they pressed forward to a thicket of trees near the bank of the river. In an open spot the stubby undergrowth was smashed and broken.

"Look at the circular wagon tracks. The wagon turned here and headed north, back to the road," Ed said pointing. They searched the area in a wide circle.

"What are we looking for?" Ed asked.

"I'm not sure. A body, a grave, a campsite, or something that seems out of place."

"Perhaps they dumped her body in the river or she tried to swim away and drowned," Ed suggested.

Again they split up to cover more ground. Tomás walked up river and Ed moved down river. Tomás spotted a clump of dead branches and dried grass piled up under a low hung tree. It seemed oddly placed.

Drawing closer, his nose picked up a sickly stench coming from under the tree. He yelled out for Ed, and pulled a bandana over his nose.

"What did you find?" Ed asked.

"I don't know."

"Damn that smell!" Ed complained following Tomás under the tree.

Tomás pulled on one of the branches and then another, lifting gently. Under the last branch he spotted a bare foot. Jumping back, like he had been bit, he almost knocked Ed over and they stumbled backward.

"Jesus, Thomas," Ed yelled out.

"She is there," was all Tomás said turning away from the site.

"What! Are you sure?"

"You go in there and look for yourself," Tomás told him.

Ed covered his nose with a bandana and crawled under the tree. Tomás watched him remove more of the branches and grass from the body. He kept his distance not wanting to see or believe.

Ed came out and bent over gagging. They sat on a log staring toward the body under the tree. Neither spoke for a few minutes.

Finally Tomás asked, "Well, do you still think it was Indians?"

"No," Ed replied.

"Ed, you stay here and look around for anything that might help us figure out who did this. I'll go home and get my wagon," Tomás said.

CHAPTER 39

Don Bernardo and the *vaqueros* arrived back at the house shortly after noon to find *don* Alejandro had not arrived yet. "Good," he muttered to himself. Stiffly, he climbed up the well-worn staircase. Large pictures of generations of his family hung on the wall. He never looked at his father's painting. His grandfather's painting hung next to his father's. He had never known him, but *don* Bernardo thought he looked like him a bit. He liked his grandfather's striking smile under the mustache and small triangular beard. His hair was dark brown and slightly curly. *Don* Bernardo stopped and stared at the painting. The eyes stared back at him. Something in the eyes he had not noticed before – something familiar.

Shaking his head, he climbed the stairs to his bedroom. He rang the bell for his manservant and then sat on the bed. He wanted to rest a bit until *don* Alejandro arrived.

"*Señor?*" the manservant asked hurrying into the room.

"Remove and polish my boots," he ordered. "Bring me a wet towel."

"*Sí, señor.*" The manservant helped him wash and *don* Bernardo lay back on the bed.

"Wake me when *don* Alejandro arrives," he commanded.

Exhausted, he closed his eyes. He hated his tired and twisted body. "*Peón desgraciado,*" he muttered. "Shot me and left me a cripple. If I ever find that boy, I will make him suffer as I have suffered," he swore. "Yes, I'll make them pay – him, his mother, and stupid sister. They will all pay."

At least María was of good use. She was an ample lover and a fertile woman. The bastards by her were his only children. She was pregnant with a third child. Sometimes he watched her young boy playing in the courtyard – his boy. He wished Carmela had given him children as legitimate heirs.

When he opened his eyes the sun no longer shone in the windows. He had fallen asleep. Ringing for his manservant, he sat on the side of the bed.

"I told you to wake me when *don* Alejandro arrived," he scolded the manservant.

"He has not arrived, *señor.*"

"*¿Qué?* It is late."

"*Sí, señor.*"

Don Bernardo stumped down the stairs and into the courtyard pacing back and forth. Where was *don* Alejandro and the gold? The sun was low on the horizon. *Don* Alejandro should have been here hours ago with the gold to purchase the horses.

He waited until dark for *don* Alejandro to come. Sitting alone at the dining table, he flew into a rage over supper, yelling at the servants over every detail.

Where was the *Americano*? Surely, if he had been delayed at the bank, Gregorio would have sent a messenger. The more he pondered, worry lines popped out on his forehead. What if the *vaquero* was missed? Surely *don* Alejandro would wonder why his *vaquero* had not returned.

After a disturbed sleep, *don* Bernardo rose early the next morning and sent Mariano to town. "Find the banker; get him out of bed; see if he has the gold," he ordered Mariano. *Don* Bernardo waited at the house in case *don* Alejandro arrived this morning.

Mariano returned several hours later and *don* Bernardo met him on the veranda. "*Señor,* Gregorio gave *don* Alejandro the gold yesterday morning, as planned," he reported to his boss. "He said *don* Alejandro was on his way to see you. It was about ten o'clock yesterday morning."

Don Bernardo was dumbfounded, wondering what might have happened – an accident, lost, *bandidos*?

Stupid *Norte Americano* probably bragged about the gold in town. He did not know the ways of Mexico. *Bandidos* had ways of knowing such events and may have followed him from town. They would have robbed him, probably killed him, or left him for dead.

"*¡Mierda!*" he cursed how stupid he had been. "I should have sent a man to protect him."

"Come, we will search the road to town," he said to Mariano. "Go get Enrique and Ernesto."

They left the *hacienda* and rode toward Torreón. When *don* Bernardo rode past the guest house, he did not notice the door was closed and the children were not playing in the yard. Once they crossed under the entrance to the *hacienda, don* Bernardo told the men to split up – two left and two right. He knew if *bandidos* followed *don* Alejandro from the bank, they would have attacked him, left him for dead, and taken the gold – his gold.

They rode in zigzag patterns across the plain. Mariano checked near the lake, nothing. *Don* Bernardo scoured the foothills. They rode all afternoon, returning to the *hacienda* just before dark. *Don* Bernardo was exhausted. His body ached.

"Brandy," he growled at his servant when he arrived back to the main house.

The next morning *don* Bernardo rose and dressed. His head hurt, but his back hurt worse. He knew he must go to town and talk to the banker himself. He should have done it yesterday. He rang for his manservant and told him to get Mariano and to call for his carriage.

Mariano was waiting when he walked outside. *Don* Bernardo climbed into the carriage and Mariano followed his boss on horseback. An hour later the carriage pulled up in front of the bank. *Don* Bernardo stormed into the bank and immediately pushed into Gregorio's office.

"What kind of bank are you running?" he demanded.

"What do you mean? I run a good bank, *don* Bernardo," the banker insisted.

"Where is my gold? Where is *don* Alejandro and my gold?" he growled at the nervous banker.

"I told your man yesterday, *don* Alejandro came here in the morning, picked up the gold, and left."

"Where did he go?" *don* Bernardo demanded.

"To your *hacienda, señor.* He said he was going directly to meet you."

"*Mierda*, why didn't you send a bodyguard with him?" *don* Bernardo cursed. "With that much gold, *bandidos* probably robbed him on the road."

Gregorio was insulted. "Perhaps you should have sent one of your men to protect him, *señor.*"

Don Bernardo turned on his heels without a word. Mariano waited by the door. "Where do you want to search now, *jefe?*"

"Follow me."

The hotel was only across the plaza, but *don* Bernardo took the carriage. A conversation with the hotel clerk confirmed *don* Alejandro packed, paid, and left two days ago. He paid for two rooms. He left the same morning as his *vaquero*. He left the hotel on foot. His horse and wagon were stabled at the livery.

"Check the livery for his horse," *don* Bernardo ordered Mariano. "Meet me at the restaurant."

"*Buenos días, señor,*" a waiter greeted *don* Bernardo.

"*Desayuno y café,*" he ordered breakfast.

Where the hell was *don* Alejandro? The thought of losing the gold enraged him. He needed the gold to pay Carmela. Well into his breakfast Mariano rode up. He walked to the table and waited to be acknowledged.

"Well, I assume his horse is gone," *don* Bernardo said gruffly. Mariano knew his *jefe* was angry and must not be crossed in any way. He held his hat carefully in his hands and kept his eyes low.

"Yes, and his wagon. The livery man said he took the wagon and horse a couple days ago," Mariano replied.

Don Bernardo grumbled and fumed. "Disappeared, just disappeared," he gruffed.

"Go back to the *hacienda* and gather as many men as you can. Scour the hills and find him, dead or alive," *don* Bernardo commanded.

Mariano was going to ask his *jefe* whether he should take the old buggy at the livery back to the *hacienda*, but thought better of it. He rode quickly back and gathered some men. If they did not find the *Norte Americano*, *don* Bernardo would be furious.

By the time *don* Bernardo returned to the *hacienda*, he was angry and exhausted. He climbed the stairs to his bedroom and rang for his manservant. He undressed and stretched back on the bed.

"Go and bring María."

"*Sí, patrón,*" the manservant replied.

Staring at the ceiling, he fumed. His back was hurting and he needed María to massage it. She knew how to stop the pain and then he would take his anger out on her.

"*Patrón, María no está en casa,*" the manservant said breathless upon his return.

"*¿Como qué no está en casa?*" *don* Bernardo asked the manservant what he meant that she was not home.

"No one is there, *señor.*"

"Not even the old woman and the children?"

"No, no one, *señor.*"

"Go find her and find the children," he yelled. "Bring her to me."

What was going on? First, *don* Alejandro was missing, now María and the children. Nothing made sense. Worst of all the gold was gone – his gold was gone.

"*Pinche babosa.* Where was María? Where was her mother?"

The trouble-making old woman was a thorn in his side. In fact, the whole family had been nothing but trouble to him. Her *pinche* son shot him and made his life miserable. It was only because María bore him a son that he tolerated them. He should have tossed them out in the cold.

He heard shouting and horses in the courtyard. Perhaps Mariano found *don* Alejandro. *Don* Bernardo pulled on his boots and limped downstairs.

"*Jefe,* we have ridden in every direction and have found nothing," Mariano reported.

"Nothing!"

Mariano held is head low. "*Nada señor.*"

"Go look again," *don* Bernardo screamed, "and don't come back without him."

CHAPTER 40

Xihuitl, the Healer, obeyed the Chichimeca chief and turned away from the village. He walked the donkey to a level spot under a nearby cottonwood tree. Untying the bundles carried by the donkey, the old medicine man erected his small traveling tent. The two curious brothers helped him. The tent, more like an awning, stretched on a rope between two trees. It took all three to carry the man and carefully place him under the tent. Xihuitl made sure the tent shaded the injured man from the sun.

Bending over the injured man, Xihuitl looked again at the star pattern on the man's chest left by the shattered turquoise amulet. Xihuitl believed the star shape on the man's chest was a sign from the Aztec Goddess Coatlicue, the Goddess of life and death as taught by the ancient Aztec legends. Xihuitl's parents secretly practiced the old ways, the ways of their ancestors, the Aztec. They named him Xihuitl, meaning comet, because he was born in a year when a comet was visible to the south of Mexico City. They chose to speak *Nahuatl,* the ancient language of the Aztecs.

At the age of twelve, Xihuitl's parents took him to Tonauac, a shaman who practiced the Aztec healing methods. After their first meeting, the old shaman took Xihuitl as an apprentice. The years Xihuitl practiced with Tonauac were the best years of his life. He soaked up all the knowledge Tonauac imparted on him and by the age of twenty Xihuitl was curing people by himself.

Tonauac instilled in Xihuitl a belief in the power of the ancient Aztec Gods. The star was the Goddess Coatlicue's symbol, and Xihuitl remembered her statue standing at the foot of the Sun pyramid facing the Moon pyramid in Teotihuacán with a star on her chest. The Goddess's sign was clear and Xihuitl was bound by the power of the Goddess to save this man.

Xihuitl, now fifty-six years old, took Tonauac's advice

and became a traveling healer. "Take the knowledge I have taught you and take it to the people," Tonauac told him before he died. He had spent the last thirty years, mostly on the back of a horse, traveling from village to village tending to the sick and injured. His mission brought him to a Chichimeca village just southeast of Torreón several weeks ago. Now, the Goddess brought him this injured man to take care of.

The Healer asked the young Chichimeca brothers to gather wood and bring it to him. He also asked them to refill his water gourd. The boys happily trundled off on their assignments. He asked Pomac to retrieve a pot and some herbs from his tent in the village.

"I cannot leave this man," he told the boys. Actually, Xihuitl was tired. His old body ached from the long and bumpy ride. Lifting the almost dead man had hurt his back and he knew the boys had energy to burn.

By the time the boys returned, the Healer had prepared a place in the dirt and ringed it with rocks for a fire. Pomac returned with his arms full of sticks and grasses, while Katu dragged a large dead branch. Pomac piled the grasses and sticks in the pit and quickly flinted it into a small fire.

"Can we stay here with you tonight?" Katu asked him. We will sleep by the fire and keep it going for you." Xihuitl smiled and nodded in agreement. He knew any distraction, in the otherwise simple world of these two young boys, was welcome. "Can you find me some roots?" he asked them. "I'll make a stew."

The boys ran off in excitement. Xihuitl poured water into a pot and set it on the fire. It boiled quickly. From a small pouch, he took dried leaves of water nettle to fight infection. He stirred the pot and set it on the edge of the fire where it continued to boil slowly.

The injured man under the tent had not moved. Xihuitl unsaddled the man's horse and using the saddle and a blanket, propped the man's head up slightly. His head was still bleeding a bit where it had hit the rock.

He removed the man's shirt, carefully cutting the

sleeves so he did not have to move him. The mangled silver star amulet hung around his neck. Five pieces of turquoise were embedded deep into his chest. Xihuitl carefully pulled the amulet over the man's head. Cradling it in his hand, he did not think he had ever seen anything like it before. The bullet had molded it into a mangled lump of silver. There was a bloody hole in the man's chest where the amulet had stopped the force of the bullet.

After a few minutes, he took the pot from the fire and dipped strips of the man's shirt into the hot herbal medicine. He placed the wet strips on the man's chest. The hot strips would soak the crusted blood and cleanse the wounds. The Healer repeated this procedure several times. After the third time, he was able to gently dig the five pieces of turquoise out of the man's chest, adding them to the other pieces he had saved in a small leather pouch.

The man's chest did not look too bad. The small wounds would heal quickly. The larger one, where the amulet gouged the man's chest, he packed with herbs and wrapped it with the hot strips. At least he did not have to dig out the bullet. It was lodged in the amulet.

Xihuitl finished with his medicine and exited the tent. He turned the amulet over in his hand. A silver star encrusted with turquoise was not a symbol of any tribes he knew in Mexico. He thought it could be from northern tribes, like the Navajo or Apache, but why was this man wearing it? He was not an Indian. He was a *mestizo*, but somewhat taller than most mixed-blooded Mexicans and his clothing was different from that worn by the local *vaqueros*.

Katu and Pomac returned with a few vegetables – shriveled onions, cassava roots, and wild turnips. Xihuitl cleaned them and put them in a pot to boil.

"You have done well," he praised the boys. "Watch, I will show you some magic." Xihuitl entertained the boys with simple tricks. They howled and screamed with delight. "Ah, to be young again," he mused. "Life was so simple."

For three days, Rafe raged with fever. Xihuitl dressed his wounds daily and when the man was slightly conscious, he poured little sips of water down his throat. Rafe was not sure if he was dreaming or awake. He stared at a tan cloth over his head wondering why it flapped in the wind. At times, he felt the presence of an old man, other times children. He had blurry dreams of snow, guns and horses.

Xihuitl wondered at the words the man repeated. "Chiwiwi. Chiwiwi." He acted like he was calling to someone, growled and groaned and then calmed into sleep.

On the fourth day, Rafe awakened more fully. He looked at an old man stooped by a fire, but did not know him. He tried to talk, but no words came to his mouth. The old man gave him water and fed him a bit of broth. Rafe was grateful and liked the tune the man hummed. By the fifth day, Rafe was almost fully conscious. The old man came to him and helped him to sit up and drink a little water.

"¿Como te llamas?" Xihuitl asked him his name.

Rafe pondered the question. What was his name? Odd, he must have a name, but he could not remember.

"I don't know," Rafe answered. Everything in his mind seemed fuzzy. He had a terrible pounding in the back of his head and there was a ringing in his ears.

"I am Xihuitl," the old man said patting Rafe's shoulder.

Rafe attempted to get up, but fell back. It felt like someone had kicked him on his chest. Exhausted by the effort, he lay back on the blanket.

"What happened to me? Where am I?" Rafe asked confused.

"You were shot," the old Healer said. "You hit your head on a rock. Do you remember being shot?"

"No." Everything was a blur and his head throbbed.

"No worry, you will remember in time," Xihuitl told him.

"Where am I?" Rafe asked again.

"You are outside a Chichimeca village. Two Chichimeca boys found you."

"Who are you?" Rafe asked.

"I am Xihuitl, a *tepahtiani*, a healer. I was visiting this village when the two boys found you. The Chichimeca do not like outsiders and know nothing of medicine. You would have died, if I had not been visiting here. The Goddess was with you."

"Gracias," was all Rafe said. He tried to remember who he was, but only vague memories of faces, houses, and horses floated in his brain. The more he tried to remember, the more his head ached. Exhausted, he eased back down on the blanket and promptly fell asleep.

Katu and Pomac came running to the tent. A young rabbit dangled in Katu's hand. "I caught a rabbit for you Healer," he bragged.

"Well done boys. The rabbit will make a good stew. Now go, and play quietly for he needs his sleep. Come back for rabbit stew tonight." Xihuitl shooed the two happy boys off.

He turned to look at Rafe. "If you do not know your name, I will call you Citlalin. It means star in *Nahuatl*, because it was your star amulet that saved you," he said to the sleeping man.

Chapter 41

Three days from Torreón, María finally stopped complaining, and was feeling a little better, but the bumpy ride hurt her back. She noticed Carlos, the young *grandee*, treated her and her mother with dignity. Antonio was enthralled with the trip and often rode up in the driver's seat with Carlos, excitedly chattering along the way. Tiny Alicia wanted to sit in her mother's lap, but thankfully Celiá enticed the baby to sit with her.

"Tomorrow we'll be in El Paso," Carlos told them. Celiá and Carlos exchanged a worried look. Rafe had not caught up with them. He should have two days ago.

Celiá had asked, but Carlos shrugged and said, "He'll be along. Don't worry."

The trip was uneventful, but Carlos kept a close eye on their back trail. Nothing that looked like a posse of *vaqueros* ever came into view. Only wagons that plied the trail, up and down, and some lone riders. The women appreciated that the wagon was stocked with blankets and food, because they had taken nothing from the *casita*. Carlos even produced a few toys and sugar sweets for the children.

Carlos told Celiá, "We'll stop in El Paso and rest for a few days at Jose's. He and Lupe will be happy to see you."

"It will be good to stop and rest. Rafael will meet us there," Celiá said hopefully.

"Yes," Carlos replied, "perhaps he is already there." Carlos prayed that Rafe had taken a back route to El Paso. Perhaps he had to run from *don* Bernardo and avoided the main road, but deep inside Carlos knew something was wrong. The last time he saw him, Rafe was headed to the *hacienda* to meet *don* Bernardo and round up the horses.

Don Bernardo turned to his manservant and bellowed, "Where are María and the children? Where could they go?"

"They are not here at the *hacienda, patrón*," the servant

informed him.

Don Bernardo limped his way to the guest cottage and opened the door to find everything in place – clean, tidy, but empty. Their clothes, the children's extra shoes, their blankets, everything was in place. Even tortillas sat on the table, dry and hard.

"They can't have vanished!"

"No one has seen them in a few days. The boy in the barn thinks they took the buggy to town a couple days ago to see the doctor," his servant said. "Two, maybe three days ago. The buggy has not been returned."

"*Me cago en esa vieja y su hija que es puta,*" he screamed a Spanish curse on the old woman and her whore of a daughter.

At sun up the next morning, *don* Bernardo called for his horse to be saddled. He rode with Mariano and Enrique to the livery in Torreón.

"*Buenos días. ¿Has venido para su vagón, señor?*" the liveryman asked him if he had come for his buggy.

"When did you get the buggy?" the *don* demanded.

"I think it was three days ago. The man said you would pick it up soon."

"What man?" *don* Bernardo asked his face reddening and puffed out.

"*Don Alejandro, señor,*" the liveryman replied.

Mariano held his breath. If the liveryman told *don* Bernardo that he knew the buggy was here, *el jefe* would shoot him dead.

Murder raged in *don* Bernardo's heart. He knew now, he had been tricked by *don* Alejandro, but who was he? Then, he thought about the look on the *vaquero's* face just before he shot him. Those eyes belonged to someone he knew.

Turning to Mariano he said, "You two head north and find *don* Alejandro. He has María. Bring her and the children back and kill the *Americano* and the old woman."

Don Bernardo mounted and spurred his horse into a gallop. He rode as fast as his frail body could stand to where he left the body of the *vaquero* in the canyon. He wanted to search the *vaquero's* body and his belongings for any clues to help him find *don* Alejandro. Reaching the spot where he shot the *vaquero*, the body was gone and so was the saddle. The only sign left was a dried puddle of blood and hair on a rock where the *vaquero* hit his head when he fell.

"*Ayyyeeee*," he screamed and it echoed throughout the canyon.

Unbeknown to *don* Bernardo, Carlos and his precious cargo reached El Paso, Texas. They continued north to Jose's *rancho*. Lupe cried when she hugged Celiá and María. Jose gave Carlos a big *abrazo*.

"Where is Rafael?" Celiá asked anxiously. "Is he here?"

"No, isn't he with you?" Jose replied confused.

"He was in Torreón at *don* Bernardo's *hacienda* looking at the horses," Carlos said. "We have not seen him since."

"Come," Lupe said wisely. "Let's get the children and María settled. You have had a long hard trip. God will bring Rafael to us soon."

Over supper, Jose and Lupe told Celiá and María they were welcome to stay as long as they wanted. "We have everything you need because of Rafael," Jose beamed and spread his arms. "Your Rafael bought all of this for us. He is a good man and God will protect him."

"We will only stay long enough to rest a few days," Carlos said. "We must go to Santa Fe. El Paso is too close to Mexico and *don* Bernardo could easily send his *vaqueros* here to find us."

Four days behind them *don* Bernardo's *vaqueros*, Mariano and Enrique, started north on the trail to El Paso searching for María and the children.

CHAPTER 42

Xihuitl had been nursing Rafe for almost two weeks before he was able to walk, but with pain in his chest. His chest was black and blue from the impact of the bullet and Xihuitl thought he had a broken rib. The back of his head had a large crusty scab.

The Healer showed Rafe the bent and twisted amulet that had saved his life, but Rafe did not recognize it. "It was covered in turquoise," the Healer told him, "but the turquoise was shattered by the bullet."

Together they searched his saddlebags. A clean shirt, a few pieces of jerky, and a pistol gave Rafe no clues about his identity. His shirt and jacket, which had been ruined by the bullet, spoke that he was a *vaquero*. Xihuitl told Rafe he was a *mestizo*, part Indian and part Spaniard. Rafe nodded with a blank look on his face. "Yes, but who am I?" When Rafe slept, he dreamt of horses, hills, snow, and unknown faces that were clear and then blurry.

"Citlalin, tomorrow I must continue my travels, but I cannot leave you here with the Chichimeca. Do you think you can travel?" Xihuitl asked his patient.

"I will try," Rafe answered struggling to stand upright without pain. Riding would be hard, but the Chichimeca were not friendly. "Why are the Chichimeca afraid of me?" he asked.

"The ancient Spaniards chased the Chichimeca into the hills. For many generations they have lived as nomads. Now, they try to live in peace, but the ancient stories make them afraid of Spaniards," Xihuitl said. "It is so with many of the tribes."

"Come out and eat. It will be dark soon. You must get a good night's rest for we will leave in the morning."

Rafe slept and the foggy dreams came again. Tonight, an evil-faced man shot at him, and then the image disappeared. When Rafe woke the next morning, the old Healer was packed and ready to go.

Xihuitl handed Rafe a simple, worn *sarape*. The dark blue wool was faded with years of use. With the *sarape*, the old man handed him a simple cotton *camisa*, *pantalones*, and a straw hat. "Wear these," he said. "You will travel as my apprentice."

The Healer set a steady pace, knowing the jarring pain would tire the young man.

"Where are we going?" Rafe asked.

"We are going to the southeastern foothills of the Sierra Madre," Xihuitl answered. "I am a traveling medicine man. Many of these people do not have any healer and the old ways have been forgotten."

"Do you have a home?"

"I was born in a small village east of the ancient holy city of Teotihuacán, but I spend most of my life on the back of a horse," he chortled. "You are much better company than that gray donkey."

Many miles later, the Healer saw Rafe sagging in his saddle. "How are you?" he asked.

"My head hurts, but my chest hurts worse," Rafe answered.

"Do you want to stop?"

"No," Rafe mustered. The Healer set a slower pace. He knew of a village not too many miles ahead. He hoped they could reach it before nightfall.

The sun blazed down over the distant horizon before they saw smoke rising from a distant village. "A Tepehuán village," Xihuitl said. "We will be welcome there, but do not speak, just nod, and keep your straw hat low over your face," he instructed Rafe.

The pain in Rafe's chest was excruciating. He was in no condition to do anything but nod. All he wanted was to get off this horse and lie down.

CHAPTER 43

By the time Tomás came back with his wagon, Ed had pulled Carmen's body out from under the tree and covered it with his coat. They carefully placed her in the back of the wagon and covered her body with a canvas tarp. They agreed to keep the body and the location of the crime scene a secret for now.

"Did you find any clues as to who might have done this?" Tomás asked Ed.

"There are what looks like boot heel marks, but rain has mostly washed them away. It looks like her clothes were thrown in the river. I found this torn shirt clinging to a branch down river a little way. It looks like the one she often wore," Ed replied.

They took Carmen's body to Johnny Fields house in San Marcial for examination. Walking out of the back room drying his hands, Johnny looked at Tomás and Ed who were waiting in his living room.

"The body has decayed," Johnny said. "For sure the woman was raped. Her vagina is bruised and her face and arms are bruised. She died of a skull fracture. She was hit twice, so not sure which blow killed her," he talked in a matter-of-fact way. "The most interesting thing I found was a piece of someone's ear in her mouth," Johnny reported.

"What?" Ed asked shocked. "An ear?"

"Well, I'm pretty sure it's an ear. I think she bit her attacker before she died."

"So you're sure it wasn't Apaches," Ed asked the medic.

"Well, I never saw an Indian attack like this, so I guess I'd say it wasn't redskins." Johnny replied.

"Ed, help me put her in the wagon. I want both of you to keep quiet about the ear," Tomás said. "It may be our only clue." Both men agreed.

"Johnny, please make out a report and Ed and I will

sign it as witness. I will give it to the Sheriff when he comes from Socorro." Tomás extended a hand to the medic. *"Gracias."*

After Tomás left with the wagon, Ed went to the hotel and cleaned up. There was a note on the counter for him to ride out to the construction site signed by John Sutton.

Following the road, Ed had trouble getting the gruesome image of Carmen out of his mind. He rode by the turnoff to the crime scene and shuddered. He wondered who would do such a thing and about Lucas, half out of his mind looking for his wife.

Now that he knew the Apaches were not at fault, he realized the village had a bigger problem. There was a rapist and murderer amongst them. He sure hoped the sheriff from Socorro would get here soon.

Tomás took Carmen's body to the part time undertaker. Together they carried the covered body into the embalming room.

"Peeuuwww," the undertaker said. "This one's pretty ripe. Is it the woman?"

"Yes, can you preserve the body until we find her husband?" Tomás asked.

"Yes, but not for long, maybe a week at the most, maybe less" he said.

"Was it *Indios?*" The undertaker peeked at the woman under the canvas.

"No," Tomás said, "but you must keep this quiet until the sheriff gets here."

When Ed arrived at the construction site, he found John and Cynthia standing in the living room of the half-finished ranchhouse. Only the well digger was working out in the yard, otherwise the site was quiet. He listened at the doorway as Cynthia was telling John how she wanted to decorate the rooms. She was giddy as she twirled around the unfinished living room. Ed quietly watched Cynthia throw her arms around John in a happy hug.

"Ed, glad yew made it," John said when he spotted him near the door.

"It's wonderful," Cynthia purred in a southern drawl.

"Yes, it is coming along just like the drawings," John added.

"I can't wait until it's done," Cynthia said grabbing her husband's hand. Wanting to please her, John's mood changed abruptly.

"Why cain't we git these greasers back to work? Damn superstitious greasers are scared of their own shadows. Git a fire under that new carpenter and git this work done." John demanded. "Like I told yew yesterday, pay these greasers more iffin yew have to. I want this place finished!"

"I'll do my best, Mr. Sutton," Ed said seriously.

"I expect this place done by the end of the month. No excuses. If yew have to force these damn greasers at gunpoint, then do it!"

John Sutton turned his back on Seeley, loaded his wife into the buggy, and snapped the reins. Ed stood watching them disappear, and shook his head hoping he could get the workers back on the job soon, now that Carmen's body had been found and it was not Indians.

At Big Ed's Saloon, Butcherknife Bill and Jed were having a drink when a man burst in with the news of the woman's body. "Not Apaches!" he shouted. "The woman was raped and beaten."

Bill's stomach churned. The ruse to blame the Apaches had not worked. Bill did not want to hang for killing a greaser all because of Ponyboy George.

More and more locals drifted into the saloon as the news spread. Big Ed was not there, but a young local tended bar. Several more locals came in with pistols and wooden clubs.

"We think its you, you *Tejanos* that killed her," one big villager said turning to Bill and Jed.

"Don't go spoutin yer bazoo greaser," Bill said, but the room of angry eyes were all looking at him.

"You *Tejanos* get out of our town," the man retorted. "You've been nothing but trouble since you came here."

Bill had always seen the Mexicans cower and tremble at their sight, but this group was angry and not afraid. He could see it in their eyes. They outnumbered him and Jed by four to one. Bill was not used to backing down, especially to greasers.

"Go back to yer dirt farm, greaser," Bill grumbled. "We ain't dun nuttin to this lousy shitheel town."

Fifteen angry men surrounded the two Texans at their table. "We're done taking your shit," Ramiro said with a club in his large hand. "You've been causing trouble, shooting up our town, and scaring our women. Now get out!"

Bill and Jed looked at the mob. Bill burned with fury, but this was not the time to teach these greasers a lesson.

"Cum on Jed," Bill said. "The stench of Mescans is getting to me." The mob made a path for the two men to leave.

Bill and Jed mounted up and rode down the street. The group of men turned back to the saloon laughing and slapping each other on the back. *"Eeeyaa,"* one yelled. In the distance they heard gunfire as the Texans rode out of town.

By the time Ed got back to his saloon, word of the dead woman's body and it wasn't Apaches who killed her, had spread all over town, despite Tomás' wishes to keep it quiet.

About fifteen locals hung in the saloon talking about making a posse.

"A posse after who?" Ed asked.

"After them *pinche Tejanos,*" Ramiro said. "They've brought only trouble since they got here."

"Sí," another said. "We have to send them all back to *Tejas,* like we ran off those two."

"What?" Ed asked.

"We told the *Tejanos* to leave. That big one and another," Gerardo piped up.

Ed noticed several of the men had pieces of wood and a couple had old pistols stuffed behind their belts.

"You men are no match for those cowboys," Ed said. "Besides it coudda been anyone who did it, even someone not from our town."

CHAPTER 44

As Rafe and Xihuitl neared the Tepehuán village, they saw huts made of cut logs with straw and mud roofs. Children ran to them and around the horses, giggling and pushing each other. When they reached the center of the village, a small man with a feather-adorned palm hat stepped out of a large hut and signaled a greeting.

"*Cualli tonalli Cacique* Kukuduli," Xihuitl called out a greeting in his native *Nahuatl* language to the village chief.

"*Cualli tonalli,*" the Chief answered. Xihuitl signaled at Rafe to remain on his horse. The Healer and the Chief went inside the large hut.

"I am glad you are here, my friend," Kukuduli said. "Who is with you?"

"My apprentice, Citlalin. He was bucked from his horse and is in need of rest," the Healer said.

"It will be so." Kukuduli clapped his hands to call a woman who was waiting outside. He told her to make the young apprentice comfortable.

The woman came out from the chief's hut and motioned for Rafe to follow. Pain seared in his chest with each step of the horse after the long day of riding. Rafe slid off his horse and followed her into a small hut. Gingerly, he crawled onto a bed of skins and almost immediately fell asleep.

In the Chief's hut, a servant brought two cups of a warm drink and handed them to the Healer and the Chief. They sat across from each other discussing old times and past visits of the Healer.

"I am glad you have come, Xihuitl. My grandson was also thrown from a horse. Ugai, our medicine man, has been chanting and making spells for three days, but I fear the boy grows worse. He has much pain," the Chief said.

"Take me to the boy. I will have a look at him."

Xihuitl gathered his sack of medicines from the donkey and followed Kukuduli down a path past several small huts. Kukuduli pushed aside the woven grass door to a hut for Xihuitl to pass and wafts of incense filled the air. Ugai was bent over a young boy who looked to be about ten or eleven years old. The boy was moaning and crying. Ugai was wearing a palm cap, formed to his head just above the ears, with a thin cone shape about six inches tall and three black feathers stuck out the top. He was chanting and waving his hands over the boy's body.

"Ugai, I bring Xihuitl, the Aztec healer. Perhaps he can help you with my grandson," the Chief said interrupting the medicine man. Ugai's trance-like actions continued until Kukuduli touched his shoulder, bringing Ugai out of his trance and the chanting stopped.

"I bring Xihuitl, the Aztec healer, to help you, Ugai," the Chief repeated.

"His are not the ways of our people," Ugai protested.

"Ugai, we respect the ways of the Aztec healer and he has helped us in the past. Let Xihuitl examine my grandson," the Chief demanded.

Ugai nodded obediently and moved aside. After the examination, Xihuitl determined the boy had a broken leg, probably broken ribs, and many bruises. He told the Chief the boy would live and requested the cloths and sticks he needed to set the leg.

"First, I must make a tea to reduce his pain and make him sleep," the Healer said. Several hours later, they left the boy who was sleeping quietly. His leg was set and bound tightly with leather straps. Cloths soaked in herbs were wrapped tightly around his chest to relieve the pain of the broken ribs and to heal the bruises.

"Keep the cloths wet with the herb water," Xihuitl instructed a woman who was helping. "Give the boy more tea if he is in pain."

In the hut where Rafe slept, images of a room in the Isleta village haunted Rafe's dream. His body lay on a bed of soft skins. A girl with long dark hair turned her head to look at him. She opened her mouth as if to speak to him, but a hand shook Rafe's shoulder instead. "Citlalin, Citlalin, wake up." The words sounded far off.

"Citlalin, it's time to wake up," the voice came again. The images disappeared and Rafe awakened groggy. The Healer was pushing his shoulder. "Citlalin, come. Kukuduli has ordered a feast in our honor," Xihuitl told him.

As Rafe and Xihuitl walked to the center of the village the women smiled, looking up from their labors, and children tugged at their pantlegs. The villagers were dressed in loose woven cotton *pantalones* and *camisas* with colorful kerchiefs around their necks. The women wore colorful skirts. Most wore hats woven out of palm leaves. The sounds of joyous laughter and cooking meat filled the air.

Rafe was suddenly ravenous. He and the Healer had not eaten since morning. The Chief smiled and motioned for them to sit. In the middle of the open area, men were stacking wood for a large fire. Women brought them cooked roots, pieces of venison, and flat corn tortillas. Rafe devoured the food and a woman offered him more.

As night darkened, the fire was lit. The village men sat circling the bonfire. The fire licked strands of orange into the sky and tiny flaming embers spit high into the night. Soon a drum and bowstring played a mesmerizing tune. Young girls dressed in tunics adorned with feathers and beads danced around the fire in cadence with the drumbeat. As Rafe watched the ritual dance, another flashed in his mind. Maidens with red cords in their hair swirled across his mind, but just as quickly the image disappeared. Shaking his head, he wished he could remember.

For several days, Rafe and Xihuitl stayed in the Tepehuán village. Rafe help the Healer with the Chief's grandson. The boy's fever finally broke and Rafe carved a simple crutch from a young sapling for the boy. The villagers spoke some Spanish, but Xihuitl warned him to watch and listen. "Keep to yourself," he warned. "They will accept you as my apprentice, but may not as a *mestizo.*"

A week later, Xihuitl and Rafe saddled their horses and Xihuitl packed the donkey. Several villagers gathered in the early morning light. One of the women gave Rafe a woven bag with red and white stripes and a red cord for carrying on his shoulder. Rafe nodded and thanked the woman. Another woman handed Xihuitl a food sack. Slowly, they walked the horses out of the village headed west.

The ten days at the Tepehuán village allowed Rafe to rest and heal. He noticed riding was not as painful. The scab on Rafe's head was almost gone and only the deepest wound on his chest had not healed. The rest and food at the village had helped heal his body, but not his memory.

CHAPTER 45

The *vaqueros* returned empty handed to *don* Bernardo's *hacienda*. They had stayed on the trail an extra day, afraid to give their *patrón* the bad news. They went as far north as El Paso and found nothing.

"Did you find the uncle, the one who came here?" *don* Bernardo growled.

"*Sí, patrón*. We went to the uncle's ranch, but they were not there. He said he did not know where they were."

"Did you search El Paso?"

"*Sí, patrón*. We hid and waited for over a day. They are not in El Paso. They are gone."

The old *don* dismissed the *vaqueros* and called for brandy. He paced the length of his parlor – hobbling, drinking, and cursing Celiá. *"Me cago en esa familia desgraciada y la puta madre que los parió." Don* Bernardo went into a tirade saying, "I shit upon that wretched family and the whore of a mother that bore them."

He raged against Celiá. It was her *bastardo* son who shot him and left him mangled, and now he knew she took María and the children away from him. *"Aaayyee,"* he growled knowing she bested him again.

Long ago, Celiá was young and beautiful, more beautiful than her daughter María. Young *don* Bernardo watched her tending to her chores at the *hacienda*. With each passing day, his lust for her escalated. He had grown tired of Carmela's body and she had not bore him a child. One day the young *don* caught Celiá alone near the lake.

Don Bernardo still remembered the curve of her breast. Her skin was velvety smooth. She fought him, pounding her small fists into his chest. He tried to be gentle. *"Shhh, querida,"* he whispered. "I will not hurt you." He kissed her sweet lips, moving down her neck to her nipples. She squirmed and hit at him, only making him want her more.

His *garrancha* strained in his pants, while he tried to

caress and calm her. When he was bursting with desire, he thrust inside her and she screamed. Her soft folds enveloped his *garrancha*, exquisitely tightening around it. He thrust and waited and then thrust again. With each thrust his desire heightened. Her sweet wetness rubbed tightly all around his *pene*. She screamed and tried to bite him, squirming to get away, but he held her tight.

Her fiery dark eyes flashed at him in anger. Quieting her with his mouth over hers, he finally exploded inside her – excruciating, powerful, and delightful. He held her tightly trying to catch his breath.

Mounting Carmela had become boring. She was amenable, but had lost her passion. Usually, she lay quietly while he relieved his manhood needs. Taking Celiá awakened all of his lust. He imagined many nights of sweet love in her arms. She would learn to love him. He would teach her to satisfy him and give him sweet kisses. He was a good lover, of that he was sure.

Underneath him, Celiá's black eyes glared. The *haciendero* brute held her captive. The more she squirmed, the tighter his hold. She could barely breathe. Slowly, he raised his head and kissed her, demanding her mouth meet his. She screamed, but there was no one to hear her. It would not do any good anyway. He was the *haciendero* and no *peón* would stop him.

Don Bernardo tried to kiss her and soothe her. He ran his hand gently over her breast, playing with the nipple. Tenderly, he kissed her again and his *garrancha* swelled quickly. More gently this time, he pushed inside her wet folds. She did not scream, but there was fire in her eyes. *Don* Bernardo pulled her legs around him and pulled her to him. He drew long and steady thrusts, each one rippling quivers throughout his body. The sensation was almost impossible to bear, and he did not want it to end. He slowed down to calm himself and then started again. He wanted it to last forever. Finally, he could no longer hold his passion and burst within her. A guttural groan escaped from his lips, and spent, he fell on her.

Celiá wanted to kill him, but he was the *haciendero*. He

had total power and control over the *peóns,* as if they were his slaves – in essence they were. Without money and land, they worked for the pittance a *haciendero* provided.

Finally, *don* Bernardo released her from his grasp. She jumped up and ran. She spit near him when she left.

Three weeks later, Celiá married Antonio Estrada de Escalante, a young *peón* at the *hacienda.* She knew Antonio was interested in her. When she knew she was pregnant, she agreed to the marriage. Antonio suspected the baby was not his, but loved Rafael all the same.

Don Bernardo fumed at the marriage. Raping a young girl was one thing, but raping a married woman was not allowed. Celiá had bested him and he hated her. When she bore a son, he wondered if it was his, and she even named the boy, Rafael, like *don* Bernardo's grandfather. He watched as the boy grew into a lad. Yes, he was a Reyes, *don* Bernardo knew it, but he swore he would never acknowledge the bastard, never.

Chapter 46

Ramón Moreno, the deputy sheriff from Socorro, arrived in San Marcial on Wednesday morning trailing two prisoners with him. After tying them to a tree in Tomás' yard, the deputy gratefully accepted a cool lemonade before sitting down in one of the overstuffed chairs in Tomás' living room. Tomás handed him the official report written by Johnny Fields, San Marcial's medic.

"Raped and beaten," he said after reading it. "The report says the woman had what looked like a piece of ear in her mouth," the deputy said.

"Yes, Johnny took it out and cleaned it up and thought that's what it looked like," Tomás said.

"What part of the ear was it?" the deputy asked.

"We think it was from the top," Tomás answered.

"Have you looked to see if any man is missing the top part of his ear?"

"I know every man in San Marcial. I would know if it was someone from town."

"What about Apaches?" the deputy asked.

"Possible, but she didn't have any wounds like an Apache attack. No arrows, no scalping," Tomás said. "I think it might be one of the Texans."

"Have you checked them?"

"No. They are scattered on the range and besides I don't think they will cooperate. I can't prove anything, but I think one of them took a shot and wounded Bartolo when we were looking for evidence. Can you check the cowboys?" Tomás asked the deputy.

"No, I'm sorry. I need to get the two prisoners to Socorro for a hearing. As soon as I get done with that I'll come back and you and I can go check the cowboys," the deputy said.

Tomás thanked him and hoped the deputy would be back soon and they could find the murderer.

Ed Seeley stood behind the bar when John Sutton

came downstairs. John walked directly up to the bar and said, "Damn greasers still won't work. Yew said they would go back to work after that woman was found. It warn't Apaches, I heard tell." His voice was hard and angry.

"People are still upset," Ed replied. "They still don't know who raped and killed her."

"Dreadful, just dreadful," Cynthia chimed in. Neither man had heard her come down the stairs. "I don't blame the people for being scared. The women are scared. I heard them talking at the mercantile."

"Shut up. Stupid greaser women are scaring their men," John snapped at her, then softened his tone. "They shouldn't be afraid of Apaches any more, my dear." Cynthia was shocked at her husband's attitude. She was scared to go much further than the mercantile without him with her.

"I need to git these greasers back to workin on the ranchhouse," Sutton told Ed. "I don't care what it costs. Git em workin again," he almost shouted. "We need breakfast," he said without any cordiality.

John and Cynthia sat a table and Ed brought breakfast. "I'm sorry, darlin iffin I snapped at yew," John said. "I just don't understand these lazy greasers that won't work."

Cynthia patted his hand appeasing him. "It will get finished," she said brightly. "I'm going to the mercantile and order fabric for the draperies. The seamstress said she'll make them up for us."

The batwing doors slammed against the wall and Butcherknife Bill strode in. "Them damn greasers broke down the corral and scattered the hosses," Bill reported sliding up in front of Sutton. "Dragged the corral posts into a pile and burned them."

"What!" Sutton replied. "When?"

"Late last night. By the time the boys got outta bed, they ran like rabbits, but the new corral is gone and mosta the hosses, too. Jed and Pewee are roundin em up."

"Git the boys together," Sutton growled. "Pull em off the range. Meet me at the camp."

John stood up. Cynthia reached for his arm. "John B, maybe it wasn't the people from town," she said. "Don't start trouble or they'll never finish the house."

"Keep yer place woman," he grumbled at her. "This is man's business." Turning, he walked out of the saloon.

Ed came over to pick up the breakfast dishes. "Sorry ma'am. The people in the town think one of the cowboys may have killed the woman."

"My husband's cowboys?" she asked.

"Yes," Ed replied.

"But, they are all good men," she said. "John B says so."

Ed did not know what to say. Good was a relative term. "Don't worry ma'am, I'm sure the murderer will be found," he told her.

Ed overheard both the locals and the cowboys. Anger was boiling over, one side against the other. The Texans had come to town full of spit and zeal and guns firing. The quiet peaceful locals did not like it, and he understood. If one of the Texans killed the woman, war was going to break out in San Marcial.

"Ed," Cynthia interrupted his thoughts. "My mother is not feeling well. Is there someone in town? A doctor?"

"Not a doctor exactly, but an ex-Army medic. He's good. Name's Johnny Fields. Get your mother ready and I'll take you there."

John Sutton rode to the camp where Bill had gathered all but the two men who were rounding up strays in the far foothills – one was Ponyboy George. By the time Sutton rode in, the men were loading up and angry.

"Kill em damn greasers," one tall cowboy yelled out. "Teach em good."

Sutton tethered his horse and the men quieted. He was mad, knew his men were plenty worked up, but this was to be their home and he remained in control.

"We need to learn em greasers whos boss round here," he told his men. "They need scaring, but not killin. Shoot their dogs and livestock and burn down their barns, scare em, but I don't want no killin," he repeated. A general grumble echoed within the men.

"I mean it and don't burn the saloon and hotel down, it's all we got. Now, mount up and let's go."

Ed walked Cynthia and her mother to Johnny Fields modest house. Johnny talked to them and checked her mother. It was not one of her good days.

"Your mother is senile," he said softly.

"Yes, I know. She's getting worse," Cynthia said. "Can you give her something to keep her calm. She gets upset when I'm not around. Everything here is new and different to her and I think she gets scared."

He walked to a cabinet and pulled out a jar. "It's not medicine, but herbs. Some of the local women mix it into a tea. It's only chamomile flowers and bitter root. They say it helps such things," Johnny told her.

Cynthia thanked him and asked what she owed. "Oh, nothing," Johnny said. "Bring her anytime." Cynthia walked her mother back to the hotel and tucked her into bed. The walking seemed to exhaust her mother. She would give her the tea later.

With her mother settled, Cynthia walked out of the hotel and down the street to the mercantile. Arturo, the merchant, greeted her kindly.

"Good day, *Señora* Sutton. How can I help you today?"

"I'm going to need things for my new house," she said. "First, I need material for drapes. Do you have a book?"

"*Sí.*" He pulled a heavy book out from behind the counter. "You can sit in the back if you would like."

"Yes, please." Arturo carried the heavy book to a small table in the backroom of the store. Surrounded by crates and barrels, Cynthia quietly leafed through the pages of fabric samples. Suddenly, the sound of gunfire and galloping horses erupted outside. Cynthia jumped up and ran to the front room of the mercantile. Shots rang out. Then more shots.

"*¡Eyyyaaa!*" she heard someone scream. More screams erupted down the street. She heard more shots and then glass breaking. Cynthia was frozen in the doorway. Arturo looked back and saw her. *"¡Agacharse!"* he yelled for her to get down, but she did not understand him.

Arturo moved around the corner of the counter toward Mrs. Sutton. Suddenly shots whizzed into the mercantile's windows and glass flew in all directions. Blood spurted from Arturo's arm, but he reached Mrs. Sutton and pulled her down with him to the floor.

Minutes ticked by like hours. Cynthia smelled smoke. Arturo held her down until the shooting stopped. Finally, he tried to move. Blood covered the left side of Cynthia's dress.

"You're hurt," she said. He looked pale and his eyes were only partly focused. When she tried to sit him up, he just groaned.

"I'll get the doctor," she told him and propped him gently against the doorjam. Cynthia ran out the door and down the street to Johnny Field's house. "Help, help," she screamed. "Arturo's been shot."

Several locals with wounds looked at her suspiciously. "You two, go get Arturo and carry him here," Johnny commanded two local men.

"Are you all right?" Johnny asked Cynthia.

"Yes. Arturo protected me."

CHAPTER 47

Xihuitl and Rafe traveled for over a week, stopping at several small villages along the way, before making camp in the high desert. Each day Xihuitl related stories of the Indian peoples of Mexico as they rode. At night Rafe stared into the inky sky dotted with millions of stars and wondered who he was. Rafe liked that the Healer gave him the name of Citlalin, meaning star, after the silver star amulet which saved his life, but still wished he knew his real name.

"Someday, you can tell me where you got the amulet," Xihuitl had told him. Rafe hoped that day would come soon.

In Rafe's sleep, he continued to see unknown people and places. Some images were pleasant, but one was evil, menacing his dreams. Those images lingered with him during waking hours, and he could not reconcile them.

As Rafe gathered wood and built a small fire, he watched the Healer expertly sling rocks into a covey of quail killing two of the plump birds. Deftly he dressed the birds and skewered them on a stick and placed them on the fire Rafe built. Rafe grew more and more amazed at the Healer's agility and resourcefulness, and was thankful the man had saved his life. A debt he could never repay. According to the Healer, the Goddess Coatlicue saved him. The wounds from the shattered turquoise amulet had now healed, but left scars in the shape of a star on his chest forever. Rafe did not understand the ways of the Healer and the Aztec rituals he followed and often wondered about the prayers the Healer chanted in *Nahuatl*.

Later, eating the tasty quail Rafe asked, "Healer, how can I ever repay you for your kindness?"

"You are blessed by the Goddess and it is my duty to obey her command. It is she who saved your life. You are still healing and I cannot leave you until you regain your memory," the Healer told him. Rafe wondered how long that would be, and was beginning to realize if his memory did not return soon, he would have to go search for himself.

They camped in the high desert for three days, resting. The vistas from the high desert camp were spectacular. Rafe wondered if he had ever been in this part of Mexico before, but nothing looked familiar. From their camp, he could see mountains to the west and low flatlands to the east. Xihuitl told him the mountains were called the *Sierra Madre*.

Leaving their camp, it took several days to reach the foothills of the mountains. They climbed through a forested area until they reached a canyon. Xihuitl told him these canyons were known as *Barrancas del Cobre*, the Copper Canyons, and home to many Tarahumara Indian villages.

They descended down on a thin trail and were met partway down by several men running up the trail.

"Cualli tonalli," Xihuitl greeted them in *Nahuatl*.

"Cualli tonalli," one of the men replied. The man said something else that Rafe did not understand, but it did not sound like the *Nahuatl* language Xihuitl had been teaching him.

"Their chief sent them to greet us and we are to follow," the Healer said to Rafe. With the men running quickly down the canyon trail, Rafe and the Healer followed on horseback until they reached a small village below. It was located near a narrow river where two thin waterfalls splashed off the north wall of the canyon. In the center was a small, whitewashed Catholic Church surrounded by log huts with grass roofs. Upon seeing the church, Rafe was startled by a memory of a similar church flashing across his brain. The memory faded and then was gone leaving him shaken, but wanting more.

As they rode into the village, Rafe noticed the men wore knee-high white cloth *pantalones* and simple white tunic shirts. A colorful bandana was either tied around the neck or head. The women wore ankle-length skirts of colorful zigzag patterns and brightly colored shawls. Several women carried babies tightly bound in shawls on their backs. Nearer one big hut, several women kneaded dough while others ground corn on stones. Young boys were running and kicking a small brown ball in an open area, delighted when one overtook the ball from another. Little attention was paid to Rafe and Xihuitl as they rode into the village.

When they reached the center of the village an old man, with white hair and stooped shoulders, emerged from a large hut. A bright red band was wound around his head adorned with a crest of short turkey feathers. He raised his hand in greeting.

"My runners told me of your visit, great medicine man," the *cacique* said. "I am glad you have come again."

"You are most gracious, Tepórame. This is my apprentice, Citlalin," Xihuitl said pointing to Rafe. The Healer had already told Rafe the Tarahumara were a friendly people and he would be accepted there.

"Come, rest and eat," Tepórame offered.

They followed the chief to the center of the village and into a small hut. The Healer told Rafe to unload the donkey and bring in his supplies. A young boy took the unloaded animals to a pen near the river. Inside the hut, soft goat hides were piled upon a sleeping platform and a small fire burned in the center. A woman brought a tray of fruits and cups containing a drink.

While they were eating, Tepórame told Xihuitl about his niece's baby. "The baby cries constantly, and our medicine man has not been able to help. Will you have a look at him?"

"Have your niece bring the baby to me," the Healer said.

Tepórame told a woman to fetch the mother and child. In a short time, the flap to the hut opened and a young woman with a crying baby entered. Chief Tepórame introduced his niece to Xihuitl and Citlalin and then left.

The mother was shy and kept her head low as she handed the six-month-old baby to the Healer. The baby's cheeks were sunken and his body thin, but his belly was bloated. The Healer asked the mother what was wrong and she told him the baby cried night and day and could not be soothed.

Rafe watched Xihuitl gently push on the baby's belly. The baby responded by wailing loudly. The Healer laid the baby on the plush skins and gently massaged his belly. The baby wailed louder.

"Here, you do it," the Healer said to Rafe. "Rock the baby and gently massage his belly. It is full of gas. He is like a young horse who has eaten too much green grass," the Healer told him.

"Bring me some goat milk," Xihuitl said to the mother.

When she returned, Xihuitl took some pouches from his supplies and mixed a solution with the goat's milk. Rafe watched curiously from the bed where he sat rocking the baby. The Healer put the solution in a drinking skin. Picking up the baby in his arms, he forced the infant to sip drops of the solution from the squirting skin. At first the baby squirmed mightily and wailed, but then started to calm. Soon the baby boy stopped crying and sipped aggressively at the skin's potion.

Finally, the Healer held the baby and patted his back. He rocked and patted until the baby fell asleep, then handed the sleeping baby to his mother.

"Bring him to me when he awakens," he told the mother. "Go and let him sleep."

When the woman and baby left, Rafe asked the Healer what was wrong. "The woman eats the native grains. Her baby cannot tolerate her breast milk and it causes much gas in his belly. We will see if the baby can tolerate the goat's milk."

"What herbs did you mix with the milk," Rafe asked fascinated.

"*Batamote y bayetilla*. They will sooth his stomach."

"My mother tended the sick," Rafe blurted out causing Xihuitl to look at him questioningly.

"You remember?"

"No," Rafe said confused. "I just know it somehow."

Rafe and Xihuitl wandered out into the courtyard where the boys were still playing the ball game. They stopped to watch, sitting on a large log. A short time later the Chief joined them. Rafe asked him to explain the game.

"The game is called *rarájipari*. It is a game, but it is really training for our young boys. We are runners and our people are called Tarahumara. We were named by the Spanish from the word *rarámuri*, which means runners in our native language," he explained in Spanish.

"What is the object of the game?"

"It is a simple game played by two teams. The players kick the ball and try to get it past the line of the other team. The players cannot use their hands. The ball is made of carved oak or some kind of hard root. It is about the size of my hand. Kicking the hard ball strengthens the boys' feet."

Suddenly a great shout was heard on the field. One of the teams had scored a goal. The boys yelled and laughed, and then the game started again.

"The length of the field can be several hundred yards for a simple game, like this one, but for a serious game it can to be from one village to another. The game will last for several days," the Chief said.

"Do they stop and rest?" Rafe asked.

"They stop once a day for some food and drink," he replied. "They train their bodies to run without stopping."

"Why do you train to run?"

"We are runners," the Chief said again. "When we hunt, we can run down a deer or an antelope. It will tire before the runner, and then we catch it and kill it. It is our tradition. We had no horses and the land was large with many mountains and canyons. We run to survive."

"But, I saw horses in the corral by the river," Rafe said.

"Yes, the old ways are changing. Many of our tribe want to keep the ways of the runner and others say we need to have horses and weapons. If the people stop running, they will grow soft and lazy."

They watched the game for several hours. Rafe was amazed at the boys' stamina. They never stopped or acted winded, but kept running back and forth kicking the ball and struggling to take it away from another player. Finally, as the sun set over the canyon wall, the Chief told them to follow him.

In the village center, several women sat by small fires. They rolled and flattened patties of corn and cooked them on flat stones for the communal meal. Clay dishes of grilled wild turkey and the corn patties were brought to them. Rafe was ravenous and quickly devoured the sweetened corn patties, mixed with native grains. The turkey was smoky and tender.

After the meal, Rafe and the Healer sat around the campfire with the Chief and several elders. Women brought the men a strong drink, called *tesguino*, in clay cups and some of the men smoked pipes. The corn drink made Rafe feel relaxed and sleepy. He watched the flames of the fire licking upward in a mesmerized trance.

Two men came running to Chief Tepórame. They spoke in the native language and one pointed at the Healer. The Chief turned to Xihuitl and said, "My runners have returned from the canyon. A runner has fallen and is hurt. Xihuitl will you go and help the injured runner?"

"Yes, we will go at first light."

Tepórame spoke to his runners, explaining to them to be ready to lead the Healer and his apprentice in the morning and sent one back to the canyon to stay with the injured runner.

Later when Xihuitl and Rafe returned to their hut, the mother and baby were waiting. The baby clung quietly to his mother and she was smiling. She told the Healer the baby slept for five hours and woke up happy. She bowed and kissed his hand, over and over. Tears ran down her face. Xihuitl showed the mother how to mix the herbs in the goat's milk and gave her a pouch containing the herbs.

When Rafe lay back on the soft goat skins to sleep, he willed himself to remember his mother. He had told the Healer his mother tended the sick. He knew in his heart this was true, but could not remember anything else. *"Mierda,"* he cursed in total frustration.

CHAPTER 48

The trip north from El Paso was uneventful, but Carlos was wary and watchful for *don* Bernardo's *vaqueros*. He grew more relaxed as each mile north passed under the wagon's wheels. María sat with Antonio in her lap looking at a large lake created by the Rio Grande. As they followed the river north, large flocks of birds soared and flew and then landed in the shallow marshy waters. Antonio was delighted by the show.

It was late in the afternoon of a clear, brisk November day when Carlos turned the wagon toward the village of San Marcial. Small puffy white clouds lingered over the western mountains in sharp contrast to the intense aqua blue sky. Pulling into the village, Carlos was shocked. The window to the mercantile was shattered. A small white dog lay dead in the street. Big Ed's Saloon sign was hanging sideways. Every building had damage.

A few merchants scrutinized the oncoming wagon, then went back to work sweeping up. Otherwise the town was quiet. Carlos drove by Big Ed's and made the turn toward Tomás' *hacienda* where he stopped the wagon in the yard and helped Celiá and María down. The door opened and Teresa came out to greet them.

"*Bienvenidos.*" Teresa welcomed them and ushered them into her home helping with the children. "Tomás will be home soon," she told Carlos. Teresa took María to lie down before she helped Celiá with the children. Carlos was anxious to talk to Tomás about what had happened in town. He unbridled the horses and gave them well-deserved hay and oats in the horse barn.

It was well after dark when Tomás arrived home. The women and children had already eaten and were sleeping in the upstairs bedroom.

"*Dios te ha traído a nosotros,*" Tomás greeted his cousin warmly thanking God they were safe. Carlos noticed dark circles under Tomás' eyes and worry lines creasing his handsome face.

"Come let us drink to your safe return," Tomás said. "Where is Rafael?"

Carlos related the events in Torreón. Rafe should have joined them on the trail, but had not. It was a relief for Carlos to finally express how worried he was. He had been keeping a positive attitude for Celiá and María, but deep inside his heart ached. Death. It was the only reason he could think of that kept Rafe from joining them.

Teresa brought them steaming plates of food. When she placed the plate in front of her husband, Carlos noticed a glance exchanged in their eyes. Tomás placed his hand on her arm, but said nothing.

They had barely started to eat when angry voices erupted in the yard and loud knocking rattled the door. Tomás rose wearily and went to answer it.

"Pinche Tejanos," a man's voice shouted. Carlos took another bite and rose to join his cousin. Fifteen angry men stood in the living room.

"You must do something," one man said. "Where is the sheriff?" another asked.

"The deputy is gone," Tomás explained.

"They killed the woman and they have to hang."

"Who?" Tomás asked. "Who is the murderer?"

"Los Tejanos. They killed my milk cow," a short man said. "They must pay."

"Arturo and Hector were shot. Hector cannot take care of his pigs," a large man with long hair said. "Who will help his family?"

"Calmate, calmate. We must help each other," Tomás said. "We cannot fight the Texans. They have many guns and you are farmers and shopkeepers."

Each day brought more hostility between the townspeople and the cowboys, and he feared more senseless death. "I will talk to Mr. Sutton," Tomás said.

"Desgraciado. He will not help. They are his men," the large man said.

"He will see reason." Tomás tried to sound confident. "His own wife might have been killed."

No one had seen Sutton on the day the cowboys shot up the town, but it was Sutton's men who shot Arturo and Hector.

"Go home and tend to your families. I will talk to Mr. Sutton."

Grumbling to each other, the angry mob finally left. Tomás closed the front door and sighed. He looked at Carlos standing in the doorway. Tomás explained about the woman's rape, death, and the retaliation of the townspeople who burned the cowboy's corral and scattered their horses. Then the cowboys swept down on the town and shot at everything in sight and two people were hit. A small war was brewing.

Carlos nodded, now understanding the damage he saw in town as they arrived. "What about the sheriff?" he asked.

"His deputy was here, but couldn't stay. There is no law here, only guns."

"I will go with you to talk to Mr. Sutton," Carlos said.

"No, you must take Rafael's family and go to Santa Fe. This is not your fight. You must leave in the morning.

CHAPTER 49

A new dream came to Rafe last night. He rode an Appaloosa high into snowy mountains. The horse was strong and powerful beneath him. He drank lemonade with a young woman with light brown curly hair by a river. While they sat, a giant thunderclap struck and lightning filled the sky. Running, he was running like the boys in the Tarahumara ball game. Running, but he never got anywhere.

In the dream he saw the evil face again. The evil man stood over a young, dark-haired girl's body on the ground, covered with blood. Rafe was shaking in a cold sweat when he woke. The dream left him confused and he wondered if he would ever get his memory back.

At first light, Xihuitl and Rafe followed two young Tarahumara runners on an obscure trail heading northwest. Rafe watched the two young teens teasing, pushing, and laughing at each other. Leading the Healer and Rafe was slow going. The teens ran ahead, and then ran back. Rafe pondered whether he had a friend to play with when he was young, like these teens. He must have played and laughed with friends the way a carefree young boy should, but he could not remember.

Yesterday, he told the Healer about his mother nursing people. He knew it was true, but did not know why or where. He strained to bring his mother's face into his consciousness. "What did she look like?" he muttered to himself. "How can I not remember my own mother's face?"

They circumvented several deep canyons and by midday they reached their destination – a sheltered plateau where the injured runner leaned against a small tree. His leg protruded at an odd angle from the knee down. If he was in pain, he did not show it.

The Healer mixed a powder into some water and gave it to the injured runner. He told Rafe and the boys to gather wood poles to build a litter.

After he sent them off, he told the injured boy, "The medicine I gave you will help to numb the pain when I set your leg, but it will hurt. Are you ready?"

When he set the leg, the young runner screamed, but then smiled at the Healer. The Healer tightly bound the broken leg in a wooden brace made of stiff bark and leather straps.

As they placed the injured runner on the litter, a scene flashed across Rafe's brain – a burning wagon and an injured man on a litter. The vision was there and then gone.

"Healer, there is a village on the other side of the canyon. We can reach it before dark," the older of the two teens suggested.

"Let us go there," the Healer agreed.

The sun was sinking low in the sky when Rafe and Xihuitl, with the injured runner littered behind them, ascended a vista and saw a large village below. The Tarahumara teens scurried down the narrow trail. Rafe and the Healer followed on horseback, carefully descending down the steep, rocky trail trying to keep the litter level. As they rode into the village, smoke wafted from small oven chimneys and people filled the streets.

Women carried bundles on their heads in large cloth sacks. Others carried reed baskets of fruits and other foods. The women chattered happily, stopping only briefly to stare at the strangers and then resumed their tasks.

The Healer heard the people speaking his native *Nahuatl* language. The aroma of flowers permeated everywhere in the village. They were a handsome and somewhat taller people dressed in colorful cloth tunics with intricate designs. The designs were of birds, flowers, lizards, and jaguars. Some tunics were decorated with feathers and gold leaves.

The Healer was in awe. This hidden village was not a place he had ever visited on his travels. There were elaborate houses, both one story and two stories with ladders leaning against the sides. Most of the houses were made of *tezontli*, a reddish volcanic rock, and reddish-colored adobe. Everywhere there were groves and gardens lush with fragrant flowers. Even though it was winter, it was warm at the bottom of the canyon.

"I have never seen such beauty. This can't be true. This place looks like the pictures of old Aztec paintings in the government buildings at my home village," the Healer commented to Rafe. "It is a paradise."

Finally, they wound through the village to the far end and stopped in front of an ornate palace. At the entrance, two warriors who wore vests made of quilted cotton, adorned with stones and precious metals, stood guard. Each carried a shield made of woven reeds and feathers on their left side, and on the right they held a long spear. One warrior wore a painted wooden helmet carved in the shape of an eagle and the other in the shape of a jaguar.

As Rafe dismounted, he turned toward the entrance just a young woman hurried out of the doorway. The beautiful maiden walked quickly toward him. She wore a white blouse with red embroidery and a pale red skirt wrapped around her slim waist. Her sandals were laced up to her knees. Her long, jet-black hair cascaded down her back. Her skin was tan and smooth. She looked up and her eyes met Rafe's.

"Chiwiwi!" Rafe blurted out, but the young woman did not respond and walked on by.

Suddenly, all the blurred images made sense. Chiwiwi, his beloved, was dead and buried in the Isleta graveyard next to the small Catholic Church. She was killed by Benicío at the Anaya *hacienda* in Corrales last spring. He and Carlos came to Mexico to rescue his mother and sister from *don* Bernardo in Torreón. He was Rafael Ortega de Estrada from Santa Fe. Time stopped as the memories flooded back into his being.

"Citlalin, Citlalin," a voice kept saying. Rafe looked into the Healer's eyes and said, *"Sí"* and dipped his head down. Xihuitl knew the moment their eyes met, Citlalin's memory had returned.

A man exited the palace and greeted the Healer in *Nahuatl*, "How can I be of help to you?"

"Do you have a medicine man? This boy has a broken leg and fever, and he needs immediate attention," Xihuitl replied.

The man nodded and signaled a servant to summon the *tepahtiani*. He motioned for some servants to carry the injured boy into the palace. Rafe and Xihuitl followed.

As they walked Xihuitl whispered, "Citlalin, your memory has returned?"

"Yes," Rafe replied.

"I am glad, but for now you have to stay quiet as my apprentice and do only as I say. I do not know the people of this village," the Healer instructed Rafe.

They were led through several ornate rooms to a well-lit room with a small firepit. The injured runner was placed on a raised platform covered with soft skins. Shortly, a man entered carrying a leather pouch.

"This is the *tepahtiani*, our village healer," the man said to Xihuitl.

"Cualli tonalli," they exchanged greetings and Xihuitl introduced himself.

"I set the leg bone and braced it, but it will need a stronger plaster. He is flushed with a great fever," Xihuitl said to the *tepahtiani*. Xihuitl and the *tepahtiani* spoke in *Nahuatl* and Rafe did not understand, but Xihuitl seemed relaxed.

From a lit doorway a man entered the room. His white tunic was resplendent with a large gold neck piece encrusted with jewels. Around his waist he wore an intricate sash made of gold and jewels. A long cape trimmed with animal fur was draped around his shoulders and he carried a small golden scepter. A small crown with feathers adorned his head.

The *tepahtiani* and the servants bowed to the man. "I am the Revered Speaker Tezozómoc of Tenochtitlán. You are welcome here," he greeted them in *Nahuatl*.

Xihuitl bowed and pulled Rafe down with him. "I am Xihuitl, of the village of Teotihuacán, your holiness. Thank you for helping me with this injured Tarahumara boy."

"Come with me. My *tepahtiani* will take care for the

boy." Tezozómoc motioned them to follow him. They walked through the palace and outside to a courtyard. A fountain in the center was surrounded by flower gardens and stone benches. Flowers hung heavy from the balconies of the two-story palace overlooking the courtyard. The walkways were made of ceramic tiles, each with a unique design.

"My Lord, you call your village Tenochtitlán. It is the same name as the ancient Aztec city, now called Mexico City. Why is that?" Xihuitl asked.

"Yes, we are direct descendants of the Aztecs of that city. When the Spaniard, Cortés, began to destroy Tenochtitlán, the Revered Speaker Cuauhtémoc organized a party of several hundred people to escape and find a place to start a new colony," Tezozómoc explained.

A man dressed in a white tunic and red wrap around his waist stopped in front of Tezozómoc and bowed. The Revered Speaker instructed the servant to make Xihuitl and Rafe comfortable. "Whatever you need will be provided by my servant. You are welcome to stay as long as you desire," he told them before he took his leave.

The servant brought a bowl of fruit, a tray of dried meats, and an assortment of nuts, and then left them in the courtyard. When they were alone, Rafe turned to the Healer and said, "I am Rafael Ortega de Estrada from Santa Fe, New Mexico." Rafe proceeded to tell the Healer the details of why he was in Torreón, and how *don* Bernardo shot him in the canyon, and of his life in Santa Fe.

"I owe you my life," he told the Healer, "but now I must be on my way. My family must be worried, thinking I am dead. I only hope my friend Carlos helped my mother and sister escape to Santa Fe."

"Citlalin, do what you must do. I will stay in this village. This is the place where I want to live out my life. These people are *Azteca* and I belong here and it will now be my home," the Healer said and Rafe saw the Healer's eyes brighten.

Xihuitl reached into a pocket of his tunic and pulled out a small pouch. "Citlalin, you must tell me about the amulet that saved your life before you go," Xihuitl asked as he handed him the pouch containing the turquoise shards and mangled silver star.

Rafe dumped the contents of the pouch in his hand and smiled. "The amulet was given to me by the chief of the Tiwa Indians in Isleta, New Mexico, for saving his only son from drowning. He told me it would protect me and it did." Rafe replaced the pieces into the small leather pouch and tucked it into his pocket.

"That amulet has great power," Xihuitl said. "Remember this – death is near you at all times and can grab you at any instant. Death was there the day I found you, but the power of the amulet saved you. There are incomprehensible forces on this earth. Never forget that."

Rafe wrapped Xihuitl in a warm *abrazo*. There were no words between them. None were needed. Xihuitl followed Rafe and watched him climb onto his horse. Rafe left the Healer and headed north, north to Torreón.

Chapter 50

"Damn greasers!" John Sutton growled at Ed Seeley. "They've stopped workin on my house and yew are the only place in town that will sell us anythin. I cain't build my ranch with whiskey!"

"I'm sorry Mr. Sutton, but the people in town are upset at your men. They shot up the town and shot the store keeper and the butcher. They almost killed your wife," Ed reminded him. "They have the right to stop selling to you."

John Sutton was fuming mad. Everything was going wrong. When he told his men to tree the town, he expected the Mexicans to scare into submission, not retaliate. John stormed out of the saloon and mounted up. In about an hour, he caught up with Butcherknife Bill at the herd. On the hour ride to the range, his mind seethed at both his men and the damn greasers.

Finding his foreman Sutton rode up. "Yew let the men go too far," Sutton grumbled at Bill. "Yew almost killed my wife."

"Not my fault, boss," Bill protested. "Besides, them greasers deserved it."

"I'm askin yew straight, Bill," Sutton said. "Did one of my men rape and kill the woman?"

Bill swallowed hard. Ponyboy George was his friend and was stupid enough to spill the beans that they were both involved. Bill did the only thing he could, he lied. "No sir. Them greasers are jes tryin to blame us. It was probly one of them."

John thought for a minute, then said, "Tonight yew go into town and take what yew need. Do it late and no shootin, yew hear? Pick up the wire yew need for the fenceline and all the supplies yew need for the camp. If they won't sell us the supplies, we'll jes hep ourselves," Sutton ordered.

Bill grinned. It was what he wanted to hear. "Shur

nuff, boss."

Cynthia wandered down into the main room of the saloon. "Good morning, Ed," she said.

"John's already gone," Ed told her. Cynthia nodded knowing John left early. John B was in a foul mood last night and worse this morning. He cursed and fumed about the damned greasers. Cynthia found the locals to be pleasant and helpful to her. This morning she had an appointment with the seamstress for a fitting of a new dress and to talk about the draperies for the house.

Cynthia had been checking on Arturo as he made progress from the gunshot wound. He saved her from harm and probably even saved her life. John B did not even seem to care the man was hurt. Cynthia knew John B had instructed his men to shoot up the town. She did not like it, but kept it to herself.

The batwing doors slapped open and Tomás walked in. "Good morning, *Señora* Sutton, and to you too Ed," he said politely. Ed noticed his friend's face was drawn and grim.

"Good morning," Cynthia replied.

"Bacon and eggs?" Ed asked. Tomás nodded. *"Gracias."*

"Lucas is taking Carmen's body back to Socorro today," Tomás said to nobody in particular. "He's devastated. Carmen had just told him she was pregnant a couple days before she was killed."

"That poor man," Cynthia sympathized.

"Jesus, Thomas. I didn't know," Ed added.

"Mass will be held before he leaves. I wish we could find the murderer and get this thing settled. I'm afraid if we don't, there will be more violence," Tomás stated.

"Sutton's plenty mad the stores won't sell him supplies," Ed said. Cynthia listened quietly as the two men talked about the violence in San Marcial. Maybe tonight she would try to talk sense into her husband to stop this madness.

Later that morning Cynthia walked to the seamstress' small store. *"Buenos días,"* Cynthia said.

The woman greeted her graciously. The new dress was lovely and only needed a few small adjustments. The woman's work was impeccable. Cynthia chose two more fabrics, one green and one a pink check, and requested two more dresses.

"*Sí,*" the seamstress said and smiled. Cynthia wondered why John B fumed about the Mexicans so much. Everyone was nice to her.

Cynthia stopped to see Arturo. She had come every day to his small home a couple of blocks from the main street. His wife answered the door and Arturo was sitting in a chair. He was looking better and better every day. Cynthia asked him if she could help him at the store while he mended, but he waved his hand and said no.

Cynthia heard the church bells ringing as the mass for the dead woman started. As she walked back to the hotel from Arturo's, she watched the people walking into the church. Cynthia thought about going, but decided to leave the locals to their mourning. She walked to the mercantile and saw a wagon with a new piece of glass parked out front. She had not told John B that she gave Arturo the money to send for the new glass, because she knew he would get mad.

The face of the town was changed forever. She noticed Ed Seeley had fixed his sign and it no longer hung by one hinge. Funny, when she first arrived the town looked shabby to her, but now she bristled at the damage her husband's cowboys had caused.

Later that afternoon, John Sutton left his men with their instructions to take the supplies they needed and returned to town. Arriving back at the hotel, John found Cynthia taking care of her mother.

"Hello darlin," John said to his wife. Cynthia was glad he seemed in better spirits.

"Hello John B," she purred and gave him a hug. John held her firmly, feeling her breasts against his chest. It had been several days since they made love and he longed for her body.

"Let's have an early dinner, dear," he whispered in

her ear tenderly. "Then we can have all night together." He held her tight and nibbled on her neck.

"I'll meet you downstairs after I get mother to bed," she replied. Cynthia was relieved John B was relaxed and seemed happy.

After dinner, John and Cynthia returned to their room. John had smiled through dinner and did not have the cutting tone in his voice. As he undressed Cynthia, John melted into her luscious body. As soon as his men stole the supplies they needed, he could get the ranchhouse finished. He knew it would make Cynthia happy and they could get their life here in New Mexico started.

Carrying out Sutton's instructions to take what supplies they needed from San Marcial, Butcherknife Bill and twelve cowboys gathered a few miles south of town. The midnight sky was lit by a half moon. The men were tired and grouchy. It had been over a week since they had any whiskey and food supplies at the camp were low and tasteless.

"Don't see why we gotta do this in the middle of the night," Jake said.

"Sutton don't want no more trouble," Bill said. "No shootin, jes take what we need."

"Jake's right. We shudda jes taken what we needed last week. I'm sick of this crap we been eatin," Jed complained. "And what happens next time. We gunna hafta do this again. We need to learn em greasers a lesson, good this time."

"Yeah, ol' man Sutton's sleepin on a soft bed with plenty of food in his belly at the hotel," Jake said.

"And he's gots his whore, to boot, that Cinnamon's a warm ass in his bed," Jed said wryly. "We ain't seen a whore since we come to this here shitheel town."

"She's the only whore in town," Jake laughed.

Bill shook his head. He agreed with his men, but his job was to control them to do what Sutton wanted. He doubted Sutton knew how hard his job was. Bill let the men grumble until they ran out of complaints.

"Jed, yew take the wagon and circle round the back

of the mercantile store. The rest of yew have yer instructions," Bill told them.

Instead of shooting up the town, the cowboys quietly walked their horses down the main street shortly after midnight. Everything was dead quiet. Big Ed's Saloon had closed several hours ago. Jed slowly drove the wagon to the back of the mercantile. He jumped down and held the horses quiet.

Pewee and Jake headed farther down the street to the livery stable. They were to get a couple new bridles and some bits. Rip circled around the saloon. His job was to get whiskey. Bill and Jed jimmied the back door to the mercantile.

All was going as planned. Bill pointed to the bales of wire in the back storeroom. They each picked up a bale and headed to the wagon, and then returned for more. Bill shouldered a sack of potatoes. Quietly, each man picked up the needed supplies and put them in the waiting wagon.

Rip appeared out of the dark with a case of whiskey. "I'm goin back fer nother," he whispered and headed back the way he had come.

Everything was going smoothly. The night was dead quiet. Rip returned with a second case of whiskey and set it into the wagon.

"I s . . seen a c . . c . hicken c . . oop," Pewee stuttered to Jake after they took the bridles from the livery. "I sure c . . could g . go for some extree eggs in the mornin."

"Bill didn't say nuttin bout no chickens," Jake whispered.

"He s . s . said to t . . take what we need. I n . n . need eggs," Pewee grumbled handing Jake the bridles and headed into the darkness.

The small adobe house was dark. The chicken coop was quiet on the south side of the building. Pewee crept closer. When he moved the latch to the coop, a dog's head jerked up on the front porch. He gave a low growl and stood on all fours. Pewee held his breath. If he ran, the dog would see him. He stood still next to the coop, barely breathing. He could only see the dog's head as it stood on the porch.

Quickly, Pewee unlatched the coop and reached in. Grabbing a chicken in each hand he started to pull himself out of the small coop. The dog began to bark wildly. Pewee turned to run, but stumbled and slipped, holding onto the chickens.

The door to the house opened and a man with a shotgun stood on the moonlit porch. *"¡Ándale!"* he yelled at the dog to go. Pewee watched as the dog bounded from the porch in his direction. Instinctively, he dropped the chicken from his right hand, pulled his pistol, and thumbed the hammer.

The pistol barked and the dog fell about ten feet in front of him. It groaned in pain. Pewee saw the man raise the shotgun. He never thought about Bill's command for no shooting. He saw a gun and he reacted. His pistol flashed and the man fell on the porch. From inside the house a woman screamed.

Pewee jumped to his feet and ran into the darkness. He clutched the stolen chicken in his left hand, his pistol in his right.

Bill heard the shots. "Damn it," he said. "Git this wagon outta here," he said to Jed. "GO!"

The men jumped on their horses. Pewee came running with a chicken in his arm. "What the hell are yew doin?" Bill growled at Pewee.

"Old greaser t . . t . . tried to s . . s . hoot me. What c . could I do?" he whined.

"Git the hell outta here," he yelled to the men. "Now!"

CHAPTER 51

It took ten days after Rafe left the Healer to reach the canyon where *don* Bernardo shot him and left him for dead. He was not really sure how many weeks or months it had been since that day. In some ways, it seemed a lifetime. Making a small camp for the night in the foothills, he did not build a fire, nothing to give himself away, only rest for him and his horse.

The remnants of the amnesia left him somewhat confused between his past and the time with the Healer. The only unambiguous thing in his mind was the need to make sure his mother and sister were safe and to kill *don* Bernardo. He would not rest until he killed the old *don*. Tomorrow, he knew he would again be fleeing Mexico and on the run.

The next morning, *don* Bernardo was tired when he awakened. Natalia slept naked beside him. He ran his hand down her naked back and she stirred slightly. He doubted he had enough energy to mount her this morning. The pain in his back was getting worse each day. Nothing seemed to numb it enough anymore.

The horse trader from New Mexico outsmarted him and took his gold, if there ever was any. Gregorio swore he gave the sacks of gold to the *grandee*. It was all a trick, a trick to steal his bastard children and María. *Don* Bernardo blamed Celiá. She caused all of this, bearing his son after he raped her, but marrying Antonio to cover the pregnancy. Of course, he figured out the boy was his bastard. He saw the Reyes in his face, there was no mistake. As an insult, she named him Rafael after Bernardo's grandfather. It all seemed so long ago and he was tired, too tired to care about them anymore.

Don Bernardo did not care much about anything anymore. María and the children were gone. Carmela took what was left of the money and most of the horses. Without money or horses, he told his *vaqueros* to leave. He could not pay them anymore. *Doña* Juana Santos hired many of his men, which grated him. He had nothing to offer the widow. She already had everything.

A few loyal *peóns* stayed. Pablo took care of the few horses in the barn. The kitchen maid's daughter, Natalia, replaced María in his bed. She was not as good a lover as María, but she was young and sweet.

At his small camp at the mouth of the canyon near *don* Bernardo's *hacienda,* Rafe chewed on a piece of jerky after a cold night wrapped in a thin blanket. He slept fitfully, keeping a sharp ear for roaming coyotes. With his pistol by his side, the only sounds during the night were the chirping of the bugs and the crying of the great horned owls.

Gathering his few things, he mounted his horse and rode cautiously toward the *hacienda*. He hoped no *vaqueros* were around. He was still dressed in his Indian tunic and leather sandals. The broken straw hat and bandana covered most of his face. If he did meet anyone, he looked like a *peón* again and hoped, as such, they would ignore him.

From a small hill where he could see the *hacienda's* main house and barns, he stopped and watched. He could only see one horse in the corral and no workers anywhere. It was odd, given that mornings at the *hacienda* normally bustled with activity. Slowly, he rode to the path leading to the *hacienda* and stopped at an abandoned mud shack near the archway entrance. Tying his horse to a small bush where it would not be seen, he casually walked up the road toward the main house.

As he walked, it seemed that his heart would jump out of his chest. His hand felt under his *camisa* for the single-action pistol tucked in his waist. He held onto the pistol's handle hoping he did not have to use it, yet. Passing the *jacal* where he spent his childhood, it was obviously empty, as were all of the others. No children played in the dirt and no women toiled in the fields. Again he thought it odd.

Continuing up the empty path, he arrived at the guest house. The door was open and he ducked inside. It was abandoned. The things of his mother and sister were gone, and the small house stripped of anything valuable. He prayed that the empty guest cottage meant his mother and sister were safe in New Mexico.

From the doorway of the guest house, he looked around and saw no one in the courtyard or on the veranda. He swallowed hard and stepped out into the bright sunlight. He really had no plan. All he wanted was to shoot the *don*, and escape to El Paso.

He walked slowly and cautiously across the courtyard toward the main house. Sweat dripped under his shirt as he took each step up to the veranda. He remembered the lessons on death the Healer taught him and he wondered if the mangled silver star amulet in his pocket would protect him again. Pushing in the main door, he stepped into the darkened foyer of *don* Bernardo's home.

On the second floor, *don* Bernardo slapped Natalia on her naked butt. "Get me some coffee," he said pushing her to get out of bed.

"*Sí, señor,*" she replied and yawned. The *don* watched as she stretched. Her nipples were large and ripe sitting on breasts the size of large grapefruits. When he sucked on them, the brown nipples hardened. Her waist was slender and he loved the thick bush of hair between her legs. He loved to grab it when he mounted her from behind.

Natalia shook a light tan dress over her head and ran lightly in her bare feet out the door and down the stairs. She saw a *peón* walking into the entry hall, but took no interest as she ran to the kitchen to get the *don* his coffee.

Rafe stopped on his heels and watched a young girl turn the corner toward the kitchen, but she paid him no mind. Letting out a deep breath, he walked further into the entry hall. To his left was the dining room. The massive oak table and sideboard looked bare without the candelabra. It looked as if no one had taken a dinner at the table in years.

He stopped and listened carefully to the silence. Somewhere from the back of the house, he heard a pot clang and the sound of women's voices.

The grandfather clock, with the large gold pendulum swinging back and forth, was no longer at the base of the stairs. Rafe felt like this was a dream. He was here once before wanting to kill the *don* and climbing these same stairs. The first time he was full of rage, this time he only felt determination. Silently, he climbed the stairs passing paintings of people in ornate frames hanging on the wall.

On the landing outside the double wooden-arched doors, he heard *don* Bernardo's voice say, *"Mierda."* Rafe pulled his pistol, palmed the hammer, and pushed down the latch applying pressure to the right-side door. It creaked slightly as it swung open.

"Natalia?" he heard the *don's* voice say.

The opulent bed chamber, that Rafe vividly remembered in his mind, was now shabby. Dusty curtains hung from the ceiling. The crimson bedspread was thrown in a heap on the dirty Oriental rug. The oak plank floor had not been polished in a long time. Only the ornate silver cross still hung over the elaborately carved headboard just above *don* Bernardo's bed.

Rafe stood still and pushed off his hat. *Don* Bernardo stood by the bed, clad in only his pants, his upper body twisted and bent. He looked up as the door opened, expecting Natalia and instead seeing a ghost.

"YOU!" was all *don* Bernardo could say staring at the *Americano* he shot at the canyon, standing at the end of the bed with his pistol drawn and cocked.

"I am Rafael Ortega de Estrada. I came to kill you the day you raped my sister, but you did not die," Rafe growled.

The man's words shook *don* Bernardo to the core. The *Americano* he shot for the gold at the canyon was Rafael, his own bastard son, who shot him and left him a cripple.

"You *bastardo,*" the old *don* spit out. "Your mother and sister are *putas. Me cago en esas putas,*" he cursed. *Don* Bernardo moved toward the bedpost where his holstered pistol hung. Slowly he drew the gun and faced his bastard son.

"The devil will watch over you for eternity," Rafe growled at him.

Seconds ticked slowly as the old *don* and his bastard son stared at each other. Hate dripped like tears from their eyes. Suddenly, the old *don's* eyes widened and he dropped the pistol, grabbing his chest. He coughed and his voice rattled as he collapsed to the floor with a thud.

Rafe stared at the old *don's* body in disbelief, wondering if it was a trick. With his pistol ready, he stepped closer and nudged the body with his foot. A raspy rattle came from the old *don's* mouth.

"Mi hijo," *don* Bernardo whispered, my son, before he took his last breath, but not loud enough for Rafe to hear.

Rafe holstered his pistol and bent to roll the old man's body over. No breath escaped from *don* Bernardo's mouth and his eyes stared at nothingness. He was dead.

Rafe looked at him with cold indifference. He rose, turned, and walked toward the bedroom doors, pushing them open. A young girl was coming up the stairs with a cup of coffee. They passed each other at the doorway to the bedroom.

As he walked downstairs from the master bedroom, Rafe took time to look at the paintings on the wall. The people were obviously *don* Bernardo's or *doña* Carmela's relatives. Each painting had a name at the bottom painted into the picture. About half-way down the stairs was a painting of a young man on a horse. The painting was large enough to show the details of the young man's face. He looked familiar to Rafe, like he had seen see him before. At the bottom of the painting was written into the paint, *don* Rafael. Rafe paused for a moment, and then continued down the stairs to the foyer.

"¡Mamá, Mamá!" the young girl ran down the stairs calling for her mother and disappeared into the kitchen. Rafe heard the young girl crying as he walked out the front door and headed to the barn to find *don* Pablo, the horse master. He found the horse master working in the back of the barn.

"Hola, don Pablo," Rafe called out. *Don* Pablo looked

at Rafe dressed in *peón* clothes and an image of a young boy flashed in his mind confirming that the *Americano vaquero* who checked *don* Bernardo's horses was Celiá's son, Rafael.

"Rafael!" the horse master exclaimed. "Is it you?"

"*Sí. Don Bernardo está muerto,*" Rafe told him the *don* was dead. *Don* Pablo crossed himself.

"It was his time," *don* Pablo said without emotion. "Your mother and sister are gone. I don't know where. A servant said they were kidnapped."

"No, they are in New Mexico. I will join them there," Rafe said.

"You have been gone for many years. Where did you go?" the horse master asked.

"It is a long story, *amigo*. I will tell you one day. Rayo and I had a great adventure."

"Rayo is a good horse. I have another. The *don* and I hid this one from *doña* Carmela when they came to take the horses. The *don* was going to restart breeding with him. His name is Santiago, named for his sire and after the patron war saint of Spain. He and Rayo share the bloodline," *don* Pablo said. The horse master walked to a small corral at the back of the barn. He took a bridle and returned with a tall black stallion.

The stallion looked through Rafe with fire in his eyes and his muscles flexed as he pranced. Rafe went to him and patted him on the face and neck. The horse responded to Rafe's low voice and gentle touch and nuzzled his hand.

"He is magnificent," Rafe said.

Don Pablo took Rafe to the back of the barn and gave Rafe soap and a razor. "Clean up and I'll go to the house and see what I can find for you to wear," the horse master told him. In a little while, *don* Pablo returned with a *caballero traje*, a pair of black boots, and a hat.

"Here, these should fit. Get dressed and I will have Santiago saddled and ready for you," he said.

When Rafe walked out of the barn, *don* Pablo held the black stallion outfitted with a silver-studded saddle.

When *don* Pablo saw Rafe emerge from the barn he smiled. The young man was the vision of *don* Bernardo's grandfather.

"That was *don* Bernardo's father's *traje*," *don* Pablo said. "You are a *caballero*." The horse master knew this statement was true. Rafael was *don* Bernardo's son. *Don* Pablo found Celiá crying by the lake many years ago. She flung herself into his strong arms and told him she had been raped by the *don* and was pregnant. She made him promise never to tell anyone. He kept that promise, even now.

"You must come with me to New Mexico," Rafe said. "I have a horse ranch there and you can help me. There is nothing for you here."

"Not now," the horse master said. "I must stay and tend to *don* Bernardo's burial and the *hacienda*. Someone must."

Rafe climbed into the silver saddle and the black stallion pranced with anticipation. He felt the horse's powerful muscles tense.

"*Vaya con Dios*," don Pablo told Rafe to go with God.

"*Adiós*, come to Santa Fe when you are ready," Rafe said and lightly spurred the stallion. As he rode down the dirt path and away from the *hacienda*, he murmured, "I'm going home."

Chapter 52

John B. Sutton heard shots waking him from a light sleep. Cynthia slept quietly on her side next to him. He waited, straining to hear more, he heard horses and a few muffled voices. He knew it was his men. "Fuckin idiots," he cursed as he rose from the bed.

Dressing quietly, he made sure not to wake Cynthia. He walked down the stairs and out the back door. Last night after riding back from the camp, he left his horse in the small barn behind the hotel. Cries rang out in Spanish – someone was shot. More frantic voices began yelling in the distance. Quickly, he saddled his horse and rode out of town using the back street.

Tomás tried to calm the men gathered at Big Ed's Saloon early the next morning.

"*¡Ladrones! ¡Asesinos!*" The mob yelled, calling the Texans robbers and assassins. They came looking for Sutton. Ed told them he was gone and hoped Sutton stayed out of town for awhile.

"Did anyone see the thieves?" Tomás asked again. He knew the answer and he knew in his heart who had come to town and robbed the stores, but without proof he knew nothing could be done.

"It was the *desgraciados*, the cowboys," the mob said. "They shot Manuel and killed his dog for a *pinche* chicken."

"Proof," Tomás said. "The law will want proof."

"You are the law," one man out of the mob said. "You know who did this, Tomás."

"*Sí*, but we need proof," Tomás repeated.

"We go to their campsite and get the proof," one man said. "*Sí, sí,*" the others agreed.

Tomás knew it was suicide. "No, we don't need any more bloodshed. Post guards at night with rifles," he said. "Make a list of missing supplies and I will get the money from *Señor* Sutton."

"What about Manuel?" one of the men asked. "He

has a bullet in his leg. Will *Señor* Sutton pay for that too?"

Ed stood behind the bar listening to the locals. Things were going from bad to worse, quickly. With both sides at each other's throat, his business was suffering. He also lost a couple cases of whiskey in last night's raid. There was no doubt it was Sutton's cowboys, but Sutton and Cynthia were both here last night. They ate dinner with Ed and retired early.

"Did anyone see the shooter?" Tomás continued. "Can Manuel identify him?"

"It was too dark and the man wore a hat. It could be any of them."

Ed stepped up beside Tomás and said, "Thomas and I will talk to Mr. Sutton and put a stop to this war. You men are no match for the well-armed cowboys."

"Why do you care, Big Ed? You didn't get robbed and the Suttons are sleeping in your hotel."

"I lost two cases of whiskey last night, and you know the cowboys have done a lot of damage to my saloon," Big Ed retorted.

"Go back to your homes," Tomás told the mob. "Ed and I will confront Mr. Sutton when he gets back to town. All of you who were robbed, make a list and leave it on the bar. Go home to your wives and children."

The mob grumbled, but did as Tomás asked. Soon the saloon was empty.

At the campsite, Sutton found his men settling down to get some sleep after their midnight raid. The wagon with stolen supplies had not been unloaded, except for a case of whiskey. Several empty bottles littered the dirt near the fire.

"Git up you shitheels," Sutton yelled out as he dismounted from his horse.

Butcherknife Bill stood up and walked toward his boss. "It wern't my fault," he started.

"Shutup," Sutton growled. "Who did the shootin?"

"Pewee. The dumbshit went on his own and tried to steal a chicken," Bill tried to explain. "They pulled a gun on him."

"Yew cain't do nothin right," Sutton glared at Bill. "I

said no shootin."

Bill had never seen Sutton so mad. The rest of the men stood near the fire, not saying a word.

"When I give an order, I expect it to be obeyed," he growled. Everything was falling apart. Everything he planned was in jeopardy.

Sutton turned from Bill and looked for Pewee in the group. His eyes rested on the man.

"He p . . p . . pulled on me . . me . . me, boss," Pewee stuttered.

"They only greasers," another man piped up. "Yeah," a couple others agreed. The men did not like Sutton blaming them. "We're tired of boiled beef and no whiskey," Jake said.

Suddenly, the tables turned and Sutton stared at angry Texas cowboys. "We ain't had a whore in months," someone yelled out in an angry voice. "Yea we ain't had no whores since we got to this shitheel town." The men grumbled and stood around the fire looking defiant at Sutton.

Sutton knew the cowboys were angry and he was outnumbered, but he would not show any weakness. Taking a few steps, he walked directly in front of Pewee. "Yew shot the man over a chicken?" Sutton spit at Pewee. "A fuckin chicken?"

Before Pewee answered, Sutton palmed his pistol and shot the cowboy. Pewee's body jerked back and then fell next to the fire. The men fell silent.

"When I give an order, I expect it to be followed," Sutton growled with murderous rage in his eyes. No man twitched a finger. Sutton mounted his horse and left the camp.

Bill turned to the men. "Bury him."

CHAPTER 53

When Rodrigo Montoya went to visit his mother and sister at the Pojoaque Pueblo, his sister, Elena, pleaded with him to try to find Rafe. At first he ignored her pleas. "He is no good for you," he told her. "You deserve better."

Going to the pueblo was difficult for him. It dredged up old memories – memories from his childhood he wanted to forget. He worked hard to make a life in the Spanish world of Santa Fe for himself and his sister. He loved his mother, but was shunned by the tribe because he was *mestizo*.

He wanted Elena to come home with him, but she said she was too sick. He did not think she looked sick, just a bit tired. "Come home. Uncle Nico needs you at the *cantina,*"Rodrigo told her. "No, I can't," she said.

On this visit she finally admitted to him, she was pregnant. Rodrigo should not have been surprised, but he was.

"I will try to find him," Rodrigo told her, knowing Rafe was the father of her unborn child.

A couple days later, Rodrigo returned to the blacksmith and asked about the foundry. "The GSW Foundry," the blacksmith said. "North of town."

He rode to the foundry and asked to speak to the owner, but was told he was not there. Rodrigo asked about the young man named Rafe. "He went home to Mexico and has not returned and the family believes he is dead," an older man hauling coal into the foundry told him.

When Rodrigo returned to give Elena the bad news, he held her hand when he told her, "They told me he went home to Mexico and they believe he was killed there." Elena fell into his arms and wept.

About a week after Rodrigo visited the foundry, George Summers received a telegram.

"He's alive," George yelled out as he burst through the front door waving a telegram. "The message says he will return to Santa Fe by the end of the week," George said excitedly. Rafe sent the message from El Paso.

"*¡Gracias a Dios!*" *doña* Josefina cried out raising her hands to the heavens. She hugged her husband and began to cry, then pulled back. "You are sure?"

"Yes, my love, he is alive. Hurry, go tell Celiá the good news," he told his wife. George turned and left the house headed for the horse barn. He needed to find Carlos and tell him the news.

Celiá, María, and the children had been living in the guesthouse. Celiá insisted on helping in the kitchen. "I need to be busy," she told *doña* Josefina.

Everyday Celiá lit a candle to Saint Christopher and prayed for her son's safety. *Don* Jorge and *doña* Josefina were kind and obviously loved her son. *Don* Jorge told her the story about how Rafe had saved his life in the desert and battled Indians. "He is a good young man and God will watch over him," *don* Jorge had assured her.

Celiá was busy in the kitchen helping the cook when *doña* Josefina burst through the door. "Celiá, Celiá, Rafael is alive! He is on his way home." she called out in Spanish.

"*¡Gracias a Dios!*" Celiá cried out when she heard the good news and fell to her knees. *Doña* Josefina lifted her up and hugged her. The two women, mother and adopted mother, cried and laughed with joy.

"He will be here in a few days. Our prayers have been answered," *doña* Josefina said.

Tears of joy flooded Celiá's cheeks. Her son was alive. The pain of her secret was lifted – the secret which weighed so heavy in her heart. Rafael and *don* Bernardo wanted to kill each other – father against son, son against father, but neither knew. Rafael was alive and coming home to Santa Fe. Celiá could bury the secret forever.

CHAPTER 54

As soon as Rafe reached El Paso, he wired Santa Fe saying he would be home by the end of the week. Wasting no time in El Paso, he headed for his uncle's ranch north of town.

That night his aunt Lupe and the family threw a big celebration thanking the saints for his safe return. Steaming plates of spicy beef and beans were devoured with plenty of tortillas. The tequila flowed with even the younger boys taking a small shot. *"Gracias a Dios,"* his uncle praised God.

When he went to the corral to check on Rayo, the horse snorted at him and shied. His cousins had ridden him and he was well kept, but the sensitive horse was angry at Rafe. Calmly Rafe stroked his nose and spoke to him. Rayo sniffed the black stallion and jerked his head up and down. Saddling the Appaloosa, Rafe mounted Rayo and took off in a gallop. Finally, the spirited horse slowed to an easy pace. Rafe leaned down and stroked his neck. "So, you are going to forgive me?" Rafe asked his horse.

They asked him to stay for a few days, but Rafe wanted to be home. He wanted to see his mother and sister and to thank Carlos.

Riding Rayo and trailing the black stallion, Rafe breathed in the cool January air. To make better time, Rafe changed horses often on the way north. He started on Rayo and then switched to Santiago. Both horses liked to run. They nipped and nudged each other, like old friends.

Santiago would be a fine addition to his horse ranch. The black stallion stood a hand taller than Rayo and was all black, except for a small patch of white on his left foot. His mane and tail were long and curly, but it was his eyes that attracted Rafe the most. The eyes looked like large, black diamonds, or liquid pools of deep black. The stallion was proud and intelligent. When he ran, it was with wild abandon, his lean muscles moving in a fluid motion of sheer strength.

Rafe pictured his ranch in his mind. As soon as he arrived home, he would start on plans to build a house – a house big enough for his mother, sister, and the children – a house big enough for him and hopefully a family of his own, someday. The barn would be the best in town with large stalls for each horse. His brand would be known for quality. Before he left the *hacienda*, he asked *don* Pablo to come to Santa Fe and take charge of his horses. The horse master needed time, but Rafe hoped he would come soon.

It was midday when Rafe rode up the road to San Marcial, riding Rayo with Santiago trailing. It was Tuesday, he thought, no maybe Wednesday. Time and days were still a blur. All he knew was his stomach demanded food. An older man and a couple cowboys rode south out of town, coming toward him. The older man held up his hand and stopped Rafe as he rode up.

"Howdy. Those are mighty fine horses," John Sutton said. "I ain't never seen such fine horseflesh." Sutton knew horses and these two were magnificent. The black stallion carried a silver-studded saddle and pranced side to side. The Appaloosa seemed a bit calmer, but equally of fine breeding.

Behind Sutton, Butcherknife Bill dropped his head. It was the damn greaser who shot his hat off. He would recognize that Appaloosa anywhere.

"Yes, they are a breed from Mexico," Rafe replied.

"Tell yew what," Sutton said. "I'll give yew two hunerd dollars fer each." Sutton thought this was an outrageous amount to pay a greaser for horses, but they were probably worth more.

"The horses are not for sale," Rafe responded.

"Whadda yew mean not fer sale, everthin's fer sale," Sutton snorted. "Four hunerd dollars is a mighty handsome price fer that pair. Say, I up it to five hunerd fer both."

"I said, the horses are not for sale." Rafe looked the old man directly in the eye.

"Maybe yew don't know who I am. I'm John B. Sutton, biggest cattleman in these here parts," Sutton said sitting a bit taller in the saddle.

"The horses are still not for sale," Rafe said a bit more gruffly. Rafe thought about telling the man he would have yearlings for sale in the spring, but did not like the man's attitude.

Sutton eyed the two pistols on the young man's hips. This was no shitheel greaser. Even though Bill and Jed were riding behind him, three men to one, Sutton had just smoothed things over in town and did not want any more trouble. It cost him double to pay for the supplies and the damage to the town caused by the midnight raid.

Rafe spurred Rayo without saying more. Reining Rayo a bit left, he circled around the cowboys and headed into San Marcial. Tired and hungry, Rafe never looked at the two men who rode behind Sutton.

"Mighty fine hoss flesh, boss" Bill said to Sutton. "Don't seem natchral a greaser havin that kinda hoss flesh."

Sutton stared after the man and the two horses lost in his thoughts. "Whatcha say?"

"Said, that damn greaser has no right to such fine hosses."

"Yew may be right," Sutton replied as Rafe disappeared into San Marcial. Sutton spurred his horse and all three headed toward the cowboy's camp.

Stopping in front of Big Ed's Saloon, Rafe tied both horses to the post and went in. Ed was tending bar.

"Hello there, Mr. Seeley. What do you have to eat?" he asked as he eased up against the bar.

"We have sandwiches, or steak and potatoes," Ed said without looking up from his chores.

"Steak and potatoes sounds mighty fine," Rafe replied.

Ed finally looked up to see who was talking and was surprised to see Carlos' friend. "Hey, Rafael? How was your trip to Mexico?" Ed asked.

"It's a long story Mr. Seeley, and I'm hungry."

"Saw Carlos, the mayor's cousin, some time back. Was that your family he had with him?" Ed asked.

"Yes, it was."

"Your meal will be right out. Here's a cold beer." Ed placed it on the bar and went to the kitchen. Other than Rafe, the saloon was empty.

Rafe sat at a table where he kept an eye on his horses. Sipping his beer, he thought about the encounter with Sutton on the trail into San Marcial. He wouldn't put it past the Texans to come and take his horses, just like the Reynolds boys had done to him in El Paso. Shortly, Ed brought a streaming plate of beef and potatoes in gravy.

"I heaped on a bit extra. You look kinda hungry."

Rafe savored the hot meal and made short order of it. Looking around the saloon he noticed many bullet holes in the new wood.

"Hey Ed, who shot up your saloon?"

"Been like a war around here, cowboys and Mexicans, but things are quieting down, I think."

Hearing footsteps Rafe saw a beautiful woman descend the stairs into the main room. Her reddish hair contrasted her green dress that flowed when she walked. Her alabaster skin was smooth and unweathered.

"Good afternoon, Ed," she said. "Mother wants coffee and eggs."

"Right up, Cynthia."

Rafe wondered if Ed had married. The woman walked to the front windows, looked out, and then turned and walked to Rafe's table.

"Buenos días," she said purposely in Spanish.

Rafe smiled. "Good morning ma'am."

Cynthia blushed. "I'm sorry. I didn't think you spoke English."

"Would you like to sit down while you wait?" Rafe asked. He rose to hold out her chair and Cynthia thanked him.

"Are you a friend of Ed?" she asked.

"Kind of," Rafe replied. "A friend of Tomás, the mayor."

"Oh I see. I'm Cynthia Sutton."

Rafe swallowed hard. This beautiful woman was the wife of the demanding older man he met on the road into town.

"Are you just passing through?" she continued her small talk.

"Yes . . . " Rafe was interrupted by Ed Seeley. "I see you've met Mrs. Sutton." Ed said putting a covered plate on the table. "Here's your mother's eggs, done just like she likes them."

"Thank you Ed. She's not in a good mood today. I'm sure this will help."

"Pleasure to meet you . . . " Cynthia realized she did not know the man's name. "Rafael Ortega de Estrada, ma'am," he finished her sentence.

When Cynthia had climbed the stairs and gone down the hall Ed said, "Sure is a pretty woman. Nice, too."

"Is she married to the cattle boss?" Rafe asked.

"Yes . . . sure is pretty." Ed picked up Rafe's empty plate. "Had enough?"

"Yes, thank you. I need to see Tomás and then I'm heading on to Santa Fe."

With his stomach full, Rafe rode Rayo towing the black stallion down the main street and turned right to Tomás' *hacienda*.

Shortly after Rafe left, Butcherknife Bill rode up and stormed into the saloon. "Hey Big Ed, where's that greaser who shot off my hat?" he demanded.

"Don't you worry about him. He'll be gone. He's off to see the mayor and then heading on to Santa Fe," Ed replied calmly. "Don't you mess with that boy. You know he's mighty fast and we don't need more trouble around here."

Bill heard what he needed to know. The greaser was leaving town for Santa Fe and soon. Bill turned on his heels and left the saloon. He needed to find Ponyboy George and right quick.

When Rafe reached Tomás' house, a small group of men stood in the front yard. Two had rifles on the ready. They eyed the stranger, but as soon as they saw he was not a Texan, they relaxed.

"Hola," Rafe greeted them as he walked with the two

horses into the front courtyard.

The men greeted him and Rafe asked for Tomás. One of the men pointed his rifle toward the house. The door was ajar and Rafe walked into the living room.

Tomás, engaged in talking to a man holding a rifle, looked up and gasped.

"*Rafael, ¡Estás vivo!*" Thrilled he was alive, Tomás walked to him and wrapped him in a big *abrazo*, slapping him heartily on the back. "We thought you were dead."

"What is going on? Why do you have a bodyguard?" Rafe asked.

Tomás dismissed the man in the room and closed the front door. "So much has happened since you were here," he said. "They are not so much bodyguards, but deputies."

Tomás led Rafe to the kitchen. "Where have you been? Carlos and your family were frantic with worry. Where have you been all these months?"

Rafe smiled and related a short version of the story about how *don* Bernardo shot him in the canyon and left him for dead. An Aztec medicine man found him, healed his wounds, but he had lost his memory for some time.

Rafe told Tomás of the Indian villages and the Tarahumara runners. "The canyons are steep and wide," Rafe told him. "The runners traverse them hardly breathless," he said remembering the fleet runners.

"And *don* Bernardo?" Tomás asked. "What of him?"

"He died of a heart attack," Rafe said as a matter of fact. "He will never hurt my family again. Changing the subject Rafe asked, "Why do you have deputies?"

Over another cup of coffee, Tomás filled him in on the war between the locals of San Marcial and the Texas cowboys. He told Rafe about Carmen's rape and murder. He was sure she was murdered by one of the cowboys. "Carmen bit the top of the murderer's ear off. It is the only evidence I have, but I can't find the culprit.

"There has been stealing and damage by the cowboys. Several locals were injured. Sutton paid extra money to fix the damage, but you cannot replace lives and pride with money. Ed negotiated a truce with Sutton, but I doubt it will last. The locals are reluctantly selling to the Texans, as long as they behave," Tomás finished explaining the situation in San Marcial.

Rafe listened intently. He thought about his encounter with Sutton on the road this morning and thought about the cold hardness in the man's eyes. He knew the people of San Marcial had it tough, going against Sutton and his men. "Can I help?" he asked.

Rafe's offer was very tempting. Tomás needed a *pistolero*, but said, "No. This is our fight, not yours."

CHAPTER 55

Butcherknife Bill left Big Ed's in a hurry to find Ponyboy George out on the range. The greaser who shot his hat off was back in town. The uppity Mexican riding the Appaloosa and towing a black stallion that Sutton had an eye for and wanted to buy. The greaser turned down Sutton's five hundred dollar offer and Sutton was mad. Bill had an idea.

Ponyboy was staying with the herd since the woman's body had been found. Tired and dirty, he was sick of hiding, but Bill had insisted. His hair had grown longer and covered his ears – the top of one ear and the ragged top of the other and he had stopped wearing the greasy bandana weeks ago.

"Hey," Bill yelled out as he pulled his horse alongside Ponyboy.

"Whadda yew cum way out here fer?" Ponyboy replied sullenly.

"Yew member that greaser that shot off my hat?" Bill asked.

"Yep."

"Well he's back and has two mighty fine hosses. Yes sirree, mighty fine."

"Yew don't say. So what," Ponyboy grumbled not seeing how that mattered to him.

"Lookee here, if we git those hosses we kin sell em to Sutton. He was gonna pay that curlywolf greaser five hunerd. I figger he can pay us one hunerd each and we'll go back to Texas."

Ponyboy's face brightened. "Texas! I shur'd like to go back to Texas."

"Cum on, let's git goin. The greaser'll be headin north soon and we can bushwhack im and take the hosses. It'll be easy pickins," Bill said.

Rafe and Tomás finished a second cup of coffee and Rafe stood up. He could make Socorro by nightfall, if he left now, but he asked Tomás, "Are you sure you don't need my help with the Texans?"

"No, you need to get to your family. This is our problem. I hope when you come back this way things will be better," Tomás said. "You and Carlos are always welcome here."

Rafe and Tomás walked out to the courtyard. Tomás whistled when he saw the black stallion. "He's a beauty."

"Tell you what I'll do," Rafe said. "I'll bring you one of his first colts."

Tomás smiled and they shook hands. Rafe decided to ride the black and tethered Rayo to the pommel. Turning the black onto the road, he took the back street to the main road out of town, heading north.

Butcherknife Bill and Ponyboy George settled into the rocky escarpment. They could see riders coming up the trail from San Marcial for several hundred yards.

"Where'll we go back in Texas," Ponyboy whined as they waited. He was cold and tired of waiting for the greaser to show. He sure hoped Butcherknife's idea was going to work.

"I heerd Round Rock's got lottsa dance halls," Bill said. "Lottsa ranches round there too. I got a brother there."

"Shur could use a purdy Texas whore," Ponyboy said. "Me too."

Bill and Ponyboy talked excitedly about Round Rock, Texas, passing the time until their quarry appeared. They kept low when a lone rider approached from the north. The man riding a roan continued south.

"I'm hungry," Ponyboy complained. "Yew got any jerky?"

"Yeah, in my saddlebag," Bill replied. Ponyboy stood up and walked back to where the two had tethered their horses behind the escarpment. He rustled through Bill's saddlebag to find the jerky and felt a bottle. "Now, that's more like it," he muttered.

Bill spotted a rider towing a horse coming north and riding at a good clip. "Damn, Ponyboy, git back here?" Bill hissed. He looked behind him, but could not see Ponyboy or their horses. He whistled and waited and whistled again.

The black's ears perked suddenly. Rafe thought he heard it, too. It was not a natural sound. He scanned the horizon and saw no riders, but his senses heightened. He slipped the thong off the hammer of the pistol on his right hip. The black's muscles tensed under Rafe and his ears perked forward. Rafe knew the ways of horses and the black was signaling danger.

Ponyboy heard the whistle and took another swig. The sting of the whiskey swirled in his mouth giving him a pleasurable grimace. He took another long swig before he capped the top and put it back in Bill's saddlebag.

Rafe watched the escarpment for movement. Slowing the horses a bit, he maintained a steady gait.

Ponyboy walked around a big boulder. He saw Butcherknife crouched with his rifle balanced on a rock before he saw the rider on the road. He ducked down and crept up to Butcherknife's side.

"Don't shoot til I tell yew," Butcherknife Bill hissed.

Rafe's eye caught the flash of movement up on the escarpment. The road ahead narrowed nearer some boulders and both he and the black sensed danger. He had his two GSW pistols, but his shotgun was tucked in Rayo's saddle gear. All his senses were alert for trouble.

Butcherknife held his breath and Ponyboy took aim at the approaching rider. The whiskey was working and numbing his brain. All he could think about was going back to Texas. Ponyboy squeezed off a shot and missed.

"Damn yew, Ponyboy. Tol yew to wait," Bill growled.

Rafe saw the muzzle flash. Kicking the black in the flanks, he veered him right toward the river. A stand of willows gave him a bit of cover. Sliding off the black and dropping Rayo's tether, he let the horses go.

Another shot whizzed by his head, and Rafe had a good idea where the shots came from. He held his pistol and waited. Looking around, there was not much cover on this side of the trail. The rocky escarpment gave the shooters the advantage. Crawling low, Rafe made his way to a thicker patch of river willows. A shot zinged to his left.

"We got im pinned," Bill said. "Work yer way over there and we'll flank im."

Ponyboy crouched his way along the rocky escarpment. Moving right, he worked his way behind the ridgeline.

Rafe squirmed low under the willows. He left his black hat perched in a bush hoping the shooters could see it. His eyes scanned the ridge for movement. There to his left, he saw a rock skitter down the dirt. He focused on the spot and saw a shadow moving left along the ridge. Settling himself, he waited for the bushwhacker to make a mistake.

Ponyboy worked around a couple of boulders. His foot slipped turning his ankle. "Shit," he grumbled to himself. Finally, he settled behind a big boulder and peeked just over the edge and saw a hat behind a tree across the road. "I got yew now greaser."

Rafe saw the man peek over the boulder – just the top of his head. He readied his aim on the spot.

Ponyboy took a deep breath and popped up to take a shot at the hat. Rafe's pistol barked and Ponyboy's chest exploded. The deep breath, he took before aiming at the hat, was his last.

Bill could not see Ponyboy, but heard a shot – just one. He hoped Ponyboy got the greaser. "Ponyboy," Bill called out. There was no answer. "Ponyboy," he yelled again.

"Shitheel greaser," Bill cursed.

Rafe heard the voice and now knew there was another shooter. The second man just gave himself away. The voice came from Rafe's right. He crabbed his way behind the river's bank and the thicket of willows while scanning the ridgeline, but saw nothing.

Bill pondered his best move. He knew the greaser was a good shot, but had him pinned down across the trail. The greaser's horses were down by the river and Bill kept a sharp eye on them. Minutes ticked by slowly waiting for the greaser to show himself, but nothing moved.

Rafe was pretty sure the other man was behind the

big boulders to his right. It was a good place to hide. Rafe picked up a rock and threw it about twenty feet to his left. A shot rang and a bullet hit the dirt near where the rock landed. He watched the muzzle flash from behind the boulders, just where he suspected the shooter was hiding.

Bill saw something move and squeezed off a shot. He was completely protected by the boulders and had a natural rifle sight between them. The greaser would make a mistake and he wanted to plug him – plug him good.

As soon as Rafe saw the flash, he scampered behind the embankment and crawled farther right. He worked his way quickly, finally coming to a spot in the trail where it jogged a bit. He hoped the shooter could not see around the bend. "One, two, three," he counted, and then jumped and ran to the far side of the trail. All was quiet.

Bill squinted into the shadows of the willows across the trail. He thought he saw something. He waited, but nothing else moved. The horses skittered some when he fired the last shot, but only a couple feet. He wondered why the greaser had not fired back.

Bill wiggled around a boulder to get a better view of the trail, moving his viewpoint a bit to his left. There in the willows, he saw something black. Carefully he aimed and fired.

Rafe sprinted up the escarpment circling behind where he knew the shooter waited. Suddenly he heard a shot, but it was not coming his way. Good. The shooter was still firing across the trail.

Bill hit the black hat. "I got yew, yew fuckin greaser!" he yelled out, but he had to be sure before he showed himself.

"Hey greaser," he called. "I got yew pinned down." There was no response. Perhaps he killed him or the greaser was playing possum. Bill had to make sure. "Hey greaser, how bout yew and me have a draw, like real men?"

Rafe heard the voice to his right and below him as he wound his way above the boulders. He worked slowly around each one looking for the shooter.

"Hey greaser, yew chicken?" Bill called out.

Rafe rounded a boulder and saw Bill's back below him. Bill's rifle was aimed toward the trail.

"I'm not chicken and I'm not a greaser."

Startled, hearing the voice behind him, Bill whirled around to see Rafe's pistol was aimed directly at him.

"I was jes funnin," Bill said. "I was jes funnin with yew." Bill dropped his rifle to the ground.

"So, shootin people is jes funnin?" Rafe said with a Texas drawl. "Rapin and murderin women is jes funnin?"

"That warn't me," Bill said. "That was Ponyboy. He dun it, not me."

"But you knew he did it?"

"Yeah, I knew."

"Who's Ponyboy? Is he still here in San Marcial?" Rafe demanded.

"I dun know where he is?" Bill replied, hoping Ponyboy would come up behind the greaser and plug him.

"Why were you shooting at me?" Rafe asked him.

"Wanted em hosses," Bill replied. "My boss wanted em hosses, bad. Figgered he'd pay right hansum fer em."

"Come on let's go," Rafe said taking a couple steps toward the cowboy.

"Where to?"

"Back to San Marcial. They can send for the sheriff," Rafe said.

Bill saw the greaser walk down the path toward him, stepping around a large boulder, and thought he had a chance to get the drop on him. Yanking up his pistol, he palmed the hammer.

Rafe heard the click of the hammer as he stepped around a large boulder. His GSW pistol flashed and the bullet dropped Bill to his knees. Bill's pistol drooped in his hand, not fired. Rafe moved beside the cowboy, his pistol still smoking and ready.

Butcherknife Bill looked up and then fell over dead.

Chapter 56

John Sutton had been riding the range all morning with several of his drovers to check the herd. As a precaution, he never traveled alone since the trouble in San Marcial. Jed and Burt rode with him grousing about the cold, because the half-finished bunkhouse barely staved off the cold nights even with several fires going. Sutton ignored them.

Work had stopped completely on Sutton's ranchhouse. It was January and Ed told him the weather would be cold and windy until March and not much would get done anyway. At least he and Cynthia were nice and warm at the hotel.

When he returned back to San Marcial, John stiffly stepped down from the saddle at the livery. He handed the reins to the hostler and strode to Big Ed's grumpy and thirsty.

A table of locals played cards near the front door. They looked up and then continued their play as Sutton walked in. Jed and Burt were already drinking at the bar.

He was about to order whiskey, but Ed had already reached for the bottle and glass by the time John reached the bar.

Sutton had reached a truce with the town, sort of. He paid all the merchants double for the supplies his men had stolen. It grated him, but he did it. He gave each injured man fifty dollars and promised a side of beef, come spring. The merchants agreed to sell to the cowboys as long as they did not shoot up the town. So far the fragile truce was holding, but the locals were troubled about the dead woman and still believed one of the cowboys was the murderer.

"John B," Cynthia's voice came from upstairs. John turned to her voice and watched her float down the stairs. A smile crossed his weary face. She was the only good thing in this shitheel greaser town.

John's moods had been black and grouchy lately. She knew the tensions in town were costing him both in dollars and time. She found that being sweet and loving calmed him down. Walking to the bar, she wrapped her arm through his and laid her head on his shoulder.

"Hello, darlin," he said.

"I missed you John B," she purred pulling his arm tighter. John's penis stirred. Cynthia could always do that with just a word or a touch.

"Would you like something, Cynthia?" Ed asked.

"Coffee would be nice."

North of town Rafe struggled getting the two dead Sutton cowboys draped over their horses. He was sweating with the effort, even in the cold January temperatures. The sun was sinking closer to the top of the western mountains. He gathered the black stallion and Rayo from the river's edge and mounted Rayo, towing the dead cowboy's horses.

Following the trail heading south back to San Marcial, the black stallion proudly pranced alongside, untethered. He was a fine horse and Rafe appreciated *don* Bernardo's knowledge of horse breeding. He hoped that *don* Pablo would accept his offer to come to Santa Fe after things were settled in Torreón.

Linking her arm with John B's at Big Ed's Saloon, Cynthia said brightly, "The curtains for our new house are done."

"That's nice," John responded to her, thinking the damn curtains were done while the house stood at a standstill.

"John B, you haven't even looked at me. Do you like my new dress?" Cynthia pulled away from him and pouted. John wondered how Cynthia was able to get things done in this town and he could not. The dress was green and gold with frilly fluffs around the waist and collar.

John smiled a wicked grin and pulled her close and whispered, "You know I like you in nothing at all." God, he loved this woman.

"John B," she laughed and stuck her hands on his shirt and rubbed his chest. Cynthia handled him just like she did in her whore days and she knew he loved it.

The hostler at the livery saw Rafe coming down the road with two horses in tow, each carrying a dead cowboy draped over the saddle. Dropping the horseshoe he was working on, the hostler ran to get the mayor. He knew hell was coming to town.

A couple of locals were loading a wagon in front of the mercantile. They watched as Rafe approached. The rider was Mexican, the bodies draped on the horses were definitely Texan.

Rafe stopped in front of Big Ed's Saloon and dismounted. The two men at the mercantile dropped their bundles into the wagon and headed across the street.

Rafe pushed through the batwing doors and scanned the room until his eyes rested on Sutton's back.

"I brought your men back, Mr. Sutton," Rafe shouted at Sutton from the door.

Sutton turned around and saw the young greaser, the same one he met on the road this morning with the fine horses, standing at the door.

"My men?" John retorted with a quizzical look on his face.

"Yes, the two you sent to bushwhack me," Rafe growled.

"Bushwhack yew? Whatcha talkin bout greaser?" Sutton grumbled truly confused. He had not sent any men to bushwhack the greaser.

Jed and Burt set down their glasses and headed to the window and looked out. Jed knew by just looking at the horses, the bodies draped over their backs were Butcherknife Bill and Ponyboy George.

"The ones you sent to bushwhack me and steal my horses," Rafe replied calmly although he was seething inside.

"Yer a liar." Sutton turned, pushed Cynthia away, and faced Rafe straight on.

"Boss," Jed yelled. "He killed Butcherknife and Ponyboy."

Tomás reached the door to the saloon as a crowd was

beginning to gather in the street, curious about the two dead cowboys draped over their horses.

"What's going on?" he asked as he walked into the saloon. "Rafael?" he uttered surprised to see him again. "I thought you left town?"

"Sutton sent two of his men to bushwhack me up the road."

"He's lyin," Sutton growled. "He kilt two of my best men in cold blood. One was my foreman."

"And one is the murderer of the woman," Rafe said.

A hush fell in the saloon and Cynthia gasped. She could not believe that one of John's men raped and murdered that poor woman.

"Yer a damn liar," Sutton snarled.

"Tomás, go check the ears on those dead men," Rafe said.

"Check their ears? What nonsense yew talkin?" Sutton demanded.

"The woman bit the ear of the murderer before she died. One of those men is missing the top of his ear. The big man told me the one called Ponyboy killed the woman," Rafe said.

A buzz erupted in the room and four locals at the card table stood up and followed Tomás out the door.

Rafe took two steps forward. "You wanted to buy my horses this morning and I refused to sell. You decided to take them, just like you took from this town when they stopped selling to you." Rafe's disgust was obvious in his voice.

Sutton backed a step like a caged animal. He saw red. How dare this damn greaser kill his men. This damn shitheel town had been nothing but trouble from day one.

Rafe heard the batwing doors creak and footsteps behind him. "It's one of them. The one called Ponyboy George. The top of his ear is missing. He's the murderer," Tomás announced.

"What yew'll talkin bout?" Sutton hissed.

"Ed, tell him." Tomás looked at Ed.

"That's right, Mr. Sutton. The woman bit the top of

the ear of the man who raped her before she was killed. Johnny Fields found it in her mouth when he examined her."

A murmur of Spanish curses ran through the saloon. *"Hijo de tu puta madre. Chinga tu madre."* The angry curses were directed at Sutton.

John looked around at the locals yelling at him with angry dark eyes. He knew what these Spanish curses meant and saw some of the locals were armed. Looking left, he saw Jed and Burt were blocked behind the mayor. The cattleman was cornered and his head swam. Rage seethed from every pore.

Sutton locked eyes with Rafe. "Yew gonna pay fer killin my men," he growled and his hand dropped and pulled his pistol, thumbing the hammer as it came up.

Rafe saw the movement and drew instinctively. His shot caught Sutton square in the chest. Sutton's gun dropped to the floor. His eyes tried to focus on the young Mexican who shot him, but the image started to blur. Then he hit the floor, dead.

CHAPTER 57

Three days later a crowd packed Big Ed's Saloon for the inquest. For the first time the locals of San Marcial and the Texas cowboys sat together. The judge from Socorro tried to quiet the room.

"Quiet, quiet down," Tomás yelled trying to silence the crowd before the judge started, but his words were of little use.

"Bang, bang!" The circuit judge pounded his gavel on a table next to the bar.

The sound of the gavel reminded Rafe of the hearing in El Paso last spring when he was accused of murdering Henry Reynolds. The Texas cowboys wanted his head then – his head hanging from a rope. Scanning the room, he wondered about these Texas cowboys.

"We have three cases to consider," the judge began. "First, whether the man called Ponyboy, what's his real name?" the judge asked.

"George Jenkins," a cowboy called out from the crowd.

"Whether George Jenkins raped and killed the woman named . . . " The judge stopped and scanned a paper over his glasses. "Carmen Gomez."

The judge called Johnny Fields to testify about the autopsy. Johnny explained about the ear in Carmen's mouth. She had been raped, and her head had been bashed several times. The crowd was silent, except for a couple of women who gasped at Johnny's testimony.

Ed Seeley sat next to Cynthia. She was dressed in black with a veil covering her face. While Johnny was testifying, she dabbed at her eyes with her handkerchief. Ed patted her hand.

Next the judge called, "Mr. Ortega to the stand, please."

"Rafael Ortega de Estrada, your honor," Rafe said as he took the stand.

Rafe was sworn in and related the dying words of Sutton's foreman, Bill Payton, "He said it was Ponyboy who raped and murdered the woman."

"It is the opinion of this court that the deceased, George Jenkins, also known as Ponyboy George, raped and murdered Carmen Gomez. Seeing that he's dead, there isn't anything more to do," the judge declared.

Ed looked into the crowd and saw Lucas near the back. He looked ten years older than just several months ago. His face was grim, but at least now he knew that the murderer was dead.

"Now," the judge continued reading from his papers. "We have the case of the killing of the two men, George Jenkins and Bill Payton. It says here they were killed in self defense."

The judge recalled Rafe to the stand. Rafe told how Bill and George waited for him on the road north of town and bushwhacked him.

"They shot at me as I rode near the escarpment and pinned me down. George tried to flank me from behind some boulders, but I shot him when he raised up to shoot me. I then circled around behind Bill and had him covered. I told him to drop his guns and I would bring him back to San Marcial, but he drew on me. Before he died, he told me that his boss, Sutton, wanted my horses and would pay him good money to get them." Rafe recounted the encounter as simply as he could.

Some grumbling from the cowboys was heard as he related the events. Rafe knew it was his word against the two dead men.

Tomás asked the judge to call Jed to the stand. After swearing on the Bible, Jed related that he, Bill, and Sutton met Rafe on the road to San Marcial. Sutton wanted to buy the two horses from Rafe, but he would not sell. Sutton was mad.

"No, Sutton did not ask Bill to bushwhack the Mescan," Jed testified. "But, I overheerd Bill tell Jake that he hadda plan to git money from Sutton to go back to Texas."

The judge dismissed Jed. "Are there any other witnesses?"

"No, your honor," Tomás said.

The judge pondered a few minutes. The courtroom was quiet. "Seeing that one of the men was a murderer, discounts any notion he had legitimate intentions and probably intended to kill Mr. Ortega. It is the opinion of this court, Mr. Ortega acted in self defense in killing the two men who bushwhacked him on the road," the judge ruled.

Rafe expected grumbling from the Texas cowboys, but mostly the crowd was quiet.

The judge picked up another piece of paper and studied it. He looked over his glasses at Rafe and said, "You again?"

"He killed Sutton," one of the cowboys called out from the back, "and Sutton warn't no murderer." This time, grumbling erupted throughout the crowded room.

"Bang, bang," the judge hit his gavel on the table. "Quiet down now," he ordered.

The judge called Ed Seeley to the stand. Ed let go of Cynthia's hand and walked to the front of the room. After swearing himself in, Ed related the events when Rafe brought the two dead cowboys back to the saloon. "Mr. Sutton pulled on Mr. Ortega first," Ed said.

"I saw it, too," a voice in the crowd said.

"Mr. Sutton's gun was out of the holster," Ed testified. "Mr. Ortega shot in self defense."

"Sutton warn't no gunman," a voice with a Texas drawl called out.

"He shot Pewee in cold blood," Ed said. A murmur circled the room. "I heard one of you cowboys talking about how Mr. Sutton killed Pewee at the campsite for stealing a chicken during the raid on the town."

"Did they tell you that?" the judge asked.

"Not exactly, Judge," Ed said. "A bartender hears things."

The judge looked into the room and asked, "Any of you men see this?" A couple of hands tentatively rose.

Cynthia hung her head. She knew John B was a tough man, but did not think he murdered anyone in cold blood. Tears fell from her green eyes and splashed on the black veil. Yesterday, Tomás told her she now owned all of Sutton's property – the land, the cattle, the money. She was his wife, his widow, and she inherited everything.

The judge banged his gavel. "The case is ruled self defense. Mr. Ortega is free to go."

"*Ayeee,*" the mostly quiet crowd of locals yelled.

"Bang, bang," the judge hit his gavel to calm the crowd. "This hearing is adjourned."

Ed told everyone the first drinks were on the house and a yell erupted in the room. Cynthia sought out Rafe, who was standing next to Tomás in the crowd.

"Mr. Ortega," she said. "Rafe," he responded turning to her.

"I'd like to ask you to stay. I need help to run the ranch and the men."

"I'm not a cattleman, ma'am," Rafe said. "I'm a horse rancher from Santa Fe."

Tomás looked into the beautiful green eyes and asked, "So, you're staying?"

"Yes, but things are going to be different," she replied. "Can you help me hire some of the local men to work with the cowboys?"

"Work together?" Tomás asked with his eyebrows raised.

"Yes, I'll fire any cowboy who won't, or gets out of line. Things are going to be different," she said again. "There are good people in this town and I know there are some good cowboys, too."

"I'll send some men to talk to you," Tomás said.

Long shadows from the San Mateo Mountains crawled toward San Marcial bringing dark to the lower Rio Grande valley. Rafe and Tomás walked from Big Ed's Saloon. The tinny piano music echoed far down the street. For the first time, locals and Texas cowboys drank together in the saloon.

"Do you think she can make a go of it?" Rafe asked Tomás.

"I think I can get the town to help her as long as the cowboys behave themselves. It will be good for the town. Times are changing. We are all Americans. Both sides will need to accept that," Tomás replied.

"Yes, Americans," Rafe agreed. He was *mestizo*, mixed blood – Spanish and Indian, a clash of two cultures, but best of all he was now an American.

"Yes," Rafe said. "People can change."

FIN

Please continue reading a preview of the next Young Pistolero Series adventure by Robert J. Alvarado, *Death Stalks the Young Pistolero*, due to be released in 2015.

CHAPTER 1

Jed Clements promised himself to go to Round Rock, Texas, to find Luke Payton and tell him his brother, Butcherknife Bill, was killed in New Mexico. Jed was back in Austin, Texas, and mighty glad. He and nine other John B. Sutton drovers decided not to stay in San Marcial and work for Sutton's widow after the killings. Jed was riled that the greaser got away with killing Butcherknife and Sutton. Ponyboy George got his too, but Jed never cared for Ponyboy and after all he did rape and kill the woman, so it was no matter.

Cinnamon Baker, the whore who Sutton married, inherited it all – the land, the cattle ranch, and all of Sutton's money, making her a mighty rich woman. After Sutton's death, she decided to hire Mexicans to work alongside the Texas cowboys to run the cattle. That was the last straw. Jed wanted no part of working with greasers.

On the long, cold ride back to Austin, Jed weighed his decision to find Butcherknife Bill's brother. Butcherknife often bragged about his older brother, Luke, riding with the notorious Sam Bass gang, robbing and killing. Around the campfire, Bill told stories about Luke being caught after a failed bank robbery in Fort Worth and put in jail. Bill puffed out telling about how the gang had sprung Luke in a blaze of gunfire. Jed knew most of Bill's stories were embellished to impress the men and knew Luke had been sent to a federal prison in Kansas, but he never mocked Bill's lies.

Last thing Jed heard about Luke, he was living in Round Rock, a small town north of Austin, Texas. Round Rock was where the Chisholm Trail crossed Brushy Creek.

Jed had only been to Round Rock once when he was fifteen years old. It was not much of a place then, but the talk around saloons in Austin was it had grown and was now a wild place where the law looked the other way.

It took almost a month for Jed and the cowboys to make it back to Austin. Pete and Jake headed for Fort Worth, thinking they could rifle up with the Bar S Ranch. Jed was not sure what he would do, but sitting in the Devil Dog Saloon sure felt good. Jed had been making up for the New Mexican drought, as he called it, drinking and howling at the moon – chasing Texas whores. Pretty or ugly did not matter to Jed. Just having a soft woman to touch made Jed thankful to be back in Texas.

After spending the last month drunk and whoring, Jed was running low on money. Summer was coming and he needed to get signed with a spread before the cattle drives started moving. Jed remembered his own promise to find Luke Payton and tell him about Bill getting killed and thought maybe Luke could help him find a job. Luke would be beholding to Jed for bringing him the news.

It was near sunset when Jed arrived at the lawless town of Round Rock, approaching it on the south road from Austin. He did not have a plan, but hoped Luke Payton would be easy to find.

Piano music and laughter came out of saloons from both sides of the street as he slowly rode to the livery stable. Once he had his horse settled, Jed strode along the boardwalk, his Texas spurs jingling. His first stop was the Lucky Lady Emporium. It was surprisingly quiet with only a couple cowboys standing at the bar and one poker table with three players. He strolled over to the bar and ordered a beer. Looking the place over while he drank his beer, Jed was pretty sure no one in this dull saloon could be Bill's notorious brother. Pondering how to find Luke, Jed decided to ask about Luke Payton.

"Anybody know Luke Payton?" he asked loud enough for everyone to hear. The bartender's head jerked up and his eyes darted to the poker table. The two cowboys at the bar turned to look at him.

"Shur nuff do. Who's askin?" one of the poker players said not looking up from his cards.

"Spent time workin with his brother at the Circle B," Jed said. "I got sum news fer im."

The poker player looked at Jed for a long minute. It made Jed uncomfortable, but knew the poker player was not going to tell him where to find Luke until he believed he was not a lawman. Cowboys had a sixth sense about law dogs and protected each other.

Finally, the poker player responded, "He hangs out mostly at the Golden Horseshoe Saloon."

"Much obliged," Jed thanked the man and started to walk out when the same cowpoke spoke up. "Yew bess be careful. He'll kill yew iffin yew cross im," he warned Jed.

Jed strolled the boardwalk toward the main part of the town of Round Rock looking to both sides of the street for the Golden Horseshoe Saloon. Jed went by the Red Dog and the Easy Time before he saw the Golden Horseshoe across the street. As Jed walked across the street, piano music and a woman's voice floated out the door greeting him before he pushed in the batwing doors. The saloon was cloudy with smoke and loud with talk and laughter. Thinking about the poker-playing cowboy's warning, Jed sided up to the bar and casually surveyed the room hoping to identify Luke.

The action in the Golden Horseshoe was typical for a Texas saloon. The saloon girls were decent, a couple even quite pretty. A large roulette wheel spun in the far corner. Two tables of Faro were surrounded by both players and watchers. At four tables, cowboys played poker. A string of dusty cowboys leaned along the bar nursing shots or beer. Jed stood on the far end of the bar. A few cowboys looked at him, knowing he was a stranger. What they saw was a compactly-built, thirty-year-old drover in worn chaps. Sandy hair curled from under a dusty well-worn black Stetson and his beard was reddish. Jed's wiry physique made him look a lot less tough than his scrappy nature.

"Ain't seen yew round here before," the bartender said while his eyes suspiciously looked through Jed.

"Jes got in from Austin," Jed replied casually. "Worked for the Circle B." The bartender relaxed recognizing the Circle B name. Round Rock did not like strangers, especially law dogs or worse, bounty hunters. Bartenders were good at sizing up strangers and sounding the alarm to the local outlaws. The bartender served Jed a whiskey and a beer chaser and then moved down to the far end of the bar.

Jed tossed the whiskey in one big gulp and then sipped the beer turning his attention to the action in the room. Five men sat at a poker table with chips piled high in the middle of the table. He could see two of the men's faces – hard and expressionless. A tall man in a black hat and black leather vest sat across from them, and Jed could see a large stack of chips in front of him.

"Cum on, yew bettin or foldin," the man in the black vest snarled to a young cowboy across the table from him

"Yew cain't be that lucky, Luke," the cowboy retorted. "Ain't natchral."

The eyes of the other players flicked between the two men, but showed no emotion. Jed noticed most of the winnings were in front of Luke Payton. The cowboy called the bet, and Luke raised the bet a hundred dollars. The others except the young cowboy dropped out. He called Luke's bet, and laid out his cards showing a full house – three aces and two tens.

"Got yew this time," he said to Luke with a big smile.

"Not good nuff son," Luke crowed with roaring laughter. He put down four eights on the table. Luke began raking the pot toward him when the young cowboy pushed back his chair and stood up. Luke's hands went down under the table. Everyone around or near the poker table drew aside giving the confrontation plenty of space.

"Yew cheatin sumbitch! Nobody's that lucky," the fearless young cowboy said between gritted teeth as he went for his gun. As he drew his pistol, Luke pushed the table at the young cowboy causing the young man to stumble a bit. The kid had no chance. Luke's gun was out and two bullets hit the young cowboy in the chest, throwing him backward to the floor. Luke held the smoking gun up as he looked around the room, just in case any of the young cowboy's friends decide to step in. No one stepped up. Still holding his pistol, he ordered one of the other players to pick up his chips from the floor.

"Drinks are on me," he hollered out.

Jed watched Luke walk with a slight limp to the bar and immediately be surrounded by cowboys. Some patted his back, while others made a wide path for him. They all wanted free drinks. Luke puffed his chest and welcomed the attention. He was a tall man, over six feet, sporting a long mustache and a small beard under his lower lip, both showing bits of grey. He wore fitted clothing, mostly black except for a small red bandana, setting him apart from the other dusty Texas cowboys around him.

"Hey Bart, cash me in and yew bess git someone to haul that jasper outta here, afore he stinks up the place," Luke ordered the bartender as he dumped the chips out of his black hat on the bar top. The bartender poured drinks for the greedy hands outstretched at the bar, before he gathered the chips and sorted the count. He handed Luke two thousand, four hundred dollars. Luke counted five bills and pushed them to the bartender to cover the bar tab.

Luke stood at the other end of the bar from Jed, sipping shots from a bottle the bartender left on the bar. Jed noticed the greedy cowboys began to drift away from him, leaving him standing alone at the end of the bar. The cowboys in this bar were not Luke's friends, of that Jed was sure. He knew the ways of cowboys and these men feared this man more than they liked him. After what he saw, Jed had second thoughts about telling Luke the news of his brother getting killed in New Mexico. He probably should just walk out and go back to Austin, but Jed stayed at the bar nursing his beer. Luke was a bully, but Jed was not afraid.

"So long boys," Luke said after draining the shot in front of him. Picking up his hat he headed for the door. Jed tossed back the last of his beer and followed. He waited until they were out the door before he said anything to

Butcherknife Bill's brother.

"Luke Payton?" Jed called after Luke's back, hoping Luke would not turn around with gun in hand. Luke stopped and turned to face a dusty sandy-haired drover. Looking at him up and down, he had his gun hand ready to pull, but stood his ground.

"Yeah, whatcha want?"

"I'm a friend of your brother Bill, worked with the Circle B," Jed said keeping his distance from the gunslinger. Jed was heeled, but kept his hands well away from his weapon.

"So, what yew want with me?" Luke asked keeping a keen eye on the man's gun hand.

"I cum to tell yew, yer brother was killed by a Mescan down New Mexico way," Jed said in a matter-of-fact tone.

"What the hell yew sayin? Don't be bullyragging me," Luke Payton growled, grabbing Jed's shirt and pulling him eye to eye. Jed smelled Luke's breath on him, but did not flinch. He stared directly into Luke's bloodshot eyes.

"Like I said, a greaser shot Bill, down in New Mexico." Jed pulled himself away from Luke. "I'm not lyin. I rode all the way up here from Austin to tell yew what happened to your brother," Jed added.

"What the hell was Bill doin in New Mexico?" Luke blurted out.

"We drove a herd to a town called San Marcial for John B. Sutton at the end of last summer." Luke stared hard at Jed trying to process the information. His brother Bill was dead. Luke had not seen his brother for several years and he would not call them close, but Bill was his little brother and Luke had been raised to protect and defend the family. After what seemed like a long minute, Luke grinned and grabbed Jed around the neck and said, "Cum with me." Luke led Jed back into the saloon.

"Bring me a bottle and two glasses," Luke shouted out to the bartender as he and Jed walked to a table with a lone cowboy and a saloon girl. When they reached the table, Luke glared at the saloon girl. "Beat it," he said. Jed could see the cowboy bristle, but before he could speak the saloon girl jumped up and pulled on his arm.

"Jimmy, let's dance," she wisely asked the cowpoke. Tugging on his arm, the saloon girl pulled the reluctant cowboy onto the dance floor.

Luke sat down and Jed followed. A saloon girl delivered a bottle to the table and two shot glasses. Luke slapped her butt for the effort. He poured two drinks and picked up a glass.

"Now tell me who yew be and what happened to Bill?" Luke asked.

"Name of Jed Clements. I was a wrangler with the Sutton outfit down Austin way and I worked for Bill. Your brother was the ramrod for the Circle B Ranch. The boss decided to take his herd to New Mexico for better range."

Jed took a sip of whiskey trying to read Luke's face, but Luke gave nothing away. He suddenly wasn't sure what to tell Luke about the situation in San Marcial. Bill and Ponyboy had bushwhacked the Mexican who killed them. It was a fair killing by the law, but Jed did not hold with Mexicans killing Texans.

"San Marcial's nothin but a shitheel town run by greasers. One of em kilt Bill and another cowboy," Jed said.

"Why'd the greaser shoot im? Bill was mighty handy with a pistol."

"I warn't there, but at the trial the greaser said Bill and Ponyboy dry gulched im and he got the best of em."

"Why the hell would Bill dry gulch a greaser. They're easy pickins. Mostly they be scared of Texans."

"It had sumthin to do with hosses. The boss, Mr. Sutton, wanted the greaser's hosses and Bill and Ponyboy went after em. Don't know if they wanted to buy em or take em. All I know is they both ended up dead. Sutton ended up dead too. Shot down in the saloon by the same greaser."

Luke pondered Jed's story and thought it sounded a bit fantastic. How could a greaser best his brother Bill?

Suspicious by nature Luke narrowed his eyes to slits and asked, "Why did yew cum here and tell me? Yew want money or sumthin?"

"Bill was a friend of mine. We rode fer over ten years and he used to talk about yew round the campfire. He was almighty proud of yew." Jed was suddenly nervous, but tried not to show it. Luke had not responded to the news in the manner Jed expected. Any idea he had about Luke helping him find a job seemed to be evaporating. "Well I tol yew, so much obliged fer the drink," Jed said and stood up to leave.

"Not so fast," Luke growled. "Yer gonna take me to that town in New Mexico so's I kin take care of that greaser," Luke said after he took another shot of whiskey.

"I ain't going back to that shitheel town again," Jed complained thinking all he wanted was to land a drover job somewhere in Texas.

"Yes yew r cowboy, yer gonna hep me find the greaser and I'm gonna kill im." Luke pulled his pistol and laid it on the table with his hand still holding the handle. "Or do yew want to taste sum lead?"

Made in the USA
San Bernardino, CA
10 November 2014